THE LONE WOLF #11: DETROIT MASSACRE

THE LONE WOLF #12: PHOENIX INFERNO

by Barry N. Malzberg

Stark House Press • Eureka California

THE LONE WOLF

Williams said, "The way that my informant pieced this thing together, the guy who got killed must have seen this stuff in the car frame—they found that there were two hundred pounds of shit, wrapped up in the framework, stuffed into one of the joints. Anyway, my informant thinks that this guy was murdered because of what he saw. Not that it makes any difference," he said after a pause.

"So what does that mean?" Wulff said. "What does that mean to me?"

"Do you want Detroit?" Williams said.

"No. I don't want anything."

"You're lying. I can tell you're lying. You want it bad. You want to go back on the road again. You needed a little rest, but not anymore. The road's all you've been thinking of now for weeks."

"No," Wulff said shaking his head, but it was not a denial. "No, you can't—"

And then the guard came and opened the door and took Williams out of there.

And left Wulff standing in place, hearing the voices inside him again.

"Hang on for a wild ride through the dangerous darkness of America in the Seventies!"
—George Kelley

Some Notes on the Lone Wolf

By Barry N. Malzberg

Don Pendleton's Executioner series started as a one-shot idea at Pinnacle Books in 1969. By 1972 George Ernsberger, my editor at Berkley, called it "the phenomenon of the age." Eventually Pendleton wrote 70 of the books himself and the series continues today ghosted by other writers. Mack Bolan's continuing *War Against the Mafia* (the working title of that first book) had sold wildly from the outset and less than three years later, when Pendleton and Scott Meredith had threatened to take the series from a grim and obdurate Pinnacle, New American Library had offered $250,000 for the next four books in the series. Pendleton stayed at Pinnacle—the publisher faced a lawsuit for misappropriated royalties and essentially had to match the NAL offer to hold on—but the level established by the properties could not fail to have inflamed every mass market paperback publisher in New York.

A few imitative series had been launched by Pinnacle itself—most notably The Butcher whose premise and protagonist were a close if even more sadomasochistic version of Pendleton's Mack Bolan. It was Bolan who had gone out alone to avenge his family incinerated in a Mafia war while Bolan was fighting Commies in Southeast Asia. Dell Books launched The Inquisitor, a series of books on the redemptive odyssey of Simon Quinn (by a then-unknown William Martin Smith, who under a somewhat different name was to become famous in the next decade), Pocket Books and Avon began series the provenance of which is at the moment unrecollected and Ernsberger at Berkley, under some pressure from his publisher, Stephen Conlan, was ready to start his own series.

What he needed in January 1973 was someone who could produce 10 books within less than a year and although my credentials as a Pendleton-imitator were certainly questionable (they were in fact nonexistent), there was no question but that Ernsberger had found one of the few writers close at hand who clearly could produce at that frenetic level. In 1972 I had written nine novels, in 1971 a dozen, in 1970 fourteen; ten books that quickly were not an overwhelming assignment. What he wanted was a series about a law enforcement guy, say maybe an ex-New York City cop, thrown off the force for one or another perceived disgrace, who would declare war upon the drug trade. The cop could be a military veteran with (like Bolan) a good command of ordnance; it wouldn't hurt if he had a black sidekick either still on or just off the force so that they could get some *Defiant Ones* byplay going in those pre-Eddie Murphy days, and the violence was to be hyped up to Executioner level as the protagonist, after an initial festive in New York, took his mission throughout the States and maybe overseas. Ten novels, $27,500 total advance with (it is this which caught my total attention) 25% of it payable upon signature of the contract. Only a brief outline would be necessary and the tenth book was due to be delivered on or before 10/1/73.

I had never read a Pendleton novel in my life.

Hey, no problem; $6750 for a five-page outline at a time when I perceived my nascent career to be in a recession-induced collapse cleaved away scruple and, for that matter, terror. I read Executioner #7, which struck me as pretty bad, mechanical, and lifeless (like most debased category fiction it depended upon the automatic responses upon the reader, did not create characters and an ambiance of its own), wrote the usual promise-them-a-partridge-in-a-pear-tree outline, signed the contracts and began the series on 1/16/73. The third of the novels was delivered on 2/14/73.

Incontestably I could have delivered the entire series by May (the early plan was for Berkley to bring out the first three novels at once, then publish one a month thereafter) but George Ernsberger asked me to stop after *Boston Avenger* and wait for further word. There was a problem, it seemed. In the first place, I had given my protagonist, Wulff Conlan, a name uncomfortably close to that of the publisher whose name at the time I had not even known, and in the second place Conlan's victims, unlike Mack Bolan's, were real people with real viewpoints who seemed to undergo real pain when they were killed which was quite frequently. Would this kind of stuff—real pain as opposed to cartoon death that is to say—go in the mass market? Berkley dithered about this while I sulked, wrote a novelization (never published) of Lindsay Anderson's *O Lucky Man!* for Warner Books, and waited around to accept an award for a science fiction novel, which award caused me much difficulty, you bet, in the years to come. (See the letter column of the 2/74 *Analog* for any further information you want on this.)

Eventually, Ernsberger called—during dinnertime, in fact, on 3/16/73—to say that I could go ahead with the series and would I please change the name of the protagonist? Grumbling, fearing that I might never get back to the center of those novels, I started again and in fact did deliver the tenth book on 10/1/73 after all. (The first three were published in that month.) As is so often the case with imitative series, sales steadily declined from volume #1 which did get close to 70,000) but held above unprofitability through all of those ten, and I was allowed two sequels in 1974 and then two more in conclusion (at a cut advance). I insisted upon killing off Wulff in #14 against the argument of Ernsberger's assistant, Dale Copps, who reminded me of Professor Moriarty.

I signed off on #14: *Philadelphia Blowup* in 1/75. That means that I am now at a greater distance from these novels than many readers of this anthology are from their birthdates ... and for that reason my opinion of the series is not necessarily any more valid than would be the opinion of Erika Cornell on her essays in ballet class in the mid-seventies.

The purpose and development of these novels would, in any case, be clear to anyone, even the author. It is evident to me now as it was then that Mack Bolan was insane and Pendleton's novels were a rationalization of vigilantism; it was my intent, then, to show what the real (as opposed to the mass market) enactment of madness and vigilantism might be if death were perceived as something beyond catharsis or an escape route for the bad guys. As the series went on and on and as I became more secure with the voicing and with my apparent ability to circumvent surface and not get fired, Wulff became crazier and crazier. By #13 he was driving crosscountry and killing anyone on suspicion of drug dealing; by #14: *Philadelphia Blowup*, he was staggering from bar to bar in the City of Brotherly Love and killing everyone because they obviously had to be drug dealers. Finally gunned down for the public safety by his one-time black sidekick, Wulff died far less bloodily than many of his victims while managing a bequest of about $50,000 to his overweight creator. The novels sold overseas intermittently—Denmark stayed around through all 14; the other Scandinavian countries bailed out earlier; the gentle Germans found it all too bloody and sadistic and after editing down the first 10 novels quit on an open-ended contract, paid off and shut it down. I haven't seen anything financially from these since 1979 but entries in various mystery reference sources and the invitation to discuss the series in this anthology suggest that it might have found a particle of an audience. (My real pride in this series, beyond its ambition and sheer, perverse looniness is that I was able to run it through the entirety of its original contract and manage four sequels as well; no Executioner imitator other than those published by Pinnacle went past four or five volumes.) The vicious Rockefeller drug laws ("drug dealers get life imprisonment") were being debated and eventually rammed through the New York State legislature at the time I was writing through the midpoint of the series. It was a propinquity of event which led to some of the more profoundly angry passages in these novels and imputed a certain timelessness as well. (The laws were horseshit and we are still living with their existence and terrible consequence.) Calling a crazy a crazy, no matter how anguished may have been the aspect of the series which was the most admired but for me the work lives in the pure rage of some of the epigraphic statements, notably Kenyatta's. Writing these brought me close to some apprehension of how Malcolm, how H. Rap Brown, how the Soledad Brothers might have felt and how right they were: The Lone Wolf was my own raised fist to a purity and a past already obliterated as they were written, rolled over by the tanks and battery of Bolan's ordnance. (Operating under Bolan's pseudonym: "U.S. Government.") Bolan killed to kill: I think Wulff killed to be free. It all works out the same, of course.

THE LONE WOLF # 11: DETROIT MASSACRE

by Barry N. Malzberg

Writing as Mike Barry

You're my favorite law enforcement officer.
—John Ehrlichman to Richard Kleindienst

I don't want to be anyone's favorite law enforcement officer.
When you're dealing with shit, the only enforcement is
death. And even in America they haven't learned to love
death as much as their shit . . . not yet.
—Burton Wulff

PROLOGUE

They didn't know what to do with Wulff after they apprehended him in the act of trying to kill the lieutenant, so they put him in a luxurious private cell, about as luxurious as the NYPD could offer one of its most favorite customers, and there Wulff stayed for two weeks while they tried to figure out a course of action. They had to arraign him, of course. They had to do *something* with him. You couldn't have someone going around trying to kill NYPD personnel in the precincts without taking pretty strong action. Then too, Wulff had killed close to a thousand in his nine-city quest, most but not all of them directly involved with the international drug trade. There were a couple of witnesses or innocent bystanders in there; you had to keep that in mind. Also, there was the bar he had blown up in Harlem and the several top-level, almost respectable men that he had bombed out in their mansions. You couldn't have that kind of stuff going on. They had to do something.

That said, that agreed to, what the hell were they going to do? What was the best way to handle the case? There was no question but that Wulff had stirred up a good deal of sympathy, not only now in the public, which had received fragmentary but interesting reports in the press about Wulff's virtually singlehanded attempt to wipe out the drug trade from the sources, but also in the PD itself. There were a hell of a lot of cops who, if they did not have the guts to have put themselves in Wulff's position, could pretty well feel tolerant. Also, putting him up on formal charges was going to open up a lot more about Wulff's background in the narco division and the very specific events that had embarked him upon his war than the PD and its lawyers were willing to deal with at the present time.

Still, they had to do something. The lieutenant, a fifteen-year man named Smith, whom Wulff had assaulted, had been beaten up pretty badly and was still in the hospital. That was bad enough, but what was worse was that Smith, from his hospital bed, was talking up a blue streak; layers of guilt were washing out now in confession. Everything that Wulff had accused him of was true, Smith said. He had been involved with the traffic. He had been responsible, when Wulff had brought in the informant to his precinct on a possession bust, for rigging the case at higher levels, letting the informant go, and breaking Wulff down to patrol-car duty. He had only been following orders, Smith said from his bed, his little face sweating. And the order to hit Wulff's fiancée, to OD her out in retaliation after abducting her to that stinking fifth-floor room in the SRO building in the West Nineties—that had been his decision too. He was sorry, Smith said, perhaps half-delirious, perhaps only trying to come to grips with a terror he had lived with for months. He didn't mean to do it. He had merely panicked. It seemed at all costs necessary to get the informant back on the streets and Wulff out of his hair forever.

That wasn't good. That wasn't good at all, because it had been the death of Wulff's fiancée, Marie Calvante, that had sent him on his quest in the first place. It had sent him to nine cities and a thousand victims with light and heavy ordnance; it had resulted in his virtually wrecking the network on both coasts and in destroying the Havana and Peruvian pipelines. All because Smith, covering, perhaps, for higher echelons, had decided that Wulff's fiancée had to be hit and Wulff silenced. Now, seven months later, Wulff was in jail quarters and Smith was talking it all out; but at what costs? A lot of people were very unhappy with Smith.

Not all of them were members of the network. The network, what was left of it, had long since cut the lieutenant loose. No, it was the NYPD and the district attorney who did not know exactly how to handle the Smith situation, let alone Wulff's. Obviously Smith had to be charged with something. He was freely confessing to collaboration with the syndicate and conspiracy to commit murder. But charging Smith with something meant charging Wulff too, bringing it all out in open court, and that was going to be one fine fucking mess. The traffic was in pretty bad shape because of Wulff's efforts, but the PD didn't want to take the credit. The credit would have to be taken only by involving the discredited narcotics squad and the several hundred people in the PD who had worked with it at one time or another. That was a hell of a way to look good.

There was no doubt about it; it was a fine fucking mess. And there were no easy answers. So while Smith stayed in the hospital slowly recovering from a ruptured spleen, a fractured jaw, numerous internal injuries, and a broken arm, Wulff stayed in a kind of luxurious solitary while they tried to figure it all out. Occasionally Wulff was visited by his ex-partner, David Williams, the onetime rookie cop who had been driving the patrol car with Wulff the night they had taken the death call on Marie Calvante. Pure coincidence. Williams was black, and angrier than Wulff in his own way, and they had done a few flights together, most notably in Los Angeles, where Williams had left his pregnant wife in order to do battle with Wulff. But that hadn't come to a hell of a lot either. Wulff couldn't work with anyone. Now Williams was home and back with his wife and they had a son, and Williams did not know how much more he wanted of Wulff's war. Sympathy was sympathy, beating the system was great, but he had come full circle; he had a life, of sorts, to live. Of course, he visited Wulff in his private cell almost every day, offered him comfort, told Wulff that he ought to get a lawyer, stuff like that. But Wulff was hardly having any. Wulff did not want any part of it.

It was oddly comfortable in confinement, Wulff found. The facilities weren't bad, he had hot and cold running water, his own latrine, and the services of a single guard whose only job, it seemed, was to attend the cell, which was way down the corridors of a precinct in lower Manhattan. Obviously he was being given the kind of service which only top-class mobsters or politicians might get while they were hanging around waiting for their attorneys to make bail, except that in Wulff's case no one was making bail, nor was anyone likely to; he was being held without charges, and any charges that they made would have to be unbondable. That might have been the problem, the reason that the arraignment was being stalled off.

It did not bother Wulff. Enough was enough; it was pleasant to blank his mind and simply to rest. New York, San Francisco, Boston, Havana, Las Vegas, Chicago, Lima, Miami, and New York again, that was a hell of an itinerary for four months' work, even if he hadn't been fighting every step of the way, even if he hadn't been taking bodies and organization along with him. Meeting the lieutenant, finding out the responsibility for the girl's death (he had not, since the moment he had discovered her, been able to think of Marie Calvante any more as "his girl"; it was always "the girl," it was the only way to stay sane) could have taken him either of two ways, either into an even bloodier continuation of his vengeance or into a withdrawal that had only a little sanity in it. It had been quite unsettling. He had tried to kill the man; it was a pity that at the last moment they had pulled him away from what would have been bloody meat. Now, somewhere between vengeance and sanity, Wulff held ground in his cell and tried to think nothing at all.

It was better that way.

It was hard for him to pinpoint later exactly when this had ended for him.

I

Hooper came off the line gasping for a ten-minute break, went through the belts, down and around the walkways, fumes billowing around him, went into the latrine, found an empty cubicle, took out the kit, and shot three cc's of heroin, mainlining. It was the damnedest, riskiest thing he had ever done, and probably, he thought, the stupidest. He had never mainlined in the plant before. But enough was enough; he couldn't take it anymore. The first rush cleared his head and made him feel all right.

Coming from the booth, dancing a little in a two-step, moving back to his place on the line, Hooper could see the plant in a different way, through a little haze of greens and blues: American. It was not so much the Cadillacs that they were bolting together here, but America itself, the country being put together in little bits and pieces, moving through the stink and the haze of the plant, rolling down the belts and out the doors into the sunlight and the plains and the streams and the mountains and the prairies which were always in the advertisements when the things were painted and ready to make the final trip—and that final trip would take them seven years through the full circuit, just seven or eight years, Hooper thought, giggling a little, and then into the junkyard; well, that was the way it was, that was America. What was there to say? Seven or eight thousand dollars to convert a Cadillac into ten-dollar scrap in seven years; that was a stiff price, but then, it took only seventy years for the country to convert a whole person into scrap, or in most cases a little less than that—forty or fifty for the lucky ones, ten or twenty for those not so lucky. Hooper was twenty-four years old. He had been clean, fresh human meat when he had come into the plant five years ago. Now what was he?

Well, he was a little high, that's what he was, Hooper thought, a little high and freaked out, drifting now on the heroin, the first rush taking him simultaneously above and below the conditions, the way that it was apt to do, just a little weary, Hooper thought, but willing as always to resume his place, willing to do what could be done. That was America for you. Weaving slightly, he found his way back on the line, the others to the right and left of him still locked into their own rhythms, not even noticing his passage. The heat, the stink, the noise, were awful; drugs took the mask off. He stared into and partook of the hell in which he lived, and then his mind shut down again, carrying him away from there.

The foreman, Shields, had taken his place on the line while Hooper was out. Hooper hated him, nothing personal, it was all part of the system, but as Shields looked him over quickly, his little eyes blinking against the fumes, Hooper thought that the hatred could become a killing thing; there were means and moods in which he could murder this man. "Where you been?" Shields said. "You said you were just taking a leak, what the hell kept you?" His eyes flashed, each of the creases in his face held a message, then he moved away. Hooper came back into place, and Shields said, "You probably went in there to get high, that's what the fuck you did, I know you," and added something sub vocally, something, Hooper knew, about niggers, but Shields was clever, he would never say anything like that out loud. Not like the old days. "Fuck you, you son-of-a-bitch," Hooper said, but subvocally as well, and as Shields moved away, Hooper moved in, putting his hands on the bolts of the door, positioning himself toward the frame that crept down the line at a foot a second, the car still as open as a crater.

His job was to bolt on the doors of the coupe and Sedan de Villes, just lay them in place on the left front for the sedans; the entire left for the coupe, level them in so that the next man down the line could use the welder to make the first set of connections, a worse job than his because of the fumes that came off the welds. His own job was no piece of cake, because those mothers weighed forty, forty-five pounds apiece on the coupes, and wrestling them into place could give a man, even a twenty-four-year-old who wasn't quite set up for the boneyard yet, a ruined back. "Fuck you, Shields," Hooper said again, this time screaming it over the sound of the torches down the line, and the fucker did not hear a word of course, not a syllable of it, the fat son-of-a-bitch moving up and down the line now, screaming and cursing out some other poor bastards. For the couple of minutes that Shields had filled in for him, Hooper thought, those poor buggers, all of them, were going to pay.

But it was easier not to think of Shields, easier not to think of anything at all now, floating on the horse, moving the shit in his bloodstream to the rhythm of his work as he staggered the doors into place, groaning a little but sweating easily, feeling the smack lay a level in between him and the job, which, interposed, gave him a feeling of invulnerability. How could you not use the stuff? How could any man, Hooper would have liked to ask, not needed horse through the line? Well, the answer was that a hell of a lot did; this was not quite the kind of subject you went into in your free time, but he would bet that at least half of them were at least running pot and speed steady to keep going, and half of those had to be into smack a little. He was in it more than a little—he was blowing maybe two jolts a day, but that was nothing,

nothing compared to what he would be taking if he didn't have some discipline. Discipline, Hooper thought, gripping the unchromed handle of a door, moving it into position, aiming it and then holding it in place as a big, bleak Coupe de Ville rolled down toward him. You had to have discipline or the mind would go entirely, and then so would the fucking reflexes. But if you held everything in place, if you timed it out, then you could make it through. He could kill Shields. He could burn down the plant—that was what he could do; he could personally choke every son-of-a-bitch who bought a Cadillac and throw the fat bastards into a pit; that was what he would like to do, hang out incognito at the dealerships and grab the customers as they strolled through the doors, their wives in their neat little suits, steel of their faces glinting as they signed the papers for the car. Eight thousand dollars. Bastards. Still, it was a job.

He put the rage away, poised with the door now. You simply could not maintain this level of anger. If you did, the mind would go. The mind should not go. That was what the horse was for, to keep the mind in shape. Horse was the whore of the mind, bringing it into place, setting a rhythm. There was something jammed inside the frame of the Cadillac.

That was strange; he had never seen anything in these frames before. They moved on the belts like pieces of hell and sparks floating through the emptiness; now and then you might see a cigarette butt or a flake of someone's spit, but otherwise nothing; the frames were mere scaffolding, you would see nothing inside them until far, far later, when they had gone way down the line, when they had gone into the Fleetwood plant, where the interiors would be laid in as if with a knife. But nevertheless there was something in there; Hooper could see it, and as he strained his eyes, trying to locate the small parcel which he could see wedged between the spikes of the seat frame and the brackets of the hardtop, he succumbed once again to the feeling that it was an illusion. It would have to be; it was impossible that he was seeing what he did, a neat parcel riding high; it looked like something that might have been wrapped skillfully to go through the post office.

Well, there was no time to think of that. No time to think of it at all. Hooper struggled with the doorframe, the metal sliding perilously inside his palms, the car bearing down upon him at its steady, terrible rate, and everything went out of his mind—the line, the men surrounding him, even the impact of the rush upon his mind. The world had dwindled to frame and door, the fusion of the two, jamming the one into the other, just like jabbing your cock into a smooth cunt—that was exactly how it had to be, the feeling when he could get the hinges to meet on the first try, just like how it felt to slide it all the way in on that first tight conjoinment, hear her scream and then wind her legs around you .... No, he could not go on this way. He could not think, even about sex. Concentrate on the energy needed to lift the door, to seal it in, his body screaming, everything pulsing as he positioned it in his palms, oblivious of the heat; and then, as the car came in to him, he pressed the door into place, recoiling from the heat, which was now perceived only as a kind of pain.

He was damned if the package had not come open in little strips up and down its length, the heat searing away bits of the wrapping; and he was damned, Hooper would be damned, if inside it he could not see the glint of something that looked like white powder.

Impossible. It was impossible, Hooper thought, staring at it, the car trundling away now toward the welds, the heat wringing sheets of damp from his skull, running down his face, and not only the heat, not all of it. It was impossible, but he was looking at skag; that was what it was. He was looking at pure skag, wrapped into that package, rolling merrily down the line and toward the welds, and even though his jolt had slowed down his processes so that he seemed to be functioning through layers of insulation, even though it seemed that it took thirty seconds or more for him to react, his astonishment was not moving in stop-action but twitching through him; and involuntarily then, Hooper did something which he probably never would have done if he had been straight, did something which was probably the drugs talking to him. But that was not his fault; shit, a man had to do something, had to keep going any way that he could. That was all, and it wasn't his fault, damn it, it wasn't his fault if they had made of his life something which had to be supported only through skag. He hadn't asked for it to be this way, not at all. But the production line—that was all that he was offered, and even then he had had to go on his fucking knees to get the job, be part of a disadvantaged group and all that shit. "Look at that!" Hooper shrieked. "Look at that," as the paper, blackening in the fires, began to spread like the space left by a dismembered limb. "That's shit! That's pure fucking shit in that package. What the fuck is going on here?" And his scream wheeled all of them around; everyone was looking at him, the welder stupidly, with sparks coming out of the end of his instrument, the bastards to the right and left of him all staring. "Don't you see that?" Hooper screamed. "It's shit, damn it, it's shit!" And then: it was impossible, he could not keep on shouting, what was he shouting for? Hooper thought stupidly. If that was shit in that car, someone had put it there; it was no accident, and that someone would not be very happy, would not be happy at all with Hooper calling attention on the line to what could only have been a terrible mistake. And then Shields was bearing down on him. His sense of time had become compressed and all fucked up, just the way it did with a jolt after the first rush; he just was not thinking too well, events moving out of synchronization somehow. "You fool!" Shields said. "You fool, you're holding up the line!" And Hooper did not quite understand what he meant. What was Shields fucking around with now, what was this business with the line, didn't he understand what was going on here? And he turned almost dreamily to confront Shields with this, confront the man with the impossibility of his position. As he did this, something broke within him; something strange and damp in a pocket of his stomach mashed open, and he was running blood, he was running blood and fire. It was not horse, but pain that was running free within him, and as he fell, Hooper thought: This is silly, this is wrong, this cannot be. I am going to whale the shit out of the stupid son-of-a-bitch who laid on this bad stuff, but as he hit the floor, the sounds of the machinery now enveloping him, it occurred to him that whatever had happened had nothing to do with the skag—it was the skag, if anything, that was holding him off from any true understanding of what had happened to his body.

And then it all went away from him.

II

They didn't know what to do with Wulff, not yet, not by far, but they had a better idea with Smith. They could bring Lieutenant Smith in and formally charge him with conspiracy to commit murder, conspiracy to drug-peddle, obstruction of justice in the investigation of the peddling—oh, they had Smith on a hell of a lot of things, not the least of which was what Wulff had done to him in the precinct; and on the first day that Smith could stagger out of the hospital bed on his own, go down the hall under custody and take a leak, they brought him down to Centre Street and arraigned him. Those three charges would do for now; there was even heavier stuff which they could have laid on him, stuff like consorting with elements of the drug network, indeed functioning on their payroll, and actually planning if not in fact pulling the trigger on Marie Calvante, but that would have been too heavy even under the circumstances, it would have opened up a lot of questions as to Smith's supervision and contacts on the narco squad which the NYPD did not want to get into at this time. Everybody knew the narco squad stunk; it was in the process of being phased out of existence as quickly and quietly as possible; every day a new story broke about this or that member having taken graft or having been busted for actual possession—why give the press even more mileage than they had already? No, they would try to keep it in the family to the extent that they would pin everything that they could on Smith which was strictly his own and which could be tried without getting into the men he had worked with, the institution that had supported all of them.

And that gave them something to do with Wulff. If they didn't quite know what to do with him on his own hook, they could make him a material witness against Smith. If anybody was a witness against Smith it would be Wulff all right, and they must have congratulated themselves downtown the night that they had finally, about midnight, come up with that ploy; they could justify continuing to hold Wulff because of the material-witness aspect and the fact that he was being gunned for by about five thousand people, any one of whom would have gladly taken him out of the case and the chance of testifying against Smith. Oh, it was a smooth enough maneuver, and it would enable them to get their first good look at Wulff in a more public situation. So the guard told Wulff, the night before, about Centre Street, that Wulff would be taken out of the cell the next morning, and what they had planned for him; and Wulff, as he had been doing ever since he had hit confinement, merely nodded and said nothing. His face showed great acuity, his eyes intelligence, his mind clearly registered everything that was being said, but he did not talk.

It was an object of some debate in the cell block and up to higher levels of the PD whether Wulff's mind had really gone, whether that last incident in the precinct station with Smith and everything that had led up to it had actually destroyed his emotional balance and rendered him insane. There were very few who thought so, judging from Wulff's previous record and from what he had been able to accomplish on the road, on his own, in just a couple of months. "That son-of-a-bitch is biding his time," the captain downstairs had told one of his guards quietly, "and when he's through with that, he'll make his move." And the guard was inclined to believe it; all of them were. Still Wulff was not saying a word. Whatever was going on inside remained very private, even when they told him that the man who had killed his girl was going to be arraigned in open court in Wulff's presence. If there was any pleasure or apprehension in this, it would not show. They didn't bother telling him about the material-witness stuff. That, they figured, would only lead to complications.

On the morning of the arraignment, Williams came to Wulff's cell with a guard, got keyed inside, waited until the guard went away mumbling, and said, "I got something that I think will interest you."

Wulff said nothing. He sat with his arms folded, looking at and past

Williams at the little spokes of light that bounced and glinted off the bars. He felt very comfortable with his ex-partner—there was no tension at all—but then again, he had nothing to say. Not at all personal; Williams would have been the first man he would have spoken to if anything had been on his mind.

Williams rubbed his palms together, sat on the bunk casually, and leaned toward Wulff. "I still maintain my contacts," he said. "I got a call from Detroit. Some guy called me. There was a murder at the Fleetwood plant. Some guy got a two-ton beam dropped on him while he was on the line, an assembly man. It was an unfortunate accident; the plant got closed down for half an hour while they took out the remains."

Wulff said nothing, but in a different way. There was a little activity behind his eyes, a shading of light which might have been response. Williams said, "He was impaled against a car. When they took the car out—which they had to do, because it was the only way to get the body— they found that there were two hundred pounds of shit, wrapped up, in the framework, stuffed into one of the joints. They must have been running the stuff through."

Wulff shook his head very slowly and then went back to staring. Williams said, "The way that my informant pieced this thing together, the guy who got killed, a guy named Hooper, must have seen this stuff in the frame. There was some connection between it and the way the beam fell on his head. Someone must have fucked up very bad," Williams said. "Someone must have made a drop when he wasn't supposed to, or maybe someone got awfully mad at someone else and set this up for discovery. Anyway, my informant thinks that this guy Hooper was murdered because of what he saw. Not that it makes any difference," he said after a pause. "Everything's in custody right now, the shit and the frame and the remains. They're trying to piece something together out of this, but they're not going to get very far, I don't think. For one thing, they don't want to get very far, you see."

Wulff stood and walked to the edge of the cell, then turned and came back slowly. Six-feet-four, about a hundred and eighty now, he looked no worse to Williams than he had back in Los Angeles a couple of months ago, at the peak of his crusade. Maybe a little bit ragged, but just as competent. He looked as if he could have torn the cellblock down if he wanted to. "So what does that mean?" Wulff said. "What does that mean to me?"

It was the first thing he had said in a very long time, but Williams had the cop's impassivity; he showed no reaction. "Something stinks in that plant," he said. "If they're using cars for stash, something stinks very bad. If they're going to kill a guy who sees it, that's got to be even worse. My informant thinks that hell is going to break loose."

"It's not my doing," Wulff said, "it's not my war. I'm through with it. I'm resigning."

"Just going to sit in the cell, eh?" Williams said. "You got the guy who got your girl, so that's the end of it. What do you care about the racket or the people it's killing? All you got into it for was to get the people who got your girl, and now that you've found him, now that you did, and it's only one son-of-a-bitch, you're finished. It wasn't a crusade, it was just revenge."

There was a very long pause. Wulff leaned against the wall looking at Williams in a strange, intense way, and it occurred to Williams that, yes, he had pushed it very far, he had better not push it one inch farther, this man could kill him. Even at this time, in this condition, he could kill him. "You know that's not true," Wulff said slowly. "You know that's not true at all."

"But you said you're going to stop."

"That's different," Wulff said. "Can't you see that? It's too much. It's too much already. The price is too high. I can't take the death."

"They can," Williams said. "They can take the death. There is no end to it for them. They'll do everything, kill everyone they have to in order to keep their line straight. They've proved that. So now that you're out, they have a clear path again."

"What do you want?" Wulff said harshly and walked toward Williams, put his hands on the man's shoulders, applied pressure. Williams, held in the grasp, did not move. "What do you want of me? Isn't it enough? Doesn't there come a time when you're at a stop, when you can say that there's an end to it? I can't take it. I can't take it anymore; I did everything that I could, I set them back ten years."

"Not ten months," Williams said softly. "Not ten months, if you stop, if you leave it go now."

"What do you want?" Wulff said, still holding his position. "What do you want of me? So there's hell in Detroit, so they're funneling the shit through the assembly lines. That figures, that would be the next step. Still, what's the difference? What do you want of me? Where do I come into this? They're going to arraign this guy, this bastard here this morning; I'm supposed to be present to give testimony. Do you understand, I'm going to be in court, nailing this son-of-a-bitch. The lawyers were in here to see me; that's what they want me to do. What does that have to do with Detroit? I've got an arraignment to make."

Wulff's hands still on him, Williams said, "That's what I mean."

"What? What do you mean?"

"You're going to be in open court today. Things can get a little confused in open court. Things can get a little fouled up, people can lose track of other people."

Wulff's hands fell away. "I think I hear what you're saying," he said, "but I don't believe it."

"Do you want Detroit?" Williams said.

"No. I don't want anything."

"You're lying. I can tell you're lying. You want it bad. You want to go back on the road again. You needed a little rest, but not anymore. The road's all you've been thinking of now for weeks."

"No," Wulff said shaking his head, but it was not a denial. "No, you can't—"

"I'm still living in the same place," Williams said, "the same fucking place, me and my wife and my kid, and I can't go nowhere anymore. But you can see me. You can see me, and you'll hear whatever you need to know."

"See you when?"

"Who knows?" Williams said, and stood, went to the door of the cell, knocked for the guard. "Who can say? It's a long life. It's a strange life. It's filled with strangenesses. None of us knows what may happen to us in the long run, or even in the next moment."

And then the guard came and opened the door and took Williams out of there.

And left Wulff standing in place, hearing the voices inside him again.

III

"Bastard," said Hamilton, and hit the man standing in front of him in the face again. "Stupid bastard. Stupid son-of-a-bitch. I didn't ask you to kill him. Who asked you to kill him? Who needed this?" His voice broke, and he lunged to his feet, hit the man fully in the stomach.

The man, restrained in the grip of two others, doubled over, retched at Hamilton's feet as Hamilton looked at him with revulsion. Little rivulets of sweat ran down the man's face and pooled into a little space on the floor. Hamilton looked at him, looked past him, seemed to take himself out of the room for a moment, peering into abstraction; but then, as always, he was back again, and so was the man There was no escaping; eternally you had to come back behind the walls of self and look at the sons-of-bitches who were out to destroy you. "Why?" he said to the man calmly, almost patiently, a slight lisp intruding into his voice, as it always did at times of tension. "What made you feel, you shit, that you had to do this?"

The man was named Shields; he was fat and short and in his forties and a foreman at the plant. Hamilton knew little about him, had known nothing until a day ago, when news of the situation had come through to him. Now in the man's terror he could see more than he had ever wanted to know. "I thought there was no choice," Shields said desperately. "There was a mistake, something got through on the line, it was riding in the frame—"

"I don't want to know anything about that," Hamilton said. "I don't want any excuses or explanations. I want to know why this man was killed."

"He wasn't killed," Shields said weakly. "It wasn't that; we just—"

Hamilton stepped forward and hit the man in the mouth again. There was a pulpy sound, and then his hand bore the faint marks of Shield's teeth and blood. "You fool," he said, "you stupid fool. You deserve to die for this."

The men holding Shields looked at Hamilton hopefully, and one of them made a gesture in his clothing. Abruptly Hamilton felt the disgust rising within him, the dark revulsion, and he could not deal with this any longer. He could not handle it. Not in this fashion. If there was murder in this room and Hamilton guessed that there was, it would have to be on his own terms, it would have to be the kind of murder that he could shape and understand, because only in that way, Hamilton thought, could death itself be controlled. "Get out of here," he said to the two men. "Go on, just get out of here."

They looked at him with puzzlement. Nominally they were foremen; in truth they were nothing but fools. If they had had to sustain themselves on the line, they would have been burned to death in an industrial accident years ago. That was one virtue of crime, Hamilton thought bitterly, it gave new hope to the unemployable. "Fuck out," he said. "Get the fuck out."

They let Shields go, wriggling, turned, went to the door. Looking at them, two tough-looking men in their late thirties, Shields did not see so much simple muscle as a reflection of himself, of some inward necessity. He did not want to think of that. It was nothing to pursue. "Fuck out," he said again. They went away, the door hanging like an open mouth, twitching slightly in the breezes of the hallway.

"Close the door," Hamilton said to Shields, who was standing in a graceless posture rubbing his hands up and down his arms, seemingly not sure that he had been released. "Shut the door," he said again. "I want to talk to you. Don't think about making any moves down the corridors," Hamilton said casually, and made a motion toward the desk. "There's enough armament in there to make that a very poor idea, and even if I missed, you wouldn't get very far. You wouldn't get very far at all."

"All right," Shields said. "I understand that. I got a wife and kids. I wouldn't do anything." He moved away, closed the door with an exaggerated gesture of compliance, and came back to the place where he had been standing, as if it had been assigned to him. "I'm sorry," he said. "I'm sorry about this. It was—"

"Listen," Hamilton said quietly. "Now, just listen to me. I'm a little pissed off about this, nothing serious, you understand, but serious enough. If you're fucking up an operation there, that's your business. I'm not too concerned with fuckups, only with results. If some stash got into a frame on the line, that's the kind of thing that can happen, you can get screwed up anywhere along the way in an operation like that, and I can understand that too. But to knock off a man because he happens to come across it—"

"It wasn't that way," Shields said a little too eagerly, "it wasn't like that at all. I didn't have anything to do with that. I wouldn't have wanted it that way. It was just that they got a little excited—"

"Who are 'they'?"

"Some guys," Shields said vaguely, "just some guys, nothing that I had anything to do with. They got a little overexcited, they thought that maybe his seeing something made more of it than it was. I didn't know anything about it until later; I was on a break then—"

"You fool," Hamilton said, and stood, went over to Shields, struck him again in the same place that he had hit the man before. The white of the foreman's face turned to a deeper, purplish streak; he groaned. "You stupid fool," Hamilton said. "I don't care if somebody fucks up, drops stash into the car, because that kind of thing happens. You've almost got to expect that kind of thing in any operation as complex as that. And if some fool on the line happens to get a look into the car, I don't like that at all, it isn't good publicity, it doesn't make the situation too good for us. That's for sure, but on the other hand, you can live with it. You've got to learn to live with setbacks like that in any kind of business. But what I do mind, what I mind very much, is somebody getting out of control, somebody thinking that the only way to deal with a mistake is to erase it. That's stupid thinking, Shields. That's stupid, right down to the center, and I can't afford that kind of thing. I can't afford it at all."

"Listen," Shields said, and spread his palms in a gesture that was both despairing and oddly menacing, the despair not bothering Hamilton a bit, the menace something else, because he could see in this aspect of the man, could get an idea of the way he might react in a pressure situation; yes, he was the kind of guy who might arrange to drop a beam on the head of someone who had been inconvenient. It was possible that any man crazy enough to fall into an intimidating attitude even in a situation like this might lose control of himself in that manner. "Listen, I don't have anything to do with it. I don't know shit, don't you understand that? This guy Hooper, I don't know who he is, I don't know what he saw or what it comes to, I just—"

"No," Hamilton said. Unwillingly, but out of a sense of dry compulsion, he hit the man in the face yet again, and this time Shields yelped with pain, little marks jutting out on his skin as he backed away, and now the expression in his face changed subtly. He seemed somehow less at bay, the obsequiousness draining away, the slow conviction coming into the shades and panels of his cheeks that he might have to fight. Hamilton thought: Yes, that was part of it too; driven far enough, Shields would strike back, no matter what the odds were. No matter what the situation, his temper might seize control of his functioning, and almost helplessly he would strike out in retaliation. "It won't work," Hamilton said, and backed away from the man as if he were a painter admiring his work. "I don't believe you. You did it, Shields, and now you've got me in a real stink, a far more serious pickle than there was any need to have. That was damned stupid of you."

"The beam fell! He just happened to be walking there; nobody had anything to do with it. It was just an act of God. They've got the place crawling with industrial inspectors; you know that they wouldn't do something like that unless it was an accident."

Hamilton took the gun out of his desk drawer and showed it to the man. "No," he said, and shook his head with a grave, deliberate sadness. "No, it won't work, Shields. It's just damned stupid, and it won't wash, not any of it now. You panicked and you set the whole thing up, and now the man is dead. It's all set up in a way that could be traced back to me, and I don't like it. I don't like it at all."

"How the hell," Shields said, "how the hell would I know what was in the car, how would I know what's going on? I have nothing to do with it, Hamilton. You can understand that, you can understand what I'm saying, can't you? I don't know who you are, I don't know what's in the car, I don't even know what's running through, or what there was to be seen. So that means that I wouldn't be involved, can't you tell? You can tell that, damn it, I'm sure you can," Shields said, and all of the time he had been closing ground, closing ground slowly toward him. Hamilton had watched all of it; some instruments of calculation deep in his consciousness had been working on this all of the time that Shields was babbling, trying (Hamilton thought) to mislead him, to throw him off cue. And then, in one desperate gesture, one spasm of his body, Shields leaped, his hand clawing at the air, trying, trying desperately to reach the gun.

Hamilton let him come, the scene slowing down, Shields seeming to drift through the air with odd and absent grace like a paratrooper; and then, as the man's hand came swinging clumsily forward, Hamilton shot him in the face.

The skin fragmented, and then Shields's head exploded like a piece of warm fruit.

Hamilton dodged out of the way, let the man fall. Shields kicked once on the floor and then lay still. Looking at him, Hamilton felt all passion drain from him. Now, past the impact of the bullet, Shields meant nothing. He was just damp, clinging meat on the floor; he was a piece of ruined goods which had been yanked through the machinery and had come through the other end. He meant nothing, nothing whatsoever.

It was only what he had done that had mattered. He had blown cover, and from Hamilton's point of view, that was something which absolutely could not be done. Anything could happen; you could get into difficulties that might be uncontrollable once cover was blown. Once the whole intricate network of relationships, subrelationships, traffic, and conditions was ruptured by some impatient fool like Shields, you were in a position where the entire operation could break open.

And Hamilton could not have it. He could not have it at all. This was his life, his operation, his business.

No one was going to take it away from him.

One of the men who had been holding Shields until dismissed poked his head into the door with enormous delicacy, and seeing the body on the floor, said, "I just wanted to check if—"

"It's all right," Hamilton said, standing behind the desk. "No problems."

"I didn't think there were any problems. I didn't think—"

"Nothing I couldn't handle myself," Hamilton said. "You don't have to worry about anything like that."

"I wasn't worried. I didn't say you couldn't handle it. I only thought—"

"Don't think," Hamilton said. "You're not paid to think. Your job isn't to think, it isn't to have conclusions. The last guy who did is lying there. Clean him up," Hamilton said. "Clean the dead meat up," and cursing, slammed the desk drawer, walked out of the room, past the man and into the hallway, his mind scurrying away in channels of infinite distraction. Yes, he thought, it was true, this thing had hit him more deeply than he had thought possible; he had thought that if there was one thing that he could count upon it was his ability to control situations absolutely, control them to the ground. That had been his force, his belief, but something like this . . .

Fuck it, Hamilton thought, and kept on walking. This should be the end of it, he knew. By all rights, this should be the end.

But he had the damnedest feeling that it was only the beginning.

IV

Wulff went to the arraignment under custody of his guard and with Williams to keep both of them company. The conversation with Williams had touched him at some corner of consciousness, but he did not want to think of it. Mostly because it did not concern him.

Fuck it. Whatever they were doing in Detroit they could damned well go ahead and do. It was no longer his affair. It was no longer his business; his quest was behind him. Right now, all that he wanted was to be left alone.

It was not the greatest thing this way, to be sure: living in solitary was no man's idea of finding the right destiny. On the other hand, it had its points. No one bothered him; he had a feeling of completion. And with the man who had killed his girl, had killed her as deliberately as if it had been he who had inserted the plunger in her arm—with that man in custody and now set for a long, long time off the street, Wulff had the feeling that his work was done.

No, it would never bring Marie back to him. But that was all right; maybe the man who needed her back was dead, had died in that filthy SRO apartment. So it was merely a matter of completion. Somewhere the work would have to go on, and maybe there would be someone else to do it, but he, Wulff, was finished. What did Detroit matter? The filth and corruption would go on; the stuff would keep on moving in the vein of the nation, everything would be as it had been. New interests would take over where the old had fallen; the poison would continue to flow. America was poison. If it could not get it from one set of sources, if the rivers were dammed in one place, then they would be opened up in another. That was the physics of the matter. Everything was mechanistic, determined. Stimulus. Stimulus-response. Twitch here, synapse there; and then the dead leg would quiver.

"There he is," Williams said, leaning against Wulff's shoulder, poking him gently. "Doesn't look so hot, does he? I think he's carrying a few marks that he never knew were there before."

Against his will, Wulff, sitting in the courtroom now, near the back, wedged into one of the pews against Williams, the guard standing by the door behind the two of them, looked, saw Smith being wheeled toward the judge's bench by a male attendant. There was a blanket drawn up to his lap; his head bobbed aimlessly in shallow little circles, the tight skin glinting.

"Looks old, doesn't he?" Williams said. "Looks a lot older than he did a few weeks ago, I bet."

Wulff shook his head. "It doesn't matter," he said, and tried to turn inward again, tried to pick up the bleak, even tread of his thoughts which had so contained him since the moment that he had been taken out of the precinct. Voyage in, voyage out, remain within the confines of the self. It hurt less that way. What did it matter how Smith looked? Smith was dead; all of them were dead to him now. He could not avoid seeing, however, the way in which Smith's head rolled as the wheelchair was pushed, the fashion in which the attendant's hands splayed out over the iron. Hell. The man was in hell all right. Well, much luck to him. He didn't care. He just did not care anymore.

"Makes your heart bleed, doesn't it?" Williams said, still nudging him. Wulff said nothing, looked straight ahead. "Don't tell me you're not happy," Williams said. "Don't tell me that it doesn't give you pleasure to look at the son-of-a-bitch like that. Come on. Don't try that."

"I'm not saying anything," Wulff said, "nothing at all. I don't give a damn."

"Lots of people are probably just as happy as you are to see him in that shape," Williams said. "You've left a great big hole in the organization now. A hole which someone sure as hell would like to fill."

"No," Wulff said. "Enough." It was easy, he thought. Easy to sit on this bench, the hard wood curving underneath him in cold little slivers of feeling, and denying, denying. Perhaps he could deny everything. Perhaps if he could stay on this bench long enough, if he could become a kind of artifact implanted within the courtroom like the dull, dead planks of wood, like the fat women who sat alone fanning themselves and crying in a quiet way whenever the bailiff's door clanged, perhaps if he could do that, after a certain period of time they would all go away and leave him. He would be history, no longer present time. But rising stiffly in response to the judge's entrance, standing there then as the judge, an old man with a face like a doorknob, stared out at them bleakly, he doubted that this could be so. He did not think that it could work out in this way. You were never free, he thought, you were never disentangled; there was never a moment at which you were not locked into your humanity, which was itself merely that perilous construction which hung like a rack of meat between future and past. He was no more free, Wulff thought, than he had been at the beginning of this, and probably a hell of a lot less so. It was interesting. It was interesting to realize that everything you had done under the illusion that it would gain you freedom had only locked you further in. He would have to concentrate on that a little later on.

Williams was nudging him in the back, his finger prodding like a plank of wood. "He wants you to approach the bench," he said. The guard grunted, made an indication toward the front of the room. Not his affair. "You're a material witness," Williams said. "You've got to give evidence. You're part of their case."

"No," Wulff said, "no, I don't want to do that." But he was already standing, moving toward the front of the small courtroom, Williams guiding him, the lightest and most tentative of touches on his wrist. Now, as he approached the bench, he could see Smith, see the man quivering in his chair, the blank face of the attendant poised behind; he could see that one flicker, one jolt of expression in Smith's eyes before it receded and the man mumbled something which might have been an obscenity but which Wulff knew was more likely merely a plea. Reduce them to vulnerability then, take away the devices of their insulation, and they were all the same, quivering meat on the chain, begging for protection, begging for some force which would sweep them away and save them from this mess that they had made of their lives. Vulnerability and terror, that was it, and underneath a plank of wood. "He wants you to approach the bench," he said. The guard grunted, made an indication toward the front of those sheets stretched so tight, the flickering light of self-preservation. "Look at him," Williams said. "I want you to look at him."

And Wulff turned, looked at the man sitting in the wheelchair, the judge looming over them as if from a great height, the same kind of judge he had faced so many times when he had been with the PD, the bleak, blank face of the civil servant who would time and again hold the cases over, dismiss the cases, continue the cases, do anything but enact them. But it was not the judge with whom he was concerned, but Smith. They exchanged one look, one searing look, Wulff seeing his own reflection reduced in the man's eyes, those eyes winking terror, underneath it loathing, and in that moment Wulff felt that he could see the man falling away. Smith had never mattered; he had not mattered at all. All the time he had merely been an interposition between Wulff and something larger. It was that larger thing which mattered, that larger force whose light Smith blocked that he would have to understand. And then he heard a sound, one crack, a sound he had heard in dreams and on the street so often that his body had reacted long before his brains had; he was already diving toward the floor, taking cover like an infantryman scrambling before a land mine. "Someone get the gun!" a voice was screaming. "Get the gun, get the gun!" And down on the flat, gray surfaces of the courtroom, Williams toppling to his side, Wulff could hear two more shots, closely spaced and somewhat nearer than the first, and then there was the dull sound of explosion near him, the sound of impact. Looking up, he saw Smith's skull slowly, grandly fall open, and from it spurts of fire seemed to move toward the ceiling. No fire, of course, merely blood and brains spewed out in a halo, and he thought, almost stupidly: *They want to kill Smith, not me. If it had been me, I would have been dead already. No, it's someone after Smith; they want to shut him up. I wonder who it could be, I wonder what he knows.* . . . His thoughts were oddly precise, marshaled in the cop's way, but there was no time to think of it, no time to consider, not that he wanted to anyway. It was something very far, far away, and dull. Something fell on top of him as casually and brutally as if it were a hand coming across his face; it hit him between the shoulderblades and rolled, and he realized that that must be Smith toppling from the wheelchair. How interesting, he thought, his mind scuttling away from the situation in a strange and detached fashion; it might have been another mind, it might have been a different incident; how strange that all of this is happening now, now, when it is supposed to be over. This might have sent him into a reverie, might have enabled him to lie on the floor and think it all through quietly, but there were more sounds around him, bellows, screams, and little hisses; then Williams was shouting: "Make a run for it! *Make a run for it!*"

What the hell are you talking about? Wulff wanted to ask in an abstracted way. What do you mean, "make a run for it? Run for what? Run from where?" But his partner was hitting him now, slamming him repeatedly on the back, and then he could feel the pressure of Williams' hand tugging.

"You stupid fool," Williams was screaming, his mouth poised in a frantic O, his eyes glaring bright. "This is the time to do it. If you don't do it now, you never will, and you could get killed here!" And then, like the tumblers of a pinball machine slamming into place together, it fused for Wulff: He understood what Williams was saying; he understood what was happening. Someone was making a run on the courtroom, someone who was very interested in making sure that Smith did not testify. Someone who did not have Smith's best interests at heart was attempting a desperate play to shut off the case right here, and Wulff was part of Smith's case. All of them were. He was in the line of fire now, but even beyond that, even if his own presence were not to be considered, if the gunner was out merely for Smith and not for Wulff— even so, he must take this opportunity in the uproar to escape, because another would not come for a long time.

They would tighten after this. They would put Wulff so far under wraps that he might never see daylight again. If he did not do it now, he might be taking in his very last little piece of freedom.

And he did want to be free. He realized that, all of this passing through him in the tumbling event of the courtroom, forms scattering, hysterical shouts, someone in the distance being surrounded by police, uniformed and plainclothes, who were gasping, shoving, trying to move in tighter, but circling the gun, which was still being waved free in little circles above the gunman's head. He wanted to be free; he could no longer exist like this. He had been underground for a long time, he had been deep in the bowels of his own denial, but it could not continue to exist. The stakes were too high, they had not declined at all; only he, Wulff, had changed, and not in a way which was to his or anyone's credit. If he did not take this opportunity, it would not return.

And his quest would have been as for nothing. Everything would be the same. In another year the new order would have risen, would have sealed all of the cracks, and it would be the same as always—except the more terrible, because they would have learned from their mistakes, from the chinks in the armor which he had discovered.

A scream of absolute rage came from Wulff as he sprawled there in the heat and the haze of the courtroom, his fists clenched, his eyes closed not against sight but against what he saw as a vision of the future— America as a 137th Street and Lenox Avenue of the mind, forms reeling and scattered through filth, the filth rising, the great plunger throbbing . . .. He could not bear it. If everything he had done would come only to this repeated monstrosity, then it was worse than having done nothing at all, it would make a mockery of his battle, would even mock the dead, because if nothing else, they had died in the furtherance of what was right. No, Wulff thought, no, he could permit that only by losing himself entirely, obliterating his past, obliterating Marie himself, who might have died so that the battle could begin. Bellowing, he rose to his feet; bellowing, he ran through the stench of the courtroom; bellowing, he ran toward the door. And in the screams and the shouts, the confusion and the terror, the only one who might have noticed him was Williams, but Williams himself was too occupied with protecting his own position, which, if he had thought about it, was so close to Wulff's as to be indistinguishable.

Wulff knew, now, that he would never stop running.

V

Detroit. Something was going on in Detroit. It all tracked back there; hell was breaking loose in the motor city, and Wulff's first thought when he had come clear of Centre Street, running, still running, was that this would be the next stop, but in the meantime there was much to be done, much to be accomplished before he could make his way twelve hundred miles west to Motown. Looked at objectively, the odds against him getting there were overwhelming; he was wearing prison fatigues, he had no money, he had no clear sense of direction, he had wasted weeks of his one, his irreplaceable life, dreaming in his cell as if the world did not exist anymore, as if it would stop at the time of his own cessation. And this was not true; it had gone on, everything was moving ahead. Had they not tried to kill Smith? Would they not have killed him, given the same opportunity? What the hell was going on in Detroit?

No, in a war, in a long-range quick-combat war like this one, you improvised, you played it by ear, but above and beyond everything else, *you kept on moving*. So what Wulff did in the next two hours was to do exactly that: improvise, make the changes the way that they had to be made, but concentrating always on the one single goal, which was to get himself back together again and get out to the Midwest before they took away everything that he had built. When you played it by ear, you functioned in a kind of haze, the smoothness of your functioning sometimes in its well-oiled fashion almost replacing consciousness, so that what you did you did as if it were someone else, but that someone else could be trusted to do it right, being a part of you, and you only the observer.

So the stranger who was Wulff did the following things within the next couple of hours: he stole a car at Worth Street simply by stepping into an old Ambassador which was idling at curbside and telling the terrified driver to get out. "Get out," the stranger said, "get the hell out right now before you buy more trouble than you can handle." And the driver, a man in his mid-thirties, clutching a briefcase, got out the passenger side so quickly that he hardly seemed interested in finding out what kind of trouble he was avoiding exactly, much less trying to see if Wulff had anything evidential to back up the threat. Next time, Wulff guessed, the man would remember to drive with his doors locked, but then again, on a bright, panting fall day in the downtown district, who the hell would think that something like this could happen? New York was bad, New York was going downhill, but you still had a reasonably better than even chance of getting from here to there in heavy traffic with at least your car.

But the stranger could not worry about issues like that; the stranger kept on moving. Hand-shifting the battered Ambassador, which seemed barely able to get out of second gear, wrenching on the nonpower steering, he guided the car uptown to Ninety-second Street, which was the site of his final stay in New York before he had gone score-settling with Smith; it was there that he still had a small cache of arms, clothing, and money which could get him going again—if they were still in the SRO room, that is, if he hadn't been locked out, if the room hadn't been cleaned out, if the PD hadn't tracked him to this place. And granted all of that, there was still the problem of gaining access. They had, needless to say, appropriated all of his goods downtown, although he would be damned if he would tell them where the key fit.

But the stranger Wulff had become was resourceful indeed; he was willing to take matters step by step and to gamble that even at his worst he could stay a couple of steps ahead of the two bands that were going to follow: the network and the enforcers. Each in their own way had their limitations, and of the two, the enforcers were to be feared less, because they were—he had long since faced this, even when he was on their side—almost completely incompetent. At this moment he could imagine the condition of that courtroom on Centre, the chaos, the stink, the dead body of Smith being gawked at by the court reporters, newspaper reporters, a couple of magazine stringers who would be frantically trying to reach their offices to nail down a good five-hundred-dollar assignment. He could imagine the way that the judge would look, back in his chambers, his face white and fearful, remembering only that there had been gunfire in another courtroom a few years ago and that that time a judge had been killed. There would be hundreds of uniformed police pouring through the pews looking for an explanation that simply did not exist anymore. Because the man who had shot Smith, Wulff was sure, was dead. If he was not dead by his own hand, then the cops gathered around him, all of them with guns, would have done the job. At least one of them would have panicked and fired with all the justification in the world.

So the full story would never get out. All of the stringers with all of their expense moneys would get no closer to it than Wulff was at this moment. And Wulff would follow it through in a way which would never result in getting expense moneys.

He was going to find out. He was going to get them. He was going to get the men who had gotten the man who had gotten Smith, because Smith had been *his* meat, and no one was going to get between the two of them and live.

At Ninety-second Street Wulff pulled off Broadway, idling down the block, then cut the wheel right and drifted into a spot near a hydrant, looking over at the rooming house in which he had lived, checking out the window of the third-floor room to the west, streetside, where the armaments and money were stashed if he was going to find them at all. Racing the engine lightly, holding his foot stiffly on the brake, he thought for a while, thought of the actual risks of getting into the street, going up the stairs and making a direct attempt to get into the apartment; but there was nothing else to do, there was literally no other way to play this, he thought, if it was going to be played at all. It was certainly a hell of a time for caution; caution should have operated back at the courthouse or long before that if it was going to be operative here; and with that he seemed to sever the last of his bonds with the exhaustion and revulsion he had felt since the time that they had taken him to Centre Street; he seemed to come fully back to himself, the edges of his old and new personalities fitting together with a hard click, and simultaneously with the click he cut the engine, took the keys out of the ignition and considered them for a while, then tossed them on the seat and got out of the car. It was above the Seventy-ninth Street line; that meant no tow job, but after five or six tickets the cops might get curious and check registration. Then again they might not. There was absolutely no way of judging or anticipating the incompetence of the NYPD unless you had been their employee, and then the knowledge was something to get you sick.

He got out of the car, slammed the door, walked briskly up the stairs into the rooming house. In the lobby the odor overwhelmed him along with the sign someone had posted behind the glass of the front door: ALL RESIDENTS WILL USE KEY TO ENTER. GUESTS ARE TO RING BELL AND BE PERSONALLY ADMITTED. He kicked the door through easily, the spring lock sighing back, and went up the bare flight to the room that had been his, the door sutured tight against the light, seemingly impenetrable.

Wulff looked it over for a few moments, shaking his head, and then, at a point of calculation reached somewhere at a subconscious level, kicked out again as he had done downstairs and hammered his heel into the door, grinding a little at the end and then recoiling.

The door buckled. He came in again, a little lower and toward the toes this time, and the door came open like a zipper, collapsing from the top, strips of light opening like wounds down the sides, then all of it caving backward. He had made hardly any sound at all. No one looked into the hallway; that was always an advantage of Manhattan living, whatever else you thought of it.

Wulff went into the room which had been his and found that everything was exactly as he had left it. In the closet, the rifles glinted at him like swords, the bayonets sent little echoes of circling light. In the top drawer of the bureau his money was there, fifty one-hundreds neatly stacked, winking at him like eyes.

When he had not gotten back the last time they had simply sealed up the apartment and waited for his return, sure that he would come back, sure that they could get the rent out of him then.

They had checked out the closets just to make sure that he had something worth coming back for, and then they had forgotten about it.

Oh, boy.

New York was a groove, all right.

But now he was back in action.

VI

The plan as Hamilton had worked it out carefully over a period of months was airtight, and nothing could possibly go wrong. There would be the matter of detection, maybe, but since he was a union steward and controlled almost everything on the floor, passed on everything that got up to management, he had almost a perfect hand upon it, and he would not, in fact, have gotten into this at all if he felt that that control was lacking. The stuff would be sealed into the frames only of those cars headed for Toronto, a small and random fraction of all the de Villes, Eldorados, hearses, and flower cars that rolled off the line, and they would be only random at that; only one Cadillac in five or six would receive the stash, and which one that would be was known only to Hamilton and to the foreman, Shields, who was actually putting the stuff in. Sealed up, the cars would be loaded from the plant for Toronto without even a touch-up or inspection, since that was the responsibility of the Canadian authorities. (That was the beautiful part of it, there were spot checks and final touch-ups on the American cars, but the attitude toward the Canadians was that they could go screw themselves; it was their problem, they could do anything they liked with the damned cars as long as they paid for them.) Then, in Toronto, the connection, a man whose last name Hamilton did not even know and did not want to know, would put the stuff into his own channels. Hamilton did not know anything about that. Where the shit went, who took it, what became of it, was none of his business at all. It was strictly a cash operation. He had no opinion that extended beyond the cash.

And there was plenty of it; it was payment on receipt, COD, and every Monday morning an envelope would arrive from his contact in Canada, carried by a uniformed messenger. The messenger service was incredibly expensive, having to work customs and the border as they did, but it had been Hamilton's decision to do it that way, skim it right off the top, and it was the cleanest and most satisfying feeling: nothing could compare with opening an envelope right in his own living room, with his kids still asleep upstairs at seven in the morning, and pulling the money out, denominations of one hundreds only—to the nearest hundred was his arrangement with his contact. And so it would roll in, twenty bills a week, thirty, twenty-five, thirty-seven, except for one beautiful week when he had moved out seventeen cars and ten thousand dollars had come in in one beautiful wad of a hundred bills. Twenty percent of that had to be skimmed off and passed along the line, of course, but that was a bargain too, just like the messenger service. Twenty percent for the loading and for the checker to keep his eyes off it was really like stealing money. Although Hamilton would never have admitted it, he would have paid a flat fifty if he had been put to pressure. But he never had. It was found money for the others, and no involvement. Nobody wanted to get involved. That was America for you, okay.

So it was a beautiful operation. It was one sweetheart of a beautiful operation. Running the stuff out was as profitable as running it in, and a hell of a lot safer, what with not having to worry about distribution problems or possession. As a matter of fact, it was absolutely the best deal that Hamilton had fallen into in thirty-three years of looking for an edge, and the way that he had things calculated, if things worked out, if he could only keep them going like this, in another six months to a year tops he would be able to get out of the plant for good, live quietly at home for a couple of years so that there was no undue attention caused by his early retirement, and then he could take off completely, not only from his bitch-wife, but from the kids too. Beautiful as they were, he was too far ahead in life, too old to have to deal with a twelve-, two-, and six-year-old. All girls. Beautiful kids, he loved them, he would pay through the nose so that they could have everything that they wanted for the rest of their lives. Margaret could get hers too, they all could, on just a fraction of what he was going to be able to take out of the country; but as far as he was concerned, he was going to go to someplace like Sweden or maybe Djakarta or Majorca where it was warm and catch up with some fucking. Go to all three, and twenty other places besides, be a citizen of the world. Fuck girls of every nation and description, every ability and perversion. Sometimes in his sleep at night, dreaming of them thickly, he could get hard in a way that he hadn't for twenty years, just knowing what it would be like to live that way.

And then Shields had screwed him up. That fucking Shields had screwed him up; even if this black, Hooper, *had* seen something on the line, there was no need for Shields, one of his pay-out men, to panic and cause an industrial accident. At the least Shields should have consulted with him first; they surely would have been able to work out something. But Shields had panicked, all right; like everybody else, he was just out to get his, but unlike Hamilton, he was unable to consider the long view, and now he had really fucked things up like never before. Hamilton was no fool. He knew it. He knew that he was in but deep now.

Killing Shields had been bad, a bad move. Doing it with the two others around, witnesses to murder and burial, was even worse. But it had struck Hamilton immediately that it had to be handled clean, it had to be sealed off right away, or it would get a good deal worse. Shields would have had nightmares, he would have talked to someone about Hooper. Other people would have talked. No, it was better to take the most extreme action at once and not worry about the consequences.

The truth was, and Hamilton had to admit that he knew it, he was probably doing the same thing that had gotten Shields killed; he had panicked and taken extreme action. But there was nothing else to do. He would probably have to advance his plans to leave the country by several months.

Meanwhile, though, there was too much to deal with. The Hooper business had created a real stink. Shields's death had helped a little, because there was so much mystery and excitement in the plant about that, about his body being found dumped without identification in a lot the next day, that for a while conversation had even gotten away from Hooper's accident. Hamilton himself wasn't asked about Hooper at all; they had a few perfunctory questions about his relationship with Shields and when he had last seen him, but they meant nothing, and he had dodged his way through them in an almost absentminded fashion. They couldn't pin a goddamned thing on him, no matter how they tried. There was no apparent connection with Shields at all.

It was the Hooper business which was bad. The stuff in the car, which Hooper had seen. Had the car been caught at intercept, or had assembly been finished? He didn't even know. Had they paneled up the car and had it gone out on the truck, or did they have it in some workshop with the stash, stripped down? And if they did, could they track it down to him?

No. No, they could not. He was safe there, too. His own sources of supply were absolutely airtight. They had as much as or more at stake than he did, and by virtue of what they were, they were the best damned cover in the world. No one could work past him to find out his supply source, and if they did, it wouldn't do them any good at all. He was covered that way.

He was covered all ways. He was even covered with the Shields murder, because there was no way it could be tied to him and because the two men who had buried him were in just as deep as Hamilton himself. What the hell could they do to him? Not a damned thing; that was for sure and certain. He was sealed up tight.

Tight. All that he had to do, he knew, was to wait the thing out, and everything would be fine. All roads would lead to blank facing. But it was hard, my God it was hard to play the waiting game when every cell of him screamed for action and when there was that feeling, at all times, that they were closing in. That circumstances were roping in tighter and that no matter what he did, he was in the center of the noose. It was not possible. His best instincts told him that he was completely in control; no one could touch him. But at some base level . . .

On the evening of the sixth day after the discovery of Shields's body, Hamilton got a call at home from a man who would not identify himself to Hamilton's wife. That right away was trouble; his contact had never called at home, it was an unwritten but tight understanding that there was to be as little personal involvement as possible, that all the personality should go into the decks of one-hundred-dollar bills; those were the smiles. But when Margaret handed him the phone, saying, "He won't say who he is," he could tell something from her tone, from her aspect, that she probably knew much more about what he was doing than he had ever suspected. What he had taken for ignorance might only have been indifference, because there was knowledge in her eyes. It was frightening that at some level his wife might be an unwilling collaborator. It shed an entirely different light on this circumstance, not that he wanted to get into that now. Not that he wanted to think of it at all. "Yes," he said into the phone. He still thought that it might not be his contact. Maybe it was only something down at the plant, some bastard caught holding on duty, or a sitdown strike on the line. It was not his shift, but they sometimes would call you in anyway just as a show of force. That hope went right away, though. "Hello," the voice said, "sorry to bother you at home."

"Then why do it? You should never do it."

The voice laughed. "Right," it said, "not sorry to bother you at home. Quite necessary, I'm afraid. There's been a lot of questioning here about how a certain incident was handled."

"I had nothing to do with that," Hamilton said.

"You had everything to do with it. There's been a strange death."

Hamilton swallowed and willed a fierce calm through his body. "No one I know about," he said.

"You're quite sure about that?"

"I'm not submitting to questioning," Hamilton said. His wife was staring at him. Crouched against a wall, she regarded him brightly. He did not know that the woman had so much spirit. He would not have taken her for this level of attention. "Listen," he said, "This is impossible. We can't talk here. If there's anything to say, you'll have to do it tomorrow at—"

"There's quite a bit to talk about," the voice said, "but I agree that we should do it quickly. You've fucked up, Hamilton. You've fucked up badly. The last package isn't here."

"All right," Hamilton said, "all right, it isn't there." Then where was it? He tried to keep his mind in one cycle. "That's not important. We'll make it up to you."

"Where is it?"

"I don't know," he said. "I don't know where—"

"I think you do, Hamilton. I think you know where everything is."

"You're wrong," he said. "It isn't like you think at all. This is—"

"You've fucked up very badly," the voice said again with the superb and terrible calm. "It isn't the kind of thing which can be tolerated at any level, and yet you've permitted it to happen. Why did you let it happen, Hamilton?"

"I didn't," he said. "I didn't let anything happen; none of it is my fault at all. I just did the best I could; I tried to handle this at the lowest level . . ." And then he cut himself off, because he realized that what he was saying made no sense whatsoever. He was babbling. "Forget it," he said. He would reassume command; he would show them that he was in control. "If you don't like it, you can deal with someone else. I don't give a fuck anymore."

"I'm afraid that won't work out," the voice said. "It would be very convenient if you could cut yourself out of the matter or, on the other hand, if we could pick up someone, but I'm afraid that we're all in this together. You don't seem to realize what you've done here. Now, where are those goods?"

"I don't know."

"We were afraid of that. We were afraid that you would say you didn't know."

"It's the truth!" Hamilton bellowed. "Damn it, it's the truth! I'm not holding back on you. What the fuck would it benefit me to hold back on you?"

"I don't know," the voice said. "I can't see what it would benefit you to have two men killed, but you apparently saw something in it. I can't talk for you, Hamilton. No man can talk for any other."

"It's not true," Hamilton said, babbling again. "It wasn't two, it was just one. The first death was the fault of that stupid fucking idiot, that Shields. I had to have him cooled because . . ." And he stopped again. His wife, arched against the wall now, her body compressed, was looking at him in a way that she had not for some twenty-one years. He had not seen that look of intensity and fear since their early times in bed together. "Christ almighty," he said both to the voice and to her, "I can't go on this way. I just can't—"

"Get the goods, Hamilton," the voice said. "Find out where the goods are, and get them here. That's the best advice we can give you. Otherwise . . ."

"Otherwise what?"

"Well, we don't know. We'll have to deal with that when we come to it, won't we? It doesn't suit anything to make predictions. One way or the other, Hamilton, we're going to get what we need. We're going to do it with or without you. It looks very much at this time as if we're going to have to do it without you, though, if you follow what's being said here."

"You bastard," Hamilton said. It was not a wise thing to say. It was not the kind of thing that you had any reason to tell these people, and yet it had just slipped out. His wife cringed against the wall, seemed to arc as if a shock had been put through her, and then her face broke open into little pieces. It was not only her face which was crumpling, Hamilton thought. No, it would be easier if one could think that it would end there.

"That was very stupid," the voice said. "That was stupid and unnecessary. You will regret that."

"Please," he said, "leave me alone."

"A valuable shipment has been lost. That shipment is your responsibility."

"Autonomy," Hamilton said vaguely, reaching for the word. "This is my territory. This is my responsibility. I have autonomy within it."

"You have no autonomy at all. You fucked up, Hamilton, and now you're going to pay. You're going to find that stuff and get it to us, or you're going to regret it. You'll regret it anyway. You will, a good deal."

"It's not my fault—"

"Everything is your fault, you bastard," the voice said, and hung up, the phone sending out little echoes and ripples of sounds; and then, in the emptiness of the severed connection, he could hear a discordant whine, louder, like the shrieking of some great forest animal during intercourse, or the approach of a siren. He hung up the phone, the instrument damp in his hand. And then he walked toward the living room, Margaret following him slowly, scuttling, and he retreated into a smaller and smaller opening of space until at last, in a corner, she forced him to turn with a touch and stood before him then, and every line of her face poured knowledge at him.

"What is it?" she said. "You'd better tell me now. I won't be put off, you've got to tell me what's happening. What have you done?"

And he wanted to shout at her and he wanted to tell her that it was none of her fucking bitch's business and he wanted to tell her that he had spent his whole life alone, working things always alone so that she would not have to bother with things like this and she had no right at this time to intrude upon him. He wanted to tell her that it was his fucking affair and he would handle it, and he wanted to tell her that no it was nothing to worry about, nothing at all, just let him worry about it as he had worried about everything else. He had gotten them this far, hadn't he? He had gotten them the house, the money, the cars. But even as all of this and more came bubbling, fulminating to his lips, something else happened, and Hamilton crumpled, six-feet-one, he crumpled in front of her, and then he was falling into her grasp, stunned, his sobs like those of someone else in the room that could not be him, and he was saying, "Oh, Margaret, Margaret, I'm sorry, I'm so terribly sorry, I just can't stand it anymore . . . ." And then, for the next few minutes there was a long, long tunnel of passage between the place he had been before this had happened and the place where he was going to emerge, and he did not know, he did not know if he could enter into that new, that empty, that appalling future.

VII

At the Pennsylvania tip, five hundred miles out of the city, Wulff pulled off Route Eighty and bumped down a side road in another stolen car, this one a 1966 black Fleetwood, to a roadside telephone booth. He liked Cadillacs, he liked old Cadillacs even more, all of that gloss gone to corruption, all of that complexity half-marred toward the grave; he thought that an old Cadillac could be compared to America itself, not that you had to be metaphysical in the least to appreciate the ruined grandeur of those vehicles. A Cadillac at almost every step of its eight- or nine-year journey to the boneyard was a good bargain, a well-maintained car, a car that had been given more pride and attention than any Pontiac or Chrysler. Dialing Williams' number direct with plenty of change heaped up next to him, the sun glinting across the hood of the huge car pulled up against the booth, he had the feeling of once again being almost in utter control of his life. He sighed; he was doing what he had always been meant to do. Why had he thought for a moment that he could go back on his pledge? This was his life, his work. After one ring Williams' wife picked it up and Wulff announced himself, waiting for the explosion of feeling or remonstrance that would come, but she said nothing at all, it was a different woman there, she simply said that Williams was out in the backyard and she would get him, and then he hung there for a while looking at the little twirling patches of light, looking at the dull sheen of the trunk containing all of the armaments, until Williams got on the line and Williams said, "Are you on your way to Motown?"

"Maybe halfway."

"I had every confidence in you."

"You always did. I always knew I could count on your confidence."

"Everything all right?"

"Sure," Wulff said. "I stole an Ambassador downtown, and then uptown I got myself a nice Fleetwood idling in the garage at Ninety-sixth Street. Some attendant will learn not to abandon cars while he takes a leak anymore. It's not a bad one, either; it's getting twelve miles to the gallon."

"Great," Williams said. He paused, and then his voice came in a strained, slightly higher tone. "They're running the stuff out of a Cadillac plant to Toronto in the frames of the cars."

"French Connection," Wulff said.

"Life imitating art."

"Never," Wulff said, "never."

"It was a nice tight operation for a while. Some foreman in the plant, a guy named Shields, was overseeing it. We don't quite know who the guy he was underneath is, but we have a pretty good idea."

"Who's *we?*"

"My connection," Williams said, "my connection and I."

"He isn't French, is he?"

"Oh, come on," Williams said, "come *on,*" but he giggled a little. "A guy named Hooper got killed in a plant, probably because he saw something that he shouldn't, and then Shields got cooled too. A bunch of people are pretty scared and mad; it looks like they're panicking."

"Who killed Shields?"

"Whoever is running the stuff out. The way they figure this is that Shields overreacted, and the murder of this guy opened up so many questions that they had to take out Shields also. But it can't be sealed off."

"They're running the stuff into Canada," Wulff said, "but where are they getting it from?"

"Well," Williams said, and paused, "well, that's the really interesting and unique part of this situation. No one is quite sure where the guy above Shields was getting it from, who his source is, how the distribution is worked out on that end. There are some guesses, though. My source has some pretty good suggestions."

"Police source?"

"Yeah," Williams said, "a lieutenant on the North Side."

"You're getting quite a reputation, eh? You're becoming a pipeline."

"Something like that," Williams said. "That's about all I care to be too, a pipeline. You understand?"

"I understand," Wulff said. "So the idea is to start where? At the plant?"

"Play it by ear," Williams said. "That would be the best way. Things would show up at the plant, though. They're pretty scared; they can't keep a lid on it."

Wulff watched a mail truck move slowly toward him, cresting a little rise, and said, "You've got the whole thing figured out, don't you?"

"I do the best I can."

"Why don't you join me?"

"You don't want anyone to join you," Williams said. "You're the lone wolf."

"You've got too much faith. You think too much of me. How do you know I can do anything here? How do you know that I even want to?"

Williams said, "You're out, aren't you?"

And that was the truth. He was out. The truck was moving very slowly now, the driver peering through the glass, looking at the Fleetwood with interest, the brakes groaning as it went even more slowly. Wulff realized that this was not the proper place to continue a discussion of motives, not with half an ordnance factory in the back of the car. "All right," he said, "I'll do what I can. It sounds promising, anyway. They're half in trouble as it is."

"You want the address of the plant?"

"I'll fake it," Wulff said, and hung up the phone. The truck had now stopped, was on the other side of the road, little puffs coming from its exhaust, and in the window the form of the driver had vanished. Wulff started to move from the enclosure of the area, and then suddenly he did not; some preconscious instinct held him in place while he looked the situation over carefully. There was something about the truck which did not reckon; it was mottled in a peculiar way, did not seem to bear the colors of the U.S. Mail service so much as a hastily painted version of them, and then too, the engine was idling in slow and then more rapid bursts of speed, moving from sluggishness to high rpm's in a strange uneven way, much as if someone . . . well, much as if someone behind the wheel in a strange and cramped position was gunning the engine in preparation for a fast getaway.

Wulff stayed exactly where he was and calculated the situation.

VIII

There he was with a ton of cocaine and a sleeping girl in the back of the panel truck, just trying to make a quick run through to New York, pick up the bread, dump the girl, and get out of the country, there he was, minding his own business and pleased with the camouflage, and then, Edgerton thought bitterly, then he had to run into this Burton Wulff character right on the side of highway Eighty in Pennsylvania. It was crazy.

Crazy! You spent all your life looking for the big score and settling for the small ones, dreaming a lot and performing a little, and then out of nowhere they dropped the lottery ticket on top of you, they gave you the two-hundred-dollar longshot by special-delivery mail. But meanwhile you were sitting there in the crapper with your pants down, wrapped around your ankles, barely able to move and almost beyond hope. What was he supposed to do now?

There was a ten-thousand-dollar bounty on this bastard's head. Everybody knew that; the word had been passed through all the circles of the network, what was left of it, that is—there wasn't a hell of a lot, although little coke runners like him would hardly expect to be hassled. Ten grand was ten grand, though. All that he had to do was to gun this guy down and use his Polaroid to take a couple of pictures, and there it was. They would lay the ten on him for the privilege, and maybe a little extra. They were that desperate to get him. He knew exactly whom to pass that photo to and how to make the arrangements for the pickup.

Ten grand! He even had the weapon, a good point-thirty-two Magnum small-bore, which he would never be without on this kind of a run, not that, thank God, he'd ever have to use it. But he would if he had to. Once a trooper had chased him and given him a speeding ticket, and even though Edgerton's papers had been in order and he had taken the ticket quietly, what the trooper didn't know was that all the time Edgerton was braking the truck, pulling it over to the side of the road, he had had the gun in his hand in his coat pocket and he would have killed the trooper if it had turned out to be anything more serious than a ticket.

He was ready to do it, all right. The guy had been on the phone talking away, the Fleetwood just at off-angles to the enclosure. Then, he had not been talking, but he hadn't come out, either, which meant that he might have picked up Edgerton's pitch but that he couldn't come out, because all of his weaponry—and there was probably a shitload—was in that Cadillac. So what the hell good was all his weaponry going to do him now? It was a deal. Eventually Wulff would have to come out of that enclosure; it was that simple. Edgerton could hold him under siege in the painted-over panel truck, and when Wulff came out, Edgerton would fix him. Alternatively, he could try to close in on foot or in the truck, but that would have been a trifle riskier and would have given him more exposure than he wanted. Still, it was something not to be entirely ignored. He would have done it if the situation had made it look likely.

One way or the other, or the third; it would have been a groove. It would have been *fun* toying with that initial advantage, with the outcome never in doubt. Edgerton could see where it would have been almost stimulating, almost a contest, the kind of thing he most enjoyed. He loved sports, and what was the greatest thing of all was to convert things into a sports context; that was why he thought of himself running the coke as a marathon runner moving under pressure. But he couldn't play it at all. He just couldn't do it.

He had this sleeping bitch in the back, Jessica, eighteen or nineteen years old, long blond hair, knapsack, the whole paraphernalia. She had been alone in a diner in southern Illinois, and it had been the easiest thing in the world to slide into the booth just under the gazes of the truckmen who had been staring at her, and begin to talk to her casually, intimately; unlike the truckers, he had the uniform of her kind, the sideburns, the dungaree jacket, the little beard. She had begun to come on to him right away, and it had been easy, easy; she had been, as he had suspected, dropped there on a hitch; she was looking for another hitch. East. She said she had a child back East, and a husband too, had been on the road alone all summer trying to find herself, but now it was time to go home. Her husband had been very tolerant, but if she didn't show up soon, he would cut out for good, and what would happen then? He made a pretty good living; she needed the money.

It had worked out fine; Edgerton had taken her out of there and put her in the truck, and just eight miles down the road they had found a motel, and it had been the easiest thing imaginable to take her in, day rates, and bang the shit out of her, not that she was such a terrific fuck, but then again, she beat making the long miles east alone, which he had been prepared to do otherwise but which was never much fun at all. He had looked forward to making the trek just that way, the coke under the seat in the front so she could have the whole converted back of the truck to lie in, and after the first time, when he didn't have to make an appearance anymore, they had done their banging right there in off-road rest areas or sometimes in actual forests, and it hadn't been a bad way to make eight hundred miles a day, he figured; it certainly was better than the stereo. The knowledge that she was back there sleeping, that he could stop and fuck her anytime he wanted—all she did was sleep and fuck and eat, which might be a kind of disease, but oh boy, what a disease! All of these cunts should only have it!—had been comforting. But then, rocking down the lanes on Eighty, pulling off on a sudden impulse, deciding that he *deserved* a fuck after all the good work he had done to pound the stuff this far, Edgerton had run into this Wulff character by the roadside . . . and *now* what the hell was he going to do?

It would have been so easy without the girl. But with her it was going to be a bitch; there was no way to conduct a campaign with a witness, let alone the kind of witness this girl would be: he could already hear the screams, the hysteria, the pleas. For all of her waist-length hair and her easy, cool manner, this girl would disintegrate in the face of violence the same way that she would fall apart under sex; time and again he had seen his thrusts reduce her to weeping, and this would be even worse . . . but that meant that if he were to do anything now he would have to kill her, kill her so that he could conduct his business and collect his ten thousand dollars in peace. He could not do it, Edgerton had to admit that: he was not capable of going behind those panels and killing the girl. She would not be the first person that he had killed, not even the first woman, but it would be the first murder committed coldly and with calculation . . . and he could not do that. He was no psychotic. He was no murderer; murdering was only a business. It would be a matter of business with this Wulff character. But not with the girl.

No, he could not do that. But where would this leave him, then, stalking the area, waiting for Wulff to emerge from the shelter of the boards walling off the telephone from the sounds of the road? He could not stay here indefinitely. As isolated as the area was, sooner or later a prowl car would come through, state troopers looking for trouble, and they would have questions about the setup here. Also, after dark Wulff would be able to make a bolt for the Fleetwood; even with full headlights he would not be able to open up all of the area; there would be small pockets of shadows into which he might dart, and then too, there was the need for sleep. His own alertness could not be maintained indefinitely. And sooner or later the girl would get up, come to the front, ask Edgerton exactly what the hell he was doing. He could not answer that. He had no response that he could figure out as satisfactory.

So what to do? It was like seeing ten thousand dollars turn into muddy colors, like oil running thickly with the rain and vanishing into a sewer; it was like seeing all hope and possibility draining away, and yet he could not give it up . . . not with an opportunity like this. It might change his life. A man did not want to run coke forever. He was twenty-five years old and better for other things than this, but if he did not move on, the fine edge of alertness which had kept him going would be rubbed off, and he would be a twenty-six and then a twenty-seven-year-old coke runner, and where the hell would he be then? No, it definitely would not work, Edgerton thought; it was intolerable to continue, intolerable to let it go by, because it would never happen again. And so he sat there, pinned by the wheel, looking at the changing colors in the area of the enclosure, and it was frustrating, by God it was infuriating, it was ten thousand dollars glinting at him from the waters of the sewer just before it fell away forever; it was two gigantic tits of some movie star he would never meet, bobbing and weaving, nipples erect, in three dimensions out of some huge screen before his mouth . . .. Was he going to run cocaine all his life? Edgerton thought. Was that was what he was going to be? First a twenty-two-, then a twenty-three- and twenty-four- and now twenty-five-year-old coke runner, and then up the rungs of destiny: thirty, thirty-five, forty, forty-five, fifty-six, sixty-two . . . that was it, he would be a sniveling man of sixty-two, kidneys gone, bladder like a grape, his coccyx rubbed to the bright consistency of a nail, pushing his rig through the western and far western states, the North Dakota circuit; that was it, Fargo, Bismarck, and the Black Hills . . . .

Fuck it, he thought, and the image of a sixty-two-year-old coke runner wiping snot from his nose as he pushed his old 2004 Dodge Hornet to greater and greater speeds through the blasted hills, forty, forty-one, forty-*two* miles an hour, must have thrown him over the line, because suddenly Edgerton had the gun in his hand, was uncoiling, his hand fumbling at the lever of the panel-truck door. Fuck it, he would have to *stalk* the bastard. Better to wait it out—that would be the sensible course, and one which could not fail in the long run—but this was not an idealized world in which he lived, and you had to take the bitter with the sweet, you had to keep operative, you had to do the possible . . . and he could not kill the girl. He had this prejudice; he could not kill anyone he had fucked.

Edgerton came out on the ground on the far side of the truck, the side facing away from the telephone enclosure, weaving slightly from seven hours of road fatigue, rubbing his scalp, pushing his blond hair out of his eyes. The truck provided him with perfect cover; no way that he could be seen, much less attacked, with the truck between him and the man, but the trouble was that it also blocked his own view; and as quiet as he had been, this Wulff might understand that he had left the truck, might make a break to his own Fleetwood . . . and if he did that, then all bets were off. He probably had armaments stashed away there, and once he got to the Fleetwood, he was a quicker, deadlier, more effective killer than Edgerton thought he ever could be. No; he could not wait it out. He would have to make his move now or not at all, Edgerton thought, and bringing the Magnum up against his chin in a stalking position, he came against the door and then around the hood, the grass arching against his feet, moving quickly, now slowly, quietly, looking for just that one angle, that one slash of light in which he could find his man and kill him.

Coming around the hood, moving into an open space of light, he thought that he had it for a moment: he could see Wulff framed by the booth, the partitions, thin as paint, cutting him off left and right but providing Edgerton with a shot dead-center. It must have been the excitement that destroyed him, the excitement of having the shot, the realization that he had ten thousand dollars waiting for him there; either that or it was the coke; hard to tell, a little of one and a little of the other. He raised the gun, leveled it, urged himself to take the trigger, and then, before he could complete the circle of death—hand, trigger, form, enclosure—before he could loop it all together and bring the man down, he heard a high scream from the truck, the sound of a bird in agony, and his arm twitched, he vaulted away his attention, not for a long time, just for an instant, but time enough, time enough, and something landed hard in his stomach, like a fist, and then like a fist began to flower. He felt shards and slivers of pain dig in, expanding, and then, as he fell, he realized that he had done something terribly stupid. He should not have shifted his attention. He should not have let himself be carried away from the point of focus.

But too late, too late, the screaming was still going on, but Edgerton was not in the same place; he was moving away, and as he cycled out of life in small, cautious strokes like a beginning swimmer's, it was with the thought that right up to and past the end he had been stupid. How could this have happened to him? He should have understood that no man such as Wulff would have gone anywhere, done anything at all, without a weapon in his hand.

Stupid . . . but, all right, it beat being a sixty-two-year-old coke runner.

IX

On a bleak October morning, the morning after the phone call from Canada, Hamilton went out into the North Side of Detroit for a rendezvous. He drove his new Continental cautiously, easy on the gas and brake, trying to look as inconspicuous as possible, but there was no way on the North Side that a white Continental could look inconspicuous; he should have known better than to take the car to this rendezvous; he could have taken instead his wife's Corvair, but what the hell, he might as well face it, driving the car gave him enormous satisfactions, satisfactions which often he could get nowhere else. It was a big baby too, a monster; the shield of metal, plastic, and rubber around him gave him a feeling of security that he could have gotten from nothing else. If someone was going to make a move at him—and they might, he might as well face that—he would be far better off in the Continental than otherwise.

Driving through the North Side, he could see the marks of the riots; the wound had scarred over, but the scar tissue was as thin and perilous as the city of Detroit itself, and anything could have ripped it open; then the gash would have oozed again. The city was dying. He knew that; that was no different, every big American city was dying, of course. But there was something different about Detroit, something which put it in an entirely different category: the riots had ripped up the shell of Detroit, destroyed parts of the geography, but it was coming apart from the inside as well, for the industry around which all was centered was dying. There would not be, Hamilton thought, maneuvering the Continental past a sullen pack standing outside a candy store, the bombed-out look of junk in their eyes, there would not be an automobile, as he had grown up to understand it, within ten years. That was clear. There would be something else, and Detroit would make that too, but they would never make it on the margin and in the same way that the old automobiles had been built. And that meant that the city was destroyed, and with its destruction America, because it was the car that made everything go.

One glance in the right, remote mirror to see the group receding as he drove farther into the wasteland, toward the point of his rendezvous. Moving away from him, they no longer looked menacing; indeed, they had the appearance of artifacts, human figures frozen by process into sculpture, so that a hundred years from now they might be plastered in a museum: *Junkies at Rest*; but all of this was possible only because he was shielded by glass and plastic, because the wheel was in his hands, because the car had the power of movement. If he had been on that street corner, Hamilton knew, they would have killed him. It was as simple and devastating as that. Half of the reason would have been racial, but the other half would have been pure smack. It brought death. Shit was death. But he saw no connection between what he was doing and the men on the corner. If there had been any connection to make, he would have been the first to have seen it, but anyone who said that he had responsibility for this was full of crap. If not from him, then from somewhere else. He was merely filling a place which would have been instantly seized by any one of a couple of thousand people. No one would turn it down if they were in the same position.

And besides, he was moving the stuff out of the country. No American junkie was his responsibility. If anything, Hamilton thought, he could be conceived of as a great patriot; what he was doing was getting the shit out of the country. More in Canada, less here—that was one way to look at it. It wasn't that he was trying to put the best face on it, either, trying to rationalize or escape his responsibility; if anything could be pinned on him, he would be the first to say.

But as it was, he was merely doing the country a favor, And Canada, that haven for draft dodgers, Communists, free-love advocates, and lunatics of almost any political persuasion, could fuck itself.

Pulling up to the point of rendezvous, a huge, blasted lot, shards of rubble still glinting coldly three years after it had been torn up, two years after the so-called urban reconstruction project had been supposed to start, Hamilton could see his contact's car parked just a little bit down the line, the motor idling, little plumes of smoke coming from his exhaust. This was the only part of the situation which he did not like, the fact that the meeting could not be in *his* car, the fact that Hamilton had to leave his vehicle and walk fifty feet through the rubble to the car of the other man. It was not fair, strictly speaking; he did not like to expose himself to the situation here, even for an instant, and there was no reason really why he should—he was above his contact in the line of supply—but it could not be fought, there was nothing to fight, it would do him no good at all.

He walked slowly toward the car, his body tensed, alert to sounds of any kind, watching the way that the rubble in the lot seemed to fade into landscape, the landscape into sky, all of it gray and muddled in northern Detroit, all of it reduced to homogeneity. Detroit had reduced differences; now everyone within it was boiling in the same pressure cooker, steaming toward the same dreadful end; but where, he thought, where did this kind of thinking get him? Right or wrong, there was certainly no profit in it.

He opened the door of the car and stepped inside an interior so idiosyncratic, so odorous, so compressed that it seemed to be less of a car than a room, the place where a certain kind of adolescent might retire for sixteen hours a day to consider his life and the possibilities of mass murder. His informant looked at him, a square blank man in his fifties holding a gun; and Hamilton, even as he tugged the door closed, felt a vague twinge of fright; it was unusual for the man to be actually holding his gun. It was visible at all times, bulging in his side pocket near the belt line, but Hamilton could not recall that it had ever actually been taken out before this. "Pull it shut quietly," the man said, "and then sit back on the seat."

Hamilton did so. "Put that gun away," he said when he was done.

"Making you nervous?"

"Everything makes me nervous right now."

"It ought to. I can't blame you for that." His contact shifted on the seat, faced him squarely, the gun bearing down on Hamilton. Slowly, drifting in like smoke from the corners of Hamilton's mind, was the thought that there was death in the car. This man could kill him. He could shoot him in the head and kill him. All the time, their relationship had merely been based upon the element of faith that he would not; that Hamilton, conversely, would not kill him. Now, as if in the glinting bulbs of the dashboard, was illumined the fragility of this connection. The contact had the bulbs rigged so that they blinked every time the brake pedal was pressed; apparently he was pressing it now, because the bulbs blinked like the eyes of frantic animals in the dark. Otherwise he gave no sign of movement, his leg concealed behind the other, casually flung over the seat. "You have a right to be nervous," the man said.

"Put that away," Hamilton said, "put that damned thing away." He had always had a certain authority over the man. After all, he passed him a great deal of money, money which made a significant difference in life style. He had thought that that would be enough to assure control. That had been stupid, Hamilton thought. That had been very stupid.

"I'll put it away when I feel like putting it away," the man said. "The impulse doesn't strike me right now." Then, as if picking up reverberations in Hamilton's own skull, he said, "You've been damned stupid."

"What did you want to see me about?"

"That's what I wanted to see you about. That's all. To tell you how stupid you are."

"I think I've had enough of this," Hamilton said. "I shouldn't have come here." He ducked down, moving toward the door, and shadows from the raised gun glinted at him. He eased back on the seat, feeling his shoulder blades palpitate like hands might run over the upholstery. It was a 1954 Chevrolet, customized. He was terrified, he realized. He was completely terrified.

"Damned right you shouldn't have come here. But that wasn't your first mistake. You shouldn't have killed Shields. That's making a big stink. The man was a foreman."

"I don't know anything about Shields."

"You know everything about him. You've made a lot of people learn too much about him, too." The gun descended on Hamilton's shoulder, and he heard the bone crack even before he felt the pain; then, in little igniting flames, it came, lurched down his arm. He screamed once, froglike within his throat, and then held steady against the seat. The contact adjusted the gun in his hand, business end again protruding. "You've fucked me up," he said.

"I didn't fuck anybody up. I—"

"Yeah? You've opened up things the way they've never been opened up before. I got a call from Canada last night."

Hamilton leaned back farther into the canvas covering the upholstery, only dimly aware of the tension of his body. On the periphery of his mind passed the thought that he might faint, and then the thought drifted away like a scuttling animal in the grass; he would not faint, he was far beyond that. He was in control of himself. He had not gone this far, accomplished this much, planned even his retirement and flight from the country, to end this way. "How could they know?" he said.

"That is what I want to find out. That's one of the reasons we're having this little interview right now."

"There's no way. There's no way at all."

"That's what *you* say. The man I spoke to sounded pretty thorough to me. He seemed to know more about me than I might have thought you did."

"He knew that you were passing the shit on . . . . ?"

"He knew that I was passing the shit on," the contact said. "And I want to find out who told him. Why did you tell him? Why did you do something like that? That wasn't bright, you know, Hamilton. Our relationship is based on confidentiality."

"I didn't tell him anything," Hamilton said. "He didn't get it from me."

"He sounded pretty damned mad about that murder of Shields, the foreman. As far as I can gather, that's what blew it into the open in the first place—Shields. You shouldn't have done that. I can't recommend stuff like that at all."

"Leave me alone," Hamilton said, and tried to get out of the car, made a clumsy, grappling gesture with his right arm. With the butt end of the gun his contact knocked Hamilton's arm down almost casually, Hamilton screaming with the impact. If the man had done it with other than a light touch, he would have had a broken arm.

"Stupid son-of-a-bitch," the man said. "I pass the stuff on to you, you pay me money, that's where it all ends. That's the way it was supposed to be from the start. You know that I can't get involved. You promised from the very beginning, that was the deal. That I would make the supply, but my name wouldn't get into it. What happened?"

"I didn't tell. I didn't—"

"I'm a police officer," the man said. "Do you know that? Did that ever occur to you? I can't tolerate getting my name in on any level. I thought that that was made very clear. I thought we decided on that at the very beginning."

Rubbing his arm, licking his lips, Hamilton said, "Of course that was the agreement. That was the agreement all of the time; I never broke it."

"Yes you did. Yes you did break it, and now you've got all of us in very serious trouble, but your trouble is much more serious than mine. Your trouble makes mine look like a warmup. I'm going to kill you."

Hamilton shook his head. "No you're not," he said. "You're not going to kill me, because they know who you are, and if I'm killed, there's only one person that they can trace it back to, and that's going to be you, and I'm a hell of a lot more valuable to them than you are. *I'm* the one working with them; you're only funneling it through. They'll knock you off ten times quicker than they'd knock me off, and the whole thing will blow up." Was he telling the truth? Hamilton did not even care anymore. He could barely attend to what he was saying. Attending to it would have taken more of an attention level than he had. Survive, that was the main thing. He had to survive. "Let me out of this car," he said, "and get out of here as quickly as you can, and I'll forget the whole thing. I'll forget it ever happened, and you can keep on pushing it, we can deal together just as before . . . if you let me out now."

"You must think I'm as crazy as you are," his contact said, but there was a confused expression in his face; the gun wavered subtly. "You must think I'm crazy as hell to let you walk out of here. Keep on dealing? Deal with this heat on me? You'd be setting me up, that's all."

"So don't deal. You don't like the money, you don't like the relationship, forget the whole package. I don't give a damn. It's your income you're slicing up."

"And that's not all of it," his contact said. "It's not enough that they know who I am and that they can close in anytime. There's someone else closing in too. Wulff is supposed to be heading toward Detroit. I heard that around in the department."

"Wulff?" Hamilton said, and then, like a Venetian blind admitting little cracks of light into the attack of his mind, he knew who the man was talking about. "Oh, him," he said. "The son-of-a-bitch who's been killing people from coast to coast. He hasn't been this far north yet, and I don't think he ever would be. He's not interested in Canada; it's cleaning up America that's supposed to be his bag. Anyway," Hamilton said, a little more information shooting like a kite across the panels, "he's supposed to be locked up crazy in Manhattan, something like that."

"Bullshit," his contact said "Bullshit to all of it. Bullshit to Wulff, and fuck you too." He showed Hamilton the weapon. "Between the one and the other, you've finished me off good," he said. "I guess I've got to kill you."

Hamilton had often wondered how he would face death. Now he knew. He could feel his sphincter begin to open, could feel the slow surge of waters in his bladder as they compressed, muddled together, succumbed to gravity. But he held it in. He brought in his stomach, and he held it in. Everybody had to face death. Death was an inevitable. Get it here; get it forty years from now in a coma in the hospital sheets, it was still death. In a hundred years, who would know the difference? "No you won't," he said. "I'm going to open the door and get out of this car and go back to mine, and you're not going to do a thing. You're angry, but you're not stupid. If you kill me, you lose either way. Alive I'm your only insurance ticket. You're not going to do anything."

He eased his hand up toward the handle of the door, pressed it, opened it. Twenty years with the union, twenty years of knowing how to deal with men were being called on now. If he blew this, then it proved that he had known nothing; but then, that made no difference either, did it? Dead was dead. "I'll take care of them," he said. "I'll keep them off your ass. As long as I'm here to stay between you and them, they're not going to come after you. I'll take care of your Wulff, too. All that can be handled, but it's going to be handled my way or not at all."

"You think I'll let you out of the car," the cop said. "You really think I'm going to let you walk out of here. I've got nothing to lose, don't you understand? You've blown everything."

"Nothing," Hamilton said, "nothing at all. You liked the money. You liked the suits and evenings out; it wasn't Grosse Point, but it beat a cop's salary." He pushed on the door, feeling weightless. "Now cut it out," he said. "Don't be a schmuck—that's what you tell all your suspects, right?—play it the cool way and protect yourself. Don't be a goddamned fool. Murder isn't going to get you anywhere. You cool things, you let me handle this, and we'll be all right. Otherwise it's all over."

The gun shook slightly in the cop's hand. "You think I'm going to let you walk out of this. You think that you can just get away with this."

"Murder accomplishes nothing," Hamilton said. "Murder accomplishes nothing at all." And he put his foot on the gravel, his ankle turning slightly as he put it to pressure and then moved his whole body on it, weaving slightly.

Behind him the cop said, "Murder proves nothing? Maybe you should have thought of that before you killed Shields."

Then Hamilton heard a sound which was really the gun going off in his head and killing him, but in that moment before his consciousness shifted, expanded, dwindled, and pulverized, in that instant the explosion might have been his realization of the truth of what the cop had said. My God, he was right, he had a point there, he really did, impulsive murder was being snatched back by impulsive murder ... live, die by the sword, and now the whole world, not only Detroit, was turning to shit.

X

So Wulff had a panel truck and a load of coke and a very scared girl on his hands. The coke he did not find out about until the Michigan border, when it occurred to him to make a slow, careful hand search of the crevices of the truck precisely for something like that, but the girl he had found immediately.

She had come screaming out of the truck right after he had killed Edgerton, and her panic was so immense that Wulff thought he might have to kill her too, kill her because through her screaming he could not even talk to her, make her understand, but finally, because he could not see killing a woman (unless he absolutely had to, in which case sex discriminations would vanish), he had thrown the gun away, literally tossed it into the woods and faced her empty-handed. Her screams had modulated, her eyes had taken on a very calculating expression, and for just a moment the two of them had shared an appraisal of Edgerton lying in his blood by the side of the road; then the girl had said, "What are you going to do now?"

"I don't know," Wulff had said. "I don't know what I'm going to do."

"I think you'd better haul ass out of here," the girl said. "That's what I'd do if I were you."

"And what about you?"

She ran a hand through her hair in that female gesture. "Me too," she said. "I can't drive these things, though. I can't do a damned thing. He couldn't do a damned thing either, could he?"

"He could do one thing all right."

"He was crazy," the girl said. "I think he was on drugs or something, that's what I think."

"That could be," Wulff said, "that could be," and he looked at the girl, looked at the corpse on the road, looked at the Fleetwood, and then made his decision: it would be best to leave his own car, make a transfer and get out of there in the truck rather than doing it the other way, because the truck would make more evidence than the car would. With his own stuff out of it, the car would be indistinguishable from any others, and besides that, the transmission, the crankshaft had absolutely had it; the thing had been making noises for two hundred miles. The girl was a problem, but looking at her, Wulff could see that she was not much of one; she was probably a pickup, a little blond on the run, bouncing from here to there, and this character had nailed her, but it might have been anyone else, a Harvard Ph.D. or a hit man. The road was just too open; it was a lottery on the road.

He told her that he was loading up the truck and getting out of there; she could stay or go, whatever she wanted. He even offered her the keys to the Fleetwood, told her that she was as welcome to it as anyone else around, but she backed away from that completely, saying that she barely knew how to drive, let alone drive tanks, and that there was no point in staying out here alone on the road; she would only wind up with someone worse than Edgerton picking her up. That had been the guy's name, Edgerton. She said that her name was Jessica and she was eighteen years old (Wulff didn't believe it; she was closer to twenty-four, but he could sympathize with the kind of girl who would want to put herself down in teen-age status to justify her condition, like an old bank teller saying that he was still in his forties so that he would look like less of a failure) and that she was going nowhere in particular except outward. She said that Edgerton had been heading toward New York, and Wulff said that this was no good, he was Detroit-bound, and Jessica said Detroit was fine with her, anything was fine with her as long as she kept on rolling, it didn't matter too much to her where they went. She had no expression on her face at all as he crammed in the ordnance. He had a feeling that he was going to need it. He had a good idea at that point exactly where it was going to be used.

Then it was a matter of cleaning anything personal out of the Fleetwood, which meant really nothing at all, and getting the truck secured, which was pretty simple also; and then the girl, offered her choice, said that she would sit next to him as they went highballing off on Eighty. The corpse was already in rigor, but Wulff didn't think about it too much.

Neither did the girl, apparently; at least, to the degree that Wulff could deduce mental states from outward actions, she didn't seem to be particularly disturbed at all. Edgerton's killing had been a relief to her, it appeared; it had solved a tricky problem of exactly how the hell she was going to shake him when they got to New York—he had taken it into his head that they would have a continuing relationship; at least according to him, she was the first decent fuck that he had had in years, and it had given her a sense of purpose. She spoke about the fucking in a tone so flat, so matter-of-fact, that Wulff perversely found himself excited about it; Tamara outside of bed had spoken about sex in exactly the same way, as if she were a waitress, say, talking about kitchen detail, and then in bed the woman had been absolutely wild, probably because she had, in her own head, taken all the myth out of sex, and coming to it expecting nothing, could get a great deal.

In any event, Wulff, who had thought of nothing but killing since he had come out of the courtroom, and about almost nothing other than killing for a time before that, found that he was not thinking about killing so much now; at least, it was not uppermost in his mind. Detroit would be there, but in the meantime it would take care of itself, and turning to her, he asked her if she wanted to go to a motel. She took this quite gravely, without expression, like an exquisitely trained little girl being complimented on her posture, and then said there was no need to go to a motel, they could pull off the side of the road right here and have sex if he wanted to. Edgerton had fitted out the back of the truck not only with passenger plates so that it could go anywhere but also with a double bed, which enabled the people who were riding in the truck to go anywhere too. Jessica said that this was Edgerton's joke, not hers.

Wulff didn't know how funny this was—he had picked up a certain loathing toward Edgerton; it was difficult to become emotionally involved in a healthy way with people who had tried to kill you—but he considered the offer, and then, after a while, some forty or fifty miles farther west on Eighty, he decided to take the girl up on it. It was not only a matter of energy being discharged—and since he had found Marie dead he had too often thought of sex in exactly that way—but in seeing whether he had any capacity left to feel. He had felt for the girl Tamara, of course, the girl he had found freaked out in San Francisco and whom he had carried out of there, only to bring her to her death on a beach in Miami, but it had been a very qualified kind of feeling . . . and there was also the possibility that her death had taken away the last vestige of feeling from him. In blunt language, Wulff wondered whether or not he might be impotent. He had to find out; there was an almost clinical interest in settling that case. An impotent man could not function with the kind of efficiency that a potent man could; killing was not as easy for an impotent man, no matter what the hell the myths were about it. So he pulled the truck off to the emergency lane, hoped that no state trooper would come along for a little while to check on precisely what was the emergency that had put them off the road, and went into the neatly furnished back, where he found that Jessica had already taken all of her clothes off and was lying on the stark but not uncomfortable bed, running her hands all over her body and moaning. Whether this was from real perverse passion or merely an attempt to make him feel more comfortable in the situation, Wulff did not know.

In any event, he took off his own clothes, joined her, and with an efficient ruthlessness found that he could function as well as he ever had. On an emotional level he was dead, of course; that was nothing new, but by shutting off emotions and fucking only with a small part of his mind, a single, bitter gleaming ray of intelligence lighting up the corridors of desire, he could do it any way she wanted, fast or slow, top or bottom, and her responses, automatic at first, dry and convoluted, the motions of a woman fucking as she is supposed to rather than from any real need, began to break open into a smoother and deadlier rhythm, and he put his hands up to her small breasts, squeezed them like coils, and his first orgasm was merely a draining, an unloading of blockage. Having finished quickly, he stayed within her and moved then into a slower, more intense rhythm; looking down upon her from a great height, poised between her knees, moving slowly and considerately, he began to feel the essence of the act, desire and the need for connection moving through him, and she put her arms up toward him, could not reach, fumbled away. He seized her small hands, grasped them tightly, and she began to cry then, squeeze with her thighs, demand . . . and it went on for a long while this time, much more slowly than he had done it for a long time, her little cries and shrieks like garlands of flowers all around them, and at the end there was one clear image of grief before he screamed and fell against her, winding tightly into her on the bed.

They stayed that way for a long time, and then they came apart. She ran her fingers through her hair and told him that it had been much better than she had expected; he was certainly better than Edgerton, that was for sure. In fact, he was better than anyone she had had in a long time. She would just like him to know that she had at least three orgasms, one of them intense, which, although it might seem slight, was at least fifty percent better than she had ever done before, and he had every reason to feel pride and a sense of accomplishment.

The cold-bloodedness of this might have infuriated Wulff at another time, or then again it merely might have amused him (most likely it would have amused him; it fit in with her attitude toward the world, which seemed as if she were administering it an unending true-or-false quiz), but his mind had already moved far away from sex toward the more pressing conditions of the truck, the road, his mission, the situation. Sex was all right; he had proved that he was still functional, and that was good; it was nice to know every now and then that your car could still go a hundred and ten miles an hour on the speedometer, even though in normal driving you might have to draw on that kind of power once in a hundred thousand miles, if that. Still, power in reserve was something. The more immediate problem, though, was Detroit and what to do with the girl. Within five minutes he was back behind the wheel, and Jessica, feeling affection, was riding up front with him, her head bobbing on his shoulder while he watched the panel of Eighty now fading underneath the dusk. "I don't even know your name," she said.

"Burton Wulff."

"Oh. Burton Wulff. Where are you going, Burton Wulff?"

"I'm going to Detroit," he said.

"What's in Detroit?"

"The same thing that you'll find everywhere else. Junk."

"There's also money and sex in Detroit. There are a lot of things in Detroit that you'll find anywhere else. And then you'll find things that aren't, like cars."

"Just junk," Wulff said, "that's all that interests me."

"What interests you about junk?" she said, patting his knee, winding her fingers around his flesh. "Are you a junkie?"

"Just the opposite."

"I used to be, but I got off that stuff. I never used the hard stuff, not at all. It's no good for you; it screws you all up inside. Anyway, what do you mean you're the opposite of a junkie?"

"Doesn't matter," Wulff said, "doesn't matter at all. The point is, once I get into Detroit, I got to drop you somewhere. Where do you want to be let off?"

She shrugged. "Doesn't matter," she said. "Anywhere that's convenient. I can always get a hitch."

"You're really unattached, aren't you?"

"In my head I'm unattached. That's the place for real disconnect. In life I just kind of drift."

Wulff thought of pursuing the issue, but he was moving the truck at high speed, seventy-five, eighty miles an hour over some twisting territory, and it seemed to demand fuller concentration than he could give it and at the same time dig into the girl. Also, he was simply not that interested. If she were disconnected, it was her business; he was not. He had been both ways, attached and unattached, and maybe unattached was better, although you were not talking about a girl who was maybe eighteen years old when you said this. "What's all that stuff in the back?" the girl said suddenly.

"What stuff?"

"The stuff you loaded from the trunk of your car. That was heavy ordnance, man. I know a few things."

"I'm kind of fond of it."

"You a gun runner?"

"Not exactly."

"I mean," Jessica said, "I don't give a damn how you got hold of it, you understand? It's none of my business. I was just curious."

"It doesn't matter," Wulff said again, "it just doesn't matter."

"I know he would have killed you."

"Damn right."

"He was vicious. He was crazy. I think that he was some kind of drug runner, if you want to know the truth."

"Oh?"

"Yeah," Jessica said, "he mentioned something about running coke. It was when we were having sex; things just sometimes pop out of a man's mouth when he's hot. You know how it is."

"I know how it is."

"He said he was running coke. So he was running coke, and you're running guns. I don't give a shit. Everybody's into something, right?"

"Yeah," Wulff said, thinking about the coke thing. "I guess so."

"Coke, guns, sex, it's all the same thing, right? It's all part of the same condition. You got to be into something in America or die. That's how I feel. Nixon was into something too."

"Yeah," Wulff said, his mind abstracted, thinking of the coke business and just for the hell of it holding the wheel with one hand, driving stiffly, with carefully precise motions; slowing the truck to fifty-five, he started to fumble around inside the edges of the seat, and that is when he came in his wanderings up against fifty bricks of the purest and finest that he had ever touched.

Which, added to Jessica, just complicated things entirely.

XI

Williams had heard nothing from Wulff since the call informing him that Wulff had gotten away. Not that he had expected to hear from him, not really; Wulff had better and more complex things on his mind than maintaining a close relationship with Williams. Still, it would have been nice to hear. It would have been nice to hear something.

Williams felt ambivalent. On the one hand, he had no more business being on the road with Wulff. The one time he had done it in Los Angeles it had worked out disastrously; only the fortunate intervention of an army bent on killing them had prevented them from killing each other. It had been a mad, bitter scene, which came, Williams supposed, from the fact that they could not define who was leader and who was follower. If they were to work together, they would eventually get into a tangle where there would be no intervention, and besides, he had promised his wife, and meant it, that he was going to pick up the pieces this time, that he would sit on his nice easy desk job and his potential pension and not try to clean up the system single-handedly. Trying it the police way had almost gotten him killed near the methadone center on 137th Street.

On the other hand, Williams could not completely paper over a sense of guilt. He belonged on the front lines with Wulff, he supposed. Even if it didn't work, he belonged there, because if he did not, it somehow reduced the validity of Wulff's quest. Wulff had made progress, but for all intents and purposes the world was as full of shit, minus two trunkloads, as it had been when Wulff had started. Wulff had not reduced the amount of shit in the world so much as he had merely reduced the absolute number of people handling it, but that merely meant that there would be other people in the gap soon enough to take over the wonderful and profitable work of distribution. Shit was like that. There was never any lack of customers, and if that should ever develop there would certainly be no lack of people looking for fresh customers. Call it America.

Still, ambivalence or not, he should have heard something from Wulff. Wulff was headed out to Detroit on a wing and a prayer and with a handful of ordnance; meanwhile, there were a lot of people in New York who were very anxious to find him. One was the commissioner and another was the judge in the courtroom and the third was the man who had assassinated Smith in open court, only to find out later that he had gotten the wrong man. It turned out that this man had been a freelancer originally detailed out of the far west to kill Wulff, and when Wulff had pretty well blown up the far west and every line of supply in it, there had been no one around to call the man off the job. So he had plugged away at it and eventually picked up word of the arraignment, and on the day of the hearing had managed, no one knew exactly how, to get into the courtroom respectably dressed and with a point-thirty-eight against his hip. He had kept calm, kept a professional hand on himself, waited out the entrance of the principals, and had then very neatly killed Smith with the second of two shots, which lodged in the sternum, the first one hitting the occipital regions and causing, the autopsy pointed out, little more than superficial wounds. The man was extremely distressed to find that he had killed the wrong person and that in fact he had provided exactly the excitement and distraction necessary for Wulff to make his escape. He had virtually babbled when this word had been broken to him during the interrogation. Williams had almost been able to feel a kind of sympathy for him; it was an awful thing to work toward a goal, sacrifice everything in that direction, actually achieve that goal, and then lose it all on a simple mistake. Like having colitis before you opened, after a twenty-year haul, at the Metropolitan Opera. Something like that.

In any event, it was done; the assassin, whose name and actual background mattered so little that Williams had not even cared to recall it, was in custody; Wulff had gotten out of the city; and the PD from the highest to the lowest levels was hopping mad. The guard who had been detailed to accompany Wulff to the courtroom to watch him therein had been placed on indefinite suspension and was waiting with his Local 371 representative for a hearing, the department was on an all-points alert and had transmitted, grudgingly, information to the FBI for all the good that that would do, and Williams himself had had to submit to some pretty hard interrogation on the theory that he was Wulff's closest friend in the PD, he had worked with Wulff on a few assignments (although no one could prove this), and he had also been with Wulff, nominally providing custody, on the day of the shooting. He had had to talk his way out of that one with great intensity and under the kind of pressure that he had not thought that he would ever be able to bear up under again, but he found that after the shooting, after lying on your back living with death in a hospital for weeks, anything that life had to offer looked pretty inconsequential. So he had gotten through the interview, at least to the extent that he had not given them any piece of information that they could work on, and had then gone back to the precinct house near the Gowanus Canal in Red Hook, where they planned to keep him until his pension rights came up. Which would be in approximately nineteen years and seven months. He had lived a full life during his period in the PD.

So the news from his contact in the Detroit PD that things were in an uproar there due to the discovery of Hamilton's body in a vacant lot on the North Side did not upset Williams as much as it might have if he had had the full facts of the case in front of him. For one thing, he didn't know who the hell Hamilton was. When he found out that Hamilton was the man who the contact was pretty sure was responsible for the scheme of running the drugs in skeletal frames up to Canada, when he found that Hamilton had probably been killed by the man who was supplying him, and when he learned that the supplier-murderer appeared to be a Detroit police lieutenant who had not been on the job for several days, appeared to have vanished, Williams became considerably more interested. The stink in Detroit seemed, if possible, to be greater than the stink in NYC. Of course, the one had little enough to do with the other; it was hardly to the NYPD's credit that things could be pointed out to be even worse elsewhere, but it was exactly the kind of thing that the union might have taken to the mayor at a bargaining session in an attempt to raise more funds.

"All hell is going to break loose," his contact—a rookie patrolman who had gotten in contact with Williams spontaneously some months ago because he was an "admirer"—said to him over the phone. "If they killed Hamilton, it's very serious. It means that they're going to destroy the system rather than risk losing it. They'd rather give it up altogether than let it be penetrated."

"Yeah," Williams said, "I guess that you could put it that way."

"He should stay out of Detroit. He should stay the hell out, that would be my advice to him. I mean, I think he's okay, all of us do, you know what we think of Wulff here in the PD, he's the only guy who's doing something, actually doing something for the fucking cop, doing the work the politicians won't let him do, but this one is too rough. It's too rough for anyone. If they'll kill their own kingpin, goddamn it, rather than take a chance on having the thing opened up, then anything could happen. Anything at all."

"Yeah," Williams said. He was sitting hunched at his typist's desk in the Gowanus precinct, looking at a sheaf of files on the unsolved beheading of a career girl in a furnished apartment on Atlantic Avenue two weeks ago and wondering if there was any file system which would accommodate materials like this. No one had any leads on the beheading, but then again, it was pretty well decided that this kind of work had to be attributed to a perverted and murderous type of individual, and that was a good set of clues right there. "Yeah," he said again, and pushed the papers from him, wondering vaguely if there was a tap on the phone, deciding on the instant that he did not give a damn if there was, "but there's no way to call him off anyway. I can't reach him."

"I guess not."

"I have no idea where he is. I know that he left New York, all right, and that he's headed in that direction."

"That's what I'm afraid of," his caller said almost gloomily, "and he's walking into hell here. Listen, this isn't like any other operation he's ever been in before."

"How do you know?"

"He's never had the goddamned PD on his ass."

"The whole PD?"

"Parts of it."

"He'll make out," Williams said. "You'd be surprised"; and then because the conversation was beginning to bore him, because he saw no point in it anymore, because there was something almost servile in the man's tone, something which rang of sycophancy, he said, "Look, something just came up here, I've got to handle it," and then hung up the phone before the man could even reply, not that anything could come up in a place like this except the outlines of corpses slowly taking the air in the roiling and muddy Gowanus days or decades after their immersion.

What could happen? Williams thought; the answer was that nothing could happen, not only that whatever Wulff did it would in the long run make no difference at all, but even in the short run all that he would accomplish would be realignments of power. The junk was not going to go away; there was no fashion in which the absolute amount of shit in the world would not keep on increasing day after day, year after year, and as long as it kept on growing, as long as the white mounds and bricks and flakes and sprinkles were there, there would be people in the pass-along system. Nothing would change.

Meanwhile, he would sit in this barracks at Gowanus with marks in his side of an implosion that had almost killed him and wait out all the days of his life functioning as a contact man for Wulff, taking on the sycophancy of those who reacted to him only because he was as close to Wulff as they could get . . . and living all the time with the feeling that all of the talk about hopelessness was merely a rationalization, that actually his place was on the front lines like Wulff's and that he would live all of his life knowing it and trying to circle the pain of that knowledge.

Man, it was depressing.

XII

"It was legal until 1913," Wulff said as they passed the twenty-miles-to-Detroit signpost. He had given up on anything else, and now, as he was trying to figure out what he was going to do with the girl, what his next stop would be, he had gotten into a discussion of heroin, Lord knows why. "It was a prescription narcotic and it was often used the way they use morphine now, for terminal cases with terrible pain. But a lot of unsavory people started to use it for reasons other than that, and a lot of doctors found that it could be used for better than terminal trips, and the government made it illegal. There are still people, a lot of them, who think that that's a mistake. There are people who think that making heroin possession or use a crime was the one thing guaranteed to make it what it's become today, because suddenly there was a lot of money in it. There are even people who say that the government did it on purpose because there were certain officials way up in the administration who would get a piece of the illegal action. But I don't believe that part of it."

"I never ran with heroin," Jessica said, her face bleak, her eyes on the road. "But I don't see anything wrong with it. If people want to kill themselves, it's their business."

"Sure," Wulff said, "you can't stop people jumping off bridges or chewing poison tablets. That's their right under the Constitution, I think. But there's a difference between murder and suicide. There's a difference between a man deciding to kill himself and another man deciding that he'll put the tools in the hands of someone else to make that suicide possible. A man turning profit off it at the same time. That's in a different category. If they set up heroin shops on the street corner and let those buy it who needed or wanted it for cost price, about twenty-five cents a shot, after they knew exactly what they were getting into, then that would be okay. But there's no such thing as a heroin shop, there's only a connection, and he's making his own way by getting people into it. And at the very top there are people who never touched it in their lives, people who wouldn't be caught dead associated with it who run the whole thing behind closed doors and have themselves mansions on the sea because people they've never seen are dying. Now, that isn't right. You can't say that that's a good thing."

"I suppose so," the girl said. Her hands were folded tightly into one another. Wulff looked at her sidelong and still did not know what the hell to do with her. Anything he did, it figured, was wrong; if he let her go, she knew too much, but then, he was not a criminal, he could not detain her against her will. Furthermore, he had a feeling she wanted to stay with him. But exactly where would that get them? While he thought about it, still with no solution, he kept on talking.

"You sniff it, snort it, skin-pop it, and shoot it," Wulff said. "Those are the degrees of use. You get about the same sensation from the first sniff as the tenth mainline, but you've got to go in deeper and deeper to get the same sensation, you see. Eventually, if you're allowed to run it long enough, if you have enough money and you can stay free of the police, which is more difficult than you would think, because you can run a twelve-hundred-dollar-a-week habit easy, and even medical doctors, most of them, can't afford a habit like that, but if you're allowed it all the way, you'll wind up weighing about forty pounds and in a coma with extensive liver damage. Any attempt to cure you would have to start with at least a modified withdrawal, and it would kill almost anyone even under the best medical supervision. There are about three hundred thousand heroin addicts in New York City alone. They've never estimated how many there are in the country, but the best guess is two or three million hard-core addicts and at least another two or three million who take it on a modified basis or are ex-addicts or who are on the fringes of it. That's a lot of people."

"I don't want to hear about heroin," Jessica said. "It scares me. Blowing a little pot—that's as far as I ever wanted to push it. Heroin is a killer; everyone knows that."

Wulff shook his head, played with the gearshift. The road was almost completely empty at four in the morning, unlike New York, where the major arteries were running heavy truck traffic almost all the time. "It's the same thing," he said. "Pot leads to heroin."

The girl giggled. "No one believes that," she said. "That's just the stuff you hear from priests and cops. That the path to sin starts with the first reefer."

"It's true," Wulff said quietly. He tried to keep his voice flat and level, but it was not easy; it was suddenly difficult to keep his breathing modulated. "It's the same goddamned attitude that controls heroin right from the start. Indulgence. Do anything for a kick. Freak out and feel glad. Anything for sensation. Blow a little pot; if it makes you feel good, it can't be bad. Nothing that makes you feel good can be bad. So after you've been doing that for a while, the next step is easy." He found himself unconsciously running his hand under the seat where the coke reposed in its little squares, buggering his hand. "Soft and hard," he said, "hard and soft, it's all the same goddamned thing. There's no such thing as soft drugs, any more than there's soft pornography. There are merely those who need it hard and those who can take it soft, but they're after the same damned thing."

"Crazy," she said, but not in a hostile way, rather as if she were humoring him. "I just can't take that. I can't believe it."

"You ever see an OD?" Wulff said.

"OD? What's that?"

"OD. Overdose," he said, easing the accelerator all the way back so that now they were staggering along at forty-five, little lights from the industrial plants glinting across the hood like apparitions, maintaining control of the vehicle at all costs because it was not worth throwing himself off the road to make a point. A junkie would not think that way, of course. "They've overloaded the system, you see. Usually by the time you find them they're already in deep coma, sometimes dead, and what comes off them is the smell of acetone, because there's been a complete breakdown of the liver; you see, the system hasn't been able to metabolize the stuff out, so it's all in the system, half-oxidized, just about the way it went in except that the chemistry has had a chance to work it over and mortification has started to set in. So you get this terrific smell coming from them, pure acetone if you catch them early on, but if it's more than twelve hours, you get the stench of corrupted flesh. Most of the time the needle is half in their arms. Most of your OD's of course happen on a mainline injection, although it's not unheard of for a skin-popper to get one too, particularly if he misses the right spot in his ass and instead of the gluteal maximus works it into the rectal area . . . ."

"I don't think I want to hear any more of this," the girl said fuzzily. "I don't want to—"

"Of course you do," Wulff said, slowing the truck even more, tapping the brake down about thirty now but still holding the road well. It was a sweet vehicle, no question about it, a good transporter, smooth and fluent in all gears at all speeds. "You believe in the permissive society; you think it's just a groove that people should be allowed to do whatever they want to do, different strokes for different folks and we're all children of the same God, right? Take your own trip, do your own thing, am I right? So let me tell you what it's like when a junkie takes the trip he's suited for, his final trip. The needle is generally half hanging in the arm, and the mouth of course is open; you see, one of the features of poisoned junk or an overload of the system is to induce a series of small strokes, capillaries popping, arteries starting to sever right in the weakest areas of the body, which with almost anybody under forty is in the brain. They've gone into hemorrhage, you see, they've got a nice hematoma swelling against the cranial walls, pressing on the dura mater, the sheath between the brain and the skull, the same thing that gets inflamed when you get spinal meningitis, except that this time it isn't inflamed, it's just destroyed—the hemorrhage ruptures it. It's a real groove to have a ruptured dura mater and a massive cerebral hemorrhage, and of course the OD's like it quite a bit; they get a terrific flash, I understand, just before they realize that they've had it and they collapse. Of course," Wulff said, "of course, this is just a suggestion, I mean, there isn't too much hard evidence for this. It's not too easy to get a firsthand report; the kind of people who have had the flash are a little difficult to interview. And then of course you get a rupture down below too, you get a complete loss of bowel and urinary function, so that they crap in their pants, void down their legs. That happens almost as quickly as the hemorrhage, a chain reaction, you see. It breaks down the whole system; it's really a great thing to see. And I haven't even given you half the fun of an OD; there's the business of carting them down, getting the meat wagon, you understand, scraping the body off the floor—they leave that to the cops, there's not a morgue attendant in the city who wants to handle a befouled body, and you can take your civil-service crap and throw it right out of the window, that's one dirty, sweaty, fucking job that they leave to the cops or it doesn't get done at all. And then, riding down to the morgue in the wagon, just you and the corpse, maybe your partner if he isn't puking his guts out somewhere, but usually you're handling this all alone; it's not the kind of detail, you see, where they won't mind tying up a couple of men. They'll tie up a couple of hundred men to guard the mayor when he's in the St. Patrick's Day parade, and of course when the President comes into the Waldorf to make a speech you've got the block ringed with a few thousand, all working overtime, but OD's don't generally turn up on the front pages of your own family newspaper, so it isn't too necessary to worry about the cosmetics." He was sweating lightly, ran a hand across his brow, felt it sealed in there with moisture and took it away, flinging away the droplets. It all came back. It was true; just like infantry training the army or combat or playing the guitar or sex, it was always with you. You could never leave it behind; unbidden, it rode with you, that passenger, forever, and in the nights or at times like these when the walls came down, it was always there, biting. "Forget it," he said. He could hear the girl sobbing beside him. "Forget the whole damned thing. I'm sorry," he said. "I went too far. Forget it." He slowed the truck to ten miles, drifted off the road, bounced along the gravel in the intimation of sunlight coming behind them. "Are you all right?" he said.

She shook her head violently, her hands over her cheeks, and slowly, one by one, he brought them down, to see her face gleaming like a doorknob. "All right," he said, "I'm sorry. I said I was sorry." Her face seemed riven. She shook her head again, tried to say something, couldn't.

"I'll drop you off anywhere," Wulff said. "We'll be pulling off the road in a few miles. I'll drop you at a diner or wherever you want to go. I'll even try to find you another ride. You want some money?" He felt atrociously guilty, and that was wrong; there was no reason for him to feel guilty, he had merely shown her the actual implications of what she saw only in the abstract. If everyone could see it, if people could actually see where their morals or ethics or world view or simple indifference led them, there would be no such thing as heroin addiction in the world; there probably wouldn't be any wars, either, or at least only faraway wars, where people were dismembered only at a great distance and filtered through encouraging kill ratios. But that was another issue. He could not even get into the whole matter of Vietnam or what it had meant to America; he had been in Vietnam, in combat, for years, years ago, and the moment he had gotten out, he had simply cut it out of his consciousness like a piece of meat. He would not think of it. He simply would not think of it anymore. "All right," he said, looking at her face, drying out, now merely a collection of panels tacked together in the dawn. "Okay now? I'm going to drive."

And she fell against him, and her arms were around him then; he felt her clutching at him, felt her hands moving around his body and then gathering him in; and whimpering, her mouth was at his ear. "I'm sorry," she said, "I'm so terribly sorry, I'm sorry that you had to see something like that; it shouldn't have happened, it shouldn't be that way," and she was scrabbling away at him. "Forgive *me*," she said, "forgive *me*, I didn't know, I didn't know about the pain," and her body was like a weight coming upon his, not an unpleasant weight, but a burden nevertheless. "Let's go into the back," she said. "I want you, I want you right now," and it was not perversity which had excited her, he saw, but merely the need to give comfort, and he moved slowly from the seat, he had to make Detroit, he moved into the back with her, he had to keep on going, he gathered her against him, and it was with the feeling that it was not going to be so easy, it was not going to be so damned easy at all to separate himself from her, but what did he care, what did he care? He had not talked about this for a long time, and he would never talk about it again, but it had been purged for the moment; at least for a while he was free of it, and maybe that was all that he had sought from the beginning—simple purgation, simple loss, the absolution from a culpability that he knew he would always have to carry, because if he did not, dear God, who would? Who ever, ever would?

XIII

The shit came from somewhere to the south, maybe Mexico, although Coates had never been sure. Important not to ask too many questions, he had known from the beginning. From the south it came already arranged in neat little bricks stashed in a locker at the bus terminal, the same locker or the open one nearest to it on the same day of every week, rain or shine, except for two weeks in the summer. Everybody has to take a vacation. The key came in the mail, and Coates used it to open up the locker, pick up the stuff, and transfer it to Hamilton. In return Hamilton would give him one thousand dollars in a plain white envelope, with sometimes an extra hundred or two just for the hell of it.

Coates had suspected that Hamilton was getting more than a thousand dollars a week worth of services out of him, but not to question. Fifty-two thousand dollars a year with bonuses tax free was certainly heavy enough for him, although on a patrolman's salary it was difficult to use it without raising publicity. Mostly he had had to settle for taking a small edge in small ways, better bourbon, a better car than he really could afford, while most of it was stashed deep in a safe-deposit box of a bank of which he was very fond. In a few years he could make a production of having to get the hell out of the department, get out of Detroit before it burned, get to the Canadian wilds or something and go fishing, and after he had hung around home for a while letting that bullshit story take, he would lay twenty thousand dollars on his wife and kids, more than they were worth, the three bitches, and he would take the other two hundred thousand and run. He'd stay in the country, of course; that was where most men made their mistake in abandonments, getting caught in customs or by Scotland Yard or something, but he was not stupid enough to get into anything like that. Screw Scotland Yard and exotic Mediterranean landscapes. He would hit for California with two hundred thousand and fuck his way blind through every quarter of it. It ought to last him seven or eight years anyway, conservatively invested and well handled. Beyond that, Coates did not care to think. He had his life planned out until he was thirty-nine or forty that way, and a man thirty-nine or forty he figured was half dead anyway . . . or at least after fucking his way blind through California for eight years he *ought* to be dead. He would give it a try.

It was a nice tight life scheme. He hadn't done badly for a guy who got out of high school with a lousy academic diploma that was good for nothing and another two years' voluntary draft in the army, which had taught him how to be a target emplacer for training fire. That was certainly a great opportunity for civilian employment that they were making for him, just as all the ads had promised. But the PD was hiring when he came out, and they were very sympathetic to veterans, and ninety-six hundred a year to start in those days just before the riots began looked pretty good to a twenty-year-old with the most indifferent of prospects. He had grabbed it. After that the wife and kids had come into the scene just the way that luggage might come to an airport traveler. He had never exercised conscious choice, not even during the riots when he was in the middle of the fire and figured that he would get his ass busted like everyone else, until Hamilton had made the approach to him out of nowhere, saying that he had heard that Coates was a promising man and he had an offer for him. That had been the first moment of choice. He had been twenty-five years old then. Now he was twenty-eight. He had a hundred and twenty-one thousand dollars in his safe-deposit box, and in another couple of years it would be two hundred and twenty-five thousand, less five thousand dollars for better bourbon and twenty for the wife and the two bitches. He had had a nice clean organized life.

And now Hamilton was dead.

He had no choice, Coates figured. Not after what Hamilton had done. Not after the murder of Shields, the business in the factory, the very sudden pressures which had come upon him within the department. For some reason people were screaming about the murder of Shields, and Coates knew damned well, almost as if he had been there, exactly who had killed him and probably why. Panic.

He had had to kill Hamilton. Hamilton had panicked. A panicky man, Coates remembered from the days of the riots, was capable of doing almost anything. One day he would kill Shields and the next day he would kill Coates, all for the same reason, to save his own ass, to cut off the lines of communication both ways. How could he not have done it? But now, of course, Coates was scared shitless.

It was not fear of detection. That would blow right over; Hamilton, union steward or no, was just another body in an empty lot in a city where, unfortunately, this was pretty common and incited little comment. Executives were found in empty lots. Also, Hamilton had had his share of enemies; the last place they were going to look (Coates was sure) was in the PD itself. The PD would in any event protect its own.

No, it was not that. He knew that he could sweat that one through; everything would be all right, he was positive. It was the whole matter of his income, of his life plan. Everything had been set up neat as a pin and tick, ticking along toward the deadline of age thirty, when he would make his split and start screwing, and now, thanks to Hamilton and no one else, the deal was screwed the hell up. He wasn't going to be getting the cool fifty grand a year anymore, the fifty grand that probably multiplied into a half million for Hamilton. But what the hell, he was going to get twelve-eight, plus credit toward pension plan, salary protection, increments, and full medical coverage through the PD, and that was all. If he tended bar, maybe he could work that up another three or four grand if he was very efficient and was in a tipping district. In any event, it was all shot. Sixteen grand a year wasn't sixty. And the hundred and twenty-one in the safe-deposit box simply was not enough, it was not nearly enough for the way he had had his lifetime mapped out. And at twenty-eight he was too old to deviate, to pick up another life plan. If a man was lucky he might stumble into one; it was impossible for a high-school graduate to have two.

There was only one solution, Coates figured. One way to handle the situation, to continue to have his shot and to keep things going.

He would have to run the stuff through himself.

It wasn't so hard. The people who were placing it in the lockers might not even know that it went to Hamilton or what he did with it; all that they were interested in was their own cut. As long as they got paid, it was no sweat, they would keep it coming. In the meantime, at least until a couple of payments had been made, they would keep on dropping the stuff in and Coates could continue to pick it up.

Of course, he didn't know where payment went to or how much it would be, but he was willing to take this step by step, not try to look too far in the future. First you did one thing, and then the next came along. If you moved step by step, all would be yours, whereas if you tried to see the big picture in a flash, you wound up Lyndon Johnson. That was all.

So Coates the first week did what he could. The key was mailed to him, he went to the terminal, the stuff was in the locker, he picked it up and took it home this time instead of passing it on to Hamilton. Taking it there, he realized for the first time why Hamilton had done this through Coates and not direct, why he had thought it worth a grand a week to have a runner. Of course. That way, whoever was mailing it in to those lockers had no idea of who was picking it up, and Coates double-protected by keeping it one level separated still. You had to admire the son-of-a-bitch, Coates thought. Even dead he had shown a lot of class, a good deal of free-form operating. Who would have thought that Hamilton, a mere union steward, a working stiff like Coates, would have had it in him?

Live and learn.

At home he went straight to the bedroom, threw his wife out, locked the door, and spread the stuff out on the bed. Shit, it looked good. He didn't really know horse from coke, coke from Coca-Cola, but he had seen some kilos run through the PD or on suspects a couple of times, like any cop would, and he had a rough idea of quality. This was unusual, tender, closely packed, fine white powder. In all the movies he had seen you were supposed to lick your fingertip, put it delicately in the crystals, and taste one, and so Coates did it too, finding it oddly sweetish to the taste, but otherwise he had no idea in hell of what it was supposed to mean. What did tasting it have to do with quality, and how would good shit taste as opposed to bad shit? But it wasn't worth worrying about; the important thing was that he had it.

The next thing to do was to figure out how in hell he was going to run it, and where. He could hardly put advertisements in the newspapers, and it seemed inadvisable to go up to the North Side and start peddling it by hand, although he was sure that that would have given him a brief but very profitable career. No, you had to think of some way to pass it through channels, to put it in the pipeline so that you could derive the profits but none of the penalty, so that you could work it through the existing channels of supply, which were always hungry for stuff like this, high-quality goods, but which would pay cash on the line and would enable him, who was to say, to take maybe not one but two or three thousand dollars a week out of the operation. What that cheapskate, liar, fool, murderer Hamilton was paying him had to be the least of it, just a drop in the bucket, just a shadow of the real money that was in this kind of operation. That figured. That would have to figure. If Hamilton was paying him a thousand dollars a week, there was probably ten times as much in it for him. The son-of-a-bitch.

But then, sitting on the bed, the bricks of shit looking up at him, glowing in the light, Hamilton's cheapness still making him burn, Coates had to laugh. Really, he had to laugh, sitting there, thinking of himself, thinking of the situation. How was he going to move these bricks? What was he supposed to do, go down to the PD and throw them on the table, ask for suggestions? Peddle his ass and the bricks on the North Side? Put an ad in the newspaper giving a mail drop for inquiries? No, it was crazy, all crazy, bullshit, and even if he were to do something as nutsy or more so than this, *he would not know who to pass the money on to, he would not know how much money he was supposed to pass,* and surely after one or two more shipments, that would come to one hell of a halt.

Also, the people who were sending the stuff in from wherever it was would not be too pleased with him. From their point of view, they would have been stiffed out of a good deal of money.

They would be as mad as hell, and they would come on his ass. People who were able to ship bricks of heroin and deposit them in lockers weekly in the bus terminals, mail in keys like clockwork, would not let a simple thing like failure to pay get between them and their money. They knew exactly who he was. They would kill him.

No, Coates thought, looking at the shit, no, the answer was there, it was clear, it was staring at him, and had been from the moment he had killed Hamilton, and now there was no way around it, he would have to take the stuff, he would have to dispose of it himself, not fence it, and he would have to take all the money—and that money would be his stake, because he would never be able to pass this way again. This was it. A man goeth through only one time, and so on and so forth. He was looking at his destiny on the bed. He would never get another chance to fulfill it, and he would have to get so much out of this that he would not have to worry about fulfilling it.

How much was it worth? He had no idea at all. At a guess, though, maybe there was a couple of hundred thousand dollars in it. There were ten bricks altogether, and twenty-five grand did not seem unreasonable per brick, less a percentage for bad luck. Street value had to be at least fifteen times that per brick. It was not unreasonable.

He wouldn't be squeezing it out painfully now a grand at a time. He would go for the whole thing and be done. He could advance his eight-year plan by at least two years.

Fuck it, Coates thought, it was the only way. What he would have to do, he figured, was to go to the plant itself, use his badge, edge around a little, try to find out exactly what the destination was of those cars which Hamilton had been smuggling the shit out in. That shouldn't be too hard to find out; it was all there on the forms, the line for which he was responsible. Once he had the destination, he would simply go up there himself . . . and he would drop it. That part he would play by ear; he would figure it out. But at least he knew that he had an assured source of demand there, and that was the important thing.

Yes, Coates thought, yes, that was the only way. He had been thinking like a civil servant from the beginning; almost from the day he had gotten out of high school he had had the mentality of the pensioner, and falling into the situation with Hamilton, the one thousand dollars a week had merely expanded that mentality, it had not changed it. Instead of squeezing it out a little, he had been squeezing it out a lot. But this was not a world in which you could squeeze it out anymore. You had to take it in great big chunks, like Nixon, get everything you could on the front end, and to hell with the rest of the situation, to hell with caution and with the rest of your life. In this world you had only one shot, and you had to take advantage. And if you were a little more cautious than Nixon, if you had a decent sense of timing and maybe a little bit better luck, there was no reason for you to be caught at all.

Coates giggled, overwhelmed with the ecstasy of his vision, the clarity of his insight, rubbed his palms together like a child, cackling, gloating. His sounds must have been heard outside the bedroom and caught his wife's interest, but so excellent was his mood, so sharp was his vision, that when she walked in he did not panic or lose his temper but merely one by one stuffed the bricks back into the bag and then turned to face her calmly, triumphant.

"What are those?" she said. "What are you laughing about? What are those, anyway?"

"Diamonds," Coates said. "Career- and salary-plan diamonds." And then he laughed some more.

XIV

Just outside of Detroit Jessica told Wulff that she wanted to stay with him, that she would not leave him under any conditions. There was a look of determination which sat on her face like the petulant way a child's might get between the eyebrows when he insists upon another ice cream, and Wulff, bombed out by that time and beginning to feel the dread ooze back into his pores, was not in any mood to fight with her. She was on the loose, but so was he; a handful of ordnance and a mission was not much more of a home than this girl had, and in the meantime he could not deny the fact that she had reached him, that she had touched him in a way, and that he needed the company. So he only nodded to her that that was all right if she wanted it that way, and then concentrated on the more immediate problem of getting them into Detroit inconspicuously and trying to figure out where he would move from there. She sat beside him quietly, saying nothing more now that the basic decision had been made, and he allowed his thoughts to spin out in various directions. The best way to approach the problem would be to go to the plant itself. He would have to get into the plant from which the stuff was being moved out, make contact of some sort, try to evaluate in which direction it was being pushed, who was pushing it. That was not going to be easy, of course. But then again, nothing was easy when you came right down to it.

"What are you going to do with that stuff under the seat?" Jessica said after a long time. "Are you just going to leave it there?"

"I guess so," he said. "I'll have to figure out something. In the meantime, it's safe there."

"Coke is all right. There's nothing wrong with coke. Edgar Allan Poe was supposed to live on it."

"Edgar Allan Poe went crazy and died of tuberculosis at forty after pretty well ruining his life," Wulff said, and that was about all the communication that they had until he had put the truck into downtown, moved out along a boulevard, and then far, far down saw the signs of the rooming houses beginning to come into focus. That was best, it was always best to stay in a rooming house off the downtown strip; the laws of mutual confidentiality seemed to be respected in rooming houses as they were nowhere else. You could do literally anything in a rooming house as long as you kept it within the confines of the walls and did not scream too loudly.

He stopped at the first TO RENT sign down the strip, parked the truck, left Jessica in there while he went to talk to the landlady. She seemed to be utterly devoid of affect, answering in a monotone, looking through him with brown, bleak eyes that, he decided, simply had seen too much of Detroit. When he gave her fifty dollars in advance for the first week and she gave him the keys, he went out for Jessica, and the woman showed no response to that either, although there was just the slightest twitch of attention when they started to take out the ordnance, wrapped in blankets, from the back of the truck. She stood at the open door to the lobby while they struggled in with the firearms, holding them like babies swaddled, back and forth several times, her eyes incurious and yet encompassing. But when they made the last trip to the second-floor cubicle, a hot, odorous little room which overlooked what appeared to be a pack of wild dogs living in the backyard, she was gone. Wulff decided that this might be to inform the police, but he did not care. Sooner or later you had to lose your capacity for suspecting everyone and everything; if you did not do that, if you looked for everything to provide your undoing, your undoing was certainly going to come . . . from the inside.

Up in the room he locked the door on the chain bolt while she sat on the hard, wide bed, dangling her legs on the floor. He said, "It's not too beautiful, is it?"

"I've been in worse."

"There's no reason to stay," he said. "You shouldn't feel you have to stay."

"I don't. I don't at all. I asked to come with you."

"You won't enjoy it."

"What the hell?" she said, and shrugged. "Where else would I go?"

"I'm sure you have places," Wulff said.

"I've seen them all. I've been to all the places I care to go to, and that's the end of it."

"I'm not going to be around," Wulff said. "I've got to go somewhere. Do you understand that?"

"If you say so."

"I might not be back, either. I might, and then again I might not. You've got to understand that."

"I understand everything," she said. "You've got business here, all right. I don't know what that business is, and I'll never ask you."

"All right."

"I could make a guess, though, and you could tell me if I'm right."

"I guess I could," Wulff said, "and then again, I might not." Seeing her poised in that attitude on the bed, legs now closed in the slices of light, her back arched, he felt a vagrant impulse for sex again and thought that this was the first time really since San Francisco when he had thought of sex at all. With Tamara that had been; Tamara had been back with him in Miami, but that had been a death trip for the two of them, and there had never been any inkling of connection. But now . . .

"It has something to do with drugs," she said. "You really don't like drugs. You're attacking the drug trade, aren't you? You're using all that ammunition because you're out to kill the people who are in the trade in Detroit. That's what brought you here."

"It's more complicated than that," Wulff said.

"No," she said in a strange, withdrawn way. "It's very simple, I think. Everything becomes very simple once you understand it, once you realize how simple it really is. I think I know who you are."

"All right," he said, "all right."

"I think I've been reading about you. And I think that I know why Edgerton wanted to kill you. He was trying to kill you, wasn't he?"

"He had that in mind."

"There's a price on your head, isn't there?" she said almost dreamily. "There must be ten thousand dollars, Edgerton must have thought that was good enough reason. He was a greedy, stupid little man, though, because it's a lot more than ten thousand. They would have paid him off at that, but I bet there are people who would think that you're worth ten times that."

"I don't know," Wulff said. "I never took any estimates. It's not an object of pressing interest, knowing how much it's worth to someone to kill you."

She shook her head, her eyes still holding that dreaming cast, and then slowly she got up from the bed and came toward him, moving her pelvis. "You don't have to go out just yet, do you?" she said. "You don't have to go out right now."

"It excites you," Wulff said. He should not have said it aloud, but a man living on margin did not care anymore. Once you got out past propriety, into those dead spaces where the only consequence was what you could bring about through force, you did not worry about amenities. "That's all it is. Something to excite you."

"Why not?" she said, and he could feel her close against him. "Why shouldn't it? It's better than junk, isn't it? You have to agree to that."

"Yes," Wulff said, "I guess it is. If you look at it that way, it certainly is." And then, in the hot, closed, dangerous, light-streaked room on the outskirts of Detroit, they had sex all over the bed, the floor, and damned near the walls, and all through it Wulff was thinking in a bemused way that it was her excitement upon which his own was stoked; her own necessity which was fueling his. It was funny that way; if you looked at it from that light, it meant that he was being excited by the same thing that he was accusing her of finding arousing. But it did not matter; what the hell, sex was sex, a fuck was a fuck, just like a shot was a shot to a junkie, and it was good to know after all he had been through and all that lay ahead that he could still have it and make it good, that it still meant something to him, that his world was not centered and enclosed, pebble in a shell, by junk, junk, junk.

XV

It had all seemed very clear to Coates in the bedroom, but now, going out into the world, actually contending with the fact of the assembly line, it was different. Everything was confusing, assaulting him in many colors and wedges of light, whereas it had been a simple, crystalline black and white with which he had seen the situation in the bedroom—the world neatly dwindled and very much within his control.

That was the damned trouble, Coates thought, that was the trouble with all of it, with the whole question of living itself; in the abstract it seemed to be a simple process that you could both understand and beat, but when you had to face it in the real, nothing worked anymore. Politicians must feel that way. In the bedroom, looking at the bricks piled on the bed, it had seemed that there was literally no gap anymore between desire and accomplishment, that he could go out into the world, make his few simple adjustments, and carry on from there, go to Canada, hawk the stuff, take the money, put it into small unmarked bills, run. But when you (or he) had to actually contend with the matter, had to go into the damned stinking, thunderous building where the Fleetwood coaches rolled skeletally by, their form as blunt and horrifying as skulls, it was something entirely different. Not simple. Not simple at all.

It was the civil-servant mentality all over again. Maybe he was nothing but a cop after all. Maybe he was too limited to establish a sector of control over the world, although Coates did not want to think so; any man who could establish the keenness of his insight, could so well articulate his very difficulties, could not possibly be in that category. Could he? The Fleetwood plant overwhelmed him.

It was the sheer *sound*, the impact of that sound as it assaulted him, grating, screaming, rasping sound, sound at all decibel levels and at all levels of pitch. The fumes coming off the line, the smell of smoke, asbestos, and fire—that was terrible, but it was as nothing to the matter of the sound itself, which battered at him, caused him to tremble, made him feel suddenly small and insignificant. He had thought until then that the worst possible noise would be that of the police siren generating helplessness and terror in everyone whom it passed (which was why he had liked to use it when he was on patrol duty, why he had felt that it was the best riot-control device going), but the siren would merely have been one element in the hundreds on the floor, and it would have been eaten up.

Moving through the tourist lines, trying to stay calm, losing the battle, Coates knew that he was overreacting. He wanted to scream and beg for cessation, wanted to hurl himself on the floor through which, on tracks, the gigantic mouths of the empty cars circulated, and say that he could take it no more, that he simply could not bear up under it, that someone would have to help him. But that would have done no good anyway; he merely would have been dragged away, an intrusion, something that had momentarily blocked the flow. That was, if anyone had even been able to hear him. Coates doubted that very much. It was all like one of those 1940's illustrations from the popular magazines of "Life in an Assembly Plant"; small, helpless stick figures would be seen juxtaposed to automotive skeletons that overwhelmed them, the crude representations of humanity being the least significant component of the drawing, and over their heads would be clocks indicating forty seconds to install a joint, sixty seconds to weld a door, two hours and thirty minutes through the line, the stick figures not there in the last panel, only the full-color portrait of the gleaming car itself, which seemed to deny those minuscule and helpless human forms which had run the machinery to construct it.

Yes, the car reduced humanity all the way, Coates thought; that was probably the key to the whole idea, but worse than the reduction was the sense of sheer assault. One simply could not work here. He could not imagine how anyone could get used to it. Even the stewards like Hamilton, who had had to come out on the lines only for grievance procedures or for shape-ups, must have found it unbearable. Five minutes on that line would have been too many, would have already been unbearable; ten would begin to take away the very humanity and dignity of a man, and a full day of it would leave at the end something that was in no way human. At least, that was the way he looked at it from his relatively protected cop's perspective. He guessed that the point was that after working on this line for a certain amount of time you no longer knew the difference. The human chemistry was wonderful, it could shut you off from an awareness of almost anything.

Still, there had to be a way. There had to be a way to come to terms with the situation. Somehow there was a feed line; these cars came out of the plant and went on trucks and were taken northward, and he had to find out where. That was why he was on this tour here, not to engage in philosophical insights into the American automobile industry. Fuck the industry. It was just as dirty and corrupt as anything else in the country, except that the products came out a hell of a lot prettier than most and had a sort of superficial utility, so that their real junkiness was not visible until a certain regulated period of time, usually thirty-six months, had elapsed. After thirty-six months the majority of car loans had been paid off and it was time to make the customer so sick of his old car that he could not wait to get into a new one of even more doubtful value, while the older car meanwhile got kicked downstairs to Sam's Quik-Finance, where the cycle would start on a lower level. After all, the important thing was to keep up the chain so that even the kid at the bottom, junking fifty-dollar Pontiacs for ten, would be able to look forward to stepping up to a two-hundred-dollar Oldsmobile. After seven years, or at the most ten, everything was dead, but the replacement, rather than starting in one sweep, had been phased in gradually so no one knew to what extent they were being cheated and robbed. Of course, this was not to be bitter about it, Coates thought. This was America, and everything done in America had a justification of some sort.

"Excuse me," he said to the guide, "I want to get down to the floor, I want to look at something," and before the young man in the neatly fitted uniform with the visor cap and the name stitching over his left pocket had even had a chance to react to this, Coates had vaulted over the rail, clambered down a set of stairs, and was now into the work area itself. Instantly he felt himself encircled by men, some of them holding wrenches, others in neater foremen's uniforms, all of them shouting at him, all of them sweating. They were screaming something about insurance, something about plant regulations, and as they closed in on him, Coates realized that he had done something stupid, monumentally stupid in all likelihood, reasonably stupid at the least; he had attracted attention to himself, gone far beyond those rules of inconspicuousness which he should have known were the only rules which would carry him through this. "It's all right!" he shouted, waving his arms, sparks shooting from an enclosure near him where two workmen in hell were working a weld on the roof of a Calais coupe. "I'll get right out, I just want to know which was Shields's line? *Shields?*" he screamed over the roar. "You remember him, he used to be a foreman here, he had an accident, but I'm an insurance investigator, I'm trying to get some information for his policy on behalf of his wife and kids, I have to know if it was work-related." This babble seemed to work; maybe on the Gehenna of the floor this seemed to make sense, or at least made as much sense as anything else that was going on. "Shields worked down there," a huge man holding a torch said, and motioned toward another part of the floor through the tangle. Coates nodded and began to move in that direction.

"It won't take a second!" he shouted behind him. "Don't worry about it, I'm fully covered, the company writes my own policy!" They stared after him but did not approach; apparently this satisfied them, or at least if it did not satisfy them, it was no longer their problem, because he was heading toward another part of the floor. Now Coates could hear the nearer shouts of the guard, amazingly persistent for all of his apparent blandness, the man chasing him, still on the track, but the shouts were merely vapor. Coates had other, more immediate things on his mind as he ran down toward the line which had been Shields's; there he saw the enormous, barren shells of the Fleetwoods coming toward him, glinting like teeth in the fumes of the factory, men like ants pouring in and out of them, carrying their little torches, too absorbed in their work here to notice the commotion, and Coates closed in on them, gesticulating. "Where do they go?" he asked a huge man holding a welding instrument in both hands, the welder shooting fire. "Where do they go?" The man looked at him as if he were insane; in that moment Coates could see that he might be insane, that what he was doing could not in any way be justified by normal explication, but still he had to find out. Didn't he have the right to know? How could he possibly go onward, dispose of the dope, fulfill his mission, unless he knew to where the cars were shipped? He knew that he had some larger mission in life; the conviction had come over him since he had calculated the series of steps that he would take. He was not a civil servant, not a pensioner; something large and special awaited him down the pike. If it did not, if this were not so, would these opportunities have presented themselves? "Tell me," he said, and resisted an urge to seize the man by the lapels and shake him, "tell me where they go."

"Toronto," the man said. "Toronto depot." Coates thanked him, and the man said, "What the hell is going on here, anyway? Who are you? Where you come from? Are you an inspector or something like that?"

"That's right," Coates said, turning, dodging, preparing to run. "I'm from the main office back in the East. I'm checking out delivery sites."

"You mean you don't know where the fucking things are supposed to *go*? You people back there in the management, you got to ask us employees where these things end up?"

"Well," Coates said frantically, "well, you see, that's exactly the problem. There's a great deal of distance between management and the actual production situation, that's why the old management was thrown out, as a matter of fact. We're the *new* management, and we're trying to inaugurate a policy of being closer to matters in the field."

"This is crazy," the man said. "This is crazy. I never heard of management not knowing where the *cars* are going. That's just ridiculous; nothing like that can possibly be." But Coates had no more time to straighten him out, no time to tell the man about the further and more flexible policies of the new administration that would lead to an ever-closer relationship with the workers in the field. Not only would they be finding out destinations, but they would want to know the workers' attitude toward their jobs, their feeling about the corporation, their suggestions for how they thought conditions in the plant would be improved. Oh, yes, that would have had quite a stunning effect upon the man; it would have changed his whole aspect, and Coates would have liked to do it, but they were closing in on him, not only on the floor, where a decrease in the absolute level of the noise indicated that machines had been shut off so that his pursuit could be watched; not only on the floor were they closing in on him then, but on the catwalks above they were running to gather at a particular point high above him, people pointing and staring, and Coates realized then how a worker in this plant must feel, observed all the time. The very area was laid out in a way that had as its main goal observation and a total lack of privacy. There was nothing you could do at any given time that could not be seen from almost any point above the floor.

The hell with it. With a cop's sense he had located a door in the distance which he knew opened up on newer or at least higher ground, and he headed toward that one now. Toronto depot. It would not be difficult to find out from information already readily available where the unloading point in Toronto was, and then he would move on from there, carry his precious cargo, make the contact. Once he had done so, once he had made the difficult and necessary series of arrangements which would precede disposal, his life would be utterly changed, he would never be the same again, and the true and unutterable part of the Coates that he would be would become a reality.

Running toward the door, seeing a little abscess of light twinkling, in the midst of his escape, it never occurred to Coates that he had gone mad. Nor should it. In his own mind he was acting perfectly reasonable; he was coming to terms with conditions at last.

XVI

Hamilton's wife was mad enough to go to the commissioner about the murder of her husband, except that she had a pretty good idea of what the commissioner would do and decided that it would only be a matter of continued humiliation if she were to complain about the lackadaisical investigation following the discovery of Hamilton's corpse in a vacant lot. It was not so much a personal sense of tragedy; the fact of the matter was that she did not miss him at all, nor had she particularly liked Hamilton for many years—maybe she had never liked him at all, she would have to investigate that with her psychiatrist, once she got over the immediate shock—but simply that people should not be allowed to go around doing things like that. People should not be allowed to murder men of relative financial and community standing and get away with it without at least some fuss being made, and the department was, Margaret thought, hardly knocking their brains out trying to apprehend Hamilton's murderer.

Of course, it was possible that the reason for this was that Hamilton's murder was somehow connected with the department itself, that is to say that some cop might have killed him. She was not at all naïve, she liked to think that she had been around as much as anyone else, and to have been in Detroit in the late sixties was to understand that one simple law of human contact applied: if the worst could happen, it probably had. The department might well have set him up, at least; at the most, it was a cop who had done it.

Nevertheless, she could have lived through this. Her life with Hamilton had been no fiction; she knew exactly what he had been doing, in all likelihood, there was involvement in the drug trade at one level or another, probably fostering it through the network with some kind of supply function. That was all right with her, along with all of the women that she was sure he was seeing on the outside and the fact that he had barely gone through the motions of this marriage for many, many years. Even that could have been tolerated. They had been married for a long time, Detroit was a rough place, the world itself looked crueler and crueler when you were forty-six years old, and perhaps Hamilton was doing better than most people of their generation in coming to terms with what had happened to them, better than Margaret herself. He was a realist anyway. If the world was full of dirt and deceit, he at least was going to turn something out of it. What more could one want?

So she had gone pretty well along the line to adjusting to the situation two weeks after Hamilton was buried. The insurance had been almost a quarter of a million dollars from a grab bag of policies which Hamilton had picked up over the years, the settlement from the company on their own policy had been quite generous, and Hamilton had turned out to have all kinds of bank accounts, which totaled almost half a million dollars—at least, the bankbooks that she could get hold of. She suspected that there were others that she would never see. He had no will, but that was a convenience more than anything else; if he had had a will, Margaret was pretty sure that she and the children would have been cut out of it to the exact maximum allowed by law, whereas his dying intestate meant that the whole thing, sooner or later, would fall into her hands.

So it wasn't too bad. It wasn't like being twenty-one again and looking forward to her wedding, to the wonderful life that she would have with this wonderful man who seemed so dedicated to the company at which he had already been for some three years, but it was a better end than a lot of people could have come to, including her husband. She was even thinking of how three-quarters of a million dollars might make her appear attractive in a way that she had not thought of being in more than twenty years. Her life was falling into place and doubtless would have continued to do just that, shaking out up and down the line, the northern suburb in which they lived already seeming limiting, Grosse Point beckoning, when she came up against the man who had murdered her husband and realized that her life had radically changed. It was impossible to go on in the same way of widowhood after you had met the man who had caused it; not even Margaret was detached enough for that.

The man who had murdered her husband came to her home at eight-thirty on a bright Tuesday morning, and sweating heavily in his patrolman's blues, told her at the door that he had something important to tell her. All of the children were already back at college, Hamilton's death having made as little impression upon their lives as did his existence, and the maid was not in that day, but even so she felt no nervousness about letting him in, even though she was sure from the very moment that she saw him that he was her husband's murderer. At least, that was how Margaret Hamilton looked back on it later; she would say that she had had the feeling from the moment she had seen this policeman that he was the murderer because she had suspected something like this and because in dreams she had glimpsed over and over again the moment in which the assassin would reveal himself, and he even looked like that assassin. He said that his name was Coates and that he had something to tell her.

Immediately after she had let him through, after he had kicked the door closed, he started to act peculiarly. First he said that he was not sure why he was there at all, that he was probably crazy to come to this place, that anyone would tell him that who had half a brain, but damn it, he was going to come there anyway because he had a perfect right to, and that was the end of it. He mumbled something then about her husband having ruined his life. She went over to the couch and sat quite calmly, holding her hands one within the other and hearing him out. It was inconceivable to her that she was in any danger whatsoever. Something really large and disastrous happening to someone close to you took away all sense of personal vulnerability for a while; that was one of the great purgative effects of funerals. They made you feel a little immortal, because nothing so terrible could happen to you, a tasteful person in control of her life. "I killed your husband, you know," the patrolman called Coates said. "I shot him and killed him. I had to do it, you know. He was a murderer. He had killed a lot of people."

"Shouldn't you leave now?" she said. "Why are you telling me this?"

"I have to tell you. You have to understand that I had a right to do it and that it was the best thing for all of us, that if I hadn't done it, someone else with even less consideration would have. Besides," Coates said rather wildly, his eyeballs fluttering like pennants, high-stepping in the pile of the rug, running his hand over the bullets in his belt, "besides, I can't get rid of the stuff. I mean, Canada's a huge place. It's gigantic, and even Toronto isn't narrowing it down too much. How much can you narrow down Toronto? They all thought I was crazy, but I was just trying to get information. But what the hell am I supposed to do now? There just isn't any point to it."

"I'm sure I can't help you," she said. "If you did kill him, though, shouldn't you turn yourself in . . ." And then she cut off her flow of words, because she had almost said *in to the police*, which would have been altogether quite a stupid thing to say. "I really don't think I can help you," she said. "Your answer isn't here, you know."

"But if it isn't here, where is it? Where am I supposed to go?" Coates said. His eyes appeared to be dimming; his expression was suddenly abstracted. "I mean, this is the place where the answer should be, isn't it? I can't do everything myself, you know. I've got to get some more definite clues, some more definite information on destination."

"Destination of what?"

"Listen," he said, and unless Margaret was mistaken, the man appeared to be crying, "you were his wife. You must have been very close to him, you must have known everything he was up to. After all, that's what a good marriage is, you share everything, you share information, there's a real closeness there. You must have known what he was doing and where he was putting it." He fell to his knees in a gesture that was somehow less plaintive than brutal, and raised his arms to her. "Please," he said in a barely controlled voice, "you've got to tell me where he was delivering the stuff. That's not too much to ask, is it? It's not as if I wanted to know really confidential stuff like your sex life or how much money he was making out of it."

"You're a very sick man," she said, looking down at him. "Something's got to be terribly wrong with you. I don't know what you're talking about. If I were you I would leave; I think that's best."

"No," he said, "no, I can't believe that. I can't believe that you didn't know. Look here," he said, his arms still in the air, little dank stains in the armpits, "I'm pleading with you. I'm down on my knees to you; I'm not threatening or trying to hurt you at all. I wouldn't want to hurt anyone anymore, I couldn't do that kind of thing to people. All that I want is a little information, and I'll leave you alone."

"Leave," she said, "leave right now. I don't know what you think my husband was doing or what I could tell you, but it's nothing."

"I didn't really mean to kill him," the man said. "It was just something that seemed necessary at the time. He was a very bad man. He was hurting people, you know? He was just pushing people around, and things were starting to get worse and worse, and eventually he would have hurt even more, so I did it for their sake. But if I had it to do over again, I swear, I wouldn't. It was really just an irresistible impulse. Probably temporary insanity. Please, Mrs. Hamilton. Where was he delivering it? You were probably running the thing together; that's the kind of marriage that I bet you had. I'm sure that you had a beautiful marriage, great closeness and all of that." He reached into his hip band, took out his pistol, and showed it to her. "You see this?" he said. "Do you?"

"Yes," she said, trying not to bite her lips. "Yes, I see it."

"I'll give it to you. Toronto's such a goddamned big city; they've got two million people in the metropolitan area, you know that? I'll give you the gun, just as a gift, if you'll tell me where he was unloading it. If I didn't think you knew," the man said with a horrid reasonableness, the twitch of an ingratiating smile at the corners of his features, "if I didn't think you knew, I wouldn't come in here like this, I wouldn't come in with a gun and make such an issue of this, because then I'd be crazy, you see, and I'm not really crazy, not at all. I'm just trying to make my own way in the world, just like Hamilton was."

There was nothing she could do, Margaret saw. She could not get past the man out of the house, she could not reach the telephone. Nor could she talk him out of the line of reasoning in which he was trapped like a fly in gelatin; all of her struggles or his would only imprison him more deeply. There was absolutely nothing at all that could be done, she thought, and with this there was a sense of peace, relaxation, an utter commitment to the worst of all possibilities. There was a luxury in finally seeing, accepting, merging with the worst that could happen. You could go no lower than that, ever. All of your life, she thought, or at least all of her life, she may have been looking for something so terrible that she would not have to try to cope anymore, and now here it was. She sighed, feeling animals move across her chest. "I know nothing," she said. "I know nothing at all. I don't know what you want or what you think I have to tell you, but I can offer you nothing at all."

"I was afraid you'd say that," the man said. "I was really afraid that you would say that. You're just like the rest of them, you won't try to help, you won't try to cooperate so that this thing can be over sooner. Instead, just like the rest of them, you have to fight me. Defy me at every turn," the man said like an irritated teacher, and extended the gun, leveled it, and shot her in the face.

XVII

When Wulff came back to the room after his first reconnoitering of Motown, Jessica was gone and so was the coke, which had been closeted in a sack. All of the ordnance, however, was there. The one valise she had had with her was also out of the room, which meant presumably that she had left him, but she had not even had the decency to write a note of farewell.

Well, Wulff thought, that was all right. He should have expected nothing different, and she had her own position to protect too, although the way in which she had left him only indicated that he had been something of a fool and had incurred, perhaps, bigger risks than he had any need to, something which he had not done in a long time. Usually his judgments of people were fairly acute, and he should not have left himself so vulnerable with her. On the other hand, she had obviously had little interest in him, a great deal of interest only in the coke, so this meant that his judgment had not been too far off; he had not placed himself in actual physical danger because of his lapse. Maybe in the long run it was just as well, having her out of the picture, that was to say. He had, after all, used her to the limit of the only point that she could prove to him, which was that sex existed, that he had not been cut off from its benefits and drawbacks. Not that this was any major experience for him, of course.

But in any event she was gone, and seeing the clean, stark bareness of the room after his first careful sweep through the streets of the city snapped Wulff back into perspective, gave him that utter and fine leap toward control which he had not had for such a long time, since Los Angeles at least, maybe further back than that, in Chicago. There was absolutely nothing holding him now, he thought, no connection; no sentiment about the girl or his own condition could get in between himself and the performance of his role. She could have the coke, and welcome to it. He did not give a damn. It was a shame to see all of that go back into the pipeline; if he had it to do over again he would have dumped it; but what was a little bit of coke as opposed to the reservoir of heroin running in the veins of the nation? Jessica had been right. You had to cultivate a sense of perspective. You could not, yourself, clean up the world.

Williams, whom he called, said that he had lost control of the situation. Aside from saying that Hamilton's murderer had not yet been discovered, that all sense of leads had been lost, Williams had nothing to add. He said that he had gotten some noises out of the Detroit PD, noises about how Wulff would be better advised to stay out of town, that the situation was a bad one and building, but Williams said that he pretty well discounted that. It was pretty clear that Hamilton's killer was a cop, but equally clear that he was a free-lancer, that the pattern was not tied into any long-range network of corruption within the department itself. Sooner or later they would find out the guy's identity, Williams thought; they were already running down a couple of cops who had taken unexplained leaves of absence and one who had been phoning in sick for a couple of weeks through his wife and who Williams thought might be a real prospect, but there was nothing definite and it tied in in no useful way. "I can't tell you anything," Williams said, "and you don't want to be told anything anyway. Everything's pretty quiet on this end.

They've got the guy who killed Smith, and for the moment they're happy. There's an all-points bulletin on you, and all that shit, but it's just pro forma. They're not following it up at all. They haven't even got the investigations division on it."

"All right," Wulff said, "so it's just a matter of running down the traffic."

"The traffic's stopped," Williams said. "That's my best information. With Hamilton out of the picture, they don't want to pick up on it. As a matter of fact, I think that everything's quiet."

"Nothing's ever quiet," Wulff said. He was standing in a candy store, looking through the smeared windows of the telephone booth, the dismal aspect of the interior further shrouded by the filth on the panes, and abruptly he felt himself seized by disgust, revulsion—it seemed that he had spent so much of his time standing in enclosures like this talking to Williams, standing in the midst of filth getting information indirectly and in an almost external way, while the real corrupters, safe and insulated in their pretty homes with their pretty wives and prettier mistresses made their arrangements and controlled the world. "Fuck it," he said to Williams, "I've had enough of this. I'm going to blow it out."

"What's that?"

"I'm going to blow it out. The whole plant. They'll never ship stuff through there again. They won't even think of trying a caper like that anymore. It'll cut off their entire chain of supply."

"That's wild," Williams said. He was trying to keep his voice level, noncommittal, but Wulff could detect an undertone of horror. "Are you sure that you want to do something like that?"

"It's got to be done," Wulff said, fascinated with the idea that had just come over him. It was the only way. He could see that now. Everything else was just waiting for them to come to him, waiting for the situation to be resolved from the outside, when that had never really been his way, when his way had been to create resolution. "It's the only way that it can be done. Anything else is just waiting for them."

"An awful lot of people are going to be hurt."

"A clean job," Wulff said, "incendiaries and one flash. No chain reaction, just a controlled explosion. If I place the fire right, it should stay controlled, and I'll try to hit an area where no one's standing."

"How are you going to get in there?"

"Where? The plant?"

"Yeah."

"I'll find a way," Wulff said, and paused. "Don't they have guided tours?"

"How you going to bring the stuff in that you need without being detected?"

"A briefcase," Wulff said. "Even smaller than that, an attaché case. I've got a little souvenir I saved from Wall Street, remember?"

"It's risky," Williams said, "it's very risky. Are you sure you want to do this?"

"Aren't you?"

"I don't know what you mean."

"I would have stayed in jail," Wulff said. "I didn't give a shit, remember? I was wiped out; I thought that after I got Smith, everything was wrapped up. But you didn't want it that way. You thought that I belonged back in the world, still doing my wonderful work. All of this was your idea. I would have stayed there."

"I didn't mean to take it this rough," Williams said; "there are ways and ways."

"No," Wulff said, running his hand over the glass of the booth, which, to his surprise, turned out to be plastic, a thin, crinkling sheet that curved into his palm like cellophane. "No, there's no easy way. There never was at all; it's just one way from the start, and that's the tough route. It's firearms and death. That's the only message they understand."

"You'll get killed, Wulff," Williams said. His voice sounded thin and tentative, not so much the connection as his conviction fading. "You can't go on this way."

"You sprung me," Wulff said. "It didn't have to be this way at all. I could have stayed there and been happy; they could have pensioned me off into solitary or a nice quiet sanitarium and I wouldn't have uttered a peep. They could have done anything to me they wanted; I would have been a vegetable. You wouldn't leave well enough alone, though. Everybody's got to mess with the status quo. So have it your way."

"You don't burn down a building to kill a termite, Wulff. You can't—"

"No?" he said. "That's the only damned way to make sure the termite is dead. And there isn't one of them, there are millions. You going to turn me in, Williams?"

"No," Williams said after a long, thickening pause, "that's ridiculous. How am I going to turn you in? Who would I turn you in to? That never occurred to me at all."

"So let me work," Wulff said, "let me work and let me fucking well be." That would have been a good line to hang up on, right there, but something stiffened in his arm, and he only paused there, holding the receiver. He realized that he was waiting for Williams to say something, something that would either release him or send him on his next and terrible journey without doubt, some code which only he could crack, which would release understanding; but as he stood there, he understood that he would never get it from Williams, that release would never be there and that if there would be any final apprehension of his situation it could not come from this outside force, which would eternally be an abstraction anyway, a complete fucking abstraction, but would have to come from within him. That was the only answer there would be.

"You still there?" Williams said.

"Yes," Wulff said, "I'm still here, but I don't know how much longer that's going to be," and then he put down the phone, crashing it into the receiver and he went out into the street, only dimly conscious of the way in which the proprietor was looking at him, only vaguely aware of the aspect of the pavement, the blasted-out storefronts, the exhausted stones which framed this ruined city of Detroit.

It was easy, that was all, it was easy. Once you got past the indecision, once you had decided exactly what the problem was and the best way in which to attack it, once you had taken the matter of the personal out of it completely and looked upon it merely as a war, a vicious and unending war which had to be fought mercilessly because you were struggling against the oldest and least merciful foe of all, death, once you had come to that decision, then everything fell into place. Fuck consequence, fuck circumstance, fuck remorse, and fuck the easy answers which one by one, all of them—the jail, Williams, the girl—had forced upon him. The only answers there would ever be would be the hard ones, the old blood-hard messages of death raised against death.

He went back to his room. He got the grenades, the fire bombs, and the disassembled submachine gun.

Then he went out to the panel truck, still parked discreetly a few blocks down, and prepared to go to work.

XVIII

He hadn't meant to kill her. Coates wanted to give that message to the world, scream it out through a megaphone or better yet get a slot on the six o'clock news so that he could tell everyone within the greater Detroit area how it had gone this way and how it wasn't his fault. How could they say he wanted to murder her? Once they heard his side of the story, they would understand; they would forgive him. It hadn't been in his mind at all.

Not in the least. All he had wanted was information. He had approached her in the most reasonable way, really being a gentleman about it, despite the fact that her husband had been a bastard, but he had taken the easiest and gentlest line imaginable with her. All he was seeking was a little cooperation and a little information, and it would have been so easy for her to have given him this. He would have tipped his hat and been on his way, just a good patrolman making a stop on his beat to check with the lady of the house. But she had had to get vicious with him, to deny him selfishly the information which was his right to have, only because she wanted to hold onto everything herself, only because with Hamilton dead now she thought that she could run the operation just like some kind of Ma Perkins, when by rights all of it fell to *him*, Coates; it was his by inheritance, with Hamilton dead. But the selfish cunt wouldn't understand that; she had had to take the line that it was hers and she had the right to take over where the old man had fallen. That was the kind of shit you had to put up with in today's society, this women's liberation business, they not only thought that they were better than men sexually but also in the business area, that they could not only rule men's lives but supplant them, and that was when Coates had lost his temper.

Up until then he had been perfectly reasonable, highly in control of himself, but when he saw her treachery, when he saw that she would not under any circumstances give up what she thought to be hers but would hold onto it until the very end, something within him had broken after a very long time of self-control, and he had shot her. He didn't want to do it, but she had forced him. Any fool could see that; he had had no choice.

The trouble was that now he really was in hot water. He could tell that. As upset as he was, the cool and cop part of his mind was still functioning, and he could see that there was a case against him and that it would not be pleasant. A judge, certainly a jury, would see his point and would acquit him without delay, but there would be the matter of the arraignment first, and murder one was a nonbailable offense, so he'd be sitting around in the can for a while, and he knew enough about jails to realize that he wanted no part of them. Not that if he could have gotten bail he wouldn't have gone to the D.A. and made a full confession, because right was right and he would be acquitted soon enough. But jail . . . no way. He wouldn't get near it.

But then too, he wouldn't have made his confession to the D.A. just yet. Not until he got rid of the smack and collected his five million dollars. They were worth at least that, those precious bricks, maybe six or ten million, but he wasn't going to be greedy, not with that kind of money at stake. No, he would take the five million and consider it fair enough. Once he had that stashed away, he'd gladly go to the DA and make his plea and get a lawyer (Lord knew he could afford the best then) and serve out his two or three days in jail until a jury empaneled itself and he got through a quick trial. He was a cop, he had a respect for the law taught him by his time in the department; if a citizen with five million dollars didn't have respect for the law, what the hell was the point of the whole fucking country? No *way*. Meanwhile, though, he had to get rid of the smack and get his money. That was the uppermost problem. Also, just in case there were questions about discovering her body in the living room, which he doubted would happen, because who gave a shit about her, but just in case questions developed, well, then it would be best not to be in a position to be discovered. Not until he had made his deal and gotten the five million dollars safely away; then they could do anything they fucking wanted with him as far as they were concerned, as far as he was concerned too. She was the widow of a drug dealer, for Christ's sake, who wanted to take over the business for herself! What right-thinking American jury would stand for anything like that?

Coates spent the first night after the murder, then, in an odorous cubicle in a cheap downtown hotel choking on the fumes which five years later still seemed to come from the burned-out sections to the north, spent that night formulating his final plans. As the dawn came riding along like a taxi driver briskly cutting through traffic, the plan occurred to him in its great simplicity and brilliance; the best way to find out exactly where the stuff was being dumped was to smuggle *himself* into one of the Fleetwoods and then ride it all the way to its destination. That would do it! That would solve the problem completely! If he got himself into one of the cars coming out of that particular assembly point, he would be conveyed straight to the same place where the heroin had been, and what a surprise for the recipients, to open the door expecting to find their usual neat package sealed into place behind the crushed-velour upholstery and to find instead a very angry, incorruptible Detroit policeman come prepared to wreak vengeance upon them and end their cruel game forever . . . unless of course they were willing to try to deal with him on his own terms. That would be the least that they would be expected to do; after all, these people were not fools. They would share Coates's desire to make an honorable end to the fiasco.

Pacing back and forth, banging little flakes of plaster from the walls, standing in the sift of plaster as he inhaled its odors deeply, feeling the little grains drive power into his lungs, Coates thought of the mechanics of the thing. It would be difficult to get into one of the cars inconspicuously; a man was somewhat bigger than a shipment of heroin, of course. But then again, the Fleetwoods were *enormous*; they could literally swallow one up, and he could hardly be seen through the tinted glass of the gigantic passenger compartment if he huddled within himself like an elderly passenger gripping a cane, slunk down into the crushed velour and stared fixedly ahead, his features merging with the dim interior of the car. He could certainly get away with it, he thought with excitement.

Get away with it, and what a surprise for them in Toronto! He found himself giggling, rubbing his hands convulsively as he thought about it. That would really be something, when they opened the doors, looking for their routine shipment, and found him instead, the heroin draped in a sack across his lap. They would probably freak out on the spot, think of him as some kind of avenger, the ultimate narco transported three hundred miles over the border to make his score. Their resistance, what little there might be of it, would utterly be destroyed when they saw what they had confronted; truly they would never be the same again. Five million dollars? He might get ten!

It was a wonderful idea; it was the ultimate solution. Coates almost thought of calling his wife to tell her about it, just so that she could see after all her suspicions and the vicious things she had said that she had not married a fool after all. She had married a man with an eight-year plan, a man with a stroke of genius in the bargain, and a man of such courage and persistence that even a major setback like the treachery of everybody with whom he was dealing could not slow him down from consummation. That was what she had married! And what a pleasure it would have been to outline his plan to her over the phone, even tell her that she'd be in for thirty or forty grand so that she would just shut the fuck up and stay out of his life forever, but then he remembered that the room had no phone, which was all for the better, because, he remembered, on top of that, shushing himself with an elaborate gesture for the benefit of any spies who might be observing him through one-way mirrors, he couldn't give away the plan or his location. She would just call people in on him, and he couldn't have that.

Yes, there were spies all over. There were spies in the hotel, and spies who had watched near the lot when he had shot Hamilton (but he had been clever; he had gotten away quickly), and spies no doubt who at this very moment were busily observing him and taking frantic notes for their distant superiors; but no matter what kind of notes they took, they could never defeat him, because what they did not realize was that you had forever the integrity of your own consciousness; they could never take that away from you, and no matter what they did, they would never squeeze awareness of his plans out of him. He would not even talk about them, just in case there were lip readers around. He would merely think.

All right, then; he would think. The tricky part, the only tricky part he could see to what was otherwise a very solid and admirable plan, would be getting himself into the plant and getting inconspicuously enough into one of the Fleetwoods when it had reached its final assembly point. That was something to think about. There were a lot of people around the cars then, and probably they had to survive a final inspection at that point; it was a risky thing to think that he would be able simply to walk into the car, let alone carrying a sackful of heroin, plant himself in the rear seat, pull the door closed, and set off. It would not be too likely that they would all just at the moment of his entrance shift their attention elsewhere.

But then again, Coates thought, that was an insignificant detail. A man brilliant and cunning enough to have come up with an idea like this would hardly stumble over a basic matter of mechanics. All of that would fall into place when he started to execute. If you kept your mind on the grand design of things, the details would fall into place. Time after time he had seen people with brilliant minds, fine ideas, fail to put them into action because they had staggered over the last details, or worse than that, junked or scrapped the entire idea because of details. That was the difference, he thought, between a man with five million dollars and all the women in the world to fuck and a man who would be pounding it out on a beat until pension time. He knew what he was now. He was ready to seize his destiny.

Tomorrow. He would do it tomorrow; once you had a really solid plan firmed up, once you had things in gear and knew what you were going to do, it would be foolish to let something like this go. Besides, just in case there was a stink about this second Hamilton murder, if there was a manhunt on for him, it would be best for him to keep on moving, go right ahead and do it now rather than wait them out. If you waited them out you never knew what they might stumble across, and besides that, life was too short and too precious to waste. With all the fucking that lay ahead of him, he would be a goddamned fool to delay any longer. Instantly he felt he needed some conversation just to nail it down. He went downstairs and found the clerk, a man in his eighties sitting behind the desk, which was spattered with something that smelled like beer but appeared to have had an effect more like acid upon the surface, and said, "I'm going to be a very rich man."

The clerk was looking at a picture of a naked woman in a tabloid newspaper. She had her hands across her vagina but was otherwise fully exposed, and it was the look of embarrassment on her face, the amateurishness of her face for the camera, Coates thought, which was what made the picture sexy. "Glad to hear it, Johnny," the clerk said.

"I ought to be worth five million dollars."

"You wouldn't be the first," the clerk said, running his thumb over the woman's breasts, leaving a slight indentation. His mouth pursed, he made little sucking sounds.

"It's foolproof," Coates said. "I can't possibly lose."

"Lots that made it that way too," the clerk said. "And some made it taking longer chances. The important thing is that you've got your health and you've got a plan. Look at this fucking piece of cunt. If I could get it up, I'd like to stick it right in her. Of course, it's a little difficult at my age."

Coates tugged the newspaper away from the clerk slowly and very firmly and said, "You're not listening to me."

"Give me that back."

"I'm telling you I'm going to be worth five million dollars on a foolproof plan, and you're looking at a pair of tits. What kind of guy are you?"

"Give me back that paper. I want it."

"You disgust me," Coates said, and crumpled the newspaper, threw it in the clerk's face, and cursing, ascended the stairs again, not caring whether or not the man was staring at him. What did he know? What could he do? What difference would it make to him?

It didn't matter. Nothing mattered but the money. But it was a damn shame on the very last night before you were famous that you couldn't even get some proper respect and attention, damn it.

Maybe Lyndon Johnson had felt that way, Coates thought.

XIX

Ahead of Wulff the plant had loomed up, as distinct in the dawn as at noon, a gigantic indolent animal of steel that lay over acres of land and belched waste, farted filth. He had driven right up through the gates in the truck, no trouble at all, no security to speak of, and had parked in the employees' lot, then had carefully taken the ordnance he needed, locked up the valise, tossed it in the back, removed the plates of the truck with a screwdriver, and placed them under the floorboards, which he had also unscrewed. It was not likely that they would look at this truck for a long time, even less likely that if they did they would pull it apart, least likely of all that they would have any kind of an alert out for the murdered Edgerton's vehicle (they would not even have known that he had a truck; how could they have identified the plates?), but there was nothing wrong with taking reasonable precautions. He intended to be back at work for a while; he would have liked to leave as inconspicuous a trail as possible. The trail would be a canyon deep after today, anyway.

Walking briskly into the plant, just another worker carrying his belongings, Wulff felt that he had taken on not only the appearance and routine but the mental state of an assembly-line worker; his brain felt sodden and limp in his skull, his perceptions had curled into a sodden ball like a half-drowned cat in a corner. Going in here was not to think for whatever period of time that you would be in the enclosure; already the workers that surrounded him, the men in their twenties, thirties, forties, a trickle in their desperate fifties, although they were jammed up against him as they might have been in a subway, did not notice Wulff, did not react to him, nor was there any reason why they should have. Turnover in these plants was so enormous; you might know a few faces on your line, your foreman and your steward, and one face from management, and that was it. Who noticed? For that matter, who talked? Wulff could hear a few men talking in a desultory way about the Tigers' game, but the conversation was merely in rhythm to the walking, and as they passed into the enclosure it was shut off, as with a faucet.

Wulff had expected that there might be some difficulty at this point, difficulty with a time clock, perhaps a guard at a checkpoint, but he had misconceived the Fleetwood plant; there was nothing at all. The clock would have to be somewhere way down the winding alleys of the plant; the guard was in his imagination, the lockers in which the men stowed their clothing and gear were scattered all over the bleak area winding in and around the line, and no one noticed. No one noticed anything at all. Wulff had been prepared to make a sudden attack, to launch his campaign immediately (and thus riskily), but this was much better, better than he had possibly calculated it to be. He could set up in his own time. No one was going to harass him. He could run his campaign in his own way.

It was the noise that surprised him. He had had some conception of what the noise level might be like, and anyone who had spent time on the practice-shooting range in the police academy, let alone taking combat fire in Vietnam, knew what noise was like, but this was something else entirely; the noise here was like hell, or make it more like a maternity ward with women in deep labor grouped in a common ward multiplied several thousand times; like the child, the car, that infant of America, was brought forth in pain and fury, and the screams marking its passage into the world were touched with blood, the glint of the steel that wrenched it into being adding its own terror. Wulff found it almost impossible to concentrate; he needed to quietly and efficiently set up the incendiaries, and he had a corner wedged between the men's room and the lockers where he could do just that, but it was almost impossible to concentrate with the level of noise, and there was also the heat, the mighty, penetrating heat of this gigantic delivery room, which whisked in and out of every hidden slice of ground and brought him to brilliant sweat. Impossible to make splices, impossible to work with the wiring in this cove of sound and heat, and yet he did it, gathering himself into a fetal position in which the incendiaries were wedged, the valise perched before him functioning as a cover so that any guard, any supervisor, any stroller might only have taken him for being absorbed in cryptograms during a five-minute break. If they moved in closer to question him as to exactly what he was doing, Wulff was in serious trouble, but he was calculating that they would not and that in any case union regulations, the perimeters of functions, were so tightly delineated here that, just as in the PD, no one would feel that anything not his business *was* his business. It was the only way to get along in a union situation.

He tumbled into himself, working on the fuses, carefully feeding the wires into the little grenades like a mother feeding a long, tubular breast into a baby's sucking mouth, giving the dynamite the extension that it needed. The grenades were small, but they were mighty—the best of goods from the larder of Father Justice, who was certainly equipped as virtually no one else in the ordnance business to decide what the best dynamite would be. The Father had been a great character, one of Wulff's favorites in all of his travels; it was one of the great lessons and losses of his life that he had not had more time to get away with the Father, perhaps in the weapons room back of the chapel, and have a long talk with him about the philosophy and practice of violent revolution. He was sure that the Father would have a great deal to say on the issue, was, in fact, one of the world's leading experts on the problem, but there had never been the time. He had never really had the time in any of his travels, and there was no exception with Justice. Still, it had been too bad. The Father sold only the best, though.

Occasionally men passed in front of him, their bodies lumbering, their faces abstracted, moving into the toilet or into the locker area. From the look of some of them Wulff suspected that they were going here and there to cop a fast joint on their break time or during the five minutes that the union allowed them to piss on demand, provided that they got cover. That was no secret; pot was the pivot wheel of the factories; practically everyone on the lines had been into it at some point, at least a little, and of course all of the American cars nowadays looked and ran as if they had been put together by men who were seriously involved in marijuana. Oddly, that did not bother him as much as it might have once; Jessica had had something of a point in arguing that one cop on a joint was not necessarily the first inevitable step toward mainlining . . . and even if that had not been true, here was no question but that marijuana or seeking it had made all of these men completely oblivious of the large, grim, dedicated man in the shadows who was carefully putting together a set of devices which would have blown J. Edgar Hoover clear from his grave if he had been within three hundred miles.

Wulff must have worked on it altogether for over three hours. It was the most painstaking and slow job of this type he had done since way back at the beginning in New York, when he had spent a similar amount of time rigging incendiaries to gas lines so that he would be able to blow a certain important New York dealer clear out of his townhouse. That had been fun, and this was fun too, although he had worked that time in a quiet lot at midnight and this time he was working in a crowded plant, swing shift, after breakfast time. Still, the tension and the possibility of discovery only added a certain amount of spice to the adventure.

At heart, Wulff supposed, he had the psychology of a felon. The fear of discovery made him more efficient.

Somewhere around ten o'clock he was done. The affixed grenades glinted their little messages at him, and he could feel them beating as if they were little hearts, triggering out a pulse rate of death. He fondled them, his creations, with something approaching affection, almost oblivious of the noise in that last moment of satisfaction, and then, standing slowly, easing his limbs, getting circulation moving again, he put them into the valise, closed the valise gently, and put it neatly under his arm, set the clips, moved down the corridor. No one had noticed. No one at all. The line continued to scream, odors whisked through the plant, men moved by ones and twos down the corridors with wrenches sticking out of their pockets, a few in supervisory gear giving Wulff strange sidelong looks. He realized that the reason for his isolation was probably because the workers thought that he was part of management, and management thought that he was some kind of inspector, whereas any inspector coming through the halls might think that Wulff was yet another spy from management. Paranoia, the mutual crosschecking system of the plant, had worked well for him.

Security multiplied was no security at all.

He moved up several ramps, found a walkway, moved higher, found himself on a parapet. Here he looked down upon the arena of the plant as if it were a stadium. It was empty here too; no one to share the height with him, no one looking up. He put the valise down. Very carefully he sprang the clips and took out an incendiary.

When the voice within him said that it was the proper time, he threw it.

XX

Coates walked briskly through the plant, carrying a rolled-up newspaper like an executive, striding confidently, moving toward the assembly point. He was attracting a lot of attention, he noticed, but no one seemed inclined to stop him yet. All of them knew him, of course, and had respect for him; that was the reason that they were not stopping him. If they did, if any complications arose, he had a point-thirty-eight in one pocket and a point-forty-five in the other, equipment which he would be happy to use if the necessity arose, but he did not think that it would. A little confidence would carry him through. That was all you needed, in or out of this world. Confidence and a sense of command.

He was wearing his patrolman's blues, but without the holster belt and clips. No reason to call that kind of attention his way. A cop was always worthy of respect, and the blues made him look good; he always looked crisp and vital in his blues; he knew that so well, knew how when he walked the streets wearing them every woman wanted to fuck him just to get close to a cop . . . shit, a cop was the only protection you could find in life nowadays. But wearing the holster belt was too damned provocative. A gun got everybody nervous; he even had to admit that it got him nervous. There was something about looking at an exposed gun which was like looking at an exposed cock, Coates thought, all of that power and promise were best concealed, the message was too unbearable to be confronted directly. He knew that his wife would have been proud of him, the bitch, if she could have seen him now, the way that everyone in the plant looked at him with respect, that respect coming into him in little streaks of power so that he walked confidently, erect, striding through the plant like one who might have been at the highest levels of management, but of course the bitch did not see him now. Too bad. She would never see him again. Too bad for her again, but then, if she had seen the kind of man he had become and what she was missing, it might have been unbearable for her and there would have been one of those scenes.

He hardly needed this, not at the point when he had reached the summation of his life, that height at which at last he had become everything that he was supposed to be. The power emanating from him was obvious; no one was making the slightest attempt to block his path or interrupt his progress. No one would say a word to him. The guns banged provocatively against his thighs, and with every bang he smiled, with every reassuring little sway of the metal against his flesh he felt another stab of joy. Into the car then.

He was down at the extreme end of the line, that point at which the assembled Fleetwoods came off under their own power. As they rolled off the belt, a man would run to them, leap inside, start the engine under full throttle, and then in one scream of fan belt and rubber the cars would bolt down the long line, about a fifth of a mile to another point where the maws of the trucks themselves waited. The birth cry of the cars was one of anguish, Coates thought, like the scream of a child being spanked. The cars, forced into life, bellowed from their guts, pain wrung out of their metal hearts, and you could see why American cars lasted only seven years or sometimes four if they were conceived from such abuse. The men behind the wheels fooled around not at all, declined to tease them into life; they floored the accelerator at once and whipped the Fleetwoods down that line and into the maw of the ramp that would lead to the truck, and then sprang from the enclosure, rubbing their hands, striding as if they had accomplished something noteworthy and significant that would change their entire lives. Perhaps they would, Coates thought. It was a good job. It was a job which combined all of the satisfactions of America: a huge new car in their hands for the first time and the freedom to abuse it. If they had not been allowed to floor the accelerators, cycle the cars into high rpm's at birth, Coates thought, they probably would have settled on more obscure and dangerous ways to abuse the cars that would be sold at maybe eleven thousand dollars apiece, spitting on the deep-pile rugs or touching a lit match to them or putting a carefully hidden penknife to some of the crushed-velour upholstery. It was better this way. The suckers were not the ones with the eleven thousand dollars; they had enough money to trade the cars in after a year or two and indeed would only have them in this way; the suckers were those who would pick up the cars as fourth or fifth owner six years down the line and find that the early abuse had resulted in a pale and decrepit old age. But who the hell saw these people anyway? They were invisible. Everybody throughout the system was invisible, Coates thought; that was the key to its efficiency.

He held the sack containing the shit closer to him. It was neatly piled in there, tied with rubber bands, little bricks snuggled against his person. Acapulco gold they called it, or was that marijuana he was thinking of? Yeah, mary jane, that was Acapulco gold; heroin was horse, smack, shit, skag, or (he had heard this expression once and had never forgotten it) the doctor. Whatever you called it, it was precious, the most precious commodity in the world. If the gold standard ever collapsed, the shit standard would be there to replace it.

Coates giggled with his power. People were looking at him strangely, and indeed he must have presented a strange appearance with his cop's blues and the sack, but just as he had thought they would, they figured him for a supervisor or as a guard of some sort; his real identity was unknown to them, but his aspect was so positive, his person so secure, that it was inconceivable that anyone would question his presence there. He had figured everything out. He had done it perfectly.

Giggling again, but only with excitement, not with nervousness or anything like that, because he had the whole situation under control and they could do nothing at all to shake that control, Coates began to move toward the line. His walk was jaunty yet controlled, brisk yet measured; he had all the time in the world, he knew, and until he had done what he had to, all events would stop, chronology would freeze. He controlled utterly. He held all events in the palm of his hand.

If there were people around, he did not see or sense them; he was sealed into the filaments of a bottle called Events, which he had capped himself. If there were sounds around him, protests, questions, the motion and swirl of bodies, he did not see them, because all focus had contracted, narrowed around him, and in the tight and binding sheets of concentration there was nothing existing but he, James Coates himself. So he walked toward the car, his plans firming. He was in control now. He would ease himself into the back seat, hugging the sack to his body, bring the door closed, clutch the sack underneath his arm, and just like a chauffeured passenger in this Fleetwood, he would be conveyed to Toronto. "Pardon me," he would say when they opened the door on him there, looked at him, their eyes bulging in surprise, "pardon me, I've got to see the top man here," and how he would laugh at their expression! Well, there would be time to think of that later, time to enjoy all of the anticipation during the hours of the drive. For now it was sufficient to move forward, to get inside the car.

Stride by stride he closed ground, stride by stride Coates moved toward his destiny, tight and bunched within himself, moving toward consummation. The vague stiffened forms that he had noticed before were now clamoring at him, coming to strike with stiffened arms (but what did they matter? They did not matter at all, he could make them vanish simply by concentrating his force upon them; they were nothing but abstractions), hit at him like a great gong, and he kept on moving slowly, dramatically. "Watch it now," he said quietly, with superb control, "watch it now, you don't want to do anything like that, I've got a gun," and made a gesture toward the point-forty-five in his left pocket, not that he wanted to use it unless he had to, but they were forcing him. Oh, yes, they were definitely forcing him. "Don't do it," he said again. "I want this to go nicely, I want it to be easy, there's no reason for any trouble at all," and he began to move again. They staggered away (just as he had always known that they would), and everything was fine, everything was working well, and he was really going to do it, and all was going to be in place and he would have five million dollars, and the eight-year plan would go ahead and his life was saved, brought together in a fusion of purpose, and he had never been happier in his life, and the world blew up.

XXI

From his perch on the parapet in the last instants before the fuses exploded, Wulff could see the man walking toward the line, the man in blue who looked oddly like a policeman, moving with an odd, jaunty stride, slapping people away with an odd backhanded barrage of motions, his left hand dug suspiciously into his pocket as if he were going—Wulff could tell this from old knowledge—for a gun. It was a cop's walk, a cop's gesture. With a stick in his hand the blows would have been deadly, but as it was, they were merely laughable, parodies of a strike. What was not laughable was the fact that he was walking straight toward the place where fire would be ignited, the sack jammed under his shoulder, wedged in by his elbow so that he was able to strike out with those odd, convoluted blows, but coming free every now and then as his reach extended, the sack almost going to the floor, so that he had to grasp at it. The man was walking straight toward the point of combustion, and Wulff knew that he should flee, should get out, because the first flash was going to put everybody within fifty yards of the explosion on the ground with the possibility of slivers through them. A lot of innocent people, in short, were going to be hurt for the sake of purgation, but that was all right. What was not all right was that the stupid fool, by walking into the fuses, might crush the intricate wiring, might possibly destroy all of the timers. But Wulff had no more time to think of it; if he did not move now, he knew he would merely be another statistic when the reporters and night squad started to poke around an hour or two from now, and so, slowly, almost reluctantly, he put his head down and ran. He knew that he was attracting attention this time; he had abandoned any pretense of trying to fit into the scenario of the plant, but the important thing was to put ground between himself and the fire, to save his own ass for another day, a perfectly normal human desire, no disgrace in it at all. If there was one thing he was not, it was suicidal; he had his own set of conditions to meet now, he would meet them. The delay in looking at the man in the cop's uniform walking madly toward the cars had set him back just enough so that the explosion hit him before he had quite gotten clear, a maddening set of waves like a fist in the small of his back, the dull *whoomp!* of the incendiaries touching. Then he felt the ignition of flame, as one burning thrust overtaking him, and the second, duller explosion came as the fuses touched; the time incendiaries came off together, and metal began to buckle.

He hit the ground in an army low crawl, moving stubbornly, desperately toward the exit. In a little valley of sound beneath the explosion he could hear the screams and moans of some who had been caught in the first wave. He hoped that they had not been too badly hurt. He had rigged it for property rather than personal damage; he wanted no one not directly concerned to die, but in a war the innocent would always be affected; that was the very definition of the war, something so virulent that it struck out beyond those immediately involved and began to consume the world. That was what he had to end, the existence of an enemy so ruthless that it would enlist three million junkies as nothing more than hostages to their own position. It would not come easily; every step of it would come with pain, and this, for him and for some others, would be the most painful of all. Belly to the floor, he kept on moving like a wounded animal, sensing rather than seeing the light, and came into a small open space which must have been an access doorway; then he found himself in the air, huddled behind a huge ramp that stretched upward. He had found an emergency exit. The rough air cleared him out slowly as he rolled on his back, looking up at the sky, and he could see, several yards above, how the windows, some of them, had buckled out like obscene breasts, cracks and crinkles for the veins. This made him giggle, but only for a moment; he had to keep on moving; he had to get out of here. Slowly he rose, by using his palms, off the ground, brought himself to a standing position, and then began to run.

He could run quite well, he found, better than he would have thought after the weeks of inactivity and then the tensions and pressures of setting this up in a small space; but running was not all of it. You could not dedicate your life to motion; you had to reconnoiter too, and so he turned in hard pivot to see that flames were coming out of the huge plant like fingers, the aspect of a gigantic, dismembered hand desperately reaching toward the air, trying to claw itself back to the form from which it had been severed. Even in his haste Wulff could not resist running backward for a moment to take it in; it was beautiful in a way; he could admire his handiwork.

They would never be shipping skag out of this building. They wouldn't be shipping many Fleetwoods, either. A lot of people, he thought, were going to get the message.

And then he went back to the truck he'd abandoned before the first wave of sirens could hit him and got ready to highball the hell out of there.

There would be more missions, but he felt for the first time, now, that he was on the downhill slide.

Wulff grinned, and his grin was a mask of death.

XXII

In what had once been an intricate and highly evolved assembly plant but was now a tangle of metal and fire, a sack lay twisted around a measure of iron pipe. No one saw it, and no one would see it for many days yet. After the debris had been sifted, after the police and the ambulance crews and the investigators and the insurance people had been through, the sack would still be there, and it would only be a careful sweep by a rookie squad that would finally unearth it.

The sack would cause wonderment in the department; it would be taken to the commissioner, and the commissioner himself would for the first time in many years lose his composure and begin to babble as he saw the contents of the sack. It would in subsequent years become quite famous as part of the folklore of the PD and of PD's everywhere. But that lay in the future, as did the hopes of several thousand people who did not yet know that someday they would be desperately seeking what would have been the diluted contents of that sack, people who would be put through the worst withdrawal agonies because what would have been the underpinning of the supply system during a certain month no longer existed. But at this time of course these people did not know about it, and if it had been brought to their attention they would not, except for the most alert of them, have understood what had happened to them.

The hand that had held the sack was attached to an arm, the arm to a trunk, the trunk to limbs and a head, and all of it lay in a curiously intact state about fifty yards downrange from the point where the sack was found. The cleanliness of the corpse would be an object of amazement to the investigators, as would be the fact that in an explosion so devastating that the plant would never function again as it had, this was the only body that had been found. Everybody else had scattered in the first explosion. The corpse had stayed, held its ground when all the others had run, and that explained the fact that it *was* a corpse. But as to its cleanliness, the skin as unlined and fresh as if it had been lying outdoors for only a short time after death from natural causes—there was no explanation at all.

And there was no explanation either for the fact that the corpse was smiling. James Coates, Detroit PD—they dug up an Identikit finally— had died happy, and no one could understand why, not even his grieving wife and family.

They never put the corpse together with the sack nor made the proper connection.

They never understood the happiness.

Coates had died quickly, embracing five million dollars' worth of shit.

THE END

THE LONE WOLF # 12:
PHOENIX INFERNO

....

by Barry N. Malzberg

Writing as Mike Barry

I have never understood why drugs keep coming into this
country; there must be some high degree of corruption for
those drugs to keep coming . . . .

—Howard Cosell

You're putting me on, Howie baby.

—Burton Wulff

PROLOGUE

Wulff was rolling down the interstate from Motown, laughing a little at what he had been able to do although not very much because there was not much humor in it, too much pain and blood, when the motorcyclists came from nowhere, bearing down on him left and right on the empty panels of the road near dawn.

The cyclist on the left hit a door frame hard, skittering away, and Wulff thought that he had sideswiped the man. He backed the old Fleetwood down to fifty and then twenty to see if he had done any damage and watched the cycle, behind him now, weave to the safety zone and then come to a stop, the rider falling off in the loose, reckless way that usually happens only when a man is very experienced or hurt badly. There was nothing to do. They had him cold. He thought about going on. He had nothing to do with this at all; he should be long out of Detroit by now. Of course, that was the way to look at it. Move on.

But then again the cyclists were not involved with his own odyssey, and Wulff's rule from the very beginning of this horror had been that no innocent parties were to be hurt unless they were directly in the way of the parties he had to hit. So, cursing, he braked the big Cadillac over into the safety zone, trying to keep the hurt biker leveled in his rear-view mirror. Just as he came to a stop, skittering up little explosions of pebbles from the fender skirts, the other cyclist, the one who had been on the right and who he had forgotten about, was leaning over the driver's side, a gun in his hand.

"Get the fuck out of the car," this second motorcyclist said. He was a short man with an unshaven face, but the.45 he was holding in his right hand would make up for a lot of physical defects.

Wulff sat loosely behind the wheel, trying to figure out exactly what was the best way to come to terms with this. In one way he had expected it, of course, and yet in another he had not. Trouble always came unexpectedly; that was the trouble. At the heart, man was an optimistic animal.

"Didn't you hear me?" the biker said, waving the gun a little, "I told you to come out." Looking in the rear-view mirror, Wulff could see the other one struggling up, brushing dust off his cuffs in a casual way, hunching his shoulders then and moving slowly toward them. A beautifully controlled fall. Talent. It looked like the network had finally gotten so pissed off that they were not going the cheap route any more; they were going to deal now only with expensive help. "You fucking deaf?" the short biker said. "I told you to get out of that car, you get the fuck out now. You start screwing around, I'm going to blow your head off. I don't give a damn."

Wulff guessed that this was true. The man didn't give a damn and he probably would blow Wulff's head off. Having gone this far they would probably go a little farther. The other one was closing in nicely now, out of range of the rear-view mirror, probably with a little surprise in his hand too. It didn't matter. Surprised at his detachment, at how easily he could see that it did not matter and that the situation had passed beyond him, Wulff slowly took his hands off the wheel and dropped one toward the door handle. The face of the man with the gun twitched. "Don't try anything," he said. "Come out slowly and nicely now." He backed away, a true professional, allowing room for the door to clear. That was good thinking. It meant that Wulff could not push the door hard and jar the man. Not that Wulff was thinking about that, anyway. He still had the other one to contend with. All the armaments in the trunk made no difference; he had iron on him, for that matter, but it did him no good at all. They had control over the situation, and after their beautiful first maneuver obviously had the sense not to lose control. "Easy now," the man with the gun said. "Get out nice and easy."

Wulff did that. He let his kneecap push the door open, shading just a little bit of space, and then came through slowly, his hands in front of him. There was room somewhere in here for a nice, desperate maneuver, the kind of thing that in his youth he might have worked out; he could have dropped his hands below windowline, where the biker from his new distance could not see him, grabbed hold of the gun, and come out shooting. The surprise value would have been worth something even against these professionals; if he could have dropped this one with one shot, he would have had at least a 50-50 chance using the door as cover to get the other. But he simply was not that desperate, Wulff thought. It did not matter enough to him to make the play. Maybe that showed some lack of character, but the hell with it. He had done enough.

He came out of the door slowly, his hands still up. It was empty on the interstate, sun glancing off the panels, just a little bit of haze in the distance now. Not a particularly well-traveled road, but then again passing at seventy-five, sealed into the furniture of a car, no one was going to be fool enough to help him. You were out in the open here but the isolation was complete.

The second biker was there now, his gun out. He was a little taller than the one who had gotten him out of the car but not enough to be significant. Five seven, five eight, both of them, hard, driven faces, efficient eyes, somewhere in their middle thirties, but it could have been forties or fifties too; there was a certain kind of face that started old, stopped aging altogether at twenty, and then just fell in on itself, became more and more bitter. He wished he had gone north out of Detroit instead of south. South seemed the truest way, that was for sure, but north would have led him out of the country and his luck would have been better in Canada. His luck would have been better anywhere, as a matter of fact. It looked, Wulff thought, as if the string had run out. This did not fill him with fear—he was on a one-way ticket, he was a dead man anyway—but there was a certain amount of regret here. He had been in exile so long, he had come out of prison with such difficulty to get started again and do a real job in Detroit . . . it seemed a shame to see it all end again. He wouldn't have given a damn if they had thrown away the key in jail, kept him there for a long, long time. But to get back into the swing of it and then lose was excruciating. Shit, he thought. He said nothing, holding his ground. There was a small chance that he could get one of them by going quickly for his gun, but then the other would cut him down. It didn't matter. "Check him," the shorter man said, "check him down."

The other man put his gun away, frowning slightly, and closed in on Wulff. He did not look entirely happy with the assignment but then again he was covered by the gun; he really was in no danger at all. Wulff could see the thought slowly percolating its way through the man's brain, radiating outward in levels to the broken lines of his cheeks. He was covered and therefore he was safe, but on the other hand he knew exactly who Wulff was and how dangerous he could be and that meant trouble. But the trouble Wulff might cause him was as nothing to what his partner might do if the man backed off. Wulff could see all the calculations and then he could see the man on some deep level saying *oh fuck it* and closing in and as the hands hit him he might really have submitted to it, gone with it all the way, except that the man covering them started to giggle in a hard, harsh voice, a giggle that was almost as sexual as it was from simpler excitement, as if the idea that Wulff was being caressed in the frisk somehow meant that he was being violated too, and it was this that pushed Wulff over the line. He didn't mind being ambushed and frisked down, at least not so much that he would risk getting killed to fight it. But if they were going to bring in a domination element, that was something else. Besides, if that element of excitement was part of the equation, it meant that they didn't have as much of an edge as they thought; the edge began to disappear, the element of calculation became blunted, when sexuality of any sort, no matter how transmuted, came into it. As the taller man put his fingers almost limply on Wulff's pockets, Wulff moved; in a perfect combination of rage and calculation he crouched down under the grasp and then came up hard, butted the man under his eye, brought him back just a trifle and then he was fighting the other man's hand for his .38, finding it deep in his pocket, coming out with the gun.

The taller man screamed as he realized what had happened to him, but he was still scrambling for balance, not even able to get out of the way. Wulff, gun in one hand, reached for the man with the other, pulled him toward the gun by his shirt-front, and then he had perfect cover, the man shielding him from the other. In his grasp the taller man twittered and shrieked.

"You stupid son of a bitch," the shorter man, invisible, said from behind cover. "You stupid bastard, you fucked up everything." And then he did something that Wulff hardly could have expected. He shot the taller man in the back. Wulff could feel the impact spreading all through the fingers of the hand holding the taller man, so that suddenly there was dead weight and bubbling across his arm. Desperately he held the man up, maintaining him as cover, but it was close to 180 pounds now falling against him, and his margin of protection could be measured only in seconds. The shorter man must have felt that way too. He put two more bullets into the back of the tall man, encouraging him to die faster. The weight was overwhelming. Wulff let the tall man drop and fell with him, pushing the corpse away at the last moment and putting a shot through the gun hand of the shorter man.

The shorter man screamed, and then something darker than pain overtook him, seeming to convulse his face. Concentrating slowly, desperately, he tried to work his hand around the gun, tried to get off a shot, but he could not. Something in the nervous structure had disassembled; he could not hold the gun. The gun fell from his hand into the dust of the road and the man stood there weaving, shaking his head. He was crying. "You son of a bitch," he said, "no one gets you. No one. We had you."

"Forget that," Wulff said, "it doesn't matter." He closed in on the short man, put his gun away, knelt beside him. "You got greedy," he said, "that was all. You could have killed me but you wanted something more. What did you want?"

The man shook his head. His eyes were dilating with the pain. "Nothing," he said, "I won't talk."

"Sure you will," Wulff said, almost gently. "Who sent you?"

The biker's face had a scream in it, his mouth was working all around the edges but he could not get the sound out. "No," he said, "I won't tell."

"Of course you'll tell," Wulff said. An old Rambler went by them at ninety kicking up dust and little shards of pebbles, which skittered around them. The car was almost out of sight before he had even looked up. People on the interstates minded their own business, stayed within their own compass, that's for sure. "You'll tell fast or you'll tell slow, but you will most certainly tell and I'd like to make it easier for you. That's a bad hand," he said, looking down at it. The hand was opening into little pockets of blood, leaking into the dust. "You're going to need treatment," Wulff said almost solicitously. "You could bleed to death with a hand like that."

"You son of a bitch," the man said but without conviction. "You bastard."

"I try to be," Wulff said. "It's the only way to survive murderers. Who sent you?" he said casually and hit the man in the face. The man fell over backwards, gasping. "You'd better tell me," Wulff said. "A man could be tortured to death here on the interstate and no one would notice. They patrol it about once a week, you know."

The man seemed to be calculating this. Maybe it was only the pain that made him seem to turn inward. Wulff had seen this moment time and again; even the toughest reached that point of inward seeking that came before either confession or death. The man looked over at his dead partner and said, "All right. I don't give a fuck. It's none of my affair; I never said I'd die for this." His tone was sullen even in pain. "Shit, it was a lousy deal anyway."

"Where were you supposed to take me?" Wulff said. "Obviously you wanted me alive and disarmed or you would have killed me right off; that was your mistake. Where were we supposed to go?"

"Phoenix," the man said after a little pause. "I was supposed to get you into Phoenix. Preferably alive."

"Good," Wulff said, "good." He knelt next to the man, took out a handkerchief, began to work up an improvised tourniquet almost solicitously as he leaned over, close to him. "You just tell me all about it," Wulff said. "Like, who it is in Phoenix that sent you, and who we were all supposed to see, and maybe if we get along well enough you can come along with me when we pay him a visit. Won't he like that?" Wulff said. "He'll be pleased as hell. And you'll be off the hook, too; it will be mission completed."

The biker's eyes fluttered as the tourniquet was wrapped but otherwise he said nothing. There was, of course, nothing to say.

I

Wulff had been a narc for the NYPD for two years until he had been busted for trying to arrest an informant, and on patrol car duty the first night had caught a stiff who had turned out to be his fianceé, OD'd out in a stinking SRO hotel on West 93rd Street. That had made him pretty bitter, bitter about the drug market and the men who operated it, and he had decided, not unreasonably at the time, to wipe it out singlehandedly. Since then, in stages, he had hit eleven cities and had done more than his share, but on the other hand the market was still staggering along. There was at least someone big enough left in Phoenix to try and get him collared.

Of course, everyone wanted to get him collared. He was probably the most wanted man in the history of the organization; at least ten thousand freelancers had his name and picture in their wallets, every one of them willing to take a shot for the ten grand that what was left of the organization had put on his head. The NYPD wanted him pretty badly, too, because Wulff was making more of a name for them than they particularly wanted in the area of vigilantism. And besides, he had broken out of jail after a four-week stay to start his odyssey again in Detroit out of which he had come just in time to be caught by the bikers working out of Phoenix. That meant that both sides of the law were crunching in on him like a vise, while meanwhile his own situation could hardly be described as improving. A more sensible man would have given up.

But then again a more sensible man would never have gotten into it, and all things considered Wulff had done fairly well. In New York he had blown up a townhouse and a pretty important operative with it; in San Francisco he had blown up a ship containing a million dollars' worth of junk and, incidentally, a couple of hundred men. He and the appropriated junk had gone to Boston where things had gotten even hotter for everything except the smack, which he had dropped into the Charles River. After Boston things, even in retrospect, had become a little blurred; Las Vegas was in it and Havana and Chicago and Lima and Los Angeles and Miami and New York again, the last caper the biggest and most terrible of all because it was there that Wulff had found out who had OD'd Marie out. It had been the lieutenant with whom on his last night on the narco squad he had tried to book the informant for possession. The lieutenant had not liked that very much for reasons that went to the heart of the connections in New York, and he had taken rather extreme action, not that it had done him any good in the long run. Wulff had beaten him up and put him in the hospital for weeks, and then some freelancer, working on an organization grudge, and meaning to kill Wulff, had killed the lieutenant by mistake, thus making Wulff's escape possible. Then it had been Detroit, where he had blown up a good portion of the Cadillac plant through which smack was being run into Toronto. After that one, Wulff had stuffed his ordnance and a fair amount of cocaine appropriated from a dealer who had tried to kill him into the trunk of a Fleetwood and had headed out looking only for a little peace and quiet at this stage . . . only to run into the two bikers who were not bikers at all but apparently in the employ of someone from Phoenix who wanted to put Wulff out of business about as badly as anyone who had ever run up against him. There was no peace. None at all.

Well, there never had been; Wulff had to face that. There had been no peace since the crazy time when as a young cop he had enlisted in the army, even though under civil service regulations he was exempt, just to have a first-hand look at what Vietnam was like. Was the government telling lies or was it another great fight for freedom? Everyone he worked with thought that Wulff was crazy for enlisting. Wulff, after just a few months in that drug circus in and near Saigon, thought that he was crazy too, but by that time it was too late to do anything but grit it out. He had learned a lot . . . among other things he had learned heavy and light combat and guerrilla tactics, which had come in handy later in the game.

After he had come out of the army, they had felt so guilty about what he had done, setting an example that no one else in the PD had wanted to follow and so on, that they had set him up for the job in narco, giving him what they thought was the softest and most enjoyable slot you could get in the PD short of vice, which, of course, was an inherited job altogether. Narco at that time, in the middle sixties, was a good detail; the hours were easy, the informant system was set up so nicely that you had no work to do at all, just sit on your ass, keep in touch, and every now and then bust a few people on prearranged charges without evidence when the papers stirred things up. The graft was good, the living was soft and the relationship between the informants and the narcos was very cool, very helpful for all concerned.

But what they did not realize was that Wulff, having had a good dose of Saigon, having been given a pretty good idea of exactly what the drug trade meant not in the abstract but in the way that it could do things to people, was not prepared to enjoy the life of ease and the pleasant system that meant that everyone was getting along, everyone was making out and only the junkies—and who gave a fuck about them—

were getting ripped off and they wouldn't know the difference anyway. It was a growing feeling of rage, a feeling that he was feeding the system, not doing anything at all to block it, that had gotten Wulff into the business of busting an informant for possession, not exactly the kind of thing that a narc was supposed to do unless it was prearranged. And after that, everything had led smoothly and inevitably to his ten-city odyssey and several thousand murders. But looking back at the chain, there was no way of saying that there had ever been a point at which it might have been different. Maybe if his girl had not been killed. But then again he had signed her death papers, unknowingly, when he had decided on the bust. And the horror of it was that even if he had known what was coming, even if he had known the risk, looking at the sneering, bobbing face of the informant in the bar laughing at him because Wulff was helpless, he did not know if he would have done anything different. The man had had to go to jail. There had to be an end to it, some fix to the responsibility at some point.

That was all gone, anyway. Williams was all gone, too; Williams was the black rookie cop with whom Wulff had been on patrol the night they had gotten the call on the anonymous OD, a blind squeal coming into the 67th that had been assigned them by coincidence. Williams was the one with whom Wulff had worked from the very beginning to break the organization, the one who had, playing it cautious at the beginning, finally left his pregnant wife and the nice mortgaged house in St. Albans to play it the hard vigilante way. But in the end, in Los Angeles, that had all broken down, too. Williams had seen that the system, as bad as it was, worked better for him than being outside the system, which did not work at all, and he had gone back to his wife and newborn son. Now Williams was under wraps again; he had stayed in contact with sources in Detroit who had made the Canadian run known to him. He had engineered the break from the courtroom to put Wulff back on the road again. But otherwise, essentially, he was out of it; Wulff was as thoroughly alone as he had been on the night he had seen Marie dead and had known that he would have to play it vigilante or not at all.

So he had rolled out of Detroit, once again flames in his wake, headed back toward New York, but not sure of exactly which way he was going; willing to play it by instinct as he always had in the past . . . and he had run smack into two bikers on assignment from Phoenix. Once again the enemy, his old stupid enemy, had given purpose to him, where otherwise there might not have been; once again the enemy had energized Wulff and given him a sense of mission precisely when that sense of mission had been flagging. If they were his creation, then he was theirs, the two of them welded together, hammer and the nail, anvil and the hammer, flame and the anvil . . . and now there was no disentanglement but only greater heat and the plunge down.

II

Carlin lived on one hundred acres on the irrigated Arizona desert and contemplated his holdings with delight. Carlin lived with a half million dollars and a mistress in a house the color of flame on the desert and thought of all the things that he had gone through to get there. And there was not a moment, each and every morning of his life, when the pleasure did not run through him like water, just to know what he was, where he had come from. Carlin bought and sold heroin on the open market and ran it every way that he could, down to Mexico City, up to Denver, east to New York, west to Berkeley, he didn't give a damn. It was all commerce. The country was the corpus and heroin was the blood. He might as well have been in stocks and bonds for all that it meant to him. It was a business.

Carlin was very serious about that. He refused to take the issue of heroin on an emotional level; he knew in his heart that he was not a drug peddler or a merchant of death as the press liked to call it during one of its hysterical once-a-year crusades. He was simply a product manager delivering a product in terms of the needs of a given market. Ford and Pepsi-Cola created markets and then served them; Ford and Pepsi-Cola weren't in any trouble with the feds, at least trouble that they couldn't buy themselves out of, and here he was, Carlin, not even creating the market like Ford or Pepsi were for their crap, merely servicing it. He wasn't hooking anybody into heroin; as far as he was concerned it was an evil, debilitating poison, and if he or any of the kids from his estranged marriage or anyone he knew got into it he would make sure there was hell to pay. But then again, if there was this need and all this pain, it would be almost as immoral *not* to serve it as to take care of it, and he was doing his part. The shit flowed back and forth across the border to points east and west, and through a complex of intermediaries he was good for a quarter million dollars a year without ever having seen a cube of it. He let those he hired for it make sure of the purity. He was making two hundred fifty grand a year and not sweating for it. Phoenix was a good place to live, the more pleasant after having grown up on Flatbush Avenue in Brooklyn and having spent the first thirty-nine of his forty-five years hacking it out in the miserable cities of North America trying to move his way into a position of some independence without antagonizing anyone. It hadn't been easy, and there had been along the line a little murder, but he had made it, finally, made it to the desert and a house the color of flame. And he was not going to give it up easily. There was no reason why he should. Basically, Carlin felt he had a moral right to what he regarded as his inheritance.

The war that this crazy Wulff had launched against the network had worried him, of course—Carlin was a sensible man, he kept tabs—but it hadn't bothered him too directly. He had taken reasonable precautions, stepped up his bodyguards, tried to buy his independence from certain suppliers and fences by finding new outlets, but mostly it was a matter of just watching the situation from as far away as possible, which was not difficult on the desert, and hoping for the best. He didn't want to get into anything too aggressive. Therefore, it had been a special bonus for Carlin, something really remarkable to find that the way things were working out Wulff was practically his best friend in the network, was doing more for his business than anyone ever had, more even than his estranged wife, who had inherited fifty thousand dollars that Carlin had used to buy a small shipment back in 1962, which gave him his start. What Wulff was doing was killing off the competition like crazy.

He riddled the Northeast, he went out West and blew up any fragment left of an independent West Coast network that might have made a push. He went back again to Boston and left the New England circuit reeling, then off to Vegas and Chicago where he had first enticed and then taken out violently the old man who had sat on top of everything and who even Carlin had been afraid of, worrying that the old man would notice him some day, notice how well he was doing, and move in. Louis Calabrese. He just could not have stood up against Calabrese, wouldn't have been ready for him for another fifteen years or later than that. But Wulff had taken care of that old bastard, too, he had shot up a beachful of men in Miami, gone back to New York and cleaned out the gasping survivors there. Carlin, reading about it in the newspapers and in little dispatches that he was able to cull through the network, had hardly been able to accept his own luck. He had confronted all of it with disbelief; it seemed impossible that after forty-six years everything was for once breaking completely, totally right for him rather than just wavering on the borderline as it had even during the good years. And the day he had read in the papers that they had gotten Wulff in jail in New York, Carlin had not been able to prevent himself from driving two hundred miles to Turf Paradise and laying five thousand dollars through the machines just in sheer joy at how beautifully everything had turned out. He lost the five thousand dollars but he won the reports that indicated that by the time the psychiatric teams and the jury system got through with Wulff his only source of income was apt to be the twenty-five cents per license plate that he would be knocking down for decades. And with the removal of Wulff it seemed that all Carlin's problems went away; he did not realize until he read that the man was finally under confinement how worried he had been. The desert was big and the Southwest was not a major territory. It might have been a long time, if ever, before Wulff had gotten to Carlin. But Carlin now was finally willing to admit how real Wulff had been to him. Eventually he would have come. Eventually Carlin would have had to deal with him, and if Louis Calabrese could not, would Carlin have a chance? But that was all gone now.

Everything was all gone. Carlin was a free man in a devastated field; he had every shot now at being the biggest and the best. So the word that Wulff was out again had chilled him, and it was as if the terror that he had carefully kept out of his conscious mind until then had, untrammeled, rolled in without Carlin having any defenses to fight it off. He had used all his energy the first time around, denying fright. But now the realization ripped through and he had no means to beat it off. Reading that Wulff was out left him as close to the line of panic as he had been in twenty years. At that point he had taken desperate measures, done something he never thought he would have found necessary, lost his control altogether. He had hired twenty of the best men he could find, pointed them toward Detroit, where word came through his contacts that Wulff was headed, and asked them to get him. Preferably alive so that he could see him on the desert and know that he had not been lied to, but dead, with photographs, if necessary.

He had not wanted to do this; he had not wanted to open his panic and resources to a killer team; he had not wanted to do something so provocative that if it failed Wulff would be solidly on his trail and Carlin would be on the deathlist. He was terrified of Wulff. But it was precisely this terror that had dictated his move. He could not bear to wait it out now. The man had to die.

Carlin felt a little better knowing that the team was on the job. Every single one of them had been vouched for in one way or the other. In fact, knowing that twenty men were on the trail, that he had interposed all of them between himself and this madman, had the effect of buying him the peace that he thought he had lost forever reading about the escape. Even at fifty thousand dollars out of pocket and a promised fifty on delivery to the winning team, it was cheap. Carlin felt like himself again. He wandered out to the cacti and watched sunsets. He began to think again of what it would be like to run everything from the Southwest. It was not impossible. Huey Long had almost been able to run everything from New Orleans and that was a long time ago in a less technological society. And if the Kingfish had not been such a fool he would have had it all, too. He would have done it. Carlin could do no less than that. Anything was possible.

Carlin was fucking his mistress when the call came in. He had rolled on top of her and was banging away, as deep into her as he had been for months. Her name was Janice and she was, he had to face it, little more than a stupid, slightly overweight broad in her thirties who was in no way worthy of him, had no idea of who he was or what he was doing—which was probably a benefit, come to think of it—but who had the most fantastic set of tits he had ever dealt with in his life, forty-eight inches, tits that he could drown himself in, with nipples like headlights; just a fair fuck but those incredible tits and the pliability of them, which let him do anything that he wanted to do, bounce them, toss them, throw them over her shoulders or his, squeeze them around his prick and fuck them like a crazily shaped, huge, tight cunt. All right, she was stupid, but in her own way she was exceptional and he could roll over and die in her for lust, and that was the best deal he had been able to come up with yet, what with his wife, that bitch, having mostly ruined him for women for years after their marriage. She had hated to fuck and had resented every part of it so much that sometimes Carlin would still shudder in fucking right now remembering the expression on her face when he had come. Well, that was all behind him now. Onward to better things. He had been living with Janice for two years and although nothing outside of it meant anything at all, the sex had been absolutely sensational. It was a toss-up which absorbed him more as a recreation, Turf Paradise or her tits. Maybe Turf Paradise, he had to admit. You couldn't fuck her tits nine times a day. But then again, every time he got on top of Janice he was a winner.

"All right," she was groaning as he settled against her, "listen now, take it easy." He was groaning and biting her breasts, leaving little streaks and ridges up and down the width of them and although her hand was drawing him in, her fingers pressed to the back of his neck there was a sudden pressure in the fingers, which meant that he was hurting her and she was hurting him back. "Please," she said, "enough, enough, Joe." And Carlin, almost screaming with the intensity of it, took his head back just a little, tried to focus his desire down to something he could control. Just as he ejaculated, coming within her violently without pumping, screaming and biting her breast then in fury as she dug her fingernails in and screamed back, whether in disappointment or pain he did not know . . . and just at the moment when his ejaculation was finished, swimming somewhere in the darkest part of her, the phone next to the nightstand rang.

He rolled from her, reaching for it. In a way it was almost a relief, the call coming in; he had been taking to coming within her too fast almost all the time now, an old problem that he thought he had licked but that had come back probably with all the tension of Wulff and then the leap of his plans. She didn't like it, of course, no woman liked it, but on the other hand, fuck her; he had the right. If she excited him that much, who was she to complain if he came off quick? There were a lot of women dying for it, who would have been happy to get it almost any way they could from a man like him. Shit, just read the advice to the lovelorn columns and all the women who complained that they couldn't even get their husbands to undress much less pay attention to them. But even though he was right, somehow Carlin did not want to go into this at the time. He had a few times before because Janice had really bitched about it, but somehow he didn't know quite what to say. It could get ugly. She somehow did not understand that it was his right, and anyway she with the forty-eight-inch tits and the IQ of forty-eight had no business complaining about anything. The phone was almost a relief. Often he refused to pick it up at night when there was no one around to filter it through, but tonight he made an exception, almost grabbing it, seizing it the way five minutes before he had seized her breasts. "Yes," he said, "hello?"

"Is this Joe Carlin?" a voice said. Carlin couldn't place it. It was flat, dull, and yet somehow underneath the monotone there was force in it. This man had a sense of self-possession. "I said is this Joe Carlin?"

"Yeah."

"Good. I wanted to check."

There was a pause that went on for a while until Carlin realized that the man was not going to say anything more, and for the first time he felt a dull twinge of apprehension. "What do you want?" he said, "who is this?"

"This is a friend of yours, Carlin."

"Who's that?"

"Someone you wanted to see."

"I don't know what you're talking about."

"Someone you wanted to see so badly that you sent some other friends of yours to get me and bring me there."

Carlin shook his head and said, "Listen—"

"You know exactly who this is," the voice said.

"You son of a bitch," Carlin said. The woman looked at him with interest, her hand flat on his thigh. She began to rub with sudden energy. "Cut that shit out," Carlin said sharply to her. His voice shook.

She took her hand away and looked at him with something that might have been hatred.

"Okay," the voice said, "I'll cut that shit out. I'm coming to cut it out of your heart and head, Carlin. If I were you I'd get moving now."

"I'm not afraid of you," Carlin said.

"You're about twenty men afraid of me, Carlin. You're afraid of everything. But we'll see. You'll have a chance to prove yourself. I just want you to know I'm coming," the man said. "It's been a little while and a lot of cities since I found someone who was really worth killing. Who I really wanted to kill in a personal way, not just business. So I'm glad to get caught up with you; you've given me some new interest in life. I'm coming, Carlin, I'm coming," the voice said and hung up.

Carlin put the phone down and turned slowly on the bed, looking up at the ceiling with dead, flat eyes. I should do something, he thought, I really should do something. There is a lot to be done and I can do any of it and my position really is not so bad, not so bad at all. But then again, he might be twenty miles from here now, twenty miles or two thousand, no way to say, but I shouldn't take the chance.

But he could not move. For the moment he found himself in an attitude so dull and withdrawn that it might have been grief.

The woman was touching his shoulder. Her nails were digging in. "What's wrong Joe?" she said, "what's wrong with you? Who did you hear from? What did they say?"

"Shut up, you stupid cunt," Carlin said.

III

Wulff and the biker got to know each other pretty well on the long trek south. They even got to feel that they had something in common: They both hated junk. The biker drove Wulff's Fleetwood while Wulff held the gun on the man's neck, but after a while they got so deeply into conversation that Wulff didn't worry so much about the gun, and as far as the biker was concerned he had no reason to make any sudden move. They both understood that the biker had been strictly for hire and had nothing personal against Wulff at all and would as soon have worked with as against him. He hated Carlin, too. He talked about Carlin a lot on the way down, but that was only the early and least absorbing part of their conversation.

The biker was named Owens. The other one, the taller man who had been named Yount, they had just left with the two motorcycles, by the side of the interstate for the cops to find. There was nothing tying Yount to them, and even if there had been they would be hundreds of miles away by the time an all-points went out, if it went out at all. Who cared about people like Yount? Owens asked, and Wulff, after hearing the man's background, agreed. He was hardly top-priority.

Owens was thirty-eight years old and had been around. He had been most recently a stuntman doubling for a motorcycle exhibitionist who made his living running off diving boards and canyons; the exhibitionist had been a brilliant promoter but had had something of a yellow streak, and since at a distance where most of the events were conducted one could hardly make out features in a helmet, Owens had done most of the doubling. It had been a pretty good if dangerous job without much security, but the biker had brought an end to it himself finally by taking a jump himself over seventeen parked cars on a ten thousand dollar challenge bet that demanded that he do it without a helmet. Greedy for the ten thousand if scared, the exhibitionist had done it, had turned over on the roof of the fourteenth car, had burst into flame and died. That left Owens pretty unemployed, but some contracts put him in with Carlin and he guessed that Carlin's assignment sounded like a fairly easy twenty-five hundred down. What the hell? The odds that he would ever meet up with Wulff with a search party of twenty scouring the country were almost nil.

So he had been sorry when he and Yount had come up against Wulff in the Fleetwood. Actually, Owens explained, it was really Yount's fault, the conscientious fuck had spotted Wulff on a sweep going in the opposite direction and had insisted that they turn tail and follow. Owens had wanted no part of it and had insisted to Yount that no one could identify a man passing him on the opposite side of an interstate at a combined speed of a hundred and forty an hour. But Yount said he had been an eagle scout and a point man in the infantry and that was his specialty. Rather than get into trouble with Yount, who was just the kind of prick who would have reported him to Carlin, Owens had gone along. See where that had gotten them, of course. It served Yount right; it would have served Owens right, too, being such a fool and going along if Wulff had not been such a reasonable man. Owens said he was damned grateful and he would lead Wulff right to Carlin's estate and he would even help Wulff set the grenades, that being the least he could do for the trouble they had caused Wulff and basically being in agreement with Wulff's crusade anyway. He detested drugs; the exhibitionist had been on coke and pot all the time and doing a little heroin sniffing, and where had it gotten him but out of life and Owen out of a job? Owen felt that it was a damned shame he couldn't have worked with Wulff from the start.

Wulff didn't have as much to say, there being no need for it, but he found that he liked Owens almost as much as Owens liked him; he was the first man since Williams that Wulff felt at all comfortable with. The man was cheerful, he was straightforward, he was, as he had told Wulff, in it only for the money with nothing personal at all, and furthermore, despite his bad luck on the road, he was competent. He probably could have killed Wulff if he wanted to; Owens said that, and Wulff, to himself, agreed. He hadn't because he had liked Wulff's style from the very beginning. With that as the start of a relationship it was easy to relax with the gun and let the miles go faster.

By the time they hit the outskirts of Chicago, Wulff felt at ease enough with Owens to get Carlin's private number, which he had given out to the assassination team, and put in a call himself. He had found Carlin on the phone to react almost exactly as Wulff would have hoped: with blind, complete panic. That was fine; it was all calculated. Even the possibility that Carlin would meet him with one thousand troops had been calculated, as had been the chance that Carlin would flee. Wulff liked this. He liked it fine. He understood now why Calabrese had not had him killed but sent him off to Peru. Knowing there was someone worthwhile and deadly around kept you young. He needed a rival. There was enough pain; two women dead, thousands burned, he didn't have to concentrate on that any more. The memories would come as would the *modus operandi*. It was the challenge that would keep him going.

So they kept on rolling, then, past Kansas City, moving briskly on. Wulff told Owens somewhere around Tulsa that he would be happy to let him go any time now, but Owens said no, he didn't mind the company and he didn't even mind the gun; he'd be happy to come along and help Wulff set the traps. At that, Wulff had put the gun away, taking a chance on Owens, which really was no chance at all, and had settled down to the rest of the drive, which was a piece of cake. Owens had a million stories.

In New Mexico they came across the border and came up against another of Carlin's troops. Pure coincidence. The team working in two like all the rest, was in a big Pontiac Bonneville that steamed exhaust and looked to be at the very end of the seven-year American car cycle carefully worked out by GM and followed by the others, but whatever it was the car was incredibly maneuverable. Wulff could hear the scream as it wheeled around on the two-lane highway, dwindled in the rear-view mirror, turning. It was suddenly up behind them very quickly, closing ground. It must have been moving at eighty-five or ninety miles an hour. "Floor it all the way," Wulff said.

Owens tried, little beads of sweat coming out over his forehead.

"Carlin's not so stupid," he said.

"You think it's him?"

"Who else?"

"No," Wulff said, "I guess he's not so stupid at all." The Fleetwood was rocking at eighty; the suspension, suddenly intimate underneath him, was screaming. "We can't outrun them," Wulff said. "The car won't take it."

"Main access road," Owens said, his hands stiff on the wheel. "He would have them patrolled. He just got lucky, though. I got to believe he's lucky."

"He's only lucky if they get us," Wulff said. The transition to the *us* he noted was automatic; he no longer regarded Owens as an enemy. Owens was in it with him; there had not been any question of that now for several hundred miles. Maybe that would make him a damned fool when Owens used a sudden, unexpected opening to drop him like meat and take him into Carlin, but that was the kind of chance you had to take. Everything was a chance. Everything was an odds game; if you didn't shoot craps you couldn't stay in. "They're gaining," Wulff said. Turning he took a quick look; the car had closed within a city block or so, barely a tenth of a mile back. "They must have equipment on it."

"No fucking good," Owens said. "There's never any goddamned traffic on these roads," he said with sudden urgency. "Goddamn it to hell, why does it always work out that way? When you need traffic you don't have it."

"Would traffic have stopped you?"

"Probably not," Owens said, "but we were a special case. We were very determined."

"Not determined enough."

"How lucky we got," Owens said seriously and slapped the wheel. "We can't outrun them," he said, looking at Wulff quickly, then back at the road. "You know that, don't you?"

"I thought it was worth a try."

"They're closing," Owens said, "they're closing fast now."

At ninety miles an hour the Pontiac was burning rubber, laying down little tracks behind it as it sprung up on them. There was now a distance that could be measured in car-lengths. The first shot hit, leaving a little blister in the glass, a spreading web that looked like a bloodstain.

"Sons of bitches," Owens said. His hands were flat and tight against the wheel. Otherwise there was no change in his expression and he seemed to be in control of himself. Not for nothing, Wulff thought, looking at the man, had he been a stunt man for an exhibitionist. Either that or he was one hell of a fabricator of tales. But the other looked more likely. "If they get close enough they're going to hit," Owens said flatly. "They're using rifles."

"They won't get close enough."

"I don't see how they can keep in back of us," Owens said. "They're gaining like a son of a bitch," His voice was that of a man striving successfully not to panic, moving instead the other way, toward the absence of effect. It came hard but it would last.

"Leave it to me," Wulff said, "we'll see if we can't back them off a bit."

He took out a .45 he had been holding, not the one he had leveled on Owens at the beginning when it looked as if the man might be difficult to control—a .45 was only a mess at short range, you wanted to use something much lighter and cleaner, like a Beretta automatic—and held it back on the Pontiac. Another splinter had joined the one already there, this one slightly more toward the left, the dimples intersecting. Wulff kept his head below seat level, looking up over it, held the .45 steady. "Keep on driving," he said to Owens, "just concentrate on the road. This could be kind of messy."

"It's messy already," Owens said. His hands were smooth and precise on the wheel. "Short of getting dead I don't see how it can be much worse than it is already."

"You'd be surprised," Wulff said, "you'd be surprised." But he had to admire Owen's control. The man was remarkable, there was no question about it; considering everything, he had held up very well and now the shift of roles, the shift that had put him in control of Owens seemed to alter again however subtly. Owens was in control of him now, driving the car, the situation dependent upon nothing so much as Owen's ability to maneuver the car while Wulff concentrated on the mechanics of bringing down the assailants. It was strange how things worked out. His dependency in a sense was total but in another way it was not at all, since Owens owed him as much. Wulff crouched down over the .45 leveling it into his gut and when something in his mind told him that now was the time to fire, that now the situation had worked itself that way, he listened to that inner voice as he had through all of his struggles going back to Vietnam and he let the big gun go off.

IV

Back in New York Williams was going through another kind of hell. Everything with Wulff from the first had served to only suck him in deeper and deeper, but now he was dealing with a captain from headquarters who seemed to feel that Williams was completely responsible for arranging Wulff's escape from the court building. The captain was five six or so, the sort of man who sneaked through the qualifying physical requirements by no more than half an inch either way, probably by lying. And the bitterness and fright of sneaking into the PD, the feeling all his career that he was somehow hanging in just on a technicality that could be reversed by discovery any moment, had made him ill-tempered and vicious. Williams wanted to stand up and go out of the room, tell the captain to fuck himself but he could not do this. His own career was perilous. He had taken a knife in the gut for Wulff, had dropped his civil service and gone out to Los Angeles to be Wulff's partner, had come back under the worst circumstances, and he knew that medical disability or not they could let him go at any moment. At their pleasure. While two months ago this was exactly what he had wanted, now it was anything but. He could not afford to lose the job, not now. That was simply the way it had to be; he had made his adjustments toward the side of getting locked in. Also, he had lost track of Wulff. He knew what had happened at that plant in Detroit because he had read it in the papers, but that was not enough. No word had come in. The man might have been caught in the explosion himself. Williams doubted it, but you never knew.

"I want the truth," the captain said. "I want you to tell me the truth. It will go much easier if I don't have to struggle for it."

"You don't understand," Williams said, "I told you I don't know anything."

"You engineered his escape," the captain said, "that's one thing right there. You maneuvered the whole thing."

"I maneuvered nothing," Williams said. There was the possibility that the captain was crazy. That was one thing you had to look out for in the PD all the time; the people you were dealing with might be merely stupid or corrupt, but then again they might spring into galloping insanity, which would furnish the full and final explanation of all their acts. "There was a gunman in the room. He shot Smith. He smuggled a gun into the court and he shot the defendant. There was a little confusion, as one might suspect. In the confusion Wulff escaped. I didn't have anything to do with it. Or are you suggesting that I set things up with the assailant?"

"Someone did," the captain said, rubbing his hands together. "Someone set things up."

"I didn't want Wulff out," Williams said. "Who would want him out anymore? I'm his friend. He was going to get killed sooner or later. His luck was running out." He might have gotten killed in Detroit, Williams thought. He might have been killed there, in the firebombing of the plant, and no one would know. No one had really expected him to be there, that was the problem. "I'm sorry," he said and wondered if he should risk standing, offending the captain but ending the interview. He could not stand it any more. He really could not. He was entitled to better than this. If everything that he had gone through had worked itself toward merely an outcome of this sort then he would have been better off not starting at all. That was too depressing to think about. It canceled all experience. You were better off not doing that. Not canceling your experience. You were better off accepting it for whatever it was, trying to see the benefits in it, and moving on from there. Or did that, trying to make all experience chargeable against an abstract and future knowledge, did that make him as crazy as the captain? The hell with it, he thought.

"This man is dangerous," the captain said. "This man is quite dangerous."

"To drug dealers he is."

"To all of us. He threatens the very process of law enforcement. Society is built upon structures, upon codes, upon a certain common acceptance of behavior. A man who threatens that in the name of justice risks bringing down all of society."

"Society is shit," Williams said. He put his calves back tightly against the legs of the chair, stood, flexed, and pushed back. He looked down at the captain as if from a great distance. "If this is what we ought to preserve, if this is what Wulff is attacking, then he's doing us all a great favor. I'm sorry, captain. I can't face this any more. I just can't deal with it. You'll have to excuse me. It makes me sick and I can't take it any more." He was up, moving to the door of the little office where the captain spent over 50 percent of his working life, would do it until he reached pension in a kind of hatred, which when the pension came in, would remit to nostalgia. The captain, like almost every retired civil servant, would spend the rest of his life vaguely missing what he had despised. That was the trick they played on you, if "trick" was the word for it. Williams had a better word but he didn't think that saying it would make any difference. "If there's something you think is wrong, captain," he said, "you can put in a formal complaint."

"You're a fool," the captain said. His face had clamped more tightly. "You're a stupid fool. You think that you're getting anything out of helping this man, out of covering for him? He laughs at you. He'd kill you if he had to. If he needed to, if it would stand to his advantage, he'd destroy you. He doesn't give a damn about everyone. I know what you think of him," the captain said. "I know what a lot of stupid, misguided people think about Wulff, that he's some kind of romantic, a true vigilante, the Lone Ranger of the drug market. He's a filthy murderer, probably crazy, that's what he is and he's the enemy of order."

Williams said, "Captain, I'm sick of people calling me a fool. I've been called a fool up and down by too many people for a long time, and I don't think it's in the career and salary plan that I have to take it. You haven't thought this through at all, you understand nothing, in fact, you're full of shit," Williams said quietly and went out, closed the door, went down the hall. He was shaking. From deep within, the trembling was working through, moving on many levels. He felt that he might collapse from the extent of his feeling, but then again, everything could be contained; there was nothing you couldn't live with if you kept it bottled up. All the signs were clear. He was too close to Wulff and they were going to get him now, any way they could.

On the other hand, they did have a point. They were not entirely without justification. He *had* helped Wulff escape.

It was too much, it was too complicated, the interweaving of culpability and innocence was too much for him. He was better out of it, Williams thought, going back to the dismal office where they had him on desk work, had had him since he had come back from the injury while they decided what if anything to do with him. He was better off staying away from all of them: Wulff, the PD, his wife, his own inner voices. Shut it off, shut off everything and just live your life from day to day. It was the only way to do it. But if he knew anything, he knew they wouldn't let him do that. There was no way out, no way out of it at all. You could not get off this planet alive. You could not even stay on it alive. All your life in a trap, and nibbling at the edges of it that giant animal, death.

One of the two men in the intercepting Bonneville in New Mexico was an experienced assassin. The other was not. One was cool under pressure as the result of having freelanced for almost ten years. The other, just getting into it in his late twenties, almost disintegrated under stress. One of them, in short, knew his job and the other was merely faking it. And they were both working for Carlin because Carlin was faking it too, getting what he could in a tough business at the front end and hoping for the best thereafter. But between experience and inexperience it all began to come apart in the pressure of the chase. The older man, riding shotgun, had put the shots into the rear panes of the Fleetwood that they had miraculously picked up near the state line, thinking he would panic them into scrambling for it so that he could get a nice shot at their rear tires in full flight. But it hadn't worked out quite that way. The answering fire had come immediately and, worse than that, had hit the windshield of the Bonneville on the driver's side, splintering it so that the younger man, the driver, could not see. The Bonneville swerved in a sickening way. "You stupid son of a bitch," the younger man said, "look what you've done now."

"Shut up," the older man said. "Just keep on driving and we'll run them right off the road."

"Keep on driving! I can't see!" the younger man said, fighting the wheel, the car beginning to slide. Another shot came out of the Fleetwood, splintering the glass on the passenger side, and the older man, forty-two years old, in and out of this business in good health and bad since he had come out of Korea, began to feel something he had not known since An San Loc, a little white edge of panic moving in his chest. The younger man was right; he had fucked this up, they should not have made the approach directly but should have swung around and tried it in a less direct manner. But the luck of stumbling across them, the promised fifty thousand dollars on delivery of the body, the rumors that Carlin might in combination with some others go as high as a hundred thousand if he felt particularly generous . . . all of that had unseated his judgment. He hadn't even calculated the second man he had seen in the car with Wulff so eager was he to get this damned job done and haul in the goods. Now they were in real trouble. He had really fucked this one up. How could he have been so stupid? he thought vaguely, as if he were thinking of another person. It was not in his track record to fail like this. If anything, what had distinguished his work was its caution and finesse. Its utter control. That was how he kept on getting hired, that was how he had built his reputation. This was really stupid, taking potshots at the Fleetwood. But who would have expected that they would have had the luck to run up against Wulff? When he had taken the assignment he looked on it as expense money, that was all. It was a crap game, but this Carlin would have had to be out of his mind to think that any of the teams actually had a chance of getting this guy. If he hadn't gotten taken by now he wasn't going to. Maybe he didn't exist. And yet there he was. Description, everything dovetailed against the photographs. And the answering fire, that was the key. There was just the slightest chance that they had opened fire on someone who was innocent—and that was one of the risks that had to be taken in this business. It was war, innocent people got trapped in war, that was all— but the skillful way in which the fire had been returned, the way in which the Fleetwood was being maneuvered, and what it had done to their windshield—

"I'm losing control," the younger man said, his voice peculiarly calm despite all indications in his history that he would have been the one to have broken. "I can't see a fucking thing and now I think he's got the tires."

"The tires?"

"The fucking tires," the driver said, and there was another impact, the car began to slide slowly, almost gracefully toward the side of the road. The older man knew from experience that they were going out of control; he knew what the feeling of a car was when it was no longer taking the road but succumbing to it. Something hit the windshield again and the driver shrieked. Then the Fleetwood in a trick of vision was coming upon them, moving in reverse at fifty miles an hour. What had really happened was that the car had braked down suddenly, but the illusion was complete, the feeling that the fins of the vehicle were coming upon them made the older man gasp and dive under the dashboard. Meanwhile, the driver, screaming and cursing all the way, was fighting with the Bonneville to brake it down. He wrenched the wheel and the car went into a desperate spin, lost road adhesion, turned around and landed off the road, turning completely around and landing in an improvised ditch. At the end of the last spin there was a dull sound and then a little explosion, like a grapefruit hitting a wall, and then it was very, very quiet.

The older gunman looked up and looked at the driver. Sprouting blood, he now lay back against the seat, little shards of glass coming out of his forehead like the silver sprinkles on Christmas ornaments, his head the bulb of an ornament running rich red. The older man shuddered from his crouched position but did not move. There was nothing to be done for the driver. He was dead. What was important, the only thing to do to try and save the situation was to stay under cover. Where was the Fleetwood? Where was Wulff? Maybe the Fleetwood had gone off the road, too, but that was not likely. That was not damned likely at all.

It was quiet here in the desert, quiet and hot. With the car wrecked and the air-conditioning gone, the assassin could already feel the heat beginning to work its way through to him. The windows had been up tight to facilitate the air-conditioner, of course. Now the temperature in the car must have been over ninety. In just a matter of minutes it would be a hundred and twenty, even beyond that . . . they would have to do nothing in the Fleetwood except to lay siege to him; he would not be able to live in this car for more than an hour. Amazing. It was amazing how quickly the situation could shift in one of these deals, the assassin thought; one moment you were on the prowl and the next you were at bay. Well, that was life, maybe, the constant switching of roles, the reversals that at any time could tumble you top to bottom. But this was not something you could ever learn to handle in a philosophical way, not even if you were forty-two and had been dealing with death all your life.

He looked cautiously over the ridge of the dashboard, blinked in the dazzling light, saw that the Fleetwood had pulled over at a considerable distance up the road, maybe as much as a quarter of a mile, and was just lying there, no movement at all of the doors. It was impossible to detect movement in the car at this distance, of course, but it did appear to be unnaturally quiet, no hint of shifting light within from which he might have been able to deduce movement. They might be playing possum, of course, but then again they might have been hurt, either in going off the road or by one of his shots. It was possible that he had pierced the rear window and gotten a lucky hit on one or the other, although this was not at all likely. Still, you had to have hope, and this was as likely an explanation as any other. He could not stay in the car. That much was clear; it would be impossible for him to stay in the Pontiac much longer because the heat was already beginning to dehydrate him, he could feel it wringing at him like an animal, and soon enough he would begin to feel the more severe effects, the lightheadedness, the feeling of weakness in the bowels. An hour or two was much too optimistic, the assassin thought, he might last fifteen minutes in this car, not much more. Carefully he cranked down the passenger window half an inch. A little breeze tugged at him, vaulted past his eyes, stabbed under the cheekbones where the deep and intricate nerves under the eyes lived. No help. No help at all, the assassin thought. He would have to get out of the car.

Seized with an idea, though, he pushed the body of the driver away, tried the key in the ignition. The battery fed a little power, enough to turn the amp light red, but the starting motor, after one click, seized. No good, then. The car would not move. He had to get out.

The body of the driver was already beginning to stink, a faint rancid whiff of death coming up from the corpse as the assassin had leaned over. He reeled back, reached for the door handle, lifted it, and wriggled out of the car, tumbling then to the ground. The heat surrounded him like a fist, squeezed him, little bolts of energy and sickness moved across his body. He crouched on his hands and knees, using the car as cover, crawling very cautiously so that he was not exposed in the direction of the Cadillac.

It was a mess, that was for sure. All avenues of exit seemed blocked, his mobility was gone, his command of the situation wrecked by the accident. Still, he thought, he had a few options; he still had his gun and his will and his brain, and that was something. That was not for nothing; you could not take that away from a man until the very end, the integrity of his own purpose, the fixity that had taken him through twenty years and a hundred kills in a life that was for the most a six-month business. He began to think like an assassin again. The fifty grand was still there for the taking. The quarry was still there, too. His partner was gone but that meant that he had to make no excuses and that he had to make no split. His. It was all his.

Using the Bonneville as cover he started his stalk.

VI

"I don't think he's dead in there," Owens said. "I think that at least one of them is alive."

"Probably," Wulff said. He kept the Bonneville pinned, but even with 20/20 vision and lots of terrain-searching experience in Vietnam, it was not easy to detect movement in a car a quarter of a mile down in blinding, dazzling sun. Cloudy weather might have been better, but it was never cloudy on the desert; it was either a baking heat or rain. Nothing between. "One thing is sure," Wulff said, "if he gets out we'll see a door move. And he's got to get out."

"I think so, too," Owens said. For all they had been through he was quite calm, a good man, Wulff decided; it was a pity that he hired out rather than being inner-directed. An inner-directed man like Owens with the right cause could have blown whole cities, not just ships, out of geography. "He can't stay in there," Owens said. He raced the engine of the Cadillac for emphasis; the compressor whined and little puffs of cold air came out of the air-conditioner vents as if for emphasis. Owens took his foot off the accelerator and said, "Of course, his problem is our problem. We can't sit here forever; we'll run out of gas."

"I don't think we'll sit very long," Wulff said. "I figure we'll close in and take him out."

"That's how I think, too," Owens said, "But I'd feel a hell of a lot better if I knew exactly what his condition was."

"We'll find out," Wulff said. "We'll find out soon enough. If there isn't any movement out of that car in the next fifteen minutes, we'll just close in, and if he does move we'll come in anyway. Either way—"

"Either way I don't see much of a problem."

"There are always problems," Wulff said. "I wouldn't know what to do without a problem. I haven't had a single goddamned thing yet in ten cities that wasn't a challenge, and I don't think that this is going to be easy, either. Everything's a struggle. Nothing comes without work."

"Yeah," Owens said, "but this doesn't look as bad as some of the others, does it?"

"Everything looks bad. You can die clumsy or brave, you can die fighting against a thousand or because some sixteen-year-old kid playing sniper nails you. But either way you're just as dead. The quality of the death is exactly the same."

"Not necessarily," Owens said gently, "not necessarily. But then again I'm no priest, minister, or rabbi. I couldn't get into any argument over that. And I don't think this is the time to do it, either."

"No," Wulff said. "I guess we'll table that one."

They sat in almost companionable silence for a while then, saying nothing, waiting the situation out, Owens racing the engine every now and then, listening to the valves tap, and waiting for the Bonneville to disgorge some evidence of life or death. It was an easy vigil in a way because it had a good sense of pace and direction. It was not a matter of waiting out some nameless menace in an ambiguous position. They knew exactly who they were and what they were waiting for, and there was a definite end to it. There was a man out there; eventually he would make his presence known and they would kill him. Either that or he would give no indication of his presence and that would be good enough for them, too; they could deal with the dead or injured man by closing in on him. But the situation was essentially in their hands, or so Wulff calculated; that was a pleasure, of course—it was so rare that he had controlled the tempo of a scene—but then again you had to protect yourself against the possibility of being lulled, protect yourself against taking your safety for granted. He leaned back against the seat, letting the edges of steel come against him, and it prodded him into wakefulness.

"You got to understand the way a guy thinks; the kind of guy who really wants to die," Owens said.

"Who's that?"

"This guy I worked for. He really wanted to die. Going on living was what frightened him; dealing with death gave him something to do. But after a while when he kept on beating death he got to thinking that he was cheating, that he wasn't taking death seriously enough or it would have gotten him. There's no point in fooling around with death if you're going to cheat it time and again. So he started to get more serious."

"Yeah," Wulff said, "I know the feeling. You begin to feel immortal if you take chance after chance and it doesn't catch up with you."

"No," Owens said, "it's not quite that way. I mean I know what you're saying. If you get into a lot of tough situations and start to glide out of them you wonder if you're just dreaming. But that doesn't have to do with a guy who really wants to die. That's a different situation altogether, when you're talking about a man who really wants to end his life. He can push farther and farther, but if nothing happens, if he keeps getting away with it, he's going to get the feeling that he's not taking things seriously enough, so he gets damned serious."

"I never wanted to die," Wulff said and thought that over for a while. It seemed to be an important insight and one that he was on the edge of getting absolutely, but then it slid away. "No, I don't quite mean that," he said. "It was that I calculated that I was dead already. I got killed on West 93rd Street. So that I was a dead man already. They can't kill a dead man. They can only stop him. You know what I mean?"

"Oh," Owens said, "I guess I know what you mean. But that's self-protection, saying that you're dead. You really didn't believe that, you knew you were alive, but saying you were dead, feeling that way was able to keep you operating. But that's different from really wanting to die. If you had wanted to die you would have taken care of that."

"Maybe," Wulff said, "maybe. It's hard to say. It's hard to calculate anything like that." He moved on the seat again feeling the exposed steel loops bite into his shoulder blades. "Enough," he said.

"No," Owens said, "it's never enough. You think that something's the end, you think that you've had enough and that it won't be the same and that you're moving toward the end, but every time you get that feeling it starts all over again. There's no enough. It just goes on and on. Until you die, of course."

"I don't understand," Wulff said.

"Me neither," said Owens. "I don't understand a fucking thing." Then he looked up at the rear-view mirror and something caught his glance. He said, "He moved."

"What?"

"He's out of the car and moving," Owens said. "I caught a glimpse of him. He's on the ground now. He came out of the car and took cover. He's crawling around down there now."

"Slowly," Wulff said, "he must have moved damned slowly."

"He hit the ground fast enough."

"I mean out of the car."

"He probably opened that door inch by inch," Owens said. "He probably spent fifteen minutes getting out of it, yeah. But he's out now." He leaned forward, clutched the shift lever, then dropped it into reverse. "I'm going to back up on him."

"You think so?"

"I think that's the best way."

"What if he's got heavy artillery?"

"Then he can reach us up to fifty yards anyway. Closing in won't be any more dangerous than staying here. But I don't think he's got any heavy. Generally people don't carry that around and you can be sure that Carlin, that cheap bastard, wasn't supplying anything."

"All right," Wulff said. Momentarily slack, he had returned to full alertness, the old combat feeling coursing through him. He had not handed over the decision to Owens so much as having abandoned it, but now he let the feeling of control come upon him again. "Back up very slowly," he said, "and if you see any movement, stop."

"All right," Owens said, one arm draped over the seat back, driving with the rear-view mirror, which was the way that the experienced ones did it. "Don't worry about it."

"I'm not worried about anything."

"We'll get him," Owens said. "This is just a diversion."

"I'm sure it is," Wulff said. Something hit the rear window again, another part of the glass splintered, and Wulff heard the whine of the rifle. "Son of a bitch," he said, scrambling below seat level, "he won't give up."

Owens had stopped the car, cranked it into neutral already, and then had hit the floor, squeezing himself in the place between steering wheel and seat, barely fitting in. Another round hit them, the glass splintering more densely now, little fragments momentarily visible in the air as a halo, then falling into the rear seat. Wulff, his pistol gripped in his hand, could not see the assassin yet, the assassin using the Pontiac as cover. The situation was not good. They had no cover but the assassin did. The glass splintered yet again and now Wulff could see open space, holes had been lifted out of the glass, the desert was coming in. "Bastard," he said, but he continued to concentrate. "He won't stop, will he?"

"You never stop," Owens said. "If you stop you start to think," and the fire went yet again, the bullet passed through the rear and impacted into the windshield, driving itself out on a course no more than a foot above Wulff's head. "Back it," Wulff said, "back it again."

"I'm going to go right into him," Owens said. "I don't mind, if you don't, you understand that? If you want to bear down on top of him it's perfectly okay with me, but you've got to understand that we're just giving him a larger and larger area—"

"I don't give a damn," Wulff said. It was almost as if the role-reversal was now complete; he had to explain his conduct to Owens, he had to justify himself to the man who only a few days before had been his captive, a man who had been hired to kill him. "Shut the fuck up," Wulff said and waved the pistol at Owens. Owens gave him a single look of astonishment and then his eyes blinked shut in something like an ecstasy of concentration moving inward, seeing animals stalk behind the panes of his eyes, then he floored the accelerator and the Fleetwood was bearing down at ten to fifteen miles an hour in reverse, the fastest it could go in the low gear. Wulff perilously balanced himself on the seat, aiming for a good shot. He still could not see the man.

But even if he could not see him he could see the source of the fire. Another shot came through, this one a little high, smashing into the ceiling, scattering dust over him as he ducked. Owens grunted something, but his concentration did not lapse. He kept his foot on the floor and they had now closed to within a hundred yards of the Bonneville. "Son of a bitch," Owens said, "son of a bitch, where is it coming from? Where is the bastard?"

"I don't know," Wulff said. "I don't know where he is. That's what we're trying to find out." He saw a scurry of movement, just a little twitch of shadows near the left front bumper of the Bonneville. It might have been the man moving, but then again it might only have been some reaction to his passage; the sun, off-angle, was casting shadows in a peculiar way counter to movement, and Wulff desperately tried to bring back the training he had had in combat sighting. They were still closing, and Wulff realized that the situation was cutting both ways. They were coming closer all the time, and at a certain point the assassin would no longer be able to find cover; but in exactly the same way they were losing their own cover, that distance which granted them some measure of safety.

Owens must have had the same thought. He was moving the car clamped down into the seat now, his forehead buried against his crossed arms, his eyes closed, his frame hunched over in anticipation of the killing shot. Yet to his credit—Wulff had to give the man credit, he was no fool, everything that he had said to Wulff about his training was the truth—he had not given any ground whatsoever. The only way they were going to get Owens out of that seat was to shoot him out, preferably with a howitzer and at close range, the man was not going to give. But the assassin was not going to give either. Another shot came through and Wulff twitched in reaction, taking cover deeply. Then, as if unconnected, he heard Owens' dull scream, and then the car was thrashing, bucking out of control.

His processes had been so slowed by the shock of this, he had been so funneled into concentration upon the assassin, that for an instant Wulff reacted stupidly, trying to make some connection between the shot, the scream, and the wild slewing of the car. Then, as Owens collapsed from the wheel, pinning him with his weight, the feeling of blood coursing down Wulff's body, Wulff understood what had happened and fell all the way to the panels of the floor, guiding himself to fall away from Owens, trying to find some stability. He could not move to stop the car, could not yank Owens's dead foot away from the accelerator because he was pinned in by the weight and could not lose the time to try and strain. Owens' bubbling death-sounds were moving high in his throat, sounding like a flute now.

"I'm sorry," Wulff said, not that it made any difference now—it was another man dead, that was all, forget it, concentrate on the task at hand, stay to it, don't get distracted, put it away. "I'm sorry, I'm sorry," and the next shot came in, the assassin placing his fire carefully, gaining in confidence now as well he might, and this bullet passed so closely over Wulff that if he had not fallen, had not gotten below the line of the seat, he would have been gone. No time to think of that, though, no time for calculation of any sort, what he had to do was to somehow protect himself.

The assassin was obviously running out of fire. If he had not been he would not have settled for one shot or two; he would have followed up the dead hit on Owens with only one shot but would have made that one right, then would have pumped in the remainder and finished off Wulff for sure. But he had not done that and that could only mean one thing—he had only one weapon, he had run out, he was reloading. All of this swept through Wulff in a matter of thickened seconds while the Fleetwood was still barreling in reverse at its maddened ten to fifteen miles an hour, Owens's dead foot linked to the accelerator, Owens already quiet above him. And Wulff did the only thing he could have in that instant to avoid either death by impact or by fire, nothing to lose really, double dose of death carried in the situation. He reared up from the alcove, pushing away Owens's body with an effort of strength, came up on his knees and, centering his weapon, put one shot downrange toward what he saw as an explosion of light, then braced himself against the seat as he saw that they were going to pile into the Bonneville. There was nothing to be done. There was no way around it; no way to deny the crash. In a perfect panorama of stopped time, Wulff saw it all and what would happen then, and there was nothing to do but to hang onto the seat, close his eyes as had the dead man, and hope that when the Fleetwood crunched into the Pontiac dead-on, the assassin, if he were not dead already, would be caught in the impact.

VII

Carlin had decided that he had to make a break for it. Call it crazy, what the hell. He had to get out of Phoenix until Wulff was gotten, had to lay low until he was sure that the madman was no longer on his trail. Maybe it was crazy, maybe it was cowardice, maybe what it really was was showing a lot of sense. He had entirely too much at stake now. Everything was breaking for him, if only he could save his ass. He might have the whole country in his palm, but what the hell good would that do him if Wulff got to him first? It wasn't worth thinking about any longer. Carlin wasn't going to consider it. He would go south of the border, lay out for a while. In Mexico City he knew at least three men at the highest levels, each with impregnable villas, each with a hundred gunmen. He could take his choice of any of them, hide out in perpetuity. When the time came to get out of there he could pay off any one of the men or all three in ways that would make it worth their while. No. When you considered the situation overall, when you considered all the stakes and the possibilities, he would be a fool to stay, not to go. Going made sense.

He had twenty men in teams on the trail, but what the hell were twenty? What were thousands as against this Wulff? He had taken out singlehandedly at least that many in that freighter in San Francisco; then there had been that business in Boston where they were still counting the bodies. And Las Vegas—he had blown up an entire operation in Vegas. No, twenty men, no matter how skilled, no matter who they were, could not be considered ample protection. It made sense. It made sense to get the hell out. Besides, and at the heart of it, Carlin was terrified. He was man enough to make that admission. Wulff scared the shit out of him. Anyone who wasn't scared by that man had no business being in the world. Wulff wasn't even a man, he was a beast. An animal could do anything. How could you buy off a murderous jungle beast on the full prowl?

Fuck it, Carlin thought. Fuck it, it isn't worth it. He decided to travel light, that was the best way to do it. Anything he needed he could pick up en route or on the other end. He wouldn't even call ahead because the lines might be tapped, you never knew. Not by the government— the government had had taps in for years—he couldn't give less of a shit about the government. No, it might be Wulff. Wulff somehow might have gotten lines in. Anyway, it made sense not to take any chances on it. Say nothing, travel light, get into Mexico City and then laugh about what a fool he had been. That would be the proper way to manage it. Perhaps he wasn't thinking too sanely, but then again what was sane about the Wolf Man? The only way to deal with a lunatic was to be as fast and cunning as the lunatic himself. Right? Carlin knew he was right. His judgments had carried him to a hundred acres on the irrigated desert and he wasn't going to start losing faith in himself now.

The only thing to do was to break the word to his mistress. He didn't want to take her along. On the other hand, it was too risky to leave her behind, what with her knowledge of certain things and also—he had to admit it—that he wanted her along for the sex. He had been fucking her almost exclusively for a couple of years, had lost interest in most other stuff, and he could have had anything he wanted. He wasn't sure he could perform with anyone else; in any event it was not a discovery that he wanted to make. There were certain things better off unknown; certainly by your forties you could stand as little new knowledge as possible. You had devised your life as a matter of fact for the purposes of keeping the knowledge out. Otherwise how could you live? Well, you could not live at all, that was the point. You simply could not live unless you set up certain barriers between yourself and your experience. To experience something twice was to come close to death. Carlin knew it. He knew everything that he had to know and wanted to know nothing else.

"We're going to get out of here," he said to her. He had barged in on her in the bedroom, found her lying idly amidst the pillows, picking at her hair and looking at the ceiling. She was naked under the sheets, the sheets pulled half across her breasts, the breasts falling enormously to the side. Even under all the circumstances he felt a hard-on coming. Ridiculous. It was ridiculous to feel desire for her; yet he did, and maybe it was better that way then to feel nothing. "Right now," he said. "We're going to take a trip."

"Where?" she said without looking up, "take a trip where? What shit are you talking about?" She did not have a pleasant personality. In fact, aside from her skills at fucking, she was a nasty bitch. Surely she was not the kind of person who would have appealed to Carlin on any basis other than sexual. Not at all intellectual, with no appreciation of the basic and yet more refined areas of life. "I don't know what you're talking about."

"It doesn't matter. I want you to get ready. We're going really light; anything you need you can pick up on the way."

"Where are we going?"

"Mexico City," Carlin said.

"I don't like Mexico City," she said, still not looking up. "I don't want to go anywhere. I've seen enough places; I think I'd like to stay put for a while."

"Janice—"

"Don't Janice me," she said, "don't look at me that way, Joe. You got business, you want to take a trip, take it. It wouldn't be the first time. Why do you need me? You never asked me anywhere before."

"I was never gone awhile either. I'm going to be gone awhile this time."

"No," she said and shook her head, "no, I don't think I want to go anywhere; I don't really want to go anywhere at all. I think I'll stay right here, as a matter of fact."

It was difficult to keep a lid on his temper when everything was closing in and the situation was as out of control as it threatened to be, but Carlin made the effort. Discipline. Everything came down to a matter of self-discipline and control. If you could not yourself be manipulated, then you would be able to manipulate other people. "Please, Janice," he said reasonably. "We have to go. It's for your own good and you'll appreciate it."

She shook her head. "I don't think *you* understand, Joe," she said. "I owe you nothing, you owe me nothing, that was the arrangement from the first, right? I'm not a traveling companion. If you have to go somewhere, that never stopped you in the past from just doing it and letting me know you'd be back. I never asked you to stay." She adjusted the sheet around her chin. "I'll leave," she said, "I was just going to get up in a little while and go."

"You're a fool," he said. He knew he was starting to go out of control now, but Carlin didn't care; there was a kind of luxury in going out of control. "You don't really know what's going on at all. You understand nothing." He was sweating. He could feel the sheet of it against his face, flapping as if a hand was pressing down on his features, moving that film of water like a wave breaking over his head, diving into the water, submerged by it, sinking, drowning. He came toward the bed, took her by the wrist and pulled her up. Her breasts bounced as she reared out of the bed, then hung limply, near her navel. She was not, out of bed, a very attractive woman. Aesthetically speaking she was nothing at all. Her flesh was made for lying-down sex; dressed or merely standing she was completely out of proportion. Still, what the hell. He had never said that he was in it for aesthetic reasons.

"You're hurting me," she said. She twisted her wrist around in his grasp and he went with her. Cunning, she pulled the other way and he was left floundering, without support, while she came up with her other hand, hit him a hard blow on his jaw, striking him near the nerve, stunning him, and Carlin sat down rapidly on the bed gasping, wondering, pulling at the tight flesh of his jaw and not sure exactly what had happened to him, but knowing the pain.

She moved away from him and he could swear that she was smiling, although he would have wanted her eyes to show some despair that they had come to this. "Why?" he said, "why?"

"Leave me alone, Joe."

"You had no right to do that," he said. "What reason was there to hurt me?" and he realized that he was sniveling. He, Joe Carlin was whining and crying on the bed as if he were a child, and a charge of revulsion so clear and vicious that it might have been illness swept through him; there was no reason for him to take this, Carlin thought. He was entitled to better than this; he could not possibly take shit of this sort, because if the word got around, well then, he was done . . . and the gun was in his hand, he was pointing it at her stomach, and then as he saw the rage and panic twisting across her face he realized for the first time what he had done. My, he thought slowly, that was peculiar, I wonder why she's backing away from me like that, and then he looked down at the gun and the situation slowly pulled itself into shape for him like a child clumsily tying a scout knot. "Don't," she said to him, "don't do it Joe. This is me."

"It's not right," Carlin said. He was not sure what he was talking about but the idea at least was clear to him. He had no doubt whatsoever of the idea. "It just isn't right, it isn't fair, you can't do this kind of thing to me."

"Joe," she said, and now she was backed against one of the walls, her stomach shrinking and shriveling, her nipples alert with panic, standing up as if he had been playing with them. "Joe, I don't know what you think you're doing but you can't. You can't do this, Joe. You can't do it to me."

"All I wanted," he said thickly and slowly, "all I wanted was for you to come with me. Was that so much to ask?"

"All right."

"Don't tell me all right," he said, the gun steady, the rest of him shaking, but the gun held rigid in his hand just like a cock, "don't tell me all right, you bitch, you just can't get away with it, you can't make it disappear! Things don't disappear just because you say that they weren't meant. I can't take it any more," he said. Surprising how steady the gun was. It occurred to him with clinical detachment that it was very possible that he could shoot her. He did not know which way it would go yet, you had to watch this kind of thing, but that was definitely a possibility.

"Joe," she said, lifting her arms, but very cautiously, holding them, palms turned outward against the wall, "Joe, I don't think you know what you're doing."

"Yes I do."

"I'll go with you. I'll go with you if that makes any difference. Put that gun down."

"You should have said that before. You'll say anything now with the gun turned on you."

"I'm trying to help you. I'm trying—"

"I didn't want much," Carlin said as if talking to someone else, not Janice now but some distant auditor who he could imagine as a wise, benevolent old man shaped from gases, drifting in and out of the spaces of the bedroom, turning a curious and attentive ear to his utterances, nodding wisely and sympathetically every now and then to indicate that basically, despite his silence, he was on Carlin's side. "I just wanted to be left alone. I worked hard, I had a nice thing to look forward to, a good thing going, I didn't want much. Mostly I just wanted them to leave me alone. I wanted all of the sons of bitches to let me alone, but do you understand something, they wouldn't." He wiped some sweat out of his eyes with the gun hand. Janice twitched against the wall, and then as he leveled the gun back to position, she returned to her solemn, frozen position. "They just wouldn't let me alone and now after all of it I've got to do something, you see. I've just got to do something. It's Wulff, you see, that son of a bitch, I could have held the whole thing in my palm, the two of us could have worked it out together, we could have had a deal, Wulff and me," Carlin said, and the circumspect form nodded, waved an index finger in quizzical agreement showing that he wanted more information. "Well of course," Carlin said, "I mean that stood to reason, he was working for me just as I was working for him, and so the two of us could have worked together. You dig what I mean? He was knocking off the bastards right and left, he was clearing the ground making things easier, and I could have made things easier for him, too, because once I was on top no one could have touched him. No one at all, not with me running the interference. And I could have done anything he wanted, within reason of course, even given him a piece of it, but he just didn't understand." The auditor made a *come again?* expression. "He wouldn't understand anything like that," Carlin said. "I think that the trouble with the son of a bitch is that he's truly crazy. He doesn't want to get along, he just wants to blow things up. But that doesn't make me crazy, does it? Not when I'm trying to get along as best I can. I mean, somebody has to run the operation, no? Supply and demand, that's very important, that's a brutal law of economics, that if there's a demand then somewhere there's got to be a supply. So why not me?" Carlin said, "why the hell not me? I'm just giving people what they want, and there are a hell of a lot who would have done it worse than me."

All right, the auditor nodded, satisfied, and began to dissolve into the background of the room, apparently having found Carlin's argument unanswerable. *I see what you're saying,* and Carlin alone again, some naked woman crouched up against the wall in a fetal position now, flanks touching, looking at him with bright, demanding eyes.

She was just another one of the sons of bitches out to get him, that was all. Here was yet another who was part of the enemy; the enemy was cunning and came in many guises, but underneath the amateurish mask that you could cut away like ribbons to show the living heart beneath the face was clear, the features cool and appraising. It would always be the enemy and had never been anything but, and Carlin saw it then, saw it in one burst that might have been flame but then again might only have been the defeating maneuver of the enemy as trapped it begged for escape by throwing up clouds of incense. Then he had leveled the gun in and it was exploding in his hand like a big prick, all depth, all recoil, plunging and plunging into the rotten center, and the enemy fell away, ribbons now flowing stripes, celebration in halo around the enemy's head as she fell, the auditor drifting into the sudden gloom to give an approving wink and a circle with a hand to indicate that the job had been done.

Well, of course the job had been done. Carlin had never ducked to a challenge yet, that was why he had gotten as far in the world as he had. You didn't get anywhere by fleeing, you had to take your ground and defend it, stand upon it until the very end and make that ground yours.

Giggling, he hurled the gun from him. It bounced once off the form in the room and then fell away.

Then he left the room to begin his solitary but important flight.

No one asked him anything at all. There was no reason why they should. He was utterly in command and Janice, like the rest of them, would do exactly as she was ordered and never anything else but. That was what the rest of them thought, anyway.

VIII

It wasn't a bad impact at all. Ten miles per hour head-on is enough to kill a child or unsettle a housewife. Ten miles per hour head-on is enough to shake the average suburban driver who has no sense of true speeds all the way down to his soul. But for an experienced driver who is used to driving on the edge of possibility, who knows exactly what impact is like and how to protect himself against it, ten miles per hour is manageable. Certainly it is a survivable impact, if you are fully prepared to take it. If you understand all the way to the ground exactly what it means, you can go even farther than that. You can come out of it untouched, at maximum alertness increased by the impact and ready to fight.

Wulff came clear of the Cadillac even as it was still plowing through the Bonneville, fenders crumpling, the scream of the engine trying to whip the big Fleetwood through space that no longer truly existed. Rolling from the door, the gun drawn against him, he survived that one terrible instant in any crash where the possibility exists that the gas tank might go up. Rolling clear desperately, he concentrated upon nothing so much as simply putting enough space between himself and the ruined car to give him a chance on explosion. Then, in the long aching instant when he cleared, he knew that he was home free, at least in terms of the explosion. Coming out of his tumble he allowed only a blur of the landscape to whip by him, then he leveled the gun and fired, placing the assassin by instinct rather than by sight.

Combat training. That was all it was; you got a good glimpse of the terrain, internalized the terrain so that it became part of your psychic landscape—that was the way the training sergeant had talked, anyway. Wulff had had a wild man for an infantry instructor, but the son of a bitch even with his rather Eastern orientation and rather private way of describing genitals and certain acts was a hell of a good teacher. You could move around in that landscape the way you could move around in your own head. As a matter of fact, all of the world became merely an extension of your psyche, that was the key, so that you had to control only yourself and if you did that then the landscape would take care of itself. Rolling and firing, Wulff had placed the assassin somewhere downrange and to the left of him, the only place he could have been at the moment of impact to stand clear of the gas tank. As he came up, rolling, the fire was returned. A bullet went somewhere to his left, then the next shot came in high and somehow he got under it, the bullet over him before he had really understood his gesture. That was what they said about fire, it was the same as lightning, if you heard the bullet and knew what had happened to you then they must have missed. That was the only way to look at it. He fired again, taking his third shot out of the .45 and there was a scream some yards down and to his right. Contact. He did not even check it, only pushed another shot down there and the scream arced higher, turned into a bubbling sound of rage. Wulff put one last shot down there and there was silence.

Only then did he open his eyes fully, let the landscape come into him again. He had performed all of this in a high concentration so absolute and so sealed off from the desert that it might have happened in that private place that the instructor sergeant had always urged them to use and rely upon in the same way that they would use their weapons. The two vehicles had intersected, the Bonneville and the Fleetwood meshed at an odd angle like lovers who had started an entrance but had failed of completion in a hurried ejaculation, a tumble of limbs, emptiness and open space flooding their juxtaposition then. Owens body lay crumped high in the seat. He had taken an impact that had pushed him back, and then he had reared forward, tumbled against the windshield and fallen hunched near a pane. If he hadn't been a dead man he might have been dead all over again. A ten-mile-per-hour impact could kill; Owens's attitude was evidence of exactly what could happen if you did not know how to move with a crash. There was a light stink of gasoline in the air, in the point of juxtaposition—left rear bumper of the Fleetwood, right front quarter-panel of the Bonneville. There was a rainbow streak of marks torn from the uncompounded metal that dazzled in the sun, a scheme more beautiful than anything the designers might have conceived. Neither car, Wulff suspected, would ever run again.

And crumpled to the right of the accident scene and about ten yards downrange behind the point of juxtaposition was the crumpled frame of a man now lying on his stomach, gun dangling from his fully extended fingers. As Wulff had calculated, he had used the Bonneville for cover. If Wulff had not gotten very lucky in the point of impact, if the collision had not displaced the Bonneville so that there was a wedge of light into which fire could be struck, Wulff would have been dead.

Well then. It had not been the first time he had been lucky, Wulff thought. Then again it might not be the last, although there was a point at which you had to concede that your luck might be running out. But the trouble with that, the trouble with the easy, fatalistic calculations of this sort was that you never knew it until it had happened, until you had tumbled into the cave of disaster down that trapdoor, and then it was always in surprise. Death was always a surprise; the utter cancellation of those factors which kept you however perilously alive was to be greeted in shock. That was survival. It never got any easier to yield life. Owens had been right; calling himself a dead man had merely been a rationalization so that holding on would mean less to him than it did at the heart. Owens had been surprised, too. He had died stunned, his eyes rolling into his head in horrified contemplation of the unthinkable, which was that he, Owens, a professional hunter, was dead.

Wulff spat on the ground and walked toward the dead man. His knees had cramped up slightly underneath his body so that in death the man looked as if he were humping someone, some miniscule female diminished beneath him, shriveled with the impact of his entrance or from the effort of avoiding him, and Wulff was able to grin at that; death was always like that. Death was the opposite side of a dirty joke, that was for sure; in every dirty joke there was really a scream, the scream of the toilet, the hiss of mortality. It was necessary, it had to be that way—if you did not see that comic and terrible scream in death, that rigor mortis of the frozen smile, then it would overcome you completely and you would be unable to deal at all with a life that would casually circle itself around death, make death the inevitable termination of all of it. Death as a part of life was bullshit, death was anti-life, but death also capped all of life and every individual spirit and by refraction made those lives similarly flooded with death. Oh, it was very complicated, Wulff thought. It was very complicated if you wanted to get into that kind of thing and follow it through to its natural conclusion, but the hell with it. He had lived with death so long that he never could speculate on it, not to any depth. This, if nothing else, was what kept him sane. He walked over to the corpse carefully, nudged the cheek with his shoe, and then turned the body over slowly, his gun cocked, expecting at any moment that the body might lunge to its feet, but no, that was not going to happen, that was definitely an impossibility. If he had ever seen a dead man, this one was it.

He was a big man with a smooth, empty face. Perhaps in life the face had been full of wrinkles and response, but in death as in sleep all had been smoothed out of it. The face was as bleak and empty as the bottom of a clean frying pan. The sun came down on it and sent little pockets of light into the various crevices, but the corpse did not react to the light, nor did it cast off, merely absorbing it in that quiet way the dead have, the eyes open to the intensity of the sun, taking all light, giving back nothing. One of the hands was curled on a pistol, the fingers curved through it, one of them passing through the trigger hole, the others limply but gracefully embracing the pistol, drawing it into the dead palm, which already had a greenish sheen. The man who had held this pistol had obviously understood guns, and he had died trying to shoot. There was tension in the trigger finger; like a dead fish clinging to the line it was arced against the steel, trying to drive it through a point it would never find. The arm, too, had retained a kind of urgency. Like a boxer, the dead man had tried to put the motion down from his shoulder, hitting through rather than into the object. The man had been a skilled and graceful gunman. In a way, Wulff thought, but only in a way, it was a shame that someone so obviously professional had been killed in the act of doing what he did best, because there was little enough proficiency in the world and what little there was left had to be cherished. If the proficiency had been turned in evil directions, that in no way undercut its reality. Most people simply did not know what the hell they were doing at all. In any circumstances, in any way whatsoever, those who did know were important. He kicked the gun out of the hand. It spun against the desert floor, went behind a tire of the devastated Bonneville. He should have held onto it, Wulff thought. It was almost always a mistake to dispose of weaponry, you never knew when you could use it. But then again the Fleetwood was loaded up. There was a ton of ordnance there. He hardly knew how he was going to transport it if he could not get the car to move. He could not leave it there. And he could not carry it. Well, maybe that was life itself; it was too much to carry yet too important to lay down. Not to think about the thing too much. Not getting sidetracked into thoughts about life. That led you inevitably to thoughts of death and Wulff could not deal with that any more.

There was another body in the Bonneville. Looking up, sweeping the terrain, Wulff could see that. Counter to the body of Owens in his own car there was a corpse in there; it was lying just below the level of the windshield, just barely visible at this angle unless you knew exactly what you were looking for. Yet, in another way, glowing like a headlamp from that confined space, it would have been impossible to have missed it.

Wulff walked over to the car and looked at the corpse. It had been a man once but was no longer anything at all; like the body on the desert, it had a face that had been cleaned of all expression. Yet if the body on the desert had shown a clean, bright, almost perceptive aspect in its absence of emotion, then the one in the car seemed to have been brought below the level of individuation. The body on the desert had been a face cleared of expression, whereas this one looked as if it had never had any emotion whatsoever. Wulff looked at the thing, it had been five feet, seven inches in life, an average-sized man now clinging to the seat in parody of the terror that must have grabbed him when the bullets hit. And then for reasons he could not really explain, Wulff raised his pistol and put two fast shots into the face. The body bucked on the seat. Very little blood fell. With no metabolism to punch out the blood, to try and seal over the wounds in the energy of survival, the corpse accepted those pellets as a child might have taken cookies.

No satisfaction, Wulff thought, and walked away from the Bonneville reloading his gun in an absentminded way. There was no satisfaction in any of this, not that he was looking for satisfaction, not that anything mattered. It was all past tense, Wulff thought, that was the way he had to look at it; not a matter of ongoing action—which was bad enough what with all the pain connected—but action frozen in time, everything history, history even before consummation. No, Wulff thought, the presence of death made everything inconsequential; in that look of termination the faces of the dead man in the car, the dead one on the desert, and Owens there was a finality that meant that anything held by the living was unimportant.

He put his gun away. It was hot. It was ninety-five degrees and rising on the border and still no traffic, not a single car since all of this had started, barely—Wulff looked at his watch—fifteen minutes ago. Fifteen minutes and three lives, that was all it took. Fifteen minutes and no traffic, two ruined cars, no way out.

Wulff thought that if you wanted to pursue it in that direction there were edges of panic in this situation. You could not dismiss the seriousness of this, with the heat and with the car out of commission. And with the bodies. If a highway patrol car was the first to pass by, Wulff thought, he did not want to find himself in the position of explaining to the occupant exactly what the hell had gone on. He might make his case, he might not . . . but it would take a hell of a long time, it would involve bringing him into some wretched substation and by that time the general call information would be in their hands. No. He had to get out of here.

The Bonneville or the Fleetwood? Each was wrecked, either was as good as the other. Taking a step toward the Bonneville first, he backed off. He could not under any circumstances enter that car. The aroma of death was too strong. Even if it was his only escape from the desert, Wulff thought he could not commit himself to that space, could not touch the dead man on the seat . . . . Owens, at least, was his own.

Wulff went back to the Fleetwood. Owens rested in it like a mourner at a long wake catching a snooze, the tilt of his head, cock of his eye— all he needed was a little breath in his lungs to give the total illusion of life. But he was merely dead meat, meat on the rack of the car. He meant nothing whatsoever. Wulff pushed him out of the way, jacked the keys all the way into the ignition and pushed it to start. Nothing. Not a sound.

Dead solenoid? It was the only possibility on which he could work; everything else would be too complicated. Wulff got out, strained with the hood, opened it, found the ignition block and assembled the wires. Taking another set of keys out of his pocket he bridged the gap between solenoid and battery, went around to the car to make sure that the keys were at the "on" position, then tried it again.

Slowly, groaning, mumbling, the car fired. It stalled and Wulff tried it again, but the starter motor whined and it flooded. All right. Even Cadillacs were not immune to corroded engines, ruined wires, but there was life in the old bastard yet, he could give it a try. Get a Cadillac and drive a fine car. Luxury with economy. The standard of the world for more than fifty years. Another side to Cadillac. Economy plus efficiency. Four hundred seventy-two cubic inches of power. Overhead valve V-8. Turbo-hydromatic transmission with selectra shift. He bridged the solenoid again, used a hand to carefully pump the open carburetor, clearing the air-cleaner to the side. The engine started. It rumbled and then settled into low idle, rife with misses. Twelve hundred rpm but firing.

All right. He stood aside, slammed down the hood, went to the driver's seat and pumped the gas gently until the car began to idle steadily, the high whine of the carburetor balanced off against the rattling of the misplaced aircleaner. Screw it. He was not going to open that hood again under any conditions.

Wulff settled himself into the driver's seat, had dropped the car into gear and was already crawling forward, bumpers clearing with a scream from the Bonneville until he thought of Owens. Owens was still next to him. Regardless of what he thought of the man and the circumstances in which he had died, there was no way he could convey a corpse to his destination.

He hated to do it. Owens had meant more to him than Wulff, quite possibly, was willing to admit. He did not even want to think of the pain of that revelation, shuttled it to one side, this was no time to think of Owens. Later. He might think of him later again and then he might not; it all depended. The man was dead. Dead meat. You could not sentimentalize that which was afflicted with corruption.

He got out of the car putting the gearshift into park, racing the engine a little more to steady it, tugged open the passenger side, and slid Owens out to the floor of the desert as if he were a fish coming through layers of water to the surface. The thing that he threw on the desert had no relationship to Owens, did not remind him of Owens, bore no resemblance to Owens at all. To show that he had no feeling, that he had separated the remains from the image of the Owens-that-had-been, Wulff kicked the corpse once hard in the side and then slammed the passenger door closed again, went around and into the driver's seat, pulled the door closed.

Time to go now. Time to be on the move. But something unaccountably was missing. Even though he could not quite name it, even though he could not come to grips with what was wrong the feeling that things had not yet been completed overwhelmed him, slammed at him in a sickening way. It had something to do with the corpse, Wulff guessed. It had something to do with granting honor unto the corpse. But the remains were not the person. "It's all right," he said then, wheeling the car slowly past the dead man, "it's all right. You can rest. I'll get him. I'll get the man who did this and make him pay. I'll make him feel the pain."

"I'll fix him," Wulff said to the dead man who was not really dead, "I'll fix the bastard who did this to you and make him pay for it and make him hurt," Wulff went on, and then he drove into the desert slowly, engine knocking, rough acceleration, heading toward the fearful, insulated man named Carlin who lived on a hundred acres of the irrigated desert and thinking, thinking hard about what he would be able to do to this man when he saw him.

It would be worse than Calabrese.

It would be better than Calabrese.

IX

Carlin had not been thinking properly for a while. He was the first to know that; he could tell when his mental processes were all fucked up. A man who had been in his end of this kind of business for so long knew when he was not thinking properly, knew when the mind had gone off-center. All of the time that this was going on there was an older, cooler, more competent Carlin standing outside of him, shaking his head at what had evolved, and making dismissive gestures. "Better watch it," this more competent Carlin said, "better just watch it, man, you're going wild now. There's no reason to go off in that direction, not with the edge that you have on this bastard. Still, if you insist on doing it this way I think that you had better get rid of the body before you go. Also, I think you had better get rid of the staff, all of them, just in case they start to ask questions you can't answer. I'm sure they can all be trusted, but then again you don't know about people. They can get pretty strange, pretty peculiar, they can act in ways you never thought they would. Better play it safe, Carlin," this more competent version of himself had said, "and I'm going to play it safe too, I don't particularly want to be around these premises. In fact, I think I'd better get out of here," the adviser said, and disappeared with a whisk.

He left Carlin with a corpse on his hands, but then again he knew pretty much what he had to do. The advice was well-taken—you could not disregard advice like that. He had been dealing with his auditor off and on for many years, and generally speaking anything that the auditor said was worth attending to since the auditor did not speak frequently, dedicating most of his time to simply listening with a stricken and attentive position. But then again, he was running his life, not the auditor. Carlin had to keep that in mind. What he also had to keep in mind, what was equally important, was that he knew the auditor did not really exist. He was just a projection of Carlin's own mental state, his inner turmoil, his need to imagine some calm, removed presence that would give him calm, removed advice. If there was one thing Carlin knew and was attuned to all the way, it was his capacity for craziness. At any time he could veer over the edge. No man who had gone as far as he had, who had his enemies, who had to struggle all the time just to keep the sons of bitches off his ass could eliminate the likelihood of his going crazy at any time and blowing the whole thing. The auditor kept him sane, of course. All these tricks and gimmicks kept him going. Still, you had to keep it in proportion. You could not take a crutch and call it a third leg. That was the difference.

So, after giving it due consideration, he decided that the auditor had to go to hell this time around. He would have to follow his own instincts and those were to travel light and as quickly as possible. He wouldn't get rid of the body and he wouldn't get rid of the staff. In the first place there was hardly any staff to talk about—the auditor as always had exaggerated the situation, overemphasized Carlin's importance in the world (which was flattering anyway). The only staff were two hard men, probably homosexuals—Carlin had never asked—who were employed in rotating twelve-hour shifts to answer the phone, turn away people at the doors, give him an escort if necessary, and generally beat the shit out of any interloper if all else failed, which it rarely did. Carlin knew that he should know more about them, they had been there for five years, but aside from their names, Dick and Joe (or maybe it was Joe and Dick) and their last names, which he wrote on their checks, he knew very little about them at all. They had come well recommended and they did their job. That was all that mattered to him. If he wanted to get personal he would do it with Janice or with some people he had to deal with in Mexico City; he did not have to get emotionally tied up with the servants like so many other people he could think of. It was shocking how people could be intimidated by their servants. Carlin thought that kind of thing was disgraceful. As far as he was concerned they were merely furniture.

Thinking of Janice, though, left the issue of the body, and Carlin decided that this was exactly what he was going to do: leave the issue as it was. Maybe this showed that he had gone off the deep end, that the pressure had cracked him and rendered him crazy, but if this was the case it was just something with which he would have to live, he wouldn't be the first person he had known who had gone crazy nor the last for that matter. Wulff was crazy. No, it made sense to leave the body and travel light, let Joe and Dick take care of the matter. There was a hell of a lot of blood but otherwise it could be said that Janice looked as good in death as she had in life. Which wasn't very good at all. She was a big, fat-assed broad who had those remarkable tits, which bobbled and swayed in bed and which he couldn't no matter how hard he tried stuff all the way into his mouth, but that just showed you that passion was no patron of the arts, passion was an old man with a limp and a glass eye. The hell with it. He let her lie.

He would travel light. He had his schedule all mapped out, Carlin thought, as he threw together one light valise and prepared to leave his mansion in the desert—that was how he thought of it, *mansion in the desert*, actually it was just an eight-room house with a couple of sleep-in rooms for Dick and Joe, but it was always a distinguishing thing to think of yourself as someone living in a mansion—prepared to take a flight out of Phoenix just as quickly as he could. He would head toward Mexico City; he had a hell of a lot of friends in Mexico City who owed him favors and would be glad to put him up; he would sink underground there and just wait the whole thing out. He had twenty teams of his own after Wulff; the FBI, the NYPD, and practically every agency of the government was after him as well; there were a thousand freelancers, each of them with his picture in their pocket ready to take a shot at him. No, there was no way that the guy could stay in action much longer. His time, even with his phenomenal luck and his energetic craziness could be measured in a matter of weeks. Maybe days. However long it was, Carlin could wait it out longer in perfect safety, and then as soon as word of his enemy's demise came through—as it certainly would, because Carlin had the best sources of information in the world—well, as soon as word got through that Wulff had been killed, Carlin would be on his way home with the equivalent of a million dollars in his pocket. Make that two million. Shit, make that five. There was absolutely no saying how far he could go once Wulff was out of the way. And he would be—

soon. Carlin could close his eyes and get just a whiff of what it would be like when Wulff was no longer there, and it was crazy; it made his genitals stir. So much for Janice.

Travel light. Carlin put together a suitcase with underwear and shaving materials, put in one suit, and left the room quickly. Down the stairs and into the living room, out to the veranda for a last look at the blooming desert before he left it for a while. The sound of Joe coming up behind him was almost shocking, so locked had Carlin been into the necessity for a private moment, just communing by himself with his house and his garden. But that was the way it was; there were no such things as private moments, only little abscesses yanked out of time and then lanced by intrusion, and Joe, that physician, was now destroying his own little pocket.

"You all right?" Joe said. He was a short man with a restless expression on his face, never in repose, always a kind of distraction, and Carlin enjoyed looking at him because it was nice to think that the reason that Joe could not rest was that he was always thinking about Carlin. Always looking out for Carlin's welfare.

"Yeah," Carlin said, "I'm okay."

"Anything wrong?" Joe looked at the valise. "Going somewhere?"

"For a while," Carlin said. "Something came up; I'll be going south."

"Oh," Joe said. There was a long pause. That was the trouble with his relationships with these people; he had never quite gotten clear in his own mind how to handle them. Was he their friend or their employer? If he tried to be the one he was patronizing, if the other, brutish. It all came as a consequence of growing up without servants, of course. But that did not mean that people who didn't have servants shouldn't when they were able to afford them get them. You could make the same argument for big houses. Or expensive cars. You had a right to be the best that you could. Upwardly mobile, they called it. Wasn't that the word? "South," Joe said.

"For a while," Carlin said.

"I'll go upstairs and help you pack."

"Oh no," Carlin said quickly, "oh no, that isn't necessary. You don't have to go upstairs." He pointed desperately at the valise. "I've got everything I need right here."

"Right there?"

"For a while, anyway."

"For a long trip?"

"I don't know," Carlin said. "I don't know if it will be a long trip or a short one. It all depends. But I can pick up some stuff on the way if necessary."

"Oh," Joe said, "well, all right then." He moved away from Carlin toward the stairs. "Are you leaving now?"

"I think so. I think I'll just drive to the airport and leave the car there."

"Then I'll clean upstairs."

"Oh no," Carlin said, "oh no, that isn't necessary. I don't think you have to go upstairs now."

"I don't mind. It will give me something to do."

"I'd prefer that you don't," Carlin said so sharply that Joe moved away, came instinctively toward him. "I'm sorry," he said, looking at the expressions in Joe's face, gaiety and complaint, impatience and resignation chasing themselves in the welter along with many things that he could not quite identify. The man was certainly expressive. If you could say one thing about Joe, it was that; he had the kind of face that did not conceal emotion. Often it showed emotions that he did not have, which was a problem of a different sort. "It's nothing personal," Carlin said, "I'd just prefer that you wait to do the cleaning until I'm gone."

"Until you're gone."

"You don't mind, do you?"

"Oh no," Joe said, "oh no, Not at all." He wiped a hand across his forehead, brought it away, looked at it in quizzical fashion. "Whatever you say is all right with me."

"I guess I'll be going, then," Carlin said awkwardly. He did not know exactly what to say. He had never been in a situation quite like this before. How did a murderer take leave? Not that he was exactly a murderer. He had done the only right and sensible thing under all the circumstances. Still, someone might get the wrong idea about him. He would not like that. Unless he had a chance to explain this it would really look bad. "You can give me a ride to the airport," he said.

A look of grief became manic interest on Joe's face, his cheeks quivered, lips twitched, a little wad of spittle appeared at his lips. "Ah," he said, "I thought you said that you'd be driving—"

"I changed my mind. You get a lot of vandalism at those airports."

"Oh yes," Joe said, "oh yes, you certainly do."

"Kids breaking into the cars and whatnot. They spot a car that's been parked there for a few days and they figure that the owner is on a long trip. They gut it."

"That's true. That is true."

"The attendants don't keep an eye on them. The attendants don't give a shit about any of that."

"Yeah," Joe said, "I can agree with that." He blinked his eyes, shook his head again. "You'd like me to drive you, then."

"Oh yes," Carlin said, "I thought we discussed that. I thought you could get the keys, you see, and drive me and then bring the car back."

"I can take my own car."

"Yes," Carlin said, "yes, that's true. I never thought of that. It never occurred to me that you could take your own car. But that's quite right, isn't it? That would save all kinds of difficulties. If you took your own car."

"I think so," Joe said. He looked as if he were about to cry, but then you never could tell with the man's multiplicity of expressions, he might feel very cheerful. Anyone would feel cheerful being left to the devices of Carlin's house for a period of time with no one to oversee them. Probably the son of a bitch was robbing him blind, Carlin thought. Him and the other one. And Janice too. No, scratch Janice. She was dead; that was right. He had killed her. But the other two would rip him off right down to the ground one of these days. Still, what the hell could he do or say? It was hell to get servants who were worth anything at all nowadays.

"Is Janice coming with you?" Joe asked.

Carlin shuddered, stepped back a pace. "Excuse me?" he said.

"I asked if Janice is going with you."

"What gave you the right to call her Janice?"

Now Joe looked as if he were about to giggle. That might, come to think of it, be the key to reading that face; if you went for opposites you were not too far off the track. Still, there was a light of humor and anticipation in his eyes that hardly looked as if it were against the grain. "Why nothing," he said, "nothing at all. I've never known quite what to call her. What should I call her?"

"What do you think?"

"She's not Mrs. Carlin."

"You're an asshole. Do you know that? You're a thorough fucking asshole."

Joe looked at the floor. "If you say so," he said. "I can't get into that at all."

"You're a fucking asshole," Carlin said again. He had the feeling that he was reaching for something grander than that but it was not easy, his rhetoric seemed starved. "You don't know how to handle yourself and you have no idea of respect."

Joe said, "Is that all?"

"I've always hated the idea of having the two of you around," Carlin said. "You and that other one."

"He's off duty now."

"I know that. I know he's off duty. But I felt that you could help me, that you could shield me a bit. But how much shielding have you really given me? All you do is make more problems and take wages for doing nothing at all and steal me blind when I'm gone."

"Carlin," Joe said, and now for the first time his face was smoothed out, there was nothing on it at all. He looked as if he were a machine coming to a sudden and terrible idle. "Carlin, you had better cut it out. Enough is enough."

"Maybe for you. Not for me."

"Drive yourself to the airport."

"You're fired," Carlin said.

"Not until you pay me every cent that I'm owed," Joe said, "plus a month's severance, plus the two weeks' vacation pay you promised me I'd be getting next payday. You stole that money from me."

"There's no vacation on this job."

"You said there was."

"There's no vacation on this job. What the hell do you think I am, a goddamned Rockefeller? You're not a houseboy, there's no pension here, no career and salary plan. You're just a goddamned assistant and you get an assistant's pay. You don't like it, you could have quit anytime."

"You're pushing me very hard, Carlin," Joe said. "I don't want you to do it any more. I want you to stop it."

Carlin knew that he was pushing hard but he did not mind. There was an exhilaration in going too far. It could not be denied; there was that one, clear vaulting leap when you went beyond the normal, the expected, and let everything you had always wanted to say come out. Maybe you could understand the sheer joy of lunacy, Carlin thought, the reason why most of the people in the mental hospitals, most of the people who were picked up in the act of violent murder, were grinning. There was a pleasure in going over the edge. Once you got way beyond the expected you could open up whole new areas of experience, areas that had never been touched before. Hedonism, was that the word? He didn't know, had never studied philosophy, had not had the advantages he would give to his son if he had had a son. "Fuck it," he said to Joe, grinning and grinning. He could feel the lines on his face stretching as he gave himself over to it, the frozen, concentrated smile into which he could pour the heart of him. "Fuck you. Get out of my house now."

"Not so fast."

"Sue for your pay," Carlin said. "You can see me in court and try to collect it then."

Joe's face was still blank. "You're crazy," he said, "I don't know what's wrong with you but you've gone crazy."

"No I haven't."

"Yes you have."

"Get out," Carlin said. He took out his special gun, his traveling gun, a.357 magnum, with dum-dums, expandable bullets. He showed it to Joe, smiling away. "Like it?" he said.

Joe backed slowly into the wall. His face was still empty. His face looked as if it would never show feeling again. That was fine. He had an edge now. He had the kind of edge that he should have had with this character from the first. Show them. Show them what they are. Show them where they stand, what they mean, what you are to them and they'd never make a move on you. Draw a line. "You know what happens when one of these enters your body?" Carlin said. "They expand. They turn end over end and inflate and can really blow the shit out of you."

"Small bore magnum."

"Right!" Carlin said. "That's right." The gun was steady in his hand and he pointed it at the houseman. It would be so easy now. It would really be so easy. He had only one question to resolve in his mind and that was simply whether or not he wanted to kill the man. He did not want to do anything in a lack of certainty, Carlin thought. He had to be absolutely sure so that he would not look back upon this with regret a little later and with the feeling that he had done the wrong thing. Did he want to kill the man? Yes, he thought, he probably did. He almost certainly did or he wouldn't have gotten to this point to begin with. "I'm going to kill you," Carlin said.

Joe did not seem to react. He slumped briefly against the wall. Then, in one spasm of activity his legs uncoiled and he was moving in the air, hurtling toward Carlin, the explosion of energy released from some source that Carlin could not grasp. It was a mystery where he had gotten the recoil. The man's face was a huge balloon floating toward him. As Carlin stepped aside easily, Joe's features contorted in a wholly explicable expression of sadness and agony. He should not have done it, Carlin knew the man was thinking. Putting himself in the air with an armed man stalking him was not a very bright gesture at all. He should not have left himself that wide open.

"Fool," Carlin said and turned, pointed the gun and, as Joe landed, tumbling on his feet, unloaded a round. The bullet dropped into Joe's body as if it were a cannonball. In one motion he literally exploded. Little filaments of flesh were hanging from the walls, painting the ceiling. Joe, standing, his innards hanging out through his mouth, squeaked. He tried to support himself on the floor without feet to support him. Then he collapsed in front of Carlin.

That was fine. Carlin put another round into the head of the dead man just to see what it looked like. He had often dreamed of firing the .357 magnum—it was a hell of a weapon, something you really had to respect—but he had never quite had the opportunity to do it until now.

He lived the kind of life where generally speaking he was protected against the kind of violent confrontations that the .357 was good for. Well, that meant that he had been living wrong all the time. This was a hell of a lot of fun. He should have done it before.

Through the aperture of the skull, Carlin could see Joe's brains as if they were a living thing, a vegetable-like growth moving through the foliage of his hair and outward. The brain was under terrific compression by the walls of the skull. Shooting a man in the head enabled the brains to do what they had always wanted to anyway, which was to find more space, come out for air. Laughing, he looked at the thing on the floor and grinned as the brains drove through to find their new space, the feet on the floor kicking reflexively as if in ecstasy at the way in which all of the inner tensions had been resolved. Maybe that was what made people crazy. Maybe that, more than anything else, was responsible for all the tensions of modern society, the fact that people's brains were always compressed. Why, sheer pressure on the brain, Carlin thought. That alone could make a man tense and unhappy. Look at all the facial expressions that had danced across Joe's face, look at the way that the bastard had always been trying to find an attitude, never had been quite happy with any.

Well, the poor bastard was out of his misery now for sure. Whatever the explanation, Carlin had neatly solved all of his problems.

There was nothing else to do. He holstered the .357, dragged up his valise, and left the room. If there was any purpose to his staying, he would have; he would have done everything he could have to give Joe a decent burial just as he would have done the same for Janice . . . but what the hell. What did it matter? What difference was there in any of it? Dead was dead; to pay ceremony to them was merely for the convenience of the living. It certainly would make no difference.

To Mexico City, Carlin thought, and let the other one, let Dick find the mess here and deal with it. Dick was a resourceful type; he would think of something. Maybe he would take all of the blame on himself.

Carlin headed toward the door giggling, tugging the valise, the valise rapping against his ankles, tripping him a little but not impeding his flight, speeding it in fact.

Just as he got to the door, however, the phone rang.

Shit.

Being a conscientious man now without a houseboy, Carlin went back and answered it.

✠

Narco had been just swell. Narco had been contrived as the biggest, nicest present that they could give Wulff, a returned Vietnam veteran, decorated in combat no less, as a kind of gesture of their appreciation for what he had done, which was mostly to louse up the figures on all the guys who hung out at the bars saying that Vietnam was a great cause, it was just a fucking shame that they were draft-exempt because they had a more important duty here on the front lines of America, defending it from the scum right on the doorstep, otherwise they'd be out there catching Charlie's flack. All of them looked pretty lousy next to Wulff, who had passed up the exemption on the grounds that if the war was to be seen then someone from the supposed front lines of the city ought to see it. It had created quite an uneasy feeling in the department, and there were even a few people around at the headquarters level who weren't shy about saying that Wulff had to be crazy; any man who would buy himself a piece of that when he had an exemption had to be out of his mind. Still, they felt guilty, they wanted to do something nice for him, the PD had a long and not entirely untruthful reputation for taking care of its own. So they put him on narco.

Narco was second to vice of course, which was the greatest thing in the world altogether but strictly for relatives of relatives, impossible to crack, on a hereditary basis like the washroom concessions at the top nightclubs. Narco in the mid-sixties was the biggest, boldest thing a PD flatheel could fall into. Narco was supposed to keep the city safe and pure from the ravages of King H by working not on straight busts, which would have netted only small fry and little mainliners, but instead through a network of informants who, the PR work went, would be able to lead the narcs right to major dealers, the guys who were working the shit over with both hands and were at the absolute top, kicking shit at everybody. In truth, of course, all that the informants would lead narco to were small fry like themselves who were happy to show their appreciation for the cops by giving them a few dollars, and about a quarter of that would be then kicked back to the informant for his trouble. This made everyone happy: informant, dealer, and narc who would get it on both ends because he could cheat on the informant's cut and now and then hold out on him altogether threatening a bust. The informants grumbled about it and there would occasionally be a nasty scene—almost every time you read about a narc being shot on or off duty or found in the trunk of his car, it was usually an enraged informant who didn't want to be held out on any more. But all in all it worked pretty well, better than most things in the world, anyway. It certainly worked a hell of a lot better than Vietnam. As much as he hated it, and he did from the very first day there, Wulff had to admit that the system was quite workable.

Every now and then the press would start twitching around, usually as the results of more circulation pressure coming from their intent to raise the advertising rates, and narco was supposed to go out and prove that it was keeping New York free of crime by helping to keep it free of drugs. In the beginning there were panicky scenes and shakeups every time the papers would send reporters out to East 4th Street and Avenue to pick up some stuff outside the local elementary school, and there would even be shakeups on the squad, but as the sixties went on, by the time Wulff had gotten with it, they had even that down to a system like the rest of it. What they would do would be to make a prearranged bust of a few informants who would have a stash, the stash would mysteriously disappear somewhere between the bust and the courtroom, and charges would be dropped for lack of evidence. Occasionally it was necessary, under severe pressure, to pick up a stash and hold it in the evidence room, but that worked out nicely too because when they finally did a complete search of the evidence room early in 1973 in the early glory days of the impending new drug law prescribing death for the pushers, they found out that some fans of the system had walked off with two million dollars' worth of heroin, clean. That was nice. Wulff was able to get even with some of it, but that, of course, was much later.

No, this was all back in the late sixties and early seventies, at the height of the narco operation when things were running free. And who was Wulff, who the fuck did he think *he* was to be sickened by it? Wulff was unable to come to terms with it at all. Not much more than enough to just barely save appearances for a while.

It went back to Vietnam. He had been in Saigon, he had seen what drugs had done to that demolished city. Saigon was the drug carnival and capital of the world; it was a city totally devoted to the peddling of shit and Wulff found it easy to think toward the end of his hitch that this was perhaps what the truth of Vietnam itself might be. We were not fighting for freedom there, we were fighting for shit. Western dealers were hand to hand with the Orientals for control of the rich supply fields of Turkey, and Saigon was the place where it all came together in glittering embassies and ruined corridors and the explosion of the bombs that killed children. And all in the name of bigger and better shit for the West, less kickback and payment to the sinful East, which should stay on the softer stuff anyway. Cocaine and opiate country. Coming back to New York and the narco squad after two years in the Vietnamese countryside was maybe something like coming to work in a very high-grade whorehouse after having spent two years in a field hospital treating advanced and deteriorative cases of paresis. At least that was the way it looked to Wulff.

It simply would not wash. None of it would; he couldn't take the easy lies and that the squad had been created to conceal rather than to reveal, could not face the fact that as a narc he was supposed to be dedicated not to the elimination but to the perpetuation of the drug traffic. The real hatred started then, and the grinding rage. But Wulff had a nice girl, he planned to get married; marriage to this girl looked pretty good to him and although getting off the squad and out of the PD was important, being with Marie Calvante was even more important. At least that was the way it had looked to him then. But in the long run it had only cost her her life. Agonizing, but she would have been better off alive and lost to him than dead and his forever. He still believed that. He still believed in life.

But it was all academic; the rage spilled over even as the marriage plans went along and Wulff busted a grinning informant who laughed at Wulff with the bricks of smack coming out of his jacket pockets because this was not the night for a bust and under the arrangement Wulff could do nothing. Informants were untouchable anyway, but something broke in Wulff and right in the bar he slapped the man, handcuffed him, busted him for possession and dragged him into the precinct. The informant cried. At least he had that satisfaction; he had broken the man. A hell of a lot of good that had done him.

So he had busted him, but the precinct lieutenant had busted him right out because he had denied that Wulff had turned in evidence. The informant had gone back on the streets within hours and Wulff had gone off the streets and into patrol car duty because the lieutenant had done something at headquarters, and maybe he had done Wulff a favor at that because Wulff did not think that he could have taken one more night of narco anyway without killing people. So things had worked out for the best, perhaps. Except of course that on the first night of patrol duty they had gotten a blind call to find that the OD they were talking about was his own girl, Marie, dead in an SRO. No, he would not think of that any more. That was canceled.

Wulff was pretty mad, in any event. Eleven cities and jail had hardly spiked his rage. In fact it was self-feeding; he was madder now than when he had begun. Mad enough certainly to want to kill Carlin.

Carlin was the sole remaining big dealer in the Southwest. That made him very much worth killing.

Wulff looked forward to it.

XI

The other houseman, Dick, found the bodies. The one in the living room led him inevitably to the bedroom, and the one in the bedroom led him on a slow, careful prowl through the rest of the house to make sure that Carlin himself had not been killed. The houseman did not really think he had been; everything here pointed to only one conclusion, and although Dick was not a thoughtful man he could have said, if pressed, that he had seen it coming. He had waited for it for a long time. There was every indication that someday Carlin was going to do something and if Dick had not been receiving two salaries for his services instead of just one he would not have stayed in the house. As it was, it was just barely worth it. Looking at Joe crumpled on the floor Dick could see how close the calculation had been. Fifty-fifty, that was all. Still, if you got lucky there was no reason to question that luck. He would not have wanted Joe killed, but if it came down to a simple matter of choice . . . well, Dick thought, better him than me.

Having satisfied himself that there were only two bodies and that Carlin had not hanged or shot himself but had definitely gone, Dick made the first of his two necessary calls. It was not the one to the police; the police were going to be very tricky to handle, but Dick thought he saw a way of managing this if his timing was right and if he worked it out sufficiently in his head beforehand. Certainly there was no percentage in *not* informing the police. If he could face one thing right off, it was that if he was not the one who reported the crimes suspicion would come right down on him, and even though he had, as everyone in his business ought to, a spare identity or two lying around, it was better not to count upon that except if everything else had failed. He would have to report the crimes and take a good deal of heat but that was all right. He had been taking heat in one form or another for most of his life, and the Phoenix cops, compared to some of the scenes that he had gone through, figured to be a piece of cake. There were ways. But the other call was far more important, focusing as it did on the man who was Dick's second and now only employer and who had been, even at the time there were two, by far the more important. Whatever the Phoenix PD did to him would be nothing compared to what this man would do if he were not contacted and as quickly as possible.

Dick put the call through collect to Mexico City. He did not want this showing up on the dead man's phone bill; there would be investigators crawling around. The man in Mexico City was no easier to reach than Carlin had been and had even more levels of approval and Dick waited them all out, giving his name at every juncture, telling anyone who asked him who he was, resigned to take it as long as necessary to get the call through. He had to get the contact; there was no alternative.

Calling into Mexico City with Joe's bloated and riven corpse lying in the same room with him was an uncomfortable sensation, of course, but if the roles had been reversed Joe would have done the same. They were both practical men and not at all sentimental about each other, despite the job that welded them together. It was better, Dick thought, a hell of a lot better that it was Joe than him. Too bad but it had nothing to do with him, he did not bear any responsibility here and he could feel this way without guilt. The ugly aspect of the corpse itself did not really bother him; he had been in Vietnam way back at the beginning before he had caught a lucky shell that temporarily ripped up his leg and pensioned him out. Stuff like this didn't bother him at all. You couldn't last long in Nam if corpses, no matter how gruesome, had any effect on you at all. After a long time the man who he wanted to talk to got on the line and said, "What's wrong?" The man knew damned well that if Dick were calling him it was serious. Dick had called this man only once in seven years, and that time it had involved two million dollars.

"Plenty is wrong," Dick said. "He's killed his mistress and he's killed Joe and taken off. Both bodies are in the house pretty well ripped up. I checked in this morning and found them."

The man gasped once, one small expansion of feeling coming into that open syllable, and then he was completely in control again. "I was afraid of this," he said. "In many ways I could see it coming."

I wish you had told me or Joe, Dick said—but only to himself. He would never make a comment like that out loud, it was just stupid. No matter how much he might have wanted to say it, if there was no payoff, he wouldn't.

That was simple discipline. "Yeah," he said, "yeah, he was in a bad way."

"I have long feared that. He is a highly unstable man who at any time at all was likely to commit violence. I have known him for a long time," the man said in the curious formalism of those for whom English was a second language, however exquisitely they had been schooled, "and I have long suspected this."

"Yeah," Dick said, "yeah, well," and scratched his forehead. "It happens. Things happen all the time. People get killed on the streets in New York and like that. There's always violent crime."

"You've seen no trace of him?"

"I've searched the house pretty thoroughly. Nothing at all."

"You do not think that he may have left the house and committed suicide."

"No," Dick said, "I don't think that this is a suicidal kind of man. If he were he wouldn't have gone to the trouble of leaving two bodies."

"I am very much afraid," the man said, "that he is on his way here. I think that it is very likely that this is the real meaning of the situation. I have received a few calls from him within the last few days and he was extremely agitated, apparently because of this Burton Wulff."

"Yeah."

"The question is," the man said, "whether he is coming here for sanctuary or whether he has decided that I too must die. I must consider that."

"I thought you would want to."

"What do you think?"

Dick thought about this for a while. It was a collect call, it wasn't his nickel, besides the answer might be important. "I think that he may have two things so mixed up in his mind that it really doesn't matter," he said. "He can't separate the sanctuary from the need to kill. The same thing that makes him look for sanctuary might make him a killer. I don't know. But I wouldn't imagine that he could take too much pressure."

"That is helpful. I think you are right."

"I'm pretty sure he's heading down that way, though."

"Oh yes," the man said, "oh yes, I am also sure. There is little doubt but that this is what he would do."

"Well," Dick said, "I wanted to give you the word."

"I do appreciate that very much. What do you think your own plans will be?"

"I think I'll have to report it," Dick said, looking away from the corpse, aware that he had been staring at it throughout the conversation and for the first time then beginning to feel the impact of what it was, that thing in the room. Shielding barriers had come down in his head and he realized that he was staring at a dead, horribly mutilated human body. He closed his eyes, shook his head and turned himself fully against the phone. "I have no choice."

"Well, I can certainly see your point there."

"I'm the most logical suspect, you see. Even with Carlin gone they might say that I killed all three and disposed of his body secretly to make it look like murder and suicide. And once certain things start to come out I'll look lousy. I really don't see any way that I can get away unless I go completely underground and never come out."

"I would offer my services if they would be of any assistance. You realize that you are entirely free to stay here as long as you wish."

"I appreciate that," Dick said, "and I know what you're saying but it would not work out. I would only bring pressure." Unconsciously he was mimicking the formalisms he thought and for some reason that struck him as hysterical, the way human beings unconsciously fell into the speech or habit patterns of one another, not that it was anything to laugh about. "You couldn't guarantee my safety," he said, "not if your own was threatened."

"Well," the man said after a long pause, "well yes, I do see what you are saying. I understand that you are trying to simplify the situation for me."

"Nothing can be simplified," Dick said, closing his eyes. The corpse seemed to have acquired an odor, although again this could merely be his imagination. The scene was beginning to come at him in waves now like flak pounding the horizon in Vietnam. "It can only be anticipated."

"I want you to know that he will pay for this."

"That doesn't matter," Dick said. "It doesn't matter; what does paying him back mean? They're both as dead."

"There are degrees of death. Revenge can be known to the dead; avenged they sleep at peace."

"Yeah," Dick said, "yeah, well, I don't believe that," and he found himself clamping the phone hard now. There was absolutely nothing else to say. Whatever else he had intended in this call, he hadn't planned to get into a religious discussion. That was absolutely fruitless and stupid. "All right," he said, "I wanted to tell you that."

"It was very kind of you. I want you to know that it is appreciated very much," and Dick hung up abruptly. Religious or not, mystically inclined or otherwise, one thing was sure: He was a businessman. When a conversation was terminated it was done so at his decision and without any attempt to make the breaking of the connection less abrupt. Which probably, Dick thought bitterly, putting down the phone, meant that he had chalked up a debit on this one because he had terminated the conversation, not the man from Mexico City. The man from Mexico City had been willing to go on talking, possibly feeling that Dick needed words of comfort. That was too ironic. That above all things was too ironic to be handled.

He walked away from the phone, looking down at the corpse, thinking of the other corpse upstairs, balancing off one thing against the other. The mutilation of Joe had been bad enough, but what Carlin had done to the woman was absolutely impossible. He must have hated women a lot. But then that was a general and not a specific point; women were always treated more brutally than men, all up and down the line the focus and force of aggression came upon them. They were the receptacles, and in the nightmare of a hundred million beds a night all over the world men acted away and pounded out their fury on them. Women saw how the world really was. Women fucked and died with the hammer of the world coming down upon them. As bad as it was to be a man in America, to be a woman was probably worse . . . you did not act, but merely reacted; you did not shift but merely had that which was unspeakable inflicted upon you in a private and devastating manner that ripped you out totally . . . so that the inner landscape of a woman's mind might resemble what the outer landscape of Janice's body in that bedroom was . . . no, he could not pursue it. He simply could not pursue this line of thought any more; it led nowhere. Nothing led anywhere. Or then again it all led to the cops. At the end everything did; they were always there.

Dick picked up the phone and put the call in. To think about it was to risk not doing it and that would be very dangerous. He had figured this out. He had to follow his instincts now; he could not swing away from them. He had to follow this because anything else would have been hopeless. This way, maybe, he might have a chance. Then again he might not. Either way, it was not as if he were passing up very much. Vietnam had wrecked him. He was a war casualty. He hadn't had much of a life even with two employers and plenty of money. Maybe this way he would again. Maybe not.

He told them what he had to. It was hard for them to understand. Dick was weeping.

XII

On the plane Carlin felt safe for the first time. It must have been the first time he had felt at peace for years. He had not realized the way that circumstances were impinging upon him, factors were squeezing in, until he had exploded. It wasn't the murders that had given him that hounded, pressured feeling. On the contrary, the murders were the first step on the path of release. He had gone sane. He had started to make the long road back toward sanity by killing them. Now he was getting more sane all the time, and soon he would be entirely sane. Who was to say what manner of man he might be then? No one would be able to touch him once he got all his brains together. That was happening. That was happening right now.

Unbuckling his seat belt on the empty flight to Mexico City, Carlin considered his only mistake; he probably should have killed all three. Should have waited until Dick, the other houseman, came in for duty the next day and murdered him in a clean and decisive way, one shot through the temple with a gloved hand, then put the gun into Dick's palm and make it look with the two dirty murders and the one very clean one like a classic murder-and-suicide of the sort that would have kept the cops at bay for weeks, possibly permanently. But then again, calculating everything in the intricate and brilliant arena of his mind where the lights played and dazzled now and all was almost music, then there would have been a search for him even more intensified than it would have been otherwise. They would have feared that he was the fourth victim. His every move would have been watched.

Whereas this way, with Joe and Janice dead, with Dick discovering the bodies, there was a very good likelihood that it would all be pinned on Dick . . . and they would not believe his denials, would not believe either that he simply hadn't stashed Carlin's body somewhere, really deep-sixed it because his would have been the important corpse, the one they would really have hung him for. Oh, that was brilliant thinking, Carlin thought, and wrung his hands, gave a little bubbling giggle. He did not know how truly shrewd he had been. Trust the subconscious, that was all. Always rely upon, go back to the subconscious in times of stress and if you had taken care of it, it would take care of you. He had taken care of his subconscious, all right, feeding on Janice's enormous tits for all these years, boobs that were so big it was ridiculous for a grown man to be sucking around on them . . . but his subconscious had been pleased and alerted by his efforts; his subconscious had been well sated. Had returned the favor. Carlin giggled again.

And now Montez would take care of him. Montez would offer him sanctuary, a peace so complete that it would become his life. In a villa on a mountaintop high off Mexico City he could live a life of ease with a man who owed him many favors until such time as he chose, on his own terms, to emerge. Montez would be happy, would in that curiously formal way of his be honored, he would say. And who knew? You left it up to the subconscious as always and the subconscious took good care of you . . . who knew but that he might not deal with Montez too at an auspicious moment? He had the weaponry, he had the respect, he would have the opportunity. A lot of servants, but timing was everything in these things. He could add Mexico City to his own Southwest. Damn the middleman. Why pay Montez money for shuttling when he could shuttle—and pay—himself?

He wrung his hands in ecstasy, his eyes blinking, and the stewardess came over, looked at him as if he were in pain. She was very young and unsure of herself. All these Mexican stewardesses seemed to be. "Can I get you something, sir?" she said.

Carlin put on his best smile and looked up at her. He knew he was a handsome man. That assurance had always been deep in him; hadn't Janice often said that he was as good a fuck as he was good-looking? Not that he wanted to get involved with the stewardess, have her remember him on this flight, that would be stupid . . . but still, it was irresistible. "I would like to put my head on your chest," he said.

She backpedalled, not too easy in a jet at speed, her eyes round. "Can I get you a drink?" she said. "What kind of drink did you say you would like?"

"I do not want a drink," Carlin said formally. "I did not ask for a drink; I asked for the privilege of putting my head on your chest." Montez would have phrased it this way and with a little bow. "Of course if you find that so impossible—"

The stewardess was still moving away from him. The five or six other passengers, half-hidden behind enormous seats had turned, he could see the edges of profiles showing like flowers peering through crevices in a wall. "I will get you a drink," the stewardess said, "but if you make difficulties for me in flight I must warn you that I will be forced to notify the pilot and the copilot and a full report will be made on landing."

Shit. All of it was shit; Carlin felt his mood beginning to turn rancid on him, turn inside out like a shirt collar. There was no fun or satisfaction anywhere. "I don't want a drink," he said to her loudly. "If I wanted a drink I would have asked for it. You would have known that I wanted a drink; I can make my needs known perfectly well."

"Sir," the little stewardess said, "I will get you a pillow and you can rest your head. I—"

"I don't want to rest my head," Carlin said. "I feel perfectly all right. Do you think there's anything wrong with my head? I mean, is that your implication?"

This is foolish, he thought. It was important that he make this flight as inconspicuously as possible; he did not even want Montez to know that he was coming until he came out of the plane band phoned him . . . and yet there he was carrying on a scene with a stewardess who was barely old enough to be his daughter. She could not treat him this way. No one could treat him like this; they did not have the right. If she knew what kind of man he was, what he had accomplished, what he had done, and why he was on this plane, she would treat him in a different manner, all right.

That was for sure. "Come here," he said and reached forward, got a corner of her skirt in his hand, tugged. She backed away, the skirt coming from between his fingers. The passengers were looking more intently now; their faces, still flowerlike, had popped all the way from behind their seats. He felt fixated, locked in this gaze. The stewardess backed away. Suddenly Carlin was filled with hopelessness and a kind of revulsion. He had no business carrying on this way. It wasn't doing him any good at all. The stewardess was moving toward the flight cabin. "Look," Carlin said to her, "look, please. I'm sorry."

She turned. "You can't do this," she said, "you can't do this kind of thing to me."

"I know that," he said, "I shouldn't have done it. I'm not feeling well. It must be the altitude."

"Stewardesses are not your servants. We are professional employees and entitled to be treated as professionals."

"Oh yes," Carlin said, "oh yes." He swung in his seat. "I'm not used to flying," he said, "it must be that I'm very scared, I'd never act this way any other time."

Her face buckled into something more accessible, even pitying. He had found the right line to take. Stewardesses, pilots, all airline employees liked that. Experienced travelers liked nothing better than seeing someone getting sick in a cabin, as long as it was panic and there was no cause for it. "It happens to the best of us, sir," she said.

"I think I will take that pillow, now."

"Good," she said, "good. I'll get you that." She went back up the aisle, turning from him quite gracefully, right at the pilot's cabin and into some alcove where the pillows were undoubtedly kept. The passengers had sunk beneath the seat-line again. But that was too close, Carlin thought. That was much closer than I really want to play this.

He gripped himself in his seat and sat there for a while, the plane bouncing a little in flight, wondering if he had misunderstood this situation . . . and if he had really lost control of himself.

XIII

Driving into it, Wulff thought that Phoenix was bust-out country too.

Most of America was, of course. Most of America had crystallized toward one of two poles: Harlem or Las Vegas. The better sections verged toward Vegas, the worst looked like Harlem, and those in the middle that had any kind of flexibility were trying to become like Vegas with all their might while sweeping up the crumbs and particles that were pure Harlem. One was the model, the other the penalty, and yet, in the dream that was the country Wulff thought they came together so that one could not tell, being dumped into either of them at night when the lights glowed, where they were. The Apollo Theatre or the Sands, both of them would look the same under the cover of night. They were the bust-out capitals all right, the monuments in all of the western world to the way it would all end up when the American string had been pulled. All of America was piling toward those poles, spinning centrifugally, breaking apart . . . but somehow what kept the country was its ability to sustain the belief, at least among most of those being pulled apart, that there was a real difference between the two. There was not. Wulff had seen both and he was sure of that as he was of nothing else. Still, the myth kept the country going; it kept the junkies going too, driving themselves in their inner flights toward the one or the other.

Phoenix was a would-be Vegas; unlike Harlem it had chosen to shroud reality, whereas Harlem wallowed in it. But Phoenix, although it was a city that had elements of beauty, you could see beautiful things in it anyway if you were aesthetically inclined, was really the kind of place where people who couldn't make it for Scarsdale or the Oakland Hills or Grosse Pointe would go. Fifty years ago Phoenix had been nothing; now in pastels it had been slung out across the desert: It had its millionaires, its reactionary senators, its bigoted cesspools that moved from the offices of the downtown to determine what part of the desert certain people would live in. It had its hustlers, too, who were working the El Pastorale Estates, two hundred million acres of swamp underground available now at twenty-five dollars down and a hundred and ninety-nine dollars a month for life. They were working the El Pastorales out of the boiler rooms in downtown Phoenix just as the Pocono hustlers were calling up blind leads out of stinking cellars in Paramus, New Jersey. But the air of Phoenix, Wulff thought, was the more desperate because it had started fresh, out of nothing, out of the desert, and in fifty years it had found nothing better to do than to recapitulate America. It had managed to compress two hundred years of corruption into half a century. It had set out from the beginning to be indistinguishable from the rest of America and it had succeeded. And still, with all of that, it was filled with people who could not make it to Grosse Pointe, played nominal host to a group of basketball players who were never good enough to sustain their skills in Madison Square Garden. It was a failed town.

Wulff came into Phoenix the same way he had come out of Detroit: in a busted-out Fleetwood for a busted-out town, a little sadder, a little wiser, a lot of bodies behind him, a lot of moves made. But he was really no different from the man who had left Detroit, just as the man who had left Detroit differed little from the man who had hit it. He had really been the same for a long time now. For months he had been only an angrier and more efficient version of himself. Changes were only in the direction of making him more certain of his mission. He had never been so angry in his life. And he would be angrier tomorrow.

He headed out toward the estate where Carlin lived. His plan, he guessed, was as simple and straightforward as his plans had always been; no duplicity, he would come up against Carlin's home, he would reconnoiter, check out the terrain, prepare his ordnance, move in, check things out again, and then he would blow it up. Subtlety was wasted on the Carlins just as it was on almost anything in the world, just as subtlety would have been lost in the rotten town of Phoenix itself. America was Las Vegas. He would bomb out the estate and then Carlin would understand what had happened, but only at the moment of death. Never before. He was one of those people who you would have to kill to change. Wulff accepted that simplicity. At least you knew where you stood.

He owed Carlin a vicious and painful death, of course; Carlin had hurt him more than most of those with whom he had been dealing. Carlin had cost him a man, Owens, who might have been a friend. Carlin had sent a vicious and deadly team of assassins after him. Carlin was functioning from a combination of panic and ambition, which made him more dangerous than almost anyone with whom he had dealt—more dangerous, perhaps, than Calabrese. Cicchini had merely wanted to hold onto his position but Carlin hadn't found his terminal point yet, he was still pushing, he was ambitious. That meant that he was capable of literally anything. It would be a pleasure to make him die. Wulff had looked forward to it very much. That and almost nothing else had been what had sustained him through the drive from the New Mexico border into Phoenix alone, more kills behind him, Owens gone.

Now there was merely the necessity for revenge, nothing else. Wulff knew that something was wrong, though, even before he approached the estate. He had been finding his way on Owen's directions, faking his way through back roads and the flat, long pass that would lead then directly to the small access road of Carlin's home. There had been a police presence on that road, a few more patrol cars than he would have thought necessary in Phoenix at that time of day. Driving farther he came up against a few more patrols, and then at the access road— private, Owens had said, installed at great expense to zoning laws and political maneuverings as well because Carlin wanted his privacy and controlled access and was willing to pay for it—at the access road Wulff found that it had been completely blocked by two old patrol cars, which had straddled the road in such a way that no one could get through. Wulff kept on driving.

You learned that kind of thing on instinct early; a less experienced man than Wulff might have slowed, even stopped, taken a closer look at the cars, tried to find out why the access was blocked. But Wulff kept on sailing at a steady fifty-five, holding the wheel rigidly, looking straight ahead, giving the cops nothing except a little profile, which behind the cloudy glass of the Fleetwood wouldn't mean a thing. The bullet holes in the rear might attract a little attention, but he doubted it; he had sealed them over with scotch tape at a rest stop, done a pretty good, improvised job, if he said so himself, and it looked like the kind of road damage that almost any big old car might well have picked up somewhere along the way, gravel or stones kicked up from the desert, adventures in off-road traveling, vandalism. No, the cops would not pay too much attention to the Fleetwood. And although Wulff supposed that like everyone else the Phoenix cops had his picture and nominal instructions to shoot him on sight or at least bring him into headquarters for shooting, cops in cities away from where the crimes of the fugitive had been committed just weren't interested. They had no interest in that kind of stuff, laughed at it, passed the posters around, wiped their asses with them for laughs or said they would, stuff like that. It all came out of the basic attitude of the cop; he was pretty sure that the world was out to get him, all circumstances were dangerous and threatening anyway and you had your own shit to mine, what the hell did you want to mine somebody else's shit for anyway? The hell with it. Wulff could imagine exactly how these cops in Phoenix felt. They used to laugh a lot at the FBI posters when they had come into the precinct. Fucking J. Edgar, they had said, if they were supposed to get their asses shot up doing his work then they should at least go on his payroll, the cheap, evil old bastard. And those were NYPD, the finest is what they called themselves, the best-educated, best-paid police department in the country. Imagine what they thought of this shit in Phoenix.

He kept on rolling. The patrol was interesting; the shutoff of the access road was even more so. Unless Carlin had the cops literally on his payroll, which was doubtful even in a place like this, it meant that something very bad had happened at the estate, something that demanded a police presence and a shutoff. That could mean that Carlin was dead, of course, but he would hardly be so lucky as to die without Wulff's own special attentions. More likely something else had happened involving the deaths of other people. Wulff knew that Carlin was panicking. He knew enough of the man from what Owens had told him to gather that he might panic in a very unpleasant way. There was nothing nastier and more dangerous than a weak man backed to the wall, because the weak man would do anything, like a cowardly dog under pressure, to keep from revealing that weakness. Only his self-deceit had enabled him to stay sane; he would do anything to preserve that sanity. So Carlin had probably killed some people, Wulff thought. That was his analysis of the situation, right off the bat.

All right. That meant that he would have to handle things in a different way, but the essential pattern of it would remain the same. Instead of charging Carlin direct he would have to make an end-run. Carlin was not in Phoenix if Wulff's analysis of the situation was correct; Carlin had committed crimes, he would have left the city. As powerful as he was, Phoenix was still not at the point where a man's money could buy off the institutions. That would come, of course, that was the shape that America was taking and what it would certainly be in twenty years, but now there were only pockets of that in the country in the same way that cancer in the early stages could be seen as little pockets in the body. In New York it was that way, certainly Washington, Las Vegas, the new and ultimate town of the future made it possible for law to utterly serve power . . . but Phoenix had a little bit of the frontier, vigilante ethic. It would not be likely that Carlin would be able to stay and to hold the situation with full knowledge of his crimes. Then again he might. You never knew about things like this, but Wulff had learned to proceed like a bridge player, through a series of assumptions; you took the only assumptions that would enable you to make the hand and then you played through. If you won you looked like a genius, of course. If you lost you didn't look too bad either because you got commended for your daring.

He drove through and past Phoenix, the sound of his ordnance clattering in the trunk of the Fleetwood. When he had gone as far from the center of town as he felt to be necessary—and this town like so many of the American cities built after 1900 had no center at all; Phoenix was merely a series of presumptions, apprehensions against the void, when the apprehensions eased down and the void began, that was the edge of town—he did what he had already done many times before, he got himself a furnished room in a private home. This was the best hideout of all. It beat hotels, rooms in apartment complexes, the streets, flophouses . . . nothing was better than a little one-and-a-half rented out by some solid and usually senior citizen. The cover was absolute; no one gave a damn who the golden ager was renting to or would want to since it merely helped him meet the tax burden without becoming a welfare case. Oh, Wulff loved their furnished rooms, their elegant but filthy nightstands, their ornate bureaus, the sound of the flush-toilet to the rear that never stopped flushing, not once all night. Hell might be a furnished room, but then again heaven might as likely be; it was likely that heaven was rented out in little partitions, one-and-a-halves at thirty-seven dollars and fifty cents a week, no towels supplied, sockets not quite functional but all of it on a trial basis for the Big Room.

Wulff rented his one-and-a-half from an old man with liver spots on his hands and elbows, little freckles all over the dome of his forehead, about five miles from downtown Phoenix. "You're not going to be bringing anyone in here, will you?" the old man said. "The one thing I can't tolerate is visitors."

"Oh no," Wulff said, "I don't know anybody here at all."

"I mean whores or anything like that. You won't be bringing in people to fuck."

Wulff shook his head. "I don't do that kind of thing," he said. "I don't deal with whores, anyway."

"Got nothing against fucking," the old man said, creasing and uncreasing the fifty dollars week's rent in advance, which Wulff had had to pay him before they could even get into serious dialogue. "Fucking's a good thing, a healthy thing, did a lot of it in my time right up until my wife died three years ago but by that time I got to say I didn't care for it very much. Tried to oblige her, of course, the poor woman, but it wasn't anything that I really wanted to do past sixty. But fucking's okay for young people. You're a relatively young person, aren't you?"

"I'm thirty-two."

"Oh yes," the old man said, "now that's a relatively young age, thirty-two." He blinked against the sun, which lay halfway between their angle of confrontation and ninety degrees overhead, coming into the cluttered yard behind the small house. "Thirty-two is a good age for fucking. I did a lot of fucking at the age of thirty-two. But not with whores. Never with whores."

"I don't either," Wulff said.

"Whores degrade your spirit and they also bring a bad element in. I've always been against them. I don't think there's any reason for a healthy young man to go with whores. Either he should be married and doing it in a good married way or he has lady friends, has a relationship, it just isn't a matter of dirty-minded sex if you know what I mean."

"I've got a fair amount of stuff to move in," Wulff said, thinking of what was jammed up against itself in the trunk of the Fleetwood, thinking of the grenades, the magnums, the small-bore rifle. It was nothing to leave out on the streets, even under metal, even in serene Phoenix. "If you don't mind—"

"Now with whores it's just degrading, though," the old man said, not moving away from the door. "Now there are a lot of people who talk about legalizing sex, particularly down here in the Southwest they say that it's the coming thing, open whorehouses and charge accounts and music and television and like that. I come from New York originally, you know. Me and the wife. In New York they wouldn't have such things as open whorehouses."

"I don't think they have them here."

"You're not going to look for them now, are you, Johnny?" the old man said, looking keenly at Wulff. "I mean the thing that brings you down here isn't that you're looking for some of that free and easy open sex, now, is it? Because I think you'll find that a lot of that stuff is pretty exaggerated."

"Oh no," Wulff said, "I'm not here for sex. I'm here on business."

"Good business or bad business?"

"I don't know. It all depends."

The old man smoothed the blue and white surfaces of his sport shirt against his body and said, "I hope you don't think I'm being too inquisitive here, that you think I'm being nosy or anything like that."

"Oh no. I'm from New York myself."

"I figured that. You look like a nice, intelligent young fellow of a very fine type you don't often see around here. I could have almost told you were from New York or I never would have rented you in the first place. I do some pretty careful screening, you know. You've got to keep up standards here. I mean without standards, where the hell are you?"

"That's true."

"But I could see that you're pretty decent." Puzzled, the old man looked at the five bills in his hand as if he was not quite sure what they represented, how they had gotten there. "Well I guess you'll be staying here for a week," he said.

"Maybe. Maybe not. It depends on how my business goes. But I paid for the full week in advance."

"Well if you paid for the full week in advance you ought to use it. I'm not out to make turnover money on you. The trouble is people have no respect for money any more. They think that it's something they'll always have enough of, that's their problem. You stay out the full week."

"I'll think about it," Wulff said. "I promise you, I'll really think about it."

"It would be foolish not to."

"Please," Wulff said to the old man, "please, I really do have to get settled in."

The old man looked as if he had caught a glimpse of his long-departed wife in some angle of the sun and a literal expression of fright came across the blunt angles then. "Don't have to be that way," he said. "It's your room. You can do anything you want with it."

"Please. I'm in a hurry."

"People got no goddamned patience any more, that's part of the problem. Don't have the time to sit and talk, don't have the time to really deal with others. Just rush on through. Ruining the whole goddamned country; there's no sense of place any more."

"Sure," Wulff said. "Sure, that's it." He turned from the old man, went down the steps, opened the trunk of the Fleetwood and then just stood there, looking at the old man for a while, holding the counterbalanced lid. The old man showed no disposition to leave the porch. Little leaves drifted across his face, a late October wind caressed his face and brought streaks of red to it. He made an accommodating motion to Wulff. "Just go ahead," the old man said, "don't worry about me, I'm just getting some air. I'd help you if I could but I've got a bad back. Otherwise I'm very strong, though. I could take anything you wanted in if my back weren't so weak from all that late fucking."

"I don't think you understand," Wulff said. It seemed that he had said all of this before, but then always, everything was new. "I've got some personal materials here."

"Personal materials?"

"Stuff that's important to me, anyway."

"Go on. Unload it. You don't think I give a damn what you have, do you now, Johnny?"

"You don't understand," Wulff said, "I really have a personal feeling about this stuff. I just feel that I—"

"You don't want some old bastard staring at it, is that right? That's what you think of me, you think of me as some old bastard, some old son of a bitch who just rambles on and on and can't be turned off. Hell, I was thirty-two years old once."

"I'm going to be thirty-three," Wulff said mildly. In all of his travels he had never felt so at bay. The old man had managed what none of his enemies had; they had never made him feel apologetic and vaguely ill at ease. But then again he couldn't deal with the old man the way that he had been able to handle the enemies.

"I'll just go in," the old man said. "I won't bother you. Hey, you don't have someone in that trunk, do you? You don't think you can sneak someone in, not pay rent, is that it? Well, you don't have to worry; the basic charge is for the room, not for the person. I don't care how many people stay with you."

"No," Wulff said, "no, it isn't another person. It's just some stuff I have."

"I don't mean to be nosy. I mean I don't want to push you or anything like that. I don't want you to get the idea that I'm making your business my business. It's just so hard," the old man said, "so *hard* to find anybody who will listen to you at all; maybe you have to buy a little conversation when you're old. You'll find that out, Johnny. You'll know it some day."

"Okay," Wulff said, "I don't mind. That's all right."

"Easy to be gracious. So easy to be gracious when you're thirty-two years old. You see how it gets when you start poking around those upper forties, son, you see how gracious you can be then. That's the test of a man," the old man said and went back into the house.

Wulff stayed there for a while, letting the hood slide up, the ordnance gleaming at him. The old man could well be observing through a window, his glance fixated on exactly what Wulff was bringing in there. If he did, that would be trouble . . . unless, of course, the landlord got satisfaction from the idea of heavy weaponry being in his house. That was a possibility—anything was a possibility—but not worth chancing.

But Wulff did not think that the man was looking outside. Call it a matter of instinct, call it a certain leap of perception, he did not think that that was the old man's style at all. Some skulked and some were all on the surface and some did not react at all . . . this old man said what he had to say and was done with it.

Would that Wulff would be the same when he got that far.

If he got that far. He saw no reason to calculate that he would last even to half that age.

But maybe that wasn't such a bad thing, old age being what it was in America, Wulff thought. Maybe you were far better going young and in the illusion that you had lost yourself in a pleasant, dignified old age. Because to actually enter upon it was horrifying; it was something that drove most Americans insane. No wonder they hadn't really extended the lifespan in fifty years of advancing medical science; people simply did not want to be old. They would rather be dead.

Thoughtfully, Wulff threw a blanket over the ordnance, just to be on the safe side. Grunting, he carried it through the door. He could, of course, leave it out in the street in the Fleetwood, take his chances. It had been done. He might have been able to get away with it.

But the hell with it. Phoenix was a really tough town. Anything that was founded on drawing water from the desert would have to be.

XIV

At Mexico City Carlin deplaned quietly, shamed. He could barely stand to look at the stewardess. Whatever had happened, whatever had passed through him had been like an illness, some strange malaria-like disease that left you with shaking sweats and three hours later the inability to remember exactly how you had felt. It was better to put it out of his mind completely, put it down to a reaction to what had happened, to the tension of the situation. No good would be served, certainly, by ever thinking of it again. "I'm sorry," he murmured to her as he passed her moving toward the ramp. "I'm really sorry."

"No you're not."

"Yes I am."

"None of you are ever sorry," she said, and he would have answered that one too except that he was moving out of the plane then and she was behind him. He knew that she was looking, staring at him, that the hate he had seen suggested in her glance had probably coalesced into something even more intense and dreadful . . . but there was no good in looking back. He would not think of it. He wasn't thinking of Janice, was he? So why the hell should he think of some stewardess with whom he had made a mistake, but then everybody was human and had a right to make mistakes. At least, that was the more encouraging way to look at things.

Standing in the terminal building, feeling the thin air breathe fire into his lungs, Carlin thought of the pros and cons of calling Montez. On the one hand the man would be glad to hear from him, owed him one favor or twenty, would send a car to the airport, would in every way make Carlin's trip easier. But then again Carlin had the vague feeling that calling Montez might not be the best thing to do, despite all that the man owed him, despite the certainty that Montez would fall over himself trying to accommodate Carlin. Call it suspicion, call it a vague instinctive feeling; the fact was that Montez might have picked up some news of the murder from some other source. It was unlikely, but these things happen, word spread around and there was something *disquieting* about the murders . . . Montez might even get the wrong idea about them. Of course, once Carlin had a chance to explain everything to him things would straighten out and there would be no problem in getting anything he wanted from the man in terms of sanctuary . . . but still it was the matter of approach, it was something that had to be considered.

Still, Carlin was tired of decisions. Everything was a decision; how to deal with Wulff, what line to take with the knowledge of the man's approach, whether to kill, how to kill, when to kill, what to do next . . . he had been poised on decision's edge for days and days and he was no goddamned binary computer, the coding was overloading his nervous circuitry; in short he was getting close to being knocked out. Let chance decide, Carlin thought, the air burning his lungs more and more, really a bitch, and he was not even out of the heavy, air-conditioned terminal itself, it would be even worse in the mountains outside. Let chance decide and whatever be decided let it be done fast. It was all catching up with him. Fatigue dragged at him like a hand, he felt himself beginning to collapse over his baggage. That would make a hell of a picture, wouldn't it? He would flop over those bags and the porters would come and take him to the infirmary where they would pull his identification from his pockets while he was undergoing treatment and they would run an investigation. *Run an investigation.* No, whatever else, that would not work out. He had to keep upright. He had to keep going.

Carlin took a coin out of his pockets and tossed it in the air. Heads, he would call Montez and get picked up at the airport; tails, he would get a cab and go out himself. Heads. He looked at it and in the cheater's way found himself instinctively wondering whether or not he ought to make it best out of three. Fuck it. One toss, one decision, that was what he had decided and there was no point in turning back now. He went over to one of the phones, his breath gasping and whistling in his ears now. Maybe he should not have come to Mexico City. Perhaps this was not as good as it looked at first.

But again, the hell with it. You went forward. Carlin had no idea how to work with the receiver, the paybox, the writing in Spanish that apparently called for Mexican coins; he only bellowed into the receiver until the operator, sounding confused, came on. Carlin told her who he wanted and the address and the operator after going away for a while said in a bad accent that this was an unlisted number that could not be released and Carlin cursed her and said she had better get the damned call through and she said that procedure was procedure or at least that was what he thought she had said, there was no deducing Spanish any way at all and he said that if she didn't get the goddamned call through he would order the President of the United States to drop bombs on Tijuana, he was an important *turista* with good contacts through the White House and since the President was bombing anywhere else on request he was sure that the President would be happy to oblige. This puzzled the operator—or perhaps it shamed her.

In any case, the phone at the other end began to ring and a voice answered. The operator said something like a million pesetas and Carlin began to rave and curse again until the voice said that this was perfectly all right, he would be more than happy to accept this call collect on behalf of his friend.

It was Montez all right. "Where are you?" Montez said.

"I'm at the airport. I just flew in here."

"That is very good," Montez said. "To what do we owe the exceptional pleasure of this visit?"

"I had some important things come up," Carlin said. "Some business that could be settled better perhaps face to face."

"You would like me to accommodate you? I will send a car directly to the airport."

"I'd appreciate that," Carlin said.

"Is there any length of time that you would like to stay with me? My house is your house, of course."

"It may be a little while. I don't know exactly. More than a day or two."

"Well, that will be excellent," Montez said. "It will give us an opportunity that we have never perhaps had before, which will be to simply talk with one another and to get to know one another exceptionally well. That will be a privilege. I will certainly look forward to that."

"Well, I'm sure I will, too."

"You just remain at the airport, my friend, and make yourself comfortable. If you wish, I could call one of the functionaries there and introduce you and arrange for you to wait in comfort. It will be about forty-five minutes. Perhaps a little less since I will tell my driver to hurry. I am very glad to hear from you and very anxious to see you."

"Well," Carlin said, "well, that's all right. You don't have to call anyone. I'll just sleep on a bench here or something. You can tell your driver how to find me, yes?"

"Oh, indeed," Montez said. "As a matter of fact there will be no need for my driver to have a description. I have changed my mind while speaking to you. I am so anxious to see you that I believe that I will also come. I will come with my driver and the two of us will pick you up together. That is how very anxious I am to see you."

"That's not necessary."

"For a friend anything is necessary. Nothing is unnecessary."

"That's very gracious of you."

"No more gracious than our friendship," Montez said, "which I am sure will go on to even greater and higher levels of true communication." Then he waited courteously, saying no more until Carlin realized that

Montez, polite to the last, wanted Carlin to hang up, would not be the one to first terminate the conversation. It was the kind of strange courtesy that had always been there in Montez; the courtesy of European royalty or some ruined Spanish prince. He had never trusted it but then again it hurt no one and was kind of gratifying. Besides, Montez owed him this kind of deference. He had made Montez everything he was.

"I'll see you, then," he said. "I'll be right here waiting," and hung up, walked away from the booth quickly. The phone started to ring back at once, the operator probably, like American operators, wanting some identifying information, but the hell with her. The hell with all of them. Carlin walked away, half-staggering, and took a gleaming bench to himself, folded himself over his valise, drew it into his stomach, half-dozed. The air still hurt his lungs but he seemed to be getting used to it. He would be all right if he concentrated on slow, careful, shallow breaths for a while. He was all set now. Everything was coming together. Montez had seemed perhaps just a little bit strange over the phone, a little bit peculiar in the way he had decided to pick Carlin up at the airport himself . . . but then Montez was a strange man. Give him the benefit of the doubt. Just once, Carlin thought, give everyone the benefit of the doubt.

He dozed.

XV

Wulff made his first real reconnoiter of the estate within three hours of his check-in at the furnished room. Loaded up only with light gear, a belt, a couple of hand grenades, a .357 magnum, and a small-bore rifle, as well as the dependable .45, Wulff took the Fleetwood into the canyons surrounding the estate again and found that the police cars had disappeared from the access road, that there seemed to be no police cars in the vicinity at all. If the first pass of Carlin's property had indicated furious activity on behalf of enforcement, the second showed none at all . . . which probably meant that nothing had changed objectively, merely that at upper levels it had been decided that enough of a show of involvement had been made and that patrols could be safely withdrawn. Whatever had happened had happened; events, from the police standpoint, were not to be dealt with but merely reacted to, their levels of reality manipulated in a way that would best protect the interests of the department. That was cynical, perhaps, but it was pretty much the way the situation was.

The access road was a tight, winding little creation nearly obliterated by hanging trees and foliage, which came sprouting off from the sides obscuring it. All carefully calculated of course. Carlin had wanted his privacy. Wulff shrugged, put the car into low gear, and went up the road carefully. If there were patrol cars on site, if there were sentries of any sort at the property, then he was now in severe trouble; he would have a problem to solve . . . but you could not worry about such things. You took the situation as it developed, opening before you one step at a time. To think too deeply was to risk the negation of all action. He was pretty sure that the man he wanted to kill was no longer there but that did not excuse him from the obligation of checking it out first hand.

Wulff went up the road, the engine groaning and threatening to overheat, the ordnance bouncing away in the back. At the top there was a sharp fork right, and he had to maneuver the big car to make it, coming halfway onto that second road before he lost rear adhesion, backing then for a better angle, coming in slowly, and here the road was barely one car wide; the going was really perilous. Hunched over the wheel, concentrating on that road, Wulff really did not see the house until it sprung up at him, three vaulting stories around another curve in the road, just a little bit of vegetation and open space around it, the house using most of the available space provided on the plot . . . there was a gothic feeling to Carlin's home, it might have been a castle surrounded by a moat, a castle in which dreadful things occurred. Of course, that was probably exactly the case . . . but it was a strange thing to see in Phoenix.

Abandoned. There was no one here at all. No car parked, no indication of movement on the property. They had simply closed it up and gone away. Whoever had been in the house was there no more; whoever had been assigned to do surveillance had been pulled away. Idling the engine, Wulff crept up closer, leaned the nose of the car against the bleak bronze gate that had sealed off the property. Carlin had believed in security, all right.

Wulff knew that he should go. There was nothing more to be done here; he had come on a cold trail. Dead or alive, probably alive and in flight, Carlin had abandoned his estate, and a man like this did not abandon a place of this sort lightly; it could only mean that he had no intention of ever returning. Wulff was merely setting himself up with the authorities by staying here. If on some casual sweep, some routine check, a patrol car should find him here, it was going to be very difficult, very bad. Of course, he could probably explain his presence here, but the Phoenix police would not want to listen. They would have him in jail on other counts. While local police could hardly be said to be enthusiastic about chasing down all-points bulletins, they would not mind taking a little painless credit.

He thought of throwing a few grenades into the estate, just for spite, just for satisfaction, but there was no point to that either. What would it serve? It would only bring the cops in on the trail again and would hardly inconvenience Carlin. Carlin was never going to come back here again.

Wulff shook his head in disgust, put the car into reverse and started to back it slowly down the access road. Then, in a corner of the rear view mirror he saw the car coming up fast behind him, a big, black Fleetwood much newer than his own, making the trail with that kind of proficiency that showed either great skill or familiarity with the terrain. The car was coming up behind him, swallowing up the road on both sides, no way to get past it, no way to move.

Wulff put the car into park, shut off the engine, took out the .357 magnum and waited for the car to come up behind him. There was simply nothing else to do.

XVI

As Dick had expected, the cops booked him in downtown. Whether or not they were going to go for formal arraignment, they had more than a few questions to ask him. For a while, at least, it was a very bad situation.

They told him that he was the logical suspect; it looked like murder one for sure. All they wanted to know was where the hell was Carlin? Had Dick murdered him first and dumped the body into a separate place, or had he panicked after the first two murders, waited for Carlin to show up, shot him and hidden the body for the same reason, to make it look like a crime of passion? Dick said that they didn't have that quite straight. He had merely found the bodies. He had no idea where Carlin was. As a matter of fact, he suspected that Carlin had done it himself and had set Dick up for the discovery. Dick was innocent. He hadn't had a thing to do with it except to report the crimes, which was more than a lot of people in his position would have; most of them would have turned tail and run, making things only worse for them in the long run, to be sure.

The cops weren't having much of that. The cops were extremely unhappy. With Dick in hand and with a confession they could wrap this one up quickly, get an arraignment and close the case. They had two corpses and reasonable suspicion, and as long as Carlin didn't show up for a good long time, which was highly likely, they had a terrific case. That was the way the cops wanted to play it, of course. They were looking for a closed case, not an open one, and the involvement of Carlin made it very unpleasant. Carlin had been a rich man and a great problem to the Phoenix police. He could be even more of a problem unless they could close up the case.

Carlin was running drugs. The police were pretty sure of this, but on the other hand it was not the kind of thing that was easy to prove and they did not have the muscle to even get started. If there had been federal help in the case they might have been more energetic, but the feds weren't interested in the Southwest at all; in fact the feds weren't interested in anything except Operation Intercept, which had been an incredible if backhanded bonus for the drug industry. That had left the Phoenix cops on their own, and they did not know what to do, even though all the indications were there on the record if they had wanted to research it. The best thing to do was to leave Carlin completely alone and hope that he got involved in a drug war or something, one of those upheavals in the industry that were fairly common and that redistributed power by eliminating some of it, consolidating the rest. But Carlin had an amazing survival capacity. He also lived quietly, and nothing much appeared to happen for so long that the murders looked good to headquarters. If they could only get a confession they could have the case cold. Without a confession it would be awkward, though. Dick was right; he really had no motive after working for Carlin for five years, and he certainly would not have phoned in the report himself. The cops had to admit that. Even they could see this logic.

"Listen here," the interrogating lieutenant said to Dick in the back room, a rather plush room, actually—all greens and blues and little streaks of padding on the walls into which he hit his fist occasionally. Originally the headquarters building probably was supposed to be a mental asylum, but they had run out of funding and given it to the cops, which was just about where they ranked in the schedule of American priorities; lower than lunatics but just a shade above schoolkids who otherwise might have had a building in greens and blues. "You're just making it hard for yourself. Now this is a crime of passion, we can say that you were interrupted in the act of fornication with Carlin's mistress with whom you had been having an affair for some time and you lost your head and killed her and the other because you got panicky and were afraid that Carlin would kill you. Then in a state of insanity you waited for him to return and you shot him too, disposing of the body in a different place so that it would superficially appear that he had committed the crimes. You were still insane, you were not functioning in your right mind. Then you thought you could defer suspicion by reporting the murders yourself, but you were completely insane from the moment you were surprised in flagrante delicto and that explains everything," the lieutenant said. He sighed, scratched his head, walked nearer Dick. "Now you're insane and you can't say that your employer was exactly the most desirable element in the community, right? I figure you could be institutionalized; they would decide that you needed help rather than punishment, and in just five to ten years, even a little bit less with these wonderful modern scientific practices, they could probably cure you completely and get you back into the world. Maybe you'd have a little bit of difficulty in getting a job or with your social life, with the murder rap hanging over you, I mean, but then again we're living in progressive times and everyone will know that you were insane when you did it and besides that you've been cured now. You aren't the same person." The lieutenant rubbed his palms together slowly, looked at them with a surprised, distracted expression as if their color or shape had been somehow changed before he had last considered them and said, "Why don't you make a little statement?"

"I have no statement to make."

"I can get a stenographer in and you can spill your guts out. We won't change a word of it; we'll let you go over and make corrections, as a matter of fact, if there's anything you don't like in it. All we really want is the basic stuff—times, identities, methods, like that." The lieutenant gave a long sigh, shrugged, leaned against a wall. "Don't be stubborn," he said, "everybody knew that Carlin was into running smack. He wasn't what you'd call the most desirable kind of person."

Dick had been sitting in a wooden upright chair, his back cramped against it for more hours than he could recall, his reflexes reduced to a series of messengers for pain. Nevertheless, he thought, he would hold his position. Past a certain point there was nothing they could do to you. He believed that; he had read accounts by people who had been tortured in wartime saying that if you removed the spirit from the flesh, if you backed your mind away from what was happening to you, called your body the enemy and refused to connect what was done to the flesh with your own identity, you could survive torture indefinitely. And this could not even be considered physical torture, just a kind of pressure under interrogation, which was at the most superficial level of harassment. If he held out they would get tired and go away eventually, or they would find another suspect or they would simply, in shame, release him and leave the case open. He had to believe that; it was that belief that would get him through. He hadn't done it. They could not make him say that he had done what was impossible. "No," he said, "no."

The lieutenant sighed again. "No what?"

"I discovered the bodies," Dick said. "When I came to work I found the two of them there."

"You've said that already."

"It's the truth."

"If you didn't kill those people, then," the lieutenant said, sounding almost reasonable, "if you didn't kill them, who did?"

"Carlin."

"Carlin? That makes you an accessory both before and after the fact."

"No it doesn't."

"You were working for a murderer."

"I reported the crimes as soon as I saw them."

"Premeditation would have made you involved."

"He never told me anything," Dick said stubbornly. "I only worked for him. He was not the kind of guy who would tell an employee anything."

"You worked for him for five years and he told you nothing?"

"Nothing," Dick said.

"What was his motive?"

"I don't know anything about motive. I tell you, I didn't know him very well."

The lieutenant walked toward him and said, "You're making this very difficult, you understand. You're making it far more difficult than it has any reason to be."

"I didn't do it."

"You could sign a confession and it would go much easier on you. He was not a desirable man; we all agree on that. We could let you cop a third-degree plea. Maybe he was trying to kill *you*, that almost lets in self-defense and the other stuff could have been done in a hot rage."

"I didn't do it," Dick said. Spirit from the flesh, body from the motives. If you gave them nothing they couldn't touch you. He had to believe that. He had to hold onto it. "I know he wasn't a very desirable man but I didn't do it. He did it."

"Where is he?"

"He killed them and ran off."

"If he was into drug trade you were an accessory on that, too."

"I didn't know anything about it. I just was a houseman and answered the phone."

"Make a jury believe that."

"Make them believe I committed a murder that I didn't."

The lieutenant turned, his body seemed to move through levels of discovered fatigue to a new and sudden acceptance, his aspect seemed suddenly diminished. He shook his head, ran a hand through his hair.

"All right," he said, finally, looking away from Dick, the angles of his features ruined by exhaustion and what might have been something even subtler and more terrible, the utter collapse of any belief in himself years ago, now fully accomplished, the end of the spirit, the end of the line. "All right, so you're stubborn. So maybe you really did discover the bodies and you didn't do it. Still, we don't have any trace of him and we've got ourselves a hell of a time getting him if he did do it. Does that make any sense?"

"Yes," Dick said, "yes, if he did it."

"Yeah," the lieutenant said bitterly, "but then on the other hand, it's much easier to try and pin it on you. You were there, you discovered and reported, you had some kind of a motive, it's a little tricky, but we can find some motive business for you, and we can take care of you while you're here. What's the point in trying to pin it on him?"

"He did it."

"Orders are orders," the lieutenant said. He went to the door, rolling in the exaggeratedly careful walk of the drunk or the very tired. "We always do what we're told. That's the key to everything, following orders. That's how they wanted it; that's how I tried. But I agree with you. I think you're innocent."

Dick stood, moved the chair back with his calves. "Thank you," he said.

"That doesn't fucking mean that you can go. You just stay there. You stay put. If I can't do it maybe someone else can. Conclusion has nothing to do with interrogation."

Dick stood in position and said, "That stinks. There's no justice in that if you're going to operate like that."

The lieutenant said, "What the fuck does it have to do with justice?" But he had the decency to say it bitterly as he opened the door and closed the door and somewhere in the middle of that action he was gone.

XVII

Murder like sex heightened one's sensibilities, and the moment that he saw Montez with two big, ugly, impassive men coming toward him in the terminal building, Carlin knew he was in trouble. He should have understood from the conversation, should have understood from the beginning exactly what was going to happen, but he had been stupid. From too much fatigue and excitement he had given way to too little anticipation, he had looked for Montez for help when what he should have understood was that Montez would only see him as a dangerous rival who now, having put himself alone into the hands of his enemy, could be dealt with quickly and quietly. All Mexicans were treacherous. Montez had always seemed obsequious with him, had never given Carlin any reason to feel that the man was dangerous, but then again he had never seen Montez alone either. Or announced himself to the man as coming in alone.

Stupid, Carlin thought, as the three of them surrounded him, the two silent men yanking him to his feet, Montez nodding in a peculiar and private way. Stupid, Carlin thought, as they led him through the terminal, one in front and two of them to the sides to the limousine. Stupid, he thought, when they piled him into the back seat of the limousine flanking him, Montez sitting in front, turning back to spread the glass partition and lean back to talk to him, the driver something invisible to the left moving the car. He should not have done this. He should have anticipated. Still, how long could he continue at the level of alertness with which he had operated when he killed Janice and the houseman? There were limits to anyone's will. It was not really his fault. That was no comfort, of course. None whatsoever. In the back of the limousine the men checked him quickly and professionally for weapons while Montez looked back at him through the partition, his face solemn. The limousine began to move. "You know I didn't have anything," Carlin said, "I couldn't have gotten anything through the airport detectors."

"People are resourceful," Montez said. "People have endless resources in crisis."

"You're doing this wrong," Carlin said. He had no desire to fence with the man; both of them knew exactly what was happening and why. "You can only make things worse. You're a fool. We did good business together. We could have kept on doing business. Why did you have to make it this way?"

Montez nodded to the man on his left and the man on his left hit Carlin in the jaw. It was a careful blow professionally administered; Carlin heard something crack in there, but there was only a minimal loss of consciousness and that unblocked swiftly so that he could feel the pain. The pain was terrible. He brought up a hand and rubbed the jaw, and that sent new splinters of pain through. The man on his left folded his hands like a child who had been given approval in a classroom for something difficult but necessary. A little smile worked its way through his face, but that could only be an illusion in the strange illumination of the car, refracted glitter from the dashboard the only light, the tinted glass keeping the mountains out. They were moving fast and low to the ground through hilly country. "Murderer," Montez said, "filthy fucking murderer." The elegance of his diction, the strange formalism with which he said this only made it the more horrifying. "Putrescence," he said, "diseased slime."

Carlin, sliding into unconsciousness on the seat, shook himself like a dog and said, "I can explain everything."

"You can explain nothing. Filthy disgusting pig."

"Everything," said Carlin weakly and the man on the right pinched his thigh midway between knee and groin in a painful way that Carlin had never felt before. He would not have known there was much sensation in the area. "Please," he said, "please stop it."

"Now you are weak," Montez said through the partition, "now you babble, now you beg. Would that you had shown such mercy to your victims."

"They were doing it to me," Carlin said. "I mean I did it to protect myself. To protect you."

"You are an excrescence," Montez said. The man on the left hit him on the cheekbone, the arc of pain intersecting with what was pouring from his jaw, and Carlin involuntarily retched, spewing little gobs of saliva and vomit not only on himself but on the man next to him. The one on the right moved over silently and very seriously began to choke him.

The scene wavered before Carlin and then it went away. When it came back Montez was saying, "Enough for now. We do not want to kill him just yet," and the pressure had receded. He was sitting straight and hard against the panels of leather behind him, his eyes feeling as if they were burning their way out of his skull. "Oh my God," he said then in a voice he could not believe was his own, so terrified did it sound, so childlike, so at bay. This could not have happened to him. He could not have been reduced to such a condition. "Oh my God," he said again, realizing that even if he closed his eyes it did not go away. It was happening. It was all happening to him right now and he was in the center of it.

"We will deal with you when we return," Montez said. "We will find out exactly what kind of a pig you are."

Carlin tried to say something but it caught in his throat. He could not get sound out. It occurred to him that he might be dying, and this was surprising because he had always been very frightened of death but he had comforted himself with the feeling that cowards die many times but brave men only once and that death, when it came, would be very easy. It would be like a swimmer falling into sheets of water, one gesture of parting and then done. But this was not easy. This was not easy at all; it was terrifying. He felt spittle catching in his throat and hawked it, this brought him into a partial alertness and he smelled the odor of the men in the car. They were smoking cigars blowing the smoke casually into the compartment. Montez also had lighted a cigar and was still staring through the partition, the cigar in his teeth, little casual clouds of smoke coming from it. "I didn't mean to do it," Carlin said pointlessly. "I didn't mean to do anything."

"Now you did not mean to do it. Of course you did not mean to do it; no one means murder when they must face the consequences," Montez said.

How, Carlin thought, could this be happening to him?

He had always been in control. Montez had been nothing more than his supply man.

Montez said, "Because you did not understand what you were. Because you thought that I was working for you when all the time you were working for me."

Everything wavered. Nothing made sense. "I'm sorry," Carlin said, and so he was, he guessed he really was. He began to understand what sorrow might be, but this would not do him any good, he knew, no good at all. The limousine moved on through the dense high hills surrounding Mexico City. Never did he think that it would have come to this. You lived in the open but you died in close. You lived in light and possibility but death was a little cell that squeezed around you. Funny, he thought, funny to know this now, but would it have made any difference to him to know this way back? No it wouldn't, he thought, no it wouldn't and Montez snapped the partition closed, and temporarily Carlin retreated into that final cubicle of space, layers of warmth around him but one shuddering, suffering part of his mind told him that it was only temporary and that soon enough he would be back. Back and back. Well, consciousness was better than death.

XVIII

People who knew that Wulff was a narc, the few of them who he told, were not so much interested in his job as in the fact that his being on one special squad might give him special information into the habits and working lives of some members of another. What did vice cops tell their wives or girlfriends, people wanted to know from Wulff. Did they tell them the truth of their job or keep secret about the whole thing, and if they did tell the goods, what did the wives and girlfriends think of it? The idea that night after night their husbands or fiancées or boyfriends were out being solicited to get laid, going up to hotel rooms with women whose job it was to fuck.

Of course, theoretically, the vice squad was not supposed to fuck. That would have been illegal entrapment just as solicitation would have been.

They were supposed to wait until a request for money had been made, until the money had actually been received by the prostitute, and then pull out their badges and bust them. That was the procedure according to the manual. But nobody really believed that. No one believed that a cop, if he was with an attractive prostitute—and he wouldn't bother making the bust unless she was attractive; why remove merchandise from the streets that no one wanted anyway?—was going to come back into the puritan tradition precisely at the moment when he had canceled it out. Indeed there were plenty of stories of cops who after paying over the money would show their badges and then promise not to make the arrest if they could get sex for free, and then there were others who got their kicks out of screwing and then making the bust, as if immediate punishment for sex made the sex that much more exciting. And then, too, the prostitutes were not exactly objects. They had their own minds and thoughts and opinions and desires and they would be doing everything possible to entice the cops into a kind of vulnerability that would enable them to get off. All in all, it was pretty clear what was going on in the vice squad and it was a matter of envy more than anything else . . . but still, what did the wives and girlfriends do? What did they think of all this? Were all those rumors about a high percentage of divorces on the vice squad true and also the rumors about all the VD that was being spread around?

It was impossible for Wulff to make the questions go away. In other circumstances, he was willing to admit, he might have been curious himself. But there was no way to explain to those who asked that there was no real answer. There were as many solutions to the problem as there were vice cops or wives or girlfriends of vice cops; stereotyping them into a single response was just as bad as what the vice squad did to the prostitutes, which was to make them objects subject to the single standard of entrapment or paid fucking. People were individuals first and members of a class second, Wulff would have said if he were up to a discussion of the matter, and because of that you could make no flat judgments. Of course, that would have been a lot of bullshit, but if he had wanted to turn the question away by speech he would have handled it that way.

Actually he turned the questions away simply by refusing to answer them, telling them that PD work was holy and kind of privileged and that there were laws of confidentiality surrounding all departmental policies and procedures and he was under oath not to discuss any of the internal workings . . . which was not quite true but was backed up by six feet four inches and the expression Wulff got on his face when he said it. People—or at least the kind of people who asked these questions—

were not at all likely to press the issue. And in the second place, it was not entirely true because there were certain generalities that could be applied to the vice squad that would have applied to narco as well. They were the same, vice and narco; one dealt with sex and the other with smack, but all of it was the same; all of it came down to objects being manipulated. Tits or needles, bags of smack or cunts, all of them fit into the police department view of things, which was to manipulate reality right up the pike to the point where it could not be controlled, and then simply deny reality.

So he could have told him on the basis of his experience with narco what was happening on the vice squad, too; he could have told them about the fragmentation of relationships, the busted marriages, ruined courtships, the dead men with blinded eyes drinking in their off-duty hours at short stops in Queens on Saturday nights, the men moving from one level of drunkenness to the next like a painter ascending a ladder and at the top of the ladder was merely the void, the glittering, empty space they would do anything to avoid . . . so they would scramble down the ladder and at the bottom of it there was always a fight or another drink or sometimes both. The cops fought like madmen with one another and with the public, and there was no saying what a drunken man with a service revolver might not do. Cops were getting into shootouts with each other all the time, they were killing passersby, there were a lot of people in bars picking fights with what they thought were unarmed drunks who turned out to be anything but.

He could have told them that the vice cops just like the narcs couldn't sleep at night but couldn't quite stay awake during the day either; you went through the day in the kind of fine, concentrated rage that took you through basic training or the police academy, denying the consequences of everything that was happening, thinking of all this as being funneled through a different person. The graft was there in both vice and narco: maybe a hundred, hundred and a half a week in front money from the pimps and pushers, but what could you do with it? Really, what in the hell could you do with this money?

You couldn't put too much of it into the house because your wife or girlfriend would want to know where it was coming from, and those wives who didn't say anything, who demanded only that the money come in faster and faster were even worse than those who asked too many questions. You could buy a little better car or a better class of suit, but no narc could be caught driving around in a new Eldorado; any car that was less than three years old was automatically suspect. The pay was fourteen and a half a year on the average, and with prices the way they were who the hell could afford four or five grand, even on payments, for a new car? No, only the stupid ones would let the money show up where it could count, either on the highway or in three-hundred-dollar suits. Most of them just sat on it in safe deposit boxes or pissed it away in an extra drink here, an extra toy for the kids there, and it was astonishing exactly how easy it was to make a hundred and a half a week disappear. People could and did live in New York City, even with families, even in 1970, on a hundred and a half a week, but then again a hundred and a half was something that could go out and past the counter of the Highlight Bar and Intimate Hideaway on Queens Boulevard in less than a week. Often enough you found yourself with a tab at the Highlight that steadily climbed on the last couple of days before payday. Of course the tab was a fiction, and more often than not both you and Willie the proprietor knew it, no one really tried to collect on a cop's tab . . . but still the fiction was there and you had to take it seriously. You had to take all fiction seriously. It might turn out being something exactly like life.

So that was about the way things were on vice, or on narco. It was no wonder that the entire system was geared to pushing away the crimes rather than to apprehending them. The cops were so weary, so bitter, so fragmented and so drunk most of the time that they were in a mood to do almost anything but deal with the source of their business. Besides that, the source of their business was also the source of almost half of their income, and you did not take something like that lightly.

Wulff was not sure exactly what all these speculations about vice and narco had to do with the situation at hand, which was that the car coming up the road had disgorged three men, and the three men had surrounded him and had disarmed him so quickly, so professionally, that there was nothing to do but go along with it. Resistance would have been foolish. The three men piled him back into the limousine and took him to the airport and onto a private plane, which they told him finally was going to Mexico City. Even these men were kind of curious about vice, it turned out. They knew his background and they asked him the usual questions. So rather than have a tough, tense flight to Mexico City with them watching him every moment and the possibility of death hanging in the air on the jolting, private plane, he had decided to open up and tell them the full story. What the hell. It passed the time. And the men were very interested.

XIX

Montez thought he had handled things fairly well up to this point. He had gotten Carlin, that was the important thing, and had now put him under wraps under the tightest kind of security in the basement of his mansion. He had scouted out his contacts to the north and verified that no one would mind in the least if he took Carlin out of their calculations forever. As a matter of fact, it was such a messy business altogether that they would take it as a favor if he would take over the responsibility. He could even have Carlin's territory gratis.

So that was good. That was taken care of, and then Montez had fallen into the unusual luck of having his intercept team pick up the man who Carlin had been afraid of, the man known as the Wolf, who had been responsible, as far as Montez could make out, for the triggering burst behind the murders Carlin had committed, not that Carlin himself did not have to bear the absolute responsibility for his condition. A murderer was a murderer, Montez believed that deeply, there was something about a man who would commit murder that separated him from the rest of humanity as effectively as if he were a grotesque creature of another species. Montez was proud to feel that whatever his other sins—which were not slight and which were not scattered occasionally over a period of years but seemed to have picked up in clumps, and in fact were accelerating—in spite of all those sins, Montez had at least never committed the crime of murder. There were certain things a man of honor did not do, and murder was one of them.

So Carlin was effectively separated in his mind from anything that happened to him next. Whatever Montez decided to do was not performed upon a human being but a member of a subspecies. He had tortured Carlin and he expected to kill him because there was no other just termination, but this would be no exception to his rule against murder. That rule was for human beings, not for members of this subspecies who he had wholly isolated in his mind. The fact that Carlin's murder would intersect with certain ambitions of Montez's own, which had to do with taking over what was Carlin's with the effective blessing and pledge of assistance from possible competitors in North America . . . well, that simply did not count. Montez was an ethical man; he had an intricate code of behavior in which he deeply believed and to which he had absolutely committed himself. He was going to torture and kill for ethical reasons, not for reasons of aggrandizement. If he did not believe that, he thought, if he did not really hold onto and accept that as the truth, he would be incapable of doing what he was doing.

But things had worked out nicely. Carlin was in a sub-basement, Wulff was heading toward him on private plane, he had the cooperation of North American authorities, he was free from any of the archaic law enforcement systems of North America, he was in a position he had never really thought he could attain . . . expediency and morality had intertwined. It just proved, Montez thought, it proved that there was justice in the world. He had suffered and he had gone through difficulties and times had been hard for him . . . but he had come out the other end and now everything was looking up. Not that he wanted to witness the tortures, of course. He was not a cruel man. He himself derived no personal satisfaction from human suffering.

And Wulff was heading down by charter flight. That was going to be interesting, Montez thought. He knew little of Wulff himself. Of course there were fragmentary reports. It was impossible to be in the trade without picking up a good deal of scattered information on this ex-policeman and combat sergeant who had stated the necessity to "clean out the international drug trade." That was the kind of thing you had to keep up with in your business if you took your business at all seriously . . . possible rivals, sources of opposition. But it really was hard to believe. The man had to be crazy, even for a *norteamericano* he was *loco.* That was why the reports that had started to drift in had made him laugh: ten dead in New York, a thousand in a freighter fire in San Francisco, a hundred in Boston, a hotel burnt out in Las Vegas . . . impossible. It was to laugh. No man could do all of this and survive. No man could even think of doing this. Didn't this Wulff know that the world was in the hands of the people like Montez who were truly only giving people what they wanted?

No, he did not, of course, and it was Wulff's failure to absorb this simple measure that had led to all the difficulties. Still, this was really excessive, what the man had done. Montez had to shake his head with admiration when he read the reports, saw the American newspapers from the cities where this had gone on. Any man who could do something like this phas remarkable. Any man who was capable, singlehanded, without any apparent assistance of any sort, of doing what he had done to agencies and to people was a man to cherish. It was a pity that he was on the wrong side, that he was on the unreal side of the war. His side was hopeless. But still, what an *hombre!* Montez thought that it would be an excellent thing to have a man like this working for him. The news from Havana had only increased that feeling. But what could you do? Wulff was crazy, he would rather die than work for Montez even though he would surely find out sooner or later that it would have been to his advantage to do so. Where was all of this going to get him? Surely it was going to make him as dead as his victims. Whereas working for Montez he would have become very rich. Still, you could not force a man to work against his instincts. Montez knew that very well. If Wulff felt that his life was best served by blowing up freighters and destroying houses, then Montez, no matter how reasonably he discussed things with the man, no matter how much he offered him, was not going to win.

So let it be. But it was interesting to know that his men had luckily managed to get the man at the Carlin estate. If Carlin had been so afraid of this man, Montez had thought, that he would commit murders out of fear of him, then maybe he had a reason. Maybe this man would come around to Carlin's estate sooner or later. It was worth a chance, anyway; it was not as if Montez had to do it personally. He could lease out the job at a minimum wage with a bonus. He hadn't expected it to work out; the bonus was very large, the minimum payment very small. Nevertheless, they had gotten Wulff, they had found him lurking around the estate, and they had disarmed him without a struggle. That was good. That was very good.

Montez felt in control. For a long time things had not seemed this way, what with having to pay Carlin so much of his receipts and being under Carlin's thumb, but now things had definitely changed and were coming around. It almost went to bear out the conventional Catholicism of his youth. Not that he had been a strict Catholic for many years now— honestly, how could any man in his business be religious?—but it showed that to the meek and the patient, to the workers and the committed fell within their life span the fruits of the city of Rome. Montez repressed an impulse to sing and dance around the large room that was his study. It would not be dignified for a man of his years. Singing and dancing was for women and children and for very young men at festivals. Dignified, mature men such as Montez would have other releases.

He went down into the sub-basement to see how Carlin was doing. Carlin was lying on a couch with a towel over his head, two guards standing near the wall with pistols, looking at him. Little streaks of blood were on Carlin's face, and underneath the gray clothing that Carlin had been given to wear, his body looked like a ruin. Montez shook his head in revulsion. Torture was all right, it was a political and psychological necessity, it was also justified in the case of people like this . . . but he did not like to see it. It was an ugly thing to see and caused him great personal pain.

The guards stood deferentially at the sides, looking at Montez with happy expressions as Montez walked over to Carlin to see if the man was awake. He had promised all of them, his entire staff, huge bonuses as a result of the sudden and great success that had come his way, and morale had never been higher in his quarters than it was now. Of course, morale could sink just as quickly if things started to go badly, men being what they were, employees being conditioned as they had to be . . . but Montez appreciated their pleasure and saw no reason to be cynical about it. Employees were like children; if you treated them well they were happy; if you treated them badly they were not. They had no understanding of motives or cause and effect or larger purposes. But if they did they would no longer be employees . . . and without that class of people, no amenities were possible. Montez, occasionally bitter in his long life, could see all sides of the question now. Everything made sense when looked at from the aspect of success. Success resolved all doubts and gave order to the universe.

"How are you feeling?" he asked Carlin. He did not care, of course; he could not care less about the state of Carlin's health, but this was the kind of question Americans often asked one another when they were starting an interview, and Montez admired the Americans. He had learned almost everything he had to know from them, and if this was their custom then so much the better. "Are you feeling all right?"

Carlin, who had been lying with his eyes closed, opened one to half-size and looked out at him, the eye gray and moist behind its cover. He gurgled something deeply in his throat. "I am truly sorry to hear that," Montez said.

"Leave me alone," the man said weakly. The words came out as if they were endearments torn from the throat of a lover who wanted nothing but to leave at the earliest possible moment, now crouching over an object that had become repulsive to him. "You have got to leave me alone."

"You shouldn't have murdered those people," Montez said. "You brought all of this upon yourself. If you had not brought this upon yourself everything would be well and you would be happy now."

"I shouldn't have come to you," Carlin said, slowly, his throat croaking out each syllable. Montez let it come out that way; he had plenty of time. "I should not have come to you at all."

"You had nowhere else to go," Montez said. "You thought I would give you assistance and sanctuary. You did not understand that there is truly a God of vengeance and that no one could give you sanctuary against your miserable crimes. You are beginning to understand penance now. You are beginning to understand the true significance of the word *grace*."

"I hope you die," Carlin said. "I hope you burn in hell. That is the meaning of any penance I understand."

"It did not have to be this way," Montez said again. There were little streaks and veins in Carlin's eyes; they showed the effects of a subdural hemorrhage. He had probably been beaten severely around the cheekbones, not that Montez wanted to know any of the details of punishment. It was sickening in any but the sense of moral imperative. "If you had not brought this upon yourself, it never would have happened. None of it."

"Leave me alone," Carlin said. "Leave me alone and let me die."

"You will go to hell. Why are you in such a hurry to go to hell?"

Carlin did not answer. He obviously did not want to get into any religious discussion. Montez could understand that. You could be driven beyond religion; if pain would not do it then pleasure could. "You must think about your sins," he said, "you must multiply your sins very carefully one by one in the cell of your consciousness, and if you come to truly understand them, if you come to terms with all your sins then you will be granted understanding and finally remission."

"We could have had everything," Carlin said. "Together we could have had everything."

"What?"

"We could have shared everything," Carlin said. The syllables were flowing more easily now, it was as if thinking of money had once again energized him. On his deathbed a man would always return to what had appeased him the most in life. "But you got greedy. You wanted to have it all yourself. But if it hadn't been for me you wouldn't even have been here."

"You do not understand," Montez said. "I did not do this in order to have everything. There are other things besides worldly goods. I did this for revenge."

"Liar."

"That is the truth."

"You did it for the money. Everything was always for the money. Everybody does it for the money; without that there would be nothing at all."

"You really do not understand," Montez said with regret. "You are an American and do not know that there are more timeless values, more important factors than the secular fact of money."

One of the guards said in Spanish: "Is he giving you any trouble?"

"No," Montez said, "we are having a discussion."

"If he is giving you any trouble I will go over and beat his skull in. He must be taught manners."

"No," Montez said, "that is perfectly all right. There is no trouble. We are seeking to understand each other."

"I will understand him with my fist," the other guard said. "The brains of him will understand my fist more than any amount of language, and this is a better thing."

"Montez, I hope you go to hell," Carlin said. "I hope all of you go to hell."

"Hell can be temporal," Montez said precisely, "and now you are in a temporal hell. Do you hear what my men are saying to me?"

"I don't understand Spanish."

"My men are telling me that they will be quite willing to beat you further in order to induce intelligence and understanding. They seem quite anxious to do it, as a matter of fact. They regret the failure you have had yet of spiritual ascension, and it is all that I can do to resist what they are saying. They are merely trying to be helpful, you see. Shall I let them discuss matters with you again?"

"I don't care any more."

"You have already ascended the flesh, then, you see. The spirit has become predominant if you do not care any more."

Carlin said nothing. Montez looked down at him and said, "I thought you might be interested to know that my men have located Wulff."

Energy came into the man's face and momentarily he looked like the man who had been at the airport, not the blotched and ruined specter on this cot. "No," he said.

"Oh yes," Montez said, "my men found him lurking at your estate, apparently with plans to set incendiaries of some sort. But there was absolutely no violence. They have him and they are all coming in this way. He should be here within the hour."

"That is impossible."

"No it isn't."

"It is impossible," Carlin said. "You could not catch that man if he did not want to be caught. I do not believe that any man or group of men could find him without his cooperation."

"You are exaggerating. The trouble with you Americans is that you have no true sense of proportion. You always think that your worst is the worst, your best the best. He was very easy to capture. He came along quite meekly, as a matter of fact. He will be here shortly, and I am sure that you can discuss all of this with him and find out for yourself that this is true."

"I don't believe you," Carlin said again. "I don't believe you could have trapped him."

"What you really do not believe," Montez said, "is that a man for whom you committed murders, the fear of this man driving you to ruin your life, could be so easily entrapped by someone else. This is a kind of vanity speaking. But I assure you that it is absolutely true and that he is on his way under escort here and you will see this and arrive at more understanding. Everything here has been calculated toward your greater enlightenment, toward your complete knowledge before you die, and this will be one of the best lessons we have offered you yet. Indeed, it will be perhaps your very final lesson; we shall see."

Abruptly he was bored. This kind of thing was interesting up to a point and then it was no longer interesting; it was like tormenting a fly on the head of a pin. After a while the absence of variation, the lack of challenge turned your own hatred against yourself. Whatever Carlin had done to him, whatever humiliation the man had wreaked upon Montez, it was not that man lying on the cot now but something that had once been the man. He could never get back at this Carlin who had hurt him so very much. In that sense, truly, there were no reparations in life. Death might be something else, but Montez did not care to bring it into his angle of thought. For advising Carlin that was a different thing. Carlin was much closer to death than Montez was likely to be for a while.

Montez turned and left the room without saying anything. The guards looked at him respectfully, almost worshipfully. He left the door opened behind him and ascended the stairs. Before he reached the top, the door, as he had expected, closed and he heard the low, pleading burble of Carlin's breath. He had expected nothing else. In the absence of specific orders to the contrary, the guards had returned to their wonderful work.

Enough, Montez thought. Enough of it already. They might kill him; he would have to do something, issue some orders, to make sure that they backed off clear of that. But right up until the matter of murder himself he had lost interest. He no longer cared. Let the guards do what they would. It made no difference. Depression overcame him. The man who had once oppressed him was gone for all time. Whatever happened now was merely attacking the ruin that this man had left behind.

Gloomy, Montez went back to the upper level, the balsa wood of his living room crackling pleasantly underneath him as he looked out toward the mountains and saw the limousine coming in low and fast, four forms in it. Abruptly he felt energy flowing through him again. New meat, a new contest. That was all he needed.

The infliction of pain could keep you young.

XX

Wulff had pretty well kept himself under wraps on the way in. With two men to fight off at the estate and then three when they had taken him to the field, it simply did not seem worth it to make an issue of it. He might have had a small chance with the two, but the odds were not good enough; he had dropped his gun and let them take him. Three was even more difficult, although by that time and with a particularly rough, bouncing flight in, they were all getting distracted and kind of stupid. Still, no matter what excesses of energy and luck he had, even if he were able to take over the plane, what would he do then? He did not know how to fly. It was a survival trip, that was for sure, and if he wanted to survive, it was better to play it their way, at least for a while.

Besides, he was interested. He was interested in seeing the man who had trapped Carlin. He wanted to see this Montez, whoever he was. And of course he wanted to see Carlin. It might be worth the trip, it might be worth death itself to see Carlin, and in worse condition than Wulff would ever be.

They came from the airport in another limousine, the pilot doing the driving now, heavy and fast on the damaged roads, none of them saying anything. He had talked to them a good deal about narco on the plane flight, more to keep up his own spirits than for anything else but also because they had seemed genuinely interested, these men who looked vaguely Hispanic but had no accents at all and said that they were working for Montez for the money, not for anything else, that if things worked out for them in a few years they would be able to go into business for themselves. What that business was and exactly how hired thugs branched out in the world wasn't quite clear to Wulff, but he didn't pursue the issue. Maybe like ex-narcs they retired to half-pensions, heavy drink, jobs as postal clerks and early heart attacks. He certainly wouldn't pursue it.

He sat back in the limousine and let them take him where they would. As always, after a spurt of activity it was almost pleasant to lie back, to have the feeling that fate was at least temporarily taking over and out of his own control. From too much control, from the need to do too much, there often came the reverse, which was complete lassitude, a feeling of succumbing to events, letting events completely take over. He had noted this in the faces of a good many of the men he had killed. They had accepted death almost gratefully, their faces creased into a receptivity so great that it almost might have been sexual. They had had enough of anxiety, of trying to extend the parameters of their control farther and farther, and with every extension that control had become more fluid, more tenuous, verging toward transparency . . . oh, it was agonizing to have a large operation to run, particularly if you were not sure who the hell you were running it over or against, and at the end death must have seemed almost pleasant, at least for some of them. They had lived with it for so long, they had in their way sought it so desperately and from such inner need that when it came it must have been as a lover.

Enough. He sat back in the car and watched the mountains unwind. The three men around him smoked cigarettes and said something in Spanish to one another every so often and gave Wulff beneficent, almost kindly, glances. He could see the respect they had for him. He was in their estimation one tough *hombre* if he had done what he had. Also they had to like him because at the end he had not resisted but had come with them easily. There was nothing in their business better than having a tough job turn suddenly into an easier one, like a long-planned seduction ending with the girl tearing off her clothing, leaping on you and begging to be fucked. They were high up. Wulff felt a little light-headed even in the sealed spaces of the car, the air-conditioning purring away. He could see why the American Olympic athletes had had such trouble here in 1968, had found it impossible to become acclimated even after having trained in the mountains for weeks. It was different air altogether. It took an entirely different kind of man to live here.

"We're almost there," the man next to him said, waving with his cigarette holder. They all looked the same, indistinguishable from one another. Wulff looked through the window and could just barely see an enormous construction straight ahead of them, angled off-center, something that looked like towers rising.

"He lives well, doesn't he?"

"Oh yes," the man said, "he lives very well."

"They all live very well."

"What is that?"

"People like him."

"I do know what you mean," the man said, "but that does not mean that people like us cannot live well too. Your narcotic cops, they lived very well, didn't they?"

"No," Wulff said, "you must have lost something in the translation. They didn't live very well at all. They hated their lives." He caved in further to the seat and the car kept on moving. The driver hummed something that sounded like American rock tune, faking the verses. It took all kinds, Wulff thought. Actually, these were not bad guys. As hired muscle they were far superior in all ways, cultural and intellectual, to the best that America had to offer. It had to do with the servant problem, he was sure; you couldn't get decent help in America, the culture was too mobile, too many people thought that they could do better. In the southern hemisphere it was different; the finest people were willing to work, even at humiliating jobs. After all, if you did your job well and made good contacts and perhaps killed your boss, you had a chance to go into the drug-running business yourself in a few years. Ambition was what sustained the world, Wulff thought, ambition as the reverse coin of the fear of death. They interlocked, of course; the coin fell through to only one head. If you succeeded you could beat death, that was what kept one going. But at the end it was all a cheat. He had seen the eyes of his victims.

The car cut off the drive, went up at an angle, bounced through a difficult access road not unlike that which had crept up to Carlin's property. All these men lived the same; they walled themselves off and looked for special positions of accommodation to verify their power. Wulff blanked all thoughts out of his mind and simply waited. It was best that way. It was best not to anticipate and to take situations exactly as they developed without undue anticipation, because anything else would only lead to greater difficulties.

A tall, elegant man in his middle fifties stood at the end of the drive waiting for them, rubbing his hands. He had an elegant moustache. He looked like a character out of *Carmen.* He was everything that Wulff could have anticipated.

So this is the face of the enemy, he thought, and damned if he didn't feel the impulse to giggle. If this was the enemy, if this was the face of the enemy . . . then pity the victims without any conception of roles to play.

The men murmured around him and Wulff waited for the confrontation. Not that it would prove a damned thing. Confrontation proved nothing. Only murder did. But it certainly yielded satisfaction.

XXI

They let Dick out of detention by noon of the day after his interrogation. They were quite bitter about it, so bitter that none of the interrogating personnel were even around when he checked out. He had been dumped in a sleazy cell in a basement around midnight. A guard had come by after a long time and with no breakfast to tell him that he could go. Upstairs another guard had handed him his belongings and had demanded that he sign something that upon closer inspection had turned out to be a release from all claims of false imprisonment. Dick did not give a damn. He had been around for quite awhile; he knew how the world, let alone the cops, worked. Besides, they were just as likely as not to toss him back into that cell, still without food, to meditate upon his sins some more. He signed it.

The guard said nothing to that either, just tossed the release aside as if it meant nothing, as if the release had been Dick's idea, not his, some idiosyncrasy with which they were humoring him, and Dick had walked out of the headquarters building and into the dazzling light of an October Phoenix afternoon, feeling as if he had spent not twenty-four hours but twenty-four months in detention. Prison did that to you; it destroyed your sense of time. It could hold you for six months and send you out an old man. He walked onto the street and stood there for a while, thinking how old he felt, how helpless, how stunned by the normal routine of the afternoon although he had not been away for a day—how must it be for someone who had been sent up for a year or ten years or twenty?—and then he went uncertainly into the traffic. His car was still up at Carlin's house, of course, if the cops had not confiscated it, if in fact he ever saw it again . . . he would have to take a bus home, try to look for it another time. He could go back to headquarters and ask about his car, but somehow he did not think it would do him any good. It would not do to ask the cops where the hell his car was; they were pissed off enough, they were apt to lose that vague sense of legality which held them back from doing the really terrible things they had on their minds all the time.

It was tough. It was going to be very tough; Dick could see all the complications of his new life sprouting like weeds through the tumbler of his consciousness. He had no job, he had no connections, and he was going to be poison for anybody to hire not only because he had worked for Carlin who was hated, but because once a man had been in detention, once he had been questioned for any reason whatsoever, there was the possibility that he had turned informer. The cops picked up a lot of people exactly that way, sent them back in the world on reduced or dropped charges in return for a nice, informal arrangement that would funnel information through. They were not stupid in Dick's kind of work, they weren't likely to want a man who would be quietly feeding the cops fair or foul information. And there really wasn't much work otherwise for him.

He walked toward the bus stop, thinking about his complicated and increasingly unhappy existence, vague with the feeling that the best times were behind him. Maybe to get blown out of the business the way

Joe or Janice had gone was better. They wouldn't have to worry about a lonely and useless old age, they wouldn't have to worry either about what life after Carlin would be like . . . it was bound to be unpleasant. Dick found that his walk had slowed even further. It wasn't such a good prospect after all. In interrogation, since he had seen and reported the murders in fact, he had concentrated only upon the objective of somehow coming out of this thing alive, and now he had succeeded, but he had not considered for a moment what he should have from the beginning . . . that there was nowhere to go.

"Excuse me," he said to a shambling man on the hot sidewalk whom he had bumped into, but he was not really thinking of the old man or of his apology. What he was thinking of was Montez. Montez owed him something, Dick thought, he had protected Montez. Indeed, if it had not been for him Montez might have lost everything, everything out of his hands what with Carlin somewhere in flight to an ending that might have resulted in Montez's murder. Carlin had been really crazy; he was capable of doing almost anything. If it had not been for him, Montez would have lost everything, Dick thought. But thanks to him the man was not only in control of his situation but had a chance for real power . . . power such as he could never have touched had Carlin remained sane and in control.

That was it, Dick thought, as the shambling man stood with his hands on hips and looked at him. "That's it!" he said aloud, thinking that he would go to Montez, that he would call the man right now and demand to be helped. Montez owed him that, there should be no question of the man helping him. But if for any reason Montez decided to balk—

—Well, Dick thought, in that unhappy circumstance, he certainly knew enough about the man to put him in at least as much trouble as Dick had been. Or maybe more.

Why even work? he thought, his excitement building as the shambling man, waving his arms, began to curse him. "Why even work?" he screamed, talking to himself really excitedly, the words bursting out, he could not contain himself. "If I know what I know and Montez knows that, then it isn't even necessary to put me on the payroll! He could just pay me a retainer. I deserve it," Dick said, "I deserve it for what I've done for him."

"You're crazy," the shambling man said to a small crowd that had gathered to listen to Dick and which was nodding in agreement, "you're crazy, do you know that?"

"I'm not crazy," Dick said to the voice that seemed entirely outside of him, or then again it might have been a deep version of himself with whom he had to have a brief but logical discussion. "It all falls into place, you see. The whole thing. It worked out for the best; I thought I was in serious trouble here but it really couldn't be better. I'm right in the catbird seat, in the fucking catbird seat, you know that?"

"Out of your fucking bird," the man said, "I'm going to call a cop."

"No cops," Dick said, the word touching him off at some level of reflexive twitch, "no *cops*." Cops could ruin everything, he had already had quite enough of cops, that was the truth, he could carry off his plan and make it work beautifully, no problems at all, nothing to worry him if he could just work it through uninterrupted and without people calling him crazy . . . but he couldn't have cops. That was for sure. The cops were for Montez.

He started to move toward the bus, which came panting into the stop, his hand waving, his body concentrated in a gesture that was somewhere between triumph and anticipation, thinking of the call that he was going to make to Montez from his furnished room, the call that would change two lives forever and set him, perhaps, on the glory road from which he would not depart . . . and a .38 slug fired from very high above, three or four stories high in a big, brown building hulking across the street opposite caught him in the center of the skull and tore his brain away.

He saw nothing, heard, felt nothing either, went to the stones in one tumble not knowing they were there, kicked once and lay on his back, his eyes like panes of glass. The shambling man who had hit the ground at the explosion, leaning on his elbows now, looked at the corpse and said, "I'll be damned. I'll be goddamned." He looked up at the sky. "I told you he was crazy," he said to no one at all. The crowd, what there was of it lying on the ground said nothing. "*Told* you," the shambling man said again.

But of course, Dick hadn't been.

He had merely had bad luck. A very natural and inevitable kind of bad luck, however.

Montez, in his new role as a cautious and expanding businessman, had covered all the possibilities.

XXII

"You interest me," Montez said and offered Wulff a cigarette. "I've followed reports of you, only fragmentary ones, of course, but recently I've been hearing a good deal. I've been extremely anxious to meet you."

"You could have sent an invitation," Wulff said. He leaned back in his chair. Unlike the Americans who were his counterparts, Montez seemed to have exquisite manners. He had offered Wulff a drink, a cigarette, and a chair, only the last taken, had leaned back in his own exaggerated ease, had even put his feet up on the desk and turned his attention toward Wulff as if Wulff occupied such a complete position of attention in his consciousness that Wulff's time would be his for as long as necessary. Of course the two guards, both of them armed with the pistols centered on his neck did not make Montez's mood any less forced, Wulff thought.

"You wouldn't have responded to an invitation," Montez said. "That really does not appear to be your style. Rather it seems you prefer to drop in unannounced."

"Only occasionally." Wulff said.

"You are such an interesting man," Montez said and frowned slightly. "Why does a man of your intelligence want to clean up the so-called international drug trade? And even if you could, what's in it for you? People must be happy, you know. They will try to buy their happiness in the manner and style that they can afford and to which they are accustomed. If they can't have drugs they will only have something more terrible. Besides, who are you to decide that one man's happiness is illegal? Is this under your American tradition? Your happiness comes from killing people. Why cannot another man's happiness come from injecting heroin?"

Wulff said, "I don't enjoy killing people. I—"

"—Find it necessary," Montez said. "You do it with the greatest regret, of course."

"Why don't you take your philosophy and shove it up your ass."

Montez said, "I am not mad at you, Wulff. I am trying to understand you. I am genuinely interested in you. I have found out a lot and would like to know more. That's why I've invited you down here. It isn't an opportunity I would have missed."

"Why don't you try and find out about me without two guards and a gun? Wouldn't that be an easier way?"

Montez smiled again and said, "I refuse to get mad at you. I bear you no ill will at all. I have no personal feelings against you, I am just trying to get into your psychology. If I felt that without two guards and a gun you wouldn't attack me, I would certainly talk to you that way, but you are clearly a maddened dog. You would try to kill whatever the odds and circumstances were. You can't be reasoned with unless a gun is held on you. This doesn't make you a bad person, Wulff, just an unfortunate one."

"Fuck you," Wulff said. He had had enough of Montez. He had had enough of Montez's men, Montez's arrogance, being held at bay by this empty diplomat, and he had not been in his home for twenty minutes yet. A deep and vital rage began to work within him, and Wulff knew that Montez was wrong. Guards or not, gun or not, he was going to be goaded into a situation where he possibly would attack Montez no matter what the odds were. There were limits. There were just limits to what a man could take.

"You are such an American," Montez said, "you believe in violence, always violent solutions. You think that the shortest direction between one mind and the other mind is a fist, thus converting both minds to the same point of view, but you neglect all the wise virtues we have so patiently piled up—"

Wulff stood, pushing back the chair and said, "I've had enough of you, Montez. You can take your fucking philosophy and shove it. You think you have brains but you don't. All you have is manner and manner won't get you very far."

The guards seemed to giggle behind him. Of course that could be an illusion, but then again the expression of rage that whipped across Montez's face, blank until then, was not an illusion. It was something to see a man humiliated in front of his help. They had a very intricate system of honor here. Wulff however did not give a shit. "I have nothing to say to you," he said. "You'd better kill me now, because if you don't I'm going to kill you."

"It is quite hopeless, isn't it?"

"Nothing's hopeless. I could kill you very easily."

"I am not talking about that."

"What are you talking about? You with two guards and guns and me unarmed? Is that what you call damned easy? The trouble with you sons of bitches is that you're on your own ground, you're the toughest thing going as long as you're calling off the shots, but you die whimpering, Montez. All of you die whimpering and sniveling and begging, and you will too. Your time will come."

"It is hopeless," Montez said again. "I thought we could talk, could reason with one another, could perhaps even arrive at an understanding—"

"What kind of understanding? Put me on your staff?"

"I thought I could take out some of your anger. Show you the hopelessness of your business, show you how childish your position really is . . . you are not thinking like a man but like a child, Wulff, with your belief in magic acts of violence that will make the bad things go away. There is no such absolute, Wulff. There is no magic. There are bad things and not-so-bad things and almost everything is in the middle between that."

"We have no accommodation."

"I see that," Montez said. "I see that we have no accommodation at all. You will not listen. You deal in death, but when it comes time to talk—"

"You deal in death," Wulff said. "You live on death, you juice it along, you love to throw it in veins. You like to see a junkie's eyes pop out, your blood sings when you see some fifteen-year-old kid in an alley, dead white and expanded with junk, his features all scrambled, his eyes painted all over with death. That's your discussion for you, that's where all of your wisdom and your money lies. Don't give me any of that shit, Montez, you know exactly what you are. You are filth. You disgust me. You are putrescence and slime and you can sit in a hundred rooms with a thousand guards and golden rugs all over the floor and paintings all over the walls and I still know you for scum and you know yourself for it too. That's why you can't face me alone. That's why you've got to shield yourself."

"Son of a bitch," Montez said, "do you want to see what happened to Carlin?"

"I assume you killed Carlin."

"He is not that lucky."

"So you've tortured Carlin. That doesn't mean anything to me, you bastard," Wulff said. "Carlin doesn't exist any more, don't you see that? None of this is personal; the only reason I hate you people is for what you represent and what you're doing. Once you're out of the picture, once you'll never kill a kid again I don't give a shit who you are or where you go or what you do. Don't you see that?"

"You son of a bitch," Montez said. "I want you to take a look at Carlin. I want you to see what he has become. And I want you to know what is going to happen to you too."

"I don't care," Wulff said. "You have no terror for me, you cannot give me dreams. You have no dreams to give, Montez. All you have is death, and the death you know you've lived over and over again. You're the man who is tortured and dead; you're meat on the rack. You can't touch me. You can kill me but you can't touch me."

"Get up," Montez said.

"I am up. Haven't you noticed I'm standing?" Wulff sat down in the chair, put his legs on the desk. "Here," he said, "ask me to get up now."

"Get up," Montez said. He reached into his desk and took out a small silver gun, pointed it at Wulff and waved it. "Get up and begin to move."

"And if I don't? You'll kill me where I sit?"

"I do not prefer to speculate. I do not care to discuss possibilities, not when there is enough reality around us. Get up now."

Wulff turned in his seat, looked at the guards. "What do you think?" he said to them, "should I get up?"

They said nothing, stared at him bleakly. One was old and one was young, but they were two versions of the same self, thirty years apart. Their faces were sad, their mouths under the moustaches tight, their eyes glinted messages that Wulff could not read. "I do not know if you speak English or not," Wulff said, "but I think if you do or if you have children, your sympathies are with me. You know I'm right. For all the children."

"Get up," Montez said again behind him. "Leave my men alone and stand, you dog."

"Am I right?" Wulff said and stared at them. "What do you think? Should I stand and go with him, or do I stay? And does it make any difference?"

The old guard said, "It makes no difference at all."

"But in a way it does," Wulff said. "I've lived so that I won't die obeying men like this. Would you want your children to obey a man like this? You do because you have no choice and it is a job, but if it were not a job would you stay? Would you listen?"

"I would get up," the older guard said, "I do not wish you to die. You are a good man, a man with quality. Why is it necessary for you to die?"

"Roberto," Montez said, "Roberto, you fool—"

"Leave him alone," the younger guard said to Montez. Montez's face dropped open. "You may speak to him," the younger guard said, "and you may tell him your ideas and you may even do with him as you say you must but you have no right to humiliate him. You have no right to humiliate this man."

"You are a pig," Montez said, "both of you are pigs. You are discharged from my employ."

"Good," Wulff said, "fire them. Fire them right now. Tell them to drop their guns and leave the room. Then it will be just you and me, Montez."

An expression of confusion rushed across Montez's face, was replaced by something that might have been hate if there had not been so much pain in it. "I do not know how this happened," he said, "I did not wish it to happen this way. I merely wanted to speak to you and to obtain your ideas of many issues. I did not mean this to turn into a confrontation and I did not mean it to come this way." He looked at the gun in his hand as if it were in another hand. "I did not bring you here to kill you," he said. "I came here as you did to try and seek understanding. That was all."

"There is total understanding," Wulff said. "There has always been total understanding. I know what you are and you know what I am. I hate everything you represent." He stood then, moved the chair back with his calves. "I'll go with you," he said. "I'll go with you because your guards said that I should. For them I have sympathy. They are working men who have had little choice in their lives and can do no better, and to them I can speak. I will go with you but I control this. You don't because any time I've decided I've had enough of you, Montez, I'm going to try and kill you and you're going to have to be very fast and very good because I don't think that your guards are going to defend you. I think that you're going to have to kill me yourself and you just might not be able to do that. You'll have to be awfully fast and awfully good and awfully tightly controlled, Montez, and if you do all of that you'll be able to bring it off, but you just better watch it. You'd better keep a good distance between us and you'd better keep me moving all the time."

He walked toward the door then. Behind him he heard the shuffling movement of the guards and then the creak of Montez's chair as he pushed it into the desk and followed. Montez was walking slowly and carefully, just as he had been advised. He was a good listener. Wulff didn't know how much good the guards were going to be to him, though.

<h1 style="text-align:center">XXIII</h1>

Carlin was in and out of consciousness all the time now. Once he had been able to discriminate between the dark and the light; sometimes he was awake and other times he was sleeping but as the treatments went on, as the pain grew, as the barriers of his body had created to shield him from the pain crumpled, he found that there was no longer any discrimination, that he had lost that sense of partitioning between waking and sleep through which human lives were lived.

Now he tumbled in and out, the periods blending together so that he barely knew whether he was sleeping or waking at all. Sometimes he would imagine himself striding powerfully around the room, throwing off the pain and taking control of the situation in his old, demanding way, and he knew that that had to be a waking state until he opened his eyes, thick with pain and encrusted slime, to find that he had been sleeping. Sometimes he thought he was dreaming of a pain so shuddering and intense that it was dismembering his body piece by piece, he falling into the center of it as one might fall into a particularly demanding woman, and that would have to be sleep except that he knew he was awake.

And all the time now there were the thoughts of Janice in his mind. He could smell her, hear her, see her screaming. He should not have killed Janice, he knew that now. His luck had turned bad when he had killed her. All of the time—and he had not known it—she was his luck, she had tied him to life. Now he lay in a basement and he was dying.

He was no longer conscious of men coming into the room, men leaving the room, men beating him and men leaving him alone, bits and pieces of gruel or pap being put into his mouth, tickling along the soles of his feet. He was in a pain so solid and final that it might have been pleasure or ice or anything; it was a pain that transcended pain and became something else again. This might be martyrdom, he thought, in one of his feeble periods of waking; maybe this was how the martyrs felt except that there was nothing glorious about this at all. It was all a myth. Torture was sweaty and disgusting and painful and breaking, and soon you were not a man at all and the thing that was not a man could take no pleasure from virtues. It sweated and voided and fouled itself and stank and cried and spat. That was your martyrdom for you.

So when the four men walked into the room, one of them Montez, two of them guards, a fourth someone he did not know who Montez told him was Wulff, Carlin was convinced he was dreaming again. It had to be a dream; it was impossible that this was happening. He had never met Wulff. Teams of the best men he could find had been unable to locate him, to bring him to bear. Wulff was the avenger, he was going to destroy him. How could he be in this basement? Someone or something threw water on his face and Carlin gasped into alertness, faded away again and more water came, shocking him, grinding him to awakeness. Something was propping him with pillows and then he was sitting, staring. He knew he was awake now. There were the two guards who always accompanied Montez, there was Montez himself, there was a very tall man in fatigues who looked at Carlin in a way that Carlin could not understand. He rubbed his eyes. He tried to speak but his voice wouldn't come and he fell back. There was more water in his face and more propping and then he was awake. Definitely he was awake this time, he knew it.

"This is Wulff," Montez said. "This is the man from whom you fled."

"Yes," the man said, "he's right. I'm Wulff."

Carlin said nothing. There was nothing to say. He knew that he was going to die soon in this room. In a way the man that had just come was responsible for all of it, but this did not change the situation. It changed nothing. "Wulff," he said, framing the word like a child, pursing his lips, "Wulff."

"He's going to join you, Carlin," Montez said, "you'll get a good chance to know him."

"Wulff," Carlin said again.

"Maybe you will be able to understand him," Montez said, "because I cannot. I have tried hard to reach some kind of understanding. I have tried to accommodate myself to this man, and it simply cannot be done. But perhaps when his condition approximates yours we will be able to reach some of that understanding."

"Wulff."

"No," the man called Wulff said, and turned in profile to Carlin. He was a big man, all right, a big son of a bitch, tough, no question about it, but how could he kill thousands of men? How could he do what he did, he was only one man. "No, I'm not going to stay down here with him. You've got this wrong, Montez. You misunderstand everything. You're not calling the shots here. I am."

What was this man thinking of? Carlin thought faintly. Montez was in control of everything now, two guards, three guns, Carlin tortured and helpless, Wulff about to be murdered. Didn't Wulff understand? There were certain things in this world that you simply could not fight. He blinked, tried to signal Wulff with his eyes that it was hopeless. "Please," he said then, weakly, "please don't—"

Montez smiled. "You see?" he said to Wulff, "do you see now? Even your friend is pleading with you to be reasonable. Carlin is a reasonable man. Aren't you a reasonable man, Carlin? You are trying to help him."

"Please," Carlin said, "don't do it." His voice was coming back; desperation gave him urgency. He didn't have much life, but what little was left he wanted to hold onto. That's how they got you. That was how they always sucked you in, life would hold, life would assert its power. "Please."

"This man is trying to help you," Montez said. "He has been where you will be and he is your friend. He understands the situation. He is trying to tell you with all his spirit not to make a fool of yourself."

"Put down the gun," Wulff said to Montez. "Put it down now."

Montez smiled at him and raised the gun. "You're crazy," he said, "you are crazy. Move away or I'll shoot you."

Wulff turned toward the guards. Was he crazy? Yes, Carlin thought, he had to be crazy. He had never seen anything like this. This was impossible. "Put down your guns," he said to the guards, "put them down if you won't train them on him. This is between the two of us."

The guards dropped their guns. First the younger, then the older unhooked the rifles from their shoulders. They clattered to the floor. Open-palmed, they turned toward Wulff nodding.

Montez said, "Everybody is crazy. Both of you are as crazy as he is. I will kill you both."

"No you won't," Wulff said. He raised his hand and the gesture induced such a terrible if momentary calm that Carlin had to gasp again. He must be dreaming. All of this had to be a dream. Montez did not move.

"Give me the gun," Wulff said. "Hand me the gun end over end, Montez. Otherwise I'll have to go for it and you'll be killed. If you cooperate it will be much easier and I won't kill you. I'll just make you suffer for a while."

"You are crazy."

"No," Wulff said, "you are crazy. Your power comes from your craziness, but now I have power that is making you sane. You understand that you cannot stay against me, Montez, because I am right and you are wrong. Your men understand that. You should, too."

"No."

"Then you're crazy too."

"Don't," Carlin said, "please don't. Please don't now, you'll get us all killed."

"No I won't," Wulff said. "Besides, you're dead already," and then he made a gesture at Montez, what happened then was too fast for Carlin, his dazzled senses could not follow it. One moment Montez was in position, trying to level the gun, and then Wulff had closed on him and Montez was no longer standing, the man had turned over on the floor, the gun was free, the gun was kicked away and Wulff was moving in even closer. Montez was on the floor squealing. Wulff kicked him hard in the face once and the squealing stopped. Wulff moved away, breathing hard and looked at the guards.

"I don't believe this," Carlin said. "I don't believe it."

"All right," Wulff said, "you may go."

"It is going to be very bad for us," the older one said. "They will not understand."

"There is no one to understand," Wulff said. "Are you the only ones in the house?"

"In the house, yes. Outside there are five on duty, some sentries, some working in the garden disguised. They will not know what has happened if we leave."

"All right," Wulff said, "that's good. That can be worked with." He bent over, picked up Montez's gun, put it in his pocket. "Go upstairs and just stay in the house for a while. As long as the house is secure, we'll think of something."

"It is going to be very bad," the younger one said. "It is going to be very bad."

"We will take one thing at a time," Wulff said. "We will not be concerned with the future, but only with present time and the present will become the future. Make sure the house is secure and stay up there."

"All right," the older guard said. He turned and went, the other followed him. Carlin heard the door click at the top of the stairs. He looked at Wulff, unbelieving. Montez groaned and turned on the floor. Wulff went over and very efficiently kicked him under the heart and Montez was still.

Carlin said, "I don't believe it. I don't believe what you've done."

"You had better."

"I never saw—"

"You had better believe it," Wulff said. He raised a hand, wiped a little sweat from his forehead, came in on Carlin. "It happened all right. You knew it was going to happen."

Carlin tried to move but could not. The pain, dull for a while, was efficient, terrible. He was dead. He knew it. Deep internal hemorrhage. But he was in more contact than he had been for a long time. "Why?" he said. "Why did you do it?"

"That's very simple," Wulff said, looking over at Montez, then back at Carlin. "You know the answer to that one."

"I don't know the answer to anything."

"Sure you do," Wulff said and looked at Carlin up and down and Carlin felt the fear beginning; it was impossible after what he had gone through that he could feel yet more fear, and yet he did, this was something else, this was hitting him at a level that Montez for all his ingeniousness never had. "What are you doing?" Carlin said. "Why?"

"You know why I did it," Wulff said. "You know why."

"Yes," Carlin said, deep in his throat. He could barely speak. "Yes I do."

"He tortured you and you're in bad shape and you're going to die, Carlin. You're going to die very soon." Wulff reached into his pocket, took out the gun, pointed it at Carlin. "But that isn't enough," he said. "That's no satisfaction at all. I don't want you to just die and I don't want to know that he did it to you. I want to kill you myself. It's very important that you die by my hand."

"You're crazy," Carlin said. It was not analysis but terror. He had never been so frightened in his life, even at the worst of it.

"They all say that," Wulff said. "They all say crazy when they mean sane. But that's all right. I wasn't here to debate with Montez and I'm not here to debate with you either. I'm just here to kill you."

"Why?"

"Because you killed a few good men," Wulff said, "and you're a death merchant and a killer who would have gotten crazier and crazier, and you're practically the last one left, and I think I wanted you more than anyone, even more than Calabrese because I had respect for that old bastard and he really wasn't into drugs and death, he was just into money—drugs and death were incidentals. But you're a new breed, Carlin. With you it was shit all the way, shit and death and that's the worst. I couldn't take it. I couldn't take that and I wanted you very badly."

Deep in pain, deep into the sense of his own death, Carlin said anyway, "Please don't. I'm hurt. I'm going to die. Let me die—"

"No," Wulff said, "no, it wouldn't be the same. It wouldn't feel good. Death isn't worth anything unless it feels good, Carlin. I owe you this one."

He pulled the trigger and Carlin saw nothing else, at the center of the single white hot flash there was a crevice into which he fell, but blind, blind forever he screamed and all the way down toward the end wondering, at the last of it, whether you went alone or whether you joined those who followed or whether, when you came right down to it, it made any difference at all.

He never heard Wulff shoot Montez.

THE END

The World Snake

By Barry N. Malzberg

> And the quest would, then, have been as for nothing. Everything would be the same. In another year the New Order would have risen, would have sealed all of the cracks and it would be the same as always—except the more terrible, because they would have learned from their mistakes, from the chinks in the armor which he would by then have discovered... a scream of absolute rage came from Wulff as he sprawled there in heat and haze of that damned courtroom, his fists clenched, his eyes closed not against sight, not against perception but against what he saw in terrible clarity as the future—America as a 137th Street and Lenox Avenue of the mind: forms reeling and scattered through filth, the filth rising, the filth settling, the great plunger throbbing, the rising corruption—
>
> —*Detroit Massacre*

But it came over me then with a terrible clarity not unlike Wulff's, not unlike that clarity which seemed at one point or another to strike every character in this staggering procession of ravaging event, that the country, like its Constitution, like science fiction, was the world-snake, consuming itself, head ingesting tail until it choked on itself. Drugs were the metaphor, the nation was snorting and smoking and puncturing itself into oblivion.

That insight came as I staggered through the 26 essays on science fiction history and consequence commissioned for my friend Mike Resnick's new magazine, *Galaxy's Edge,* which in a dark decade forty years later he had been recruited to edit. Science fiction by this time was in severe devolution, the field had migrated to movies and television as its core or, appositely, had been overtaken by fantasy; its very devices had become parodic or self-destructive and I began to understand that this devolution was central to the category itself.

Science fiction in its *ad astra* aspiration and paranoia was a field of exploration which almost inevitably would be self-consuming, just as the American Constitution in its origin, its makers, its very contents had embodied its destruction. The crude, cruel, limitless powers in the Executive Branch to overtake the other two parts of government through fiat, the stark inequity in the Declaration itself ("all *men* are created equal") had by the advent of Donald Trump established, perhaps inarguably, that the Constitution itself provided the very means for its destruction. Science fiction, with its hesitance and vulnerability, its ambivalence and societal incompetence as consequences of uncontrollable technological change... science fiction was no longer "a means for young men to enter science" as Hugo Gernsback proposed but rather a projective catalogue of disaster.

Self-consumption was perhaps the default mode of "social progress" which term itself was a euphemism for social destruction just as drugs, introduced in the spirit of transcendence were a means toward self-destruction. Long ago Norman Podhoretz had written, "When fascism comes to this country if it does, it will be in the guise of anti-fascism," a prediction more than half a century before the election of 2016 which proved out with terrible efficiency. The abolition of the media Equal Time Law which left Norman Podhoretz's fascists in patriot mufti with a host of options to protect our freedom. They would use their own freedom of speech to outspend, out revile and out finance an increasingly hapless left wing.

Drugs were that way too, drugs had the same terrible protocol: *turn on, tune in, drop out*, that was the mantra of the advanced in spirit and what had been a hard-run, murderous and murderously transmissive trade became rather an aspect of cool, a blushing statement of freedom.

Wulff saw this, of course, not necessarily as metaphor; Wulff was a man of the most practical working insanity and saw drugs as precisely the fuel the engines of the night needed. "Free love" was a simulation of love for seduction or rape, "tuning in" was addiction to horse, speed and LSD and if the vision of the user was clotted and intolerant, it had a kind of accuracy which went beyond his madness. "The pure products of America go insane" was William Carlos Williams' famous epigraph to the citizenry, the century, the users themselves and Wulff was the purest product of all. He was the law, he was its antithesis, he was the instrument of vengeance, he drove a stacked cattle car of propitiation. Wulff contained multitudes.

Berkley contained multitudes too; the series for which it had in innocence contracted was the series which was intended now to rip out the buried, poisonous heart of the heart of the country and left it etherized upon the table for all to inspect at ninety-five cents a throw. I am not sure if by the Fall of 1974 I had gone as mad as my character; I maintained enough of a diligent's distance to falsify a kind of objectivity. I did know that I was approaching the end of the rope's consequence, that there was only one way to go and although that had been clear from the first, the means and methodology were slower to reveal themselves in the context of a competitor for Mack Bolan's audience. But now everything was on the table. Wulff drove, I drove, we both drove on the crushed and entangled turnpike of desire, driven by our engine of the night, heading for the blasted barn. Berkley asked for an extension past the original ten novels. I did not hesitate. By that time I was so deeply embedded myself that I thought I could be the solution.

And so now to the killing run.

January 2022: New Jersey

Barry N. Malzberg Bibliography

FICTION (as either Barry or Barry N. Malzberg)

Oracle of the Thousand Hands (1968)
Screen (1968)
Confessions of Westchester County (1970)
The Spread (1971)
In My Parents' Bedroom (1971)
The Falling Astronauts (1971)
The Masochist (1972, reprinted as Everything Happened to Susan, 1975; as Cinema, 2020)
Horizontal Woman (1972; reprinted as The Social Worker, 1973)
Beyond Apollo (1972)
Overlay (1972)
Revelations (1972)
Herovit's World (1973)
In the Enclosure (1973)
The Men Inside (1973)
Phase IV (1973; novelization based on a story & screenplay by Mayo Simon)
The Day of the Burning (1974)
The Tactics of Conquest (1974)
Underlay (1974)
The Destruction of the Temple (1974)
Guernica Night (1974)
On a Planet Alien (1974)
Out from Ganymede (1974; stories)
The Sodom and Gomorrah Business (1974)
The Best of Barry N. Malzberg (1975; stories)
The Many Worlds of Barry Malzberg (1975; stories)
Galaxies (1975)
The Gamesman (1975)

Down Here in the Dream Quarter (1976; stories)
Scop (1976)
The Last Transaction (1977)
Chorale (1978)
Malzberg at Large (1979; stories)
The Man Who Loved the Midnight Lady (1980; stories)
The Cross of Fire (1982)
The Remaking of Sigmund Freud (1985)
In the Stone House (2000; stories)
Shiva and Other Stories (2001; stories)
The Passage of the Light: The Recursive Science Fiction of Barry N. Malzberg (2004; ed. by Tony Lewis & Mike Resnick; stories)
The Very Best of Barry N. Malzberg (2013; stories)

With Bill Pronzini

The Running of the Beasts (1976)
Acts of Mercy (1977)
Night Screams (1979)
Prose Bowl (1980)
Problems Solved (2003; stories)
On Account of Darkness and Other SF Stories (2004; stories)

As Mike Barry

Lone Wolf series:
Night Raider (1973)
Bay Prowler (1973)
Boston Avenger (1973)
Desert Stalker (1974)
Havana Hit (1974)
Chicago Slaughter (1974)
Peruvian Nightmare (1974)

Los Angeles Holocaust (1974)
Miami Marauder (1974)
Harlem Showdown (1975)
Detroit Massacre (1975)
Phoenix Inferno (1975)
The Killing Run (1975)
Philadelphia Blow-Up (1975)

As Francine di Natale

The Circle (1969)

As Claudine Dumas

The Confessions of a Parisian
    Chambermaid (1969)

As Mel Johnson/M. L. Johnson

Love Doll (1967; with The Sex Pros
    by Orrie Hitt)
I, Lesbian (1968; as M. L. Johnson)
Just Ask (1968; with Playgirl by Lou
    Craig)
Instant Sex (1968)
Chained (1968; with Master of
    Women by March Hastings & Love
    Captive by Dallas Mayo)
Kiss and Run (1968; with Sex on the
    Sand by Sheldon Lord & Odd Girl
    by March Hastings)
Nympho Nurse (1969; with Young
    and Eager by Jim Conroy &
    Quickie by Gene Evans)
The Sadist (1969)
The Box (1969)
Do It To Me (1969; with Hot Blonde
    by Jim Conroy)
Born to Give (1969; with Swap Club
    by Greg Hamilton & Wild in Bed
    by Dirk Malloy)
Campus Doll (1969; with High
    School Stud by Robert Hadley)
A Way With All Maidens (1969)

As Howard Lee

Kung Fu #1: The Way of the Tiger,
    the Sign of the Dragon (1973)

As Lee W. Mason

Lady of a Thousand Sorrows (1977)

As K. M. O'Donnell

Empty People (1969)
The Final War and Other Fantasies
    (1969; stories)
Dwellers of the Deep (1970)
Gather at the Hall of the Planets
    (1971)
In the Pocket and Other S-F Stories
    (1971; stories)
Universe Day (1971; stories)

As Eliot B. Reston

The Womanizer (1972)

As Gerrold Watkins

Southern Comfort (1969)
A Bed of Money (1970)
A Satyr's Romance (1970)
Giving It Away (1970)
Art of the Fugue (1970)

NON-FICTION/ESSAYS

The Engines of the Night: Science
    Fiction in the Eighties (1982;
    essays)
Breakfast in the Ruins (2007;
    essays: expansion of Engines of the
    Night)
The Business of Science Fiction: Two
    Insiders Discuss Writing and
    Publishing (2010; with Mike
    Resnick)

The Bend at the End of the Road
(2018; essays)

EDITED ANTHOLOGIES

Final Stage (1974; with Edward L.
Ferman)
Arena (1976; with Edward L.
Ferman)
Graven Images (1977; with Edward
L. Ferman)
Dark Sins, Dark Dreams (1978; with
Bill Pronzini)
The End of Summer: SF in the
Fifties (1979; with Bill Pronzini)
Shared Tomorrows: Science Fiction
in Collaboration (1979; with Bill
Pronzini)

Neglected Visions (1979; with
Martin H. Greenberg & Joseph D.
Olander)
Bug-Eyed Monsters (1980; with Bill
Pronzini)
The Science Fiction of Mark Clifton
(1980; with Martin H. Greenberg)
The Arbor House Treasury of Horror
& the Supernatural (1981; with
Bill Pronzini & Martin H.
Greenberg)
The Science Fiction of Kris Neville
(1984; with Martin H. Greenberg)
Mystery in the Mainstream (1986;
with Bill Pronzini & Martin H.
Greenberg)